I0653900

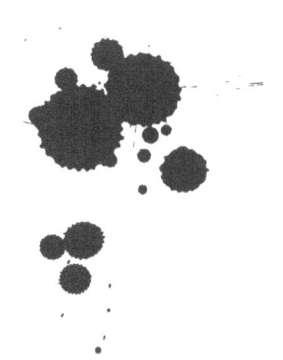

THE HAPPENING

THE WOLFSHADOW TRILOGY | BOOK 2

FOR MY BOYS.

THE WOLFSHADOW TRILOGY

Saamaanthaa

The Happening

Norm

OTHER WOLFSHADOW BOOKS

Lupinia:

The Selected Poems

of Polly Drinkwater, 2007–2015

OTHER NOVELS

Chosen

Suckage

NOVELLAS

Relict

Summerville

The Day of the Nightfish

THE WOLFSHADOW TRILOGY 2

THE HAPPENING

DT NEAL

N*P

NOSETOUCH PRESS

CHICAGO | PITTSBURGH

The Happening
© 2015 by D.T. Neal
All Rights Reserved.

ISBN-13: 978-1-944286-01-9

Published by Nosetouch Press
Chicago, Illinois

www.dtneal.com | www.nosetouchpress.com

Cataloging-in-Publication Data
Names: Neal, D.T., author.
Title: The Happening
Description: Chicago, IL : Nosetouch Press [2015]
Identifiers: ISBN: 9781944286019 (paperback)
Subjects: LCSH: Horror—Fiction. | Paranormal—Fiction.
GSAFD: Horror fiction. | BISAC: FICTION / Horror.

Cover & interior design by Christine M. Scott
www.clevercrow.com

Fourstar Ambulance just wasn't fast enough to deliver a dead man to University Hospital; fortunately, the guy came back to life four blocks from the emergency room. Mark Manning was losing his mind in the back, while Steve Clarke was just trying to drive down Marine, trying to keep from rolling their vehicle in the afternoon traffic.

They'd gotten the call from near the Polish Embassy, a frantic call about a gangland-style assassination that had taken place in front of their building, some talk about paramilitaries with assault rifles killing people in a car, some talk about terrorism.

When they'd gotten to the scene, the car was gone, driven off by whoever had done the shooting. Only the dead man was there, bullet-riddled on the boulevard. They had taken his pulse, and Steve could've sworn there hadn't been one, but the guy had gasped on the bloody curb, had coughed up blood, and the two of them had snapped into action.

There was no way somebody could have taken that many rounds and survived. To Steve's eye, there were a dozen bullet wounds, right across the man's chest. The volume of lost blood alone should have killed him. He was a good-looking guy, too, young. Dark-haired, he looked Greek, maybe Italian. He assumed it was some Mafia thing, though why they'd done the shooting in public was anybody's guess.

Steve was used to seeing strange things. In five years as a paramedic, he'd seen things. But this guy was something else. He was coming back from the fucking dead. And, if Mark was right, the guy was actually getting stronger as they got closer to the hospital. It was hard to tell, because Mark wouldn't stop yelling.

"He's fucking alive, Steve," Mark said. "He's expelling the bullets."

Steve could hear the clatter of things on the floor of the ambulance, what he assumed were the bullets Mark was yelling about. He couldn't look, couldn't see; he had to drive. But each time there was a clatter, Mark would moan. Manning had only been on the job for two years, so he was still shocked by stuff.

"Just hold on," Steve said. "We're like 5 minutes out."

"He's healing," Mark said. "Steve, he's getting better."

Steve glanced over his shoulder, swerving to dodge a cab that darted in front of them. He couldn't pause to look, he had no idea what Manning was talking about.

"Just calm the fuck down, Markie," Steve said. "Four minutes."

The man had been dead.

He'd been dead.

Steve had seen.

Then he heard something else in the back, heard a growl, heard the ripping of clothes, and he heard Mark screaming, heard bottles breaking and things overturning. Steve felt the ambulance shift, he felt the weight increase, felt the shocks soak up the load, felt something grow in the back, felt the ambulance get out from under him.

Three minutes away, and Mark wouldn't stop screaming.

Steve couldn't do more than glance in the rearview mirror, because the traffic was always tight downtown, even with the sirens blaring, people wouldn't get out of the fucking way. Everybody was so slow.

There was a snap and a gurgle and Mark stopped screaming, and Steve figured that he'd chilled out and gave the victim a sedative to calm him down.

"Markie, talk to me," Steve said. "C'mon back to me, Buddy."

He glanced in the rearview mirror, and he saw a big pair of blue animal eyes looking at him through the pane that separated the cab from the rear of the ambulance. Big blue eyes and a mouthful of teeth, hot breath right on his shoulder.

Now it was Steve's turn to scream. He rolled the ambulance in front of the Hancock Building, went right over the curb, right onto the sidewalk, right over the railing, into the fountain courtyard below. The ambulance went over, and the thing in the back of his ambulance howled and snarled as it tumbled with him. Mark tumbled, too, his lifeless body banging around the back.

They came to a jarring halt, Steve gagging on his seatbelt, which dug into his neck, while the airbag blasted him in the face. The thing in the back howled, a deafening sound in the narrow confines of the ambulance, and then Steve could feel the pressure on the metal, on the frame of the ambulance, as the thing propelled itself out the back, tearing open the doors with a swipe of its arms.

And out it went with a leap and sound of crunching metal.
It was gone. Just like that.

The thing had run through the streets, this great, big black wolf with ice blue eyes. It had run through Gold Coast, right past the boutiques and salons, snapping at people as it went—roaring, howling, snarling, charging.

People didn't know what they were seeing. Too big to be a dog. Was it a bear? Furry, fanged, monstrous—it ran, and there were the sounds of police sirens and fire trucks. Something had happened in the Loop. A disaster. Terrorists? And what was this thing?

It didn't stop running. It cut through traffic and parks in the waning light of the day, hell-bent on a destination only it could guess.

Everybody with sense moved out of its way, those lucky enough to see it. Two men, however, in an Animal Control van, pursued it. White van, black letters on the side. Not City of Chicago; this was a federal van. They drove after it, tires screeching as they took turns and blew through lights.

One of the men, the passenger, was leaning out the window of the van, carrying a high-powered rifle. He was zeroing in on the thing, at least as much as he was able, since his partner was zigzagging through traffic, which had gotten particularly bad as people saw the running thing and reacted to it.

It was like a ripple wave of chaos, as people passed from normalcy to nightmare in the wake of the monster. Some had their cell phones in hand, snapping pictures or talking, others were talking nervously to themselves. Everybody was reacting, not sure what it was that they had just seen.

It was happening, though; there was no way around that. Something was going on.

"Shoot it," the driver said. "Jesus, Frank. Fucking shoot it."

"Try driving straight," the shooter said. "Just for like 10 seconds, and I got it."

"Do you see these streets? I can't drive straight."

"We have to get a live specimen," the driver said.

"I'm trying, Zach," Frank said. "Next time, I'll drive."

A tow truck cut them off, turning, dodging the thing, which had turned and cut across the street, heading northwest. Zach slammed on the brakes to avoid rear-ending the tow truck, cursing as he did, gripping the wheel. The truck lurched.

Frank had his rifle perched on the side mirror of the van, propped up.

"Perfect," he said. "There's a truck in my fucking way."

"This is a perfect specimen," Zach said. "Did you see the size of that thing?"

"Fucking call came too late," Frank said. "I thought we had this covered."

"Not my problem," Zach said. "We got there."

"Too late," Frank said. "I thought Monica was on top of this."

"It hardly matters," Zach said. "They're getting sloppy. Every-body's getting sloppy."

The tow truck took a leisurely turn to right itself, the driver having recovered from the initial shock of what he'd seen. Zach honked and drove around him.

"I lost it," Frank said. "Shit. Do you see it?"

Zach scanned the street ahead of him. "Aw, hell."

He gunned the motor of the van, and got up to the intersection ahead. They knew what to look for, the stunned reactions, the small knots of people, talking, pointing in a panic. He looked, and he didn't see.

"The Director's going to have our balls," Frank said. "Anya's gonna geld us."

"We're not going back in until we find it," Zach said.

"How can we have even lost it? It was right there."

"You know how they are," Zach said, taking them past an alley that separated a shoe store and a handbag boutique.

Something moved at the corner of Frank's gaze, something that moved impossibly quickly, a mass of black fur and fangs.

"That's Big Black," Zach said. "It's him."

Big Black was one of the codenames they had for known Lupines at the Bureau for Extraordinary Events. The BEE had a database of known Lupines, and Zach was sure this was Big Black, who had operated in Chicago for at least a decade, and was notoriously hard to spot.

Frank had started to cry out when it had struck the van with door-crumpling force that nearly rolled the vehicle. It reached in the open window, this thing with long, muscled arms that ended in clawed hands, and reached for Frank, the claws as long as pencils, thick as knives. Without missing a beat, Zach floored the accelerator, smashed them into a yellow cab ahead of them.

In one second, there was the face of this thing, the maw and bloody muzzle, the blue eyes on him, while Frank struggled to free his rifle to fire. In the next second, he felt its claws sink into his flesh, could feel the incredible power of the thing as it ripped him out of his seatbelt, out of his seat, and took him half-through the van door, took the van door with them.

He tried to break free of it, but the thing shook him, slammed him against the pavement and parked cars, shaking the door free of him. Then it sank its teeth in his throat and killed Frank with a doglike shake of its head.

Zach stared through the hole that had been a door to his van, where his partner had been only moments before, stared right into the monstrous blue eyes of the beast that gazed right back at him, with intelligence, his partner limp in the thing's bloody jaws.

Zach drew his sidearm, a Glock loaded with silver bullets. It was like he was moving in slow motion, compared with Big Black. Orders forgotten, it became a moment of survival for Zach.

The thing dropped Frank and sprang at Zach, who stomped on the accelerator again, smashing his way past the cab ahead of him, and the SUV coming the other way. He turned sharply, which diverted the beast's attack, causing it to smash into the side of the van, instead of propelling itself into the open passenger side, as it had intended.

And it had intended that, Zach knew. He could see it in the thing's eyes. It knew.

Flooring it, Zach drove through light after light until he could no longer see the thing in his rearview mirror, then spun the wheel, screeching to the curb.

Zach jumped out, had his pistol ready. Having given himself enough breathing space, he took stock and was ready to take a few shots at the thing, once it reappeared. He waited, pulse pounding, eyes alert.

But the thing was gone.

"This is Houndstooth calling Den Mother," Zach said, holstering his pistol. "We have a man down. Repeat, we have a man down."

Ansel came back to his senses after he'd filled his belly.

It was always that way. He fought his way past the red-black curtain of pain, rage and hunger to find himself in a vacant industrial space, overgrown and weedy. His wounds had already healed, but had taken a toll, and he'd simply had to feed. His bestial body had known what it needed, and it had taken it.

He came back, naked, crouching in the weeds, barefoot amid broken glass and gravel.

It took a moment to take stock. He'd been driving Sam; they'd been arguing. Then he'd been shot. That was what he remembered. Bullets and blackness. Then he'd been running. Even for him, who knew the dance, knew the routine, it required a mental recalibration. It was like going into a dark room, blinking in the shadow, trying to make out formerly familiar shapes.

He had to find Samantha. That was most important. She'd been his responsibility. Everything that had happened had been his fault, because he had not reined her in, had failed to be there for her when he'd infected her.

Like you even could, Sam said, in his head. He could hear her voice, that saucy, clipped way that she spoke.

Ansel knew there was no way he was going to walk naked from here to home, so he willed himself to change, to let the Beast come back.

Unlike an infective, he had full control over his transformation, or, at least, more than most. Today had been an exception, owing to unusual circumstances, like his own near-death experience. Or maybe he had actually been dead. He'd been collateral damage, had gotten in the way; they'd been saving their precious bullets for Sam.

His skin parted and the furry black thing that he kept sealed inside him came spilling back out, drawing life and breath in the enveloping shadow of the waning day. His black fur concealed him so well, despite his great size. The muscle piled onto him, drawn from the flesh he'd consumed, which had healed him, made him whole. He was beautiful and monstrous, massive.

As much as he loathed to admit it, it felt good to get that release; he'd kept it bottled up inside him far too long, and it had gotten him in trouble. He was not meant to keep himself chained up that way, and the Beast had gotten peevish at that treatment, had taken matters into its own clawed hands.

It's what had led to poor Sam getting infected to begin with.

He raised his snout into the wind, took the city's scent, the blend of car exhaust, perfume, rotting leaves, water, dust, concrete and steel, pollution stink, and flesh, always flesh. He had to track down Sam, had to find her, had to settle this properly, before it got out of hand.

The trouble was, it meant going back downtown. But, now, in control once more, he was confident that he could do it. He just had to stay in the shadows. For something as big as he was, he was able to move with great stealth if he wanted to, and he needed every bit of that skill.

Without anything more in the way of a plan, with only instinct and recollection to guide him, he headed back to where he'd last been with Sam. It was the only way to track her down. From where he was, it meant he could make his way from park to park, using a big cemetery as a way of getting close enough to Lincoln Park to then skulk his way back near the embassy, on Marine Drive.

So, he ran, moving swiftly and silently, as silent as death, this hulking lycanthrope that moved with balletic grace in darkness, guided by instinct and a battery of senses that allowed him to see, hear, and smell his way flawlessly through the dark.

This was what the Beast was born to do, and Ansel had forgotten how it felt, the freedom and the joy even simple movement could bring. It was more fluid and natural than anything he'd known in his man-form, and he'd run from it, not wanting to be captive to this part of his nature. But as he indulged it, hunting and tracking, as natural as breathing, it felt good.

In a way that he'd not felt in years, he was alive again.

You have me to thank for it, I swear, Wolfman, Sam said, in his head, flirting with him as she always did, chewing on her words, cocking her head, big grin.

You won't be happy to see me, Sam. I'm coming to kill you. I made a mess; I'm going to clean it up, one way or another.

Sure you have it in you, Ansel? You got the stomach for it?

I have to, Sam. Forgive me.

He caught her scent near the embassy, picked it right up in the Chicago autumn wind. Plain as day, and bathed in blood.

There it was.

There *she* was.

He tracked her, picking up his pace, the adrenal glands firing as he geared up for the inevitable confrontation with his wayward child. He did not want to do this, but he had warned her, and she had flouted his warning. He had given her every chance in the world to pull herself together, and she'd thrown it back in his face. It was more than an insult; it was an insurrection.

Through the park he went, the trees a blur as he passed. People walking their dogs were the only ones to note his passing in the shadows, as their pets growled and barked. A chorus of barks and howls from them, their owners looking around, not seeing, too slow, too blind and deaf, unable to see what was almost right under their noses.

Ansel had no time for them; he was stalking Samantha. He'd make it quick; he wouldn't make her suffer. It had been his mistake that had birthed her to being with. He owed her the boon of a mercifully quick death.

Ever the gentleman, aren't you? For sure.

Her scent was very strong, now. There were other scents, too. Others. Blood. She'd been busy, clearly. Poor thing had lost control. She'd gone rogue.

He reached the edge of the park, mindful of flashing police lights on Marine Drive. He could get no closer from here, not without being seen. Then he remembered that there was a pedestrian tunnel that went under Marine and Lake Shore Drive, connecting this strip of the park to the proper lake shore, itself.

Without hesitation, Ansel sprang into that tunnel, bounded his way through it, through the short concrete cavern, lit by sodium lights. He cleared it in seconds, emerging closer to the lake, the roar of the waves in his ears, the chill wind of it blowing in his face. He could still smell Sam from here.

The traffic on Lake Shore Drive was, as ever, an infinite ribbon of light and noise, the constant cars, day or night, never stopping, always coming and going.

Ansel ran down until he was right across from the assembled ambulances, fire trucks and police cars, with only Lake Shore and Marine between him and the place. But with the inky dark of the lake to his back, no one could see. He climbed one of the smallish trees that grew in that place, so he could be even less conspicuous to the late-night joggers and bikers who still frequented the park after dark.

In the comfortable shadows of the tree, Ansel turned his full attention to the scene. What was going on?

There were bystanders looking, a crowd of people, and Ansel could smell Sam, could make her out as clear as day. Where was she hiding?

He would not take her there, not in front of everybody. Lord knows the people in the city had experienced enough trauma for the moment.

Ansel saw that there were three bodies being carted out of a brownstone. He remembered this place. It was an elegant building.

Reagan. It was Reagan's place. She'd hosted a dinner party there, for Sam and her ridiculous hipster asshole friends. He'd gone there with Polly. Ansel bit his lip, drawing his own blood. Polly. He'd have to see her, too. Another loose end for him to fix.

Sam was there. She was right there, but Ansel could not see her. He could only smell her. Then he saw one of the paramedics pull the sheet back over one of the bodies, and then he saw Sam, bloody-faced, her throat slit. She seemed to gaze out at him sightlessly, across lanes of traffic, blankly, lifelessly.

Whoopsie, Sam said, quite dead, in his head.

4

"Thank you for your donation," the nurse said, giving the young woman a sticker. "You have helped so many people with this."

"No prob," the woman said, grinning. "I, like, *like* to give back to my community. Totally."

The young woman looked like a fashion model, with this cleanly angular face, perfect bone structure: high cheekbones and the most arresting black eyes that contrasted with her platinum blonde hair that looked almost white. It made the girl look like an angel.

"Just be careful not to give too much," the nurse said. "Wait at least a month before donating again, Miss—"

"Zooey," the girl said. "That's my name. I think you can never give too much."

The nurse, whose name was Irene, smiled. The young woman was stunning, with this delightful shag of a haircut and voluminous bangs that playfully hung about her dark eyes. And so tall and effortlessly lean. Irene trended toward a pear shape, her hair a pile of brown curls. This woman, this Zooey, was otherworldly. Her grin was one of polished radiance. She was so comfortable in her own beautiful skin.

"I have a daughter who would kill for that color of hair," Irene said.

"That sounds extreme," Zooey said. "It's just hair."

"Easy for you to say," Irene said. "Are you a model?"

Zooey shrugged. "Could be."

Despite her radiance, there was something off-putting about the young woman, something Irene couldn't quite put her finger on. There was some hint of smug menace in the young woman's breezily affable bearing, a whiff of something unfamiliar and alien to her, almost feral.

"We're grateful for your donation, anyway," Irene said.

"See you next month," Zooey said, picking up a lollipop from the bowl that Irene had handy for donors.

She strode out of there like she owned the place, and Irene, despite herself, breathed a sigh of relief.

Zooey, meantime, took to the street and strolled down it, crunching the sour apple lollipop in two bites, then playing with the stick, half-heartedly chewing it as she went.

She'd seen what had happened to Sam. She'd gotten down there after Sam's call, only to see the fucking bloodbath of something gone terribly wrong. She'd seen the paramedics tug the sheet back, at Zooey's request, had seen her face, to be sure it was really her.

Reagan had slit her throat. Zooey had told them she was friends with all of them, just so she could see. Sweet Sam with her throat slit, gazing with this look of uncomprehending wonder on her face. And Reagan, whose face was something altogether different, a look of painful transcendence, like those Sioux warriors who'd hang themselves from hooks during their rain dance or whatever. That's what she looked like, only her skin was purpled.

"How'd she die?" Zooey asked the paramedic, this young man, who looked like he was 18 or something.

"Looks like some kind of poisoning," the paramedic said. "The coroner will know for sure."

"Fuck me," Zooey said. Then she got out of the way, melted back into the crowd of onlookers. Reagan had killed Sam? That was just fucked up. Reagan wasn't a killer. What the fuck had happened?

A bus honked at Zooey at an intersection, like when she was crossing the street. Zooey looked at the driver, a fat man behind the plexiglass. He waved at her almost daintily.

She walked over to the doors to the bus, stepped back as there was the hydraulic hiss that opened them.

"What?" Zooey asked.

"Hot chicks ride for free," the driver said.

"Yeah?"

"Oh, yeah," the driver said. "Anywhere you want."

Zooey smiled to herself, stepped aboard. The bus was empty. The doors hissed shut behind her.

"That doesn't seem very professional, Dude," Zooey said.

The guy smiled behind the half-inch thick plexiglass screen, punctured with a few holes. "Sue me; it's been a slow night."

The light turned green, and the driver started on his way.

"Where do you want to go, Beautiful?"

"Zooey," she said. "I'm Zooey."

"Where do you want to go, Zooey?" the driver said.

"Pilsen," Zooey said.

"Hah," the driver said. "Not on my route. You want the 168, the UIC/Pilsen Express."

"You said I could go anywhere I wanted." Zooey put her fingers through the holes in the plexiglass screen. "What's this thing supposed to do, anyway?"

The driver kept most of his attention on the road, glancing at Zooey furtively through one of his rearview mirrors, looking her up and down.

"It's supposed to protect us from weirdoes," the driver said.

Zooey smiled to herself at that. "Does it work?"

"Sometimes," the driver said.

"Do you think I'm, like, a weirdo, Bus Drivin' Dude?"

"Ryan," he said. "My name's Ryan."

"Do you, like, think I'm a weirdo, Ryan the Bus Drivin' Dude?"

The driver looked at her, shrugged. "I've seen lots weirder."

Zooey gripped the plexiglass and gave it another tug. The thing was locked in place. Ryan saw her tug at it and snorted to himself. He was chubby, in need of a shave. He smelled of cigarettes.

"See? I'm safe behind here. It's bulletproof. They made them the way they have those in some of the taxicabs"

"Totally," Zooey said. "You are one safe dude. It's like Ryan under glass, man. You know, like when they serve food on a platter, and it's under glass? That's what it's like. Like a cake. Or a deli counter."

Ryan laughed nervously. "You should probably sit down, now, Miss. I got passengers to pick up."

"Zooey," she said. "Call me Zooey. And don't pick anybody else up."

The driver laughed. "I'll get in trouble."

"You're already in trouble," Zooey said, taking her seat behind the yellow line painted on the floor. "I'll bet you're a Cancer, Ryan."

"How'd you know?"

"A girl can tell," Zooey said. "You're chubby. Cancerians tend to be, well, you know, egg-shaped. They're, like, at risk for it. The women are for sure, anyway. Cancerians just front. See, that's the whole thing with them—they're Crabs. And, like, what is a crab? Hard shell over soft innards. That says it all. Soft-shelled Crabs, Dude. Every Cancerian fronts, shows their hard shell to the world, because, inside, they're all squishy."

"I don't think I do," Ryan said.

"You all squishy on the inside, Ryan?" Zooey asked.

The driver pulled up to a stop, and a Goth couple boarded—rail-skinny guy with peroxide hair, and his chubby girlfriend, who had the whole raccoon eyes thing going, and a double-pierced nose.

The boyfriend checked out Zooey, glanced at her, while the girl-friend paid both of their fares and walked past, giving Zooey a disdainful once-over. She had absurdly tiny feet, stuffed into some four-inch heeled boots studded with spikes. The couple sat down at one of the double seats, midway through the bus.

Zooey made eye contact with Ryan, mouthed "Cancer" and nodded in the direction of the Goth girl, cocked an eyebrow, like she was sharing a deep secret with him. Ryan looked at the couple through the rearview mirror, then back at Zooey.

"All the freaks come out at night," Ryan said. "So, what is your sign, then, Zooey?"

"Aquarius Sun, Leo Moon," Zooey said. "Scorpio Rising. Aries Midheaven."

"I don't even know what all that shit even means," Ryan said. "I think the Zodiac is bullshit."

"It would take me too long to explain it all to you, Ryan," Zooey said. "Let's just agree that it means that I'm awesome, and destined for incredible things."

"You think so?"

"I know so," Zooey said.

"Aquarius is, like the Water Bearer, right?" Ryan asked. "Means it's a Water sign, yeah?"

"Air," Zooey said. "Fixed Air."

"Fixed Air. What the hell does that even mean?" Ryan asked. He stopped the bus, let on some more passengers. Zooey watched them pass, but kept her black eyes on Ryan.

"It means that I, like, follow something through to the end," Zooey said. "It means that, like, once I've found my true purpose, there isn't a thing in the world that can stop me. I'm like a wind tunnel."

"Wow," Ryan said. "That sounds intense."

"It is," Zooey said. "I'm incredibly intense. You can feel it, I know it, Dude. Anybody in the room with me can, like, feel it."

"What about that Leo Moon, then?" Ryan asked, half-looking at her, half-watching traffic.

"It means I love to be the center of attention," Zooey said. "I'm, like, a bit of an attention whore, I suppose. And, because I'm sure you're dying to know, you're wondering about the rest. My Scorpio Rising is how I present, like, myself to the world. First impressions, totally. It means that I'm incredibly passionate. You can tell that about me, can't you?"

"Uh, I guess," Ryan said.

"And my Aries Midheaven, hmm," Zooey said. "That gives me, like, endless confidence and the boundless desire to shine, but that I can be, well, like, impulsive, too."

Ryan laughed, a kind of porcine, snorting thing.

"Sounds like you'll be a big star," Ryan said. "Sounds like I'm lucky to have even met you."

"God, yes, totally," Zooey said. "You can feel that, can't you?"

"Oh, totally," Ryan said, mocking her tone.

"See, that's the Cancer talking," Zooey said. "All Cancerians are smartasses."

As the bus got a little more crowded, Zooey fell silent, just looked at the other passengers in turn, sizing them up—old and young, fat and thin, gay and straight, male and female, black and white. So many flavors of humanity, packed together. She felt the urge to kill everybody on the bus, licked her lips at the thought of it. But she controlled herself, kept herself contained.

Zooey rode the bus to the end of its route, watched the people board, studied them in detail, watched them get off, one by one, two by two, three by three, each of them with their own stories, their own lives, none of them with a bit of a clue. She loved taking the CTA, loved seeing the city that way.

Ryan steered the bus into a turnaround, put on the brakes. Then he turned and looked at Zooey, like just looked her up and down.

"End of the line, Zooey," he said.

"Not just yet," Zooey said. She took off her jacket, set it down on the seat next to her. Then she took off her sweatshirt, so she was sitting there in her periwinkle bra. Ryan's eyes went big, like he alternately couldn't believe his good fortune, while at the same time was terrified of being caught.

"Hey, now, uh," Ryan said. "Miss, you, uh—"

"Zooey," she said. "Say it, Dude."

"Zooey," he said, while she slipped off her sneakers, tugged off her jeans, took off her bra and her thong, dropped them on the pile of clothes on the seat. She stood there, naked in front of him.

Ryan the driver turned off the internal lights on the bus, so they were in shadow, with only the orange of sodium lights illuminating them from outside.

Zooey walked back to the partition, put her fingers through the holes again. Ryan watched in the darkness, mouth agape.

"Uh," he said. "I have a wife."

"Bet she's a Pisces," Zooey said. "She have a big ass?"

"Uh, yeah," Ryan said.

"I don't," Zooey said. "Is she pretty?"

"Not like you," Ryan said.

Zooey liked that, smiled to herself, sparkly radiant in the dark, as she gave herself over to her transformation, as smooth and graceful as could be, a limbic ballet that turned the elfin young woman into a towering, white-furred Lupine with a long snout and great big teeth.

"Nobody's like me, Dude," she snarled, and Ryan screamed.

Then she tore the partition loose, and tore Ryan the bus driver apart, before the fat man could even sing. She was at his throat, crunched that windpipe of his, felt the blood, and tore him limb from limb, took greedy bites, splashing the windshield with him as one of his hands flailed, some autonomic response, because the man was already dead; his body just didn't know what hit it, the sundered nerves were gyrating.

Zooey took three big, nicotine-tainted bites of the man, gulped him down, then tore the rest of him to bits. Then she willed herself back into her humanly wrapper, got dressed, and got out of the bus, bathed in blood, not even caring. She was so long past caring. She walked through the park with a bloody grin on her face, licking her fingers clean as she went.

It started to rain, a cold and fitful November rain, and Zooey didn't care. She just held her hands out to her side, raised her face up into it, and laughed.

She gave blood, and she spilled blood; it all balanced out in the end.

Life was, like, totally good.

Ansel went back home, without any of the people, the sheeple, being any wiser. Having already gorged himself, he had that necessary measure of control, that leash he managed to keep around the thing inside him.

Too bad the little bitch is dead, the Beast said. *I'd wanted to get my teeth in her from the start. It's why I bit her to begin with, you know.*

Somebody had done his work for him. Maybe it had been the Poles. There was a merry little band of werewolf hunters operating in the city. He had never really faced them, because he'd kept himself so quiet, he hadn't drawn their attention. But Sam had been splashing blood throughout the city, like the whole place was her canvas. And she didn't even paint, so there was no method to her madness.

As Ansel worked his way to Wicker Park, to his place, he wondered what to do next. Sam had infected a lot of people in town during her brief reign of terror. If Ansel was going to set things right, he had to hunt all of them down.

It wasn't something he wanted to do, but he couldn't handle having the city go to hell because of that one lapse of his.

At heart, the fault was his.

By all means, let me be the mop for your morality, the Beast said. *I'll make the city radiant, red in tooth and claw.*

Butchery would be the order of the day. He'd track them all down, Sam's spawn, and finish each of them off. It was the most merciful thing he could do, even though it wasn't something he particularly wanted to do. He liked Chicago; he didn't want to just pack up and move.

Urban renewal.

The Beast was thirsting for slaughter, as ever. It savored the prospect of hunting down Lupines even more than hunting down normal folk. The danger of it was enticing, intoxicating.

Before Ansel could tug on the leash, the Beast raised its head and let out a great, big howl. A full-throated, ghastly declaration of war.

You could become the alpha of her pack.

Ansel waited, listened. Several points within the city, there were answering howls. Far too many. Five? Six? A dozen? A score? Sam had been busy.

Ansel howled again, louder, more forcefully, indulging the Beast a moment more. And, again, elsewhere in the city, there were howls. Most of them east of where he was. North, south, and east. Tons of them.

Of course, dealing with Sam's pet project meant dealing with Polly, too, who was another of Sam's messes, since she'd cattily infected her out of a fit of jealousy, because Ansel really dug Polly more than he dug her. Ansel didn't like that so much, because he had affection for Polly, and Sam had claimed her. It wasn't Polly's fault.

He reached his place, bounded up the fire escape to the roof of his building, and, standing there in the shadows, gazed across the city, sniffing the air for anything he should worry about. There were no scents of Lupines here; he knew that any of them with any sense would avoid this place, would understand their danger. All of them were pups to him.

Ansel dropped to all fours, and, against the Beast's wishes, willed himself to return to his human disguise. The flesh and bone cracked and folded in on itself, like a kind of organic origami, the dreadful alchemy of lycanthropy, turning monster back into man.

You can't bury me forever, Ansel. You know that.

He never talked to himself, refused to speak to the Beast, for it was one of the games the thing played—if you spoke to it, if you acknowledged it, it was like giving it a measure of yourself, creating life for it. It was an old thing his mother had told him, how those of the true blood came to terms with their curse (or blessing, depending on whom you asked).

The Beast would trick you into speaking to it, into dividing yourself, as if you were somehow separate from the thing within you. But that was exactly the thing you could never do; you had to always remember that the Beast was you. It was not apart from you. Because if you subdivided your own soul, then there arose a place inside you that inevitably stopped being you, and gave itself over entirely to the Beast. You'd become a time-share within yourself, and once a lycanthrope did that, they were finished. The Beast would ride roughshod over you.

So, he never, ever spoke to the thing that spoke to him. It was a little game they played. It would talk to him freely, knowing that Ansel would never answer.

Silly man. I am the only friend you'll ever truly have.

He stood up and felt the chill evening air. Then he went back into his building. There was so much he had to do. First and foremost, he needed a new cell phone. He'd kept a land line out of some sense of nostalgia, was grateful for it, as he called his provider and told them that his phone had been stolen, along with his car, and that they needed to find it for him.

The company told him exactly where it was.

Ansel found his car and phone, sure enough. He had trekked out where the phone company had told him it was, in a garage in the Near West Side. He'd snuck there, mindful of every shadow, because the guys who had stolen his car were the men who had shot him.

Payback, the Beast hissed in his ear.

The garage was an old business, looked like it had been a mechanic's shop back in the 1950s, had the remains of modernity in faded colors and geometric lines. There was a symbol etched on the wall near the sign for Kowalczyk's Auto Repair: it looked like a cross with a crescent atop it and three arrows radiating upward and outward on three tines of the cross.

Ansel had remembered that from his parents, mentioning it: some secret Polish order of fanatics who hunted werewolves. He could not recall their name. *Synowie* something or other.

The shop would have been tended by smiling mechanics in matching uniforms, eager to tag-team automobiles that would have been sporting fins and sky blue paint jobs.

But now those images were nothing more than ghosts, and Ansel didn't have time to bother with ghosts. He only wanted his car back, so he pried his way in the back door of the place with a crowbar, and snuck into the darkness of the garage, smelling old gasoline and older oil, along with industrial solvents, sweat, and paints.

And there, beneath a smudgy tarp, was his car. Ansel tugged off the tarp, grateful to be reunited with his vehicle. His father had given him the Maybach the other year, having moved on to a Tesla Roadster prototype.

Not wanting to get into it with the *Synowie* Poles who had attempted to murder him and steal his car, Ansel keyed into his car, started it up.

Then he went to the garage door and opened it, ran back to his car.

Hopping in, he readjusted the seat and drove the Maybach out of there, pleased that it had gone without a hitch.

The Beast was less than happy; it had really hoped for some of those Poles to turn up, so Ansel could grease them.

Ansel popped open the glove compartment, surprised and pleased to see that his wallet had been in there, even if it was emptied of cash. He figured that the Poles had intended to dispose of the car when it suited them. They were probably going to just chop it up and be done with it, ditch the wallet and phone when that was done. Or maybe they hoped to repaint it and sell it. It was a Maybach, after all. Once the bullet holes were filled, somebody would want it.

His cell was where he'd left it, in the space between the driver's and passenger's seat, that no man's land. He was grateful for that, too; the Poles were hunters and murderers, to be sure, but they were not thieves.

There was dried blood all over the inside of the car, in the passenger side and in the back seat. The scent of it was very apparent, and it was not his blood. Sam must have wounded some of the men, because this blood was theirs, not hers.

He dialed up Polly. It was the most sensible thing he could do. She picked it up on the first ring.

"Ansel," Polly said, in barely a whisper. "Oh, my god, Ansel. Did you see? I've been trying to call you all day."

"Did I see what?"

"Sam's dead," Polly said. "Something on the news about her and Reagan and Gretta that I saw: they were in some murder-suicide pact. They wanted me to come downtown to join them."

"Yeah," Ansel said. "I saw. I want to see you."

There was hesitation on the line.

"I don't think that's a good idea, Ansel."

"I have to see you. How about that?"

"Something's wrong with me, Ansel," Polly said. "I'm sick. I think Sam gave me something. A sickness."

He wasn't going to talk about it on the cell phones. "Just let me come see you, Polly. We can talk it out. I know what's bothering you."

"How could you? I feel so sad," Polly said. "The newspaper said that Sam's throat was cut, and that Reagan poisoned herself. I can't reach anybody, Ansel. Nobody. Sheldon, Clay, and Gabe all missing. BacchUS burning down—all of their beautiful artwork, immolated. Willa burning herself to death, and Lee found murdered. Now Sam and Reagan. I'm the only one left, Ansel. I'm so unbelievably scared."

"Don't be," Ansel said. And he felt the kissing cousin to compassion in his heart. He cared for Polly, did not want to kill her. It was one thing to want to go after Sam, who had actively fucked with him; but Polly was a victim.

"Something happened," Polly said. "I'm a mess."

"I'm coming," Ansel said. "Don't go anywhere. Wait for me. Can you do that?"

"Yes," Polly said. "I'm so glad you're not dead, Ansel."

"Me, too," he said.

There was no use explaining it to her; not over the phone.

So, he set his phone to speaker and talked to her as he drove to her place, to her husband's place, up in Winnetka. She had eagerly attached herself to Ansel while Tristan was out of town, which was almost all the time, as his business kept him on the road, in other countries, more often than it kept him home.

"Is Tristan around?" Ansel asked.

"Yes and no," Polly said. "I'm really glad you aren't dead, Ansel."

"I know, you said that," Ansel said.

"I'm saying it again," Polly said.

He pulled into their place, their big stone house, Tristan's BMW parked at the back of the driveway, a black shape, shiny and polished in the light of the night. Ansel was momentarily self-conscious about his bullet-riddled Maybach.

Ansel got out of his car, grateful for some fresh air, out of the coppery scent of all of that spilled blood.

He rang the doorbell to the Drinkwater residence, waited for Polly to answer, then rang the doorbell again.

Polly came to the door, peered through the peephole. Ansel could feel her on the other side of the door.

"Promise me you won't judge me," Polly said.

"I promise," Ansel said. She really had no idea.

She opened the door and gave him a hug, burying her head in his chest. She was wearing a black embroidered blouse with sheer sleeves, and a black miniskirt that was sequined, and black suede knee boots.

"Back in black," Ansel said. "Are you going out?"

"Anywhere but here, at least until you called," Polly said.

"Where's Tristan?" Ansel asked.

Polly whisked him in, shutting the door, locking it. Her face was very pale, and her lips were bright red from the lipstick she was wearing.

"Ansel," Polly said. "Remember that you promised."

"Of course," he said.

She took his hand and walked the two of them through her house, which Ansel knew well enough, as he and Polly had spent plenty of time there when Tristan was out of town.

Then she took him to their exercise room, which was where Ansel saw the first of the blood, and could see the bloody tracks.

He saw a man's legs, wearing grey track pants with orange piping, wearing orange and grey sneakers. It was just a pair of legs. There was nothing above the waist.

Polly looked at Ansel with an expression that pushed all thought of his original plan far out of his head.

"I did this," Polly said. "I don't know how, exactly, but I did. Something boiled up inside me. Tristan and I were arguing. It was about you. And I lost control."

"You're okay, Polly," Ansel said.

"No, I'm not," she said. "I killed Tristan, Ansel. I murdered him. And I— "

Ansel hugged her again, could feel her body against his, relished how that felt.

"I know what you are, Polly," Ansel said. "I want you to know that I know."

She kept her head against his chest. "How can you?"

"I'm one, too," he said, and that made her stiffen, made her pry herself away from him, to gaze up at him with her big eyes.

"I won't say it," Polly said. "It's so gauche. It's so completely beneath me."

Ansel forced a smile, despite the grisly spectacle of her half-eaten husband on the floor. "Let's go to some other room."

That she had been planning to hit the town after butchering her husband said everything about where Polly's head was at. Ansel had to sort that out, had to sort her out.

They went back to her living room, where Polly sat at the edge of her ivory leather sofa, knitting her hands, leaning forward.

"I killed Tristan."

What was he going to say to her? Everybody's first kill was like that. It took something out of you, that first bite, that final, unspeakable taboo. For Ansel, it was something he'd grown up with, so he'd had time to process it, and had the support of his family. Polly had no frame of reference for it.

"What do we do, Ansel?" Polly asked. "I'm a poet; I'm not a monster. I do not want to go to jail."

"I know," Ansel said. "Tell me this, Polly: do you want to live, or do you want to die?"

"What kind of question is that?"

Ansel stroked her back: slow, gentle movements of his hand.

"An honest one," he said. "The most honest question I can ask you."

"I want to live," Polly said.

He had hoped she would say that. He would have honored either of her wishes, no matter what she had said. Polly did not understand that her life hung entirely on the balance of what she said. The Beast was there for her if she didn't want to live; Ansel was there for her if she did.

"In what we are, that's all that matters," he said. "It shapes everything that you are."

Polly fought for words. It was the first time Ansel had ever seen Polly at a loss for words, which was, itself, surprising.

"I won't say it," Polly said. "I will *never* say it."

"You don't have to," Ansel said.

He knew what words were to her. They were as close to sacred things to Polly.

"I lost my words," she said. "Did Sam infect you, too?"

That was a complicated question. The answer was a simple one, but it would affect everything between him and Polly, depending on how he answered. The Beast wanted him to lie, so, instead, he told the truth.

"No," Ansel said. "I infected her. Remember when you two came to my studio?"

"Of course I remember. That was just a few weeks ago."

"Exactly," he said. He could see her working it out. She was a smart woman, and it only took her seconds.

"You infected Sam, she infected me. She bit me," Polly said. "Goddammit, Ansel."

She shoved away from him, glowered at him.

"I'm sorry, Polly," he said.

"You ruined me," she said. "I see it, now. You infected Sam. Sam infected me. Sam infected Reagan. Reagan murdered Sam. Am I correct in this? Sam probably killed the others, too?"

"I don't know how it shook out with Reagan," Ansel said. "But, yes, I'm sure she killed the others. It happens with newbies—they go after the ones closest to them."

"You knew," Polly said. "The both of you. You both knew. You played all of us. Everything we did. Your little killing joke on all of us."

"It was an accident," Ansel said. "I lost control that night."

"Two weeks ago," Polly said. "Jesus God, Ansel. I want my life back. I want my friends back. How could Sam do those things?"

Her voice was angry, cold, hurt. Ansel felt terrible.

"Sam lost control," Ansel said.

"This is your fault," Polly said. Her face was a mask of torment.

"I can't make it go away," Ansel said.

"You were the monster all along," Polly said. "The real monster in our midst, the wolf in the fold. I spoke up for you, defended you. And you were playing me the whole time."

Her look was flinty, full of reproach. Ansel did not know what to say. Everything had gotten so crazy so quickly.

"We must have been so entertaining for you," Polly said. "The dinner party. The gallery showing. My sitting while you painted me."

"It wasn't like that," Ansel said.

"Out," Polly said. "Get out of here."

Ansel wanted to comfort Polly, but the look in her eyes, the expression on her face, there was no question of him doing so.

"You ruined me," she said, again, between clenched teeth. "You turned me into a thing, destroyed me."

It wasn't like with Sam. For Sam, it had been something exciting; for Polly, it could only be a curse. Ansel could see that.

Kill her, the Beast said. *Put her out of her misery. It's what she wants.*

"You want to live," Ansel said. "So that means living with it, not giving up. It means surviving."

"Out," Polly said.

Ansel would not leave without having his say. "Polly, this is your chance to be something special. Isn't that what all of you wanted? You wanted to be special."

"I *was* special," Polly said. "I already was. We all were. You destroyed us. And to think I took your side. God, I'm so embarrassed by that. I sided with you against my friends."

"I can help you," Ansel said. "I can help you understand it."

"I don't want your help," Polly said. "I can see how much you 'helped' Sam."

It was enough. The Beast was rising in him, like bile in his throat. It wanted to have a go at her, to put her down.

Let me finish this, the Beast said. *We'll do it my way.*

"If you can't handle it, I can end it for you right here and now," Ansel said. "Is that what you want? A mercy killing? Because I'll grant it."

She looked at him like he was crazy. "You say that like it's something worth having."

"You are infected," Ansel said. "It can be a blessing or a curse. It's all on you. You know how to reach me. Call me if you want to, Polly."

"Leave now," she said.

Ansel didn't want to go, but he knew that Polly would either arrive at her own peace with her condition or she wouldn't. If she found her footing, she'd reach out to him again; and if not, odds were good that she'd take care of herself, or would die trying.

"You have to be careful," Ansel said. "There are hunters out there—Poles and government agents. If they catch you, the Poles will kill you, and the feds, they'll take you to their labs. If you don't feed, the thing will compel you to change. It doesn't care; it only wants to feed."

"Goodbye, Ansel," Polly said. "I hate you."

He went back outside, feeling bad for Polly, wanting to stay, but knowing that, at least for now, he could not. In his experience, some people were better at adapting to the change than others.

The night air was getting chillier, and Ansel listened for a moment. There were no howls out here. Not yet, anyway. The suburbs were safe, at least for now.

Except for Polly, of course, the lycanthropic queen of the suburbs.

He got into his Maybach and pulled out of there. In the darkness, with the big house full of light, one would never know that there was anything wrong at the Drinkwater residence. None of Polly's neighbors would know that she'd killed and partially eaten her husband. Here, with all the pretty houses in their measured plots of land, was a kind of pastoral mummer's show.

Everybody here was "normal"—this was where the sheeple flocked, where the human livestock penned themselves. Away from "danger"—with danger being the same as "difference."

Ansel got the sudden urge to paint. It seemed self-indulgent to do in the wake of trying to contain Samantha's outbreak, but the urge was there just the same, the kernel of an idea. Seeing Polly's nice house, knowing what horrors were behind those doors—it was an inspiration.

What to do now?

All at once, his resolve wavered. All of Sam's victims were likely as confused and, ultimately, innocent as Polly. They had just been in the wrong place at the wrong time. Who was Ansel to come in and murder them?

He had been furious at Sam for infecting people, for going off the chain and creating trouble, but it was his own lapse that had allowed Sam to get infected to begin with, and his own failure to rein her in or even deal with her initially that had caused all of this.

Killing her victims wasn't a way out of his moral failures; it would only compound them. None of those people had asked for Sam to infect them. Each of them had a right to come to terms with their plight on their own, without someone like Ansel coming in and meting out some ghoulish parody of justice upon them. Sam was one thing, and she'd paid the ultimate price for it; but these others?

They weren't his responsibility, not in truth. It was an unheroic notion, but Ansel had never, ever pretended to be a hero. He was an artist and a monster who lived quietly in the midst of millions of norms. He'd been the wolf in the fold, just like Polly had said.

He drove back into the city, thoughtful, fingers drumming on the steering wheel.

Why should he even care? He had nothing to fear from an outbreak like this. Oh, sure, the Poles had surprised him, but they hadn't been hunting him; they'd been after Sam. Ansel had only been hit because he'd been an inconvenience for them, and they had assumed that he was a confederate of hers. But they'd really been hunting Sam, and rightfully so.

They'd hunt down any lycanthrope who got particularly sloppy and out of control. That was the part of the dance that Samantha never seemed to get—while lycanthropy appeared to be carte blanche to do whatever the fuck you wanted to do, in truth, even a monster had to tread lightly in the world of Man. There were protectors out there who would rise up and strike out at the monster.

That seemed absurd, was something that people on the other side—the sheeple—didn't get. As a monster (and Ansel wasn't so naïve as to think that he was anything but this), one had to navigate life far more carefully than the sheeple ever did. Sheeple did what they were told, followed the rules, obeyed the moral dictates that were handed down, whether from the Church, or the Party, or the State, or the Culture—they did what they were supposed to do, didn't rock the boat, went with the flow.

A monster lived and breathed outside of these moral confines. That was what made them monstrous in the eyes of the sheeple. Life in the moral wilderness was what made monstrosity what it was. But life in that place, at the event horizon of acceptability, spinning toward that sinful singularity, required its own kind of discipline.

What did it mean to Ansel to be a werewolf? Did he lose his mind and feast on anything that came his way? No. The unique challenge a werewolf faced was that their natural prey had the means of defending themselves, even counterattacking. The werewolf who went too wild would inevitably end up getting themselves killed, prompting such a strong reaction from the sheeple as to doom themselves. It was the equivalent of running in traffic—sooner or later, you were going to get hit.

So, to someone like Ansel, who had lived a life of measured monstrosity, not being gluttonous, avoiding innocents whenever possible, hunting those who deserved to be dead, it wasn't entirely moral, but his existence precluded true morality.

Life on the margins of monstrosity was a place he understood, and was, by most accounts, comparatively safe. Or he'd at least found some degree of balance there, where he could live a seemingly human life in relative peace, while sometimes giving in to the Beast and killing a person, but making a point to kill somebody who was actually bad—a rapist or psychopath here, a sex offender or serial killer there—he would hunt the human predators, themselves.

If he must be a monster, let him at least put that to work culling the very worst from the ranks of the sheeple, to operate in a manner that predators in nature ultimately did, which was to take the weak out of the prey species ranks, making for a stronger species, in the end. That was how he gave vent to his urges, when they came.

The historical and cultural role of the Monster was as an instrument of punishment for the transgressor. For Ansel, in practical terms, it meant that if he became aware of someone encroaching on his moral wilderness, a would-be homesteader of horror, Ansel would be the wolf at their door, and would kill them, and indulge himself.

It was how he did it, how his family did it, and it had worked well enough for them. There was some balance in it. Feed on the flesh of those who deserved to die, and the world at large would be a better place, despite the flouting of civilized law and order. It was how Ansel made peace with what he was.

He had not had the time to explain that in detail to Sam, and maybe she would not have even properly understood it if he had—for her, everything was sensation, and she was caught up in the moment, like a baby discovering its own hand, pawing at her face.

Maybe Ansel didn't have to be the Angel of Death with these other lycanthropes, and could let it play out as it did on its own. It felt like how those wildlife photographers probably felt, when they watched a boa constrictor eat a baby bird, and just had to let nature take its course.

Perhaps letting the supernatural takes its course was the best path. Ansel chewed his lip a bit, thought it over. Sam had been his responsibility, and everything she'd done afterward had been a consequence of his own failure to maintain control of himself.

But he also didn't have it in him to just murder dozens, maybe hundreds of people just to clean up his own mess. Let the crazy Poles do it. Let them fight among each other. And if anybody came for him, he would defend himself. When werewolves got out of hand, the sheeple, who always had the superior numbers, would inevitably stampede and trample them, restoring the balance.

It didn't feel terribly heroic, honorable or noble, but what did honor matter to him? He was beyond the need for honor or nobility, was free from the fetters of conventional morality. He was no hero; he was the monster.

The BEE was buzzing. They had a big board, a digital map screen that showed the status of the city, and there were indicators all over the board, lights all across Chicago.

Zach watched the lights, the bright red lights indicating an infective, listened to the frantic 911 calls that they were tapping.

The Director, Anya Walker, stalked back and forth in front of the big board, talking on the phone.

"We have an epidemic," she said. "Our recovery teams have identified at least 500 infectives at this point," Anya said.

The facility was secretly located at the lake shore, had 300 personnel, as Anya had been busy saying on the phone, pointing out the enormity of their problem. They didn't have enough recovery teams, enough agents to stop this. The agents called the place the Kennel.

Anya hung up the phone.

"That was Washington, of course," Anya said. "We're getting creamed, Zachary."

"We're doing the best we can," Zach said.

Anya, who had blonde hair and an open kind of face, wide-set brown eyes and a well-toned, middle-aged body beneath her ever-present grey suit dresses, brushed a wisp of hair from her eyes. She kept her hair back in a ponytail almost always. Zach had never seen it otherwise.

"Not good enough," she said. "We have perhaps 24 hours before we completely lose control of this thing. With that many infectives? Each minute matters on this."

"They need to send us more people," Zach said.

"They have their own problems," Anya said. "We're getting preliminary reports of breakouts in other cities, as well. Nobody's quite sure what the hell is happening. Nobody has ever seen an outbreak like this one."

BEE had the resources on-site to contain 20 lycanthropes, and nearly all the cells were already filled, minded by Dr. Mina Milkowski, the Kennel's resident biologist.

They had managed to trace this current outbreak to Patient Zero, the late Samantha Hain, but her own source of infection had not been clear to them. Their monitoring of surveillance cameras had her turning up in several locations, biting and infecting individuals seemingly at random. She had an accomplice, too, a white wolf who had been present at the Avalon incident.

That one was of particular interest to Anya, as she had been implicated in a number of incidents. She'd been biting homeless people, had bitten joggers, had infected a large number of public transit commuters, tourists on charter buses.

"Zachary, I want you to bring that one in," Anya had said. "I want Princess caught."

Anya was prone to nicknaming main targets. She'd taken to calling the white wolf "Princess."

"What about Big Black?" Zach asked, referring to the big, black-furred lycanthrope that had killed his partner and ditched him downtown.

"We'll get him," Anya said. "Tesco's hunting him."

"Tesco?" Zach asked, referring to one of the rival Wardens.

"The one and the same," Anya said. "He's hunting Big Black, and you're hunting Princess. And that is that."

Zach's hand rested on his sidearm. "I want him."

"He's not yours for the taking," Anya said. "Mina's already got a cell lined up for him. She wants to interview him before deportation to Wolf Island."

Zach scowled. "He killed Frank."

"I know," Anya said. "But Mina's research takes priority, Zach. I'm sorry about that."

The Director was in her late 40s, and yet, despite the stresses of her job, her face was smooth: she took care of her skin; it was almost too smooth for her age. Zach imagined the Director walking around with cold cream on her face, or with cucumbers on her eyes, barking orders into her cell phone, keeping up appearances in more ways than one.

"I want to know what that one has been up to," Anya said. "Most of the others are going through the usual adjustment behaviors, but Princess, no, she's got an agenda. I can just tell."

Their teams had been deployed in the field to tag infectives. It was easy enough. They would find recent mauling victims who fit the profile, would approach them disguised as medical personnel, and would take a blood sample and would inject them with a microchip to track them, like the kind they used to track pets or children. That was how they ended up on the big board. Once on the board, they could be monitored.

"Animal Control" was a euphemism for their department; everybody called the Bureau that these days, for the covert branch of the Centers for Disease Control that dealt with paranormal problems.

At least since the 1940s, the Bureau for Extraordinary Events had been in place to contain, study, and analyze lycanthropes, and had a long history with them. There had been experiments conducted, prophylaxis administered, vaccines attempted. All in the service of understanding and coming to terms with the affliction.

The case files went deep; it was only recently that they had migrated to a modern, networked computer system, and even then, they were very careful to keep the data that they accumulated inside BEE. Only the President, Vice President, and select members of Congress were privy to what they did.

These days, BEE had their methodology down pat:

1. Capture
2. Contain
3. Deport

The blood sample thus acquired, the victim tagged, then the recovery and operations teams could take care of things from there, once they had proof positive of infection.

Usually, there was a matter of quarantine and observation. And, once the source of the infection was determined, they were either held for observation and study by the zoologists on-staff, or they were deported to a kind of top secret leper colony for Lupines.

There were constitutional considerations with the deportations, naturally, a matter of due process of law. Prior to 9/11, it hadn't been an option like that. The infectives were quarantined at a remote site in the Pacific, on an island. The ones that were caught were simply too dangerous to be released back into society, so they were shipped to the quarantine site. Patrolled by Navy ships and far from shipping lanes, the classified island—Wolf Island, unimaginatively enough— was the destination for the infectives. It had been an old naval base during World War II, so there were facilities there, and the government kept the island stocked with supplies that were airdropped in. It hadn't been the tidiest of solutions, but the simple truth was that the infectives there knew they were infected, and could not be allowed to reenter society.

There were more than a thousand Lupines on Wolf Island, by the last tally, and the numbers had been spiking since November. The numbers weren't always clear, because there was a certain amount of attrition there as Lupines preyed on each other or had power clashes. There had been talk of abandoning the delivery of supplies, just to see what the Lupines would do, if they could cannibalize each other until the last one died, but at the time, there had been an unwillingness to take such measures, because they had wanted to study the infectives, too. There was also talk of nuking Wolf Island, and just being done with them.

Changes in the law, and the development of a kind of "shadow law" allowed for the option of euthanizing infectives, which saved BEE the logistical challenges of delivery of all of the infectives to Wolf Island. It was simply cheaper to euthanize them, which was applied in the case of ones who had actively hunted and killed.

It was grisly work, but efficient. Since there was no apparent cure for the genetic mutation that infected them, there was nothing else to be done—exile or execution. Infectives could be studied and they could be put down; the protocol was simple and straightforward: if an infective hadn't killed anyone, they ended up at Wolf Island. If they had killed someone, proving themselves to be a public menace, then they would eventually be euthanized. The most important part of BEE's job was to prevent the spread of infection, because if an epidemic occurred, then there was almost no stopping it.

The logic was clear: based on the research, it was determined that Lupines were no longer functionally human. Once they crossed that biological boundary, they were no longer considered applicable to US law. After that, the rest was easy.

However, they were very close reaching to that tipping point, in terms of volume. All of the tagged infectives had to be brought in before their disease fully incubated. And the facility was just not prepared to deal with this many cases this quickly. There were planes en route to deliver them to Wolf Island. And, as a compulsory expatriation, it wasn't something that could be conducted in the light of day (figuratively speaking); infectives were not given a consent form to sign; they were simply recovered and delivered to one of the planes to be shipped out. It was a very challenging arrangement.

"What do you think Princess is up to?" Zach asked, because he knew that Anya would just come out and say it.

"Revolution," Anya said. "That one's a revolutionary, a terrorist."

They watched the clip from the bus, the murder of the driver, the grainy shadow of Princess, tearing the man apart on a stuttering closed circuit television image, distorted.

"It's not going to be easy bringing her in alive," Zach said.

"That's why I'm making this your top priority, Zachary," Anya said. "Find her. Bring her in."

"Alone?" Zach said. Having lost his partner, he felt particularly unmoored.

Anya came over and patted him on the shoulder, her face full of care and concern, or a reasonable facsimile of it.

"We just can't spare the manpower, Zachary," Anya said. "We have too much on our plates as it is. You find Princess, bring her in. I need to talk to her. Get what you need from the Armory."

"What about my truck?"

"Take one of the cars," Anya said. "Don't come back without her."

"Yes, Ma'am," Zach said.

Zach left her in the situation room, wondering how he was even going to go about this. Princess had already killed one of the recovery teams, although he wasn't sure if she'd realized it at the time. They had been a pair of agents who had been buried in the Polish vigilante organization that had been busy hunting the werewolves.

Anya had tried to put agents in their ranks because those fanatics were, despite themselves, always on the front lines of this issue. They were, in the Director's eyes, kind of like an adjunct of BEE, itself: a militia, if not a well-regulated one.

The agents had not identified Princess, had only been aware that she'd been infected by Patient Zero, but when they had moved on-site to acquire the targets, something had happened, and both of them had been killed. The agents had been recovered in Calumet City, their bodies laid out with a dead lycanthrope who had been operating in the region, apparently murdered by Patient Zero and Princess.

Zach went down to the Armory, where he picked himself up an assault rifle and a tranquilizer gun, a sniper rifle with a scope, as well as some body armor. Nobody asked any questions, knew what he was up to, were more than glad that he was doing it, and not them.

Frank should have been driving, not Zach. Zach was the better shooter. He'd have been able to catch Big Black. But Frank had wanted to ride shotgun that night.

Zach was Anya's best field agent, even though it had hardly looked like it the other day with Big Black.

The tranquilizer rifle came to him in pieces, in a case with the hexagonal BEE logo on the sides of it. The whole operation always offered Zach some bitter amusement. Nobody outside of the Bureau really knew what they were charged with doing, because there was always a concern of causing a panic if everyday people, if civilians understood just what they had stalking around in their midst: Werewolves! Vampires, Zombies, Ghouls! Aliens! Oh, my!

The virus was a stubborn thing, had evaded eradication, despite the best efforts of BEE, and decades of research. Perhaps it was a bit of natural—or supernatural—selection. The sloppy lycanthropes, the real nutballs, they were easy to catch. The ones that endured tended to be the smart ones, the ones that covered their tracks and kept a low profile, or were circumspect enough about their predatory habits to not get caught.

Big Black was one of them. He was about as elusive as they came, and nobody knew where he hunted, when he did it, or where he lived. They knew he was a male, knew he was both uncommonly large and strong, but beyond that, they didn't know a thing about him.

Patient Zero had been a bit of a godsend for the Bureau, going off like a Roman Candle the way she did. It had helped them focus their efforts, had allowed Anya to get some more funding and manpower from Washington to contain the outbreak. Unfortunately, Patient Zero was implicated in the murders of her friends, which robbed BEE of the opportunity to interview them, to gather intelligence about the source of Patient Zero's infection.

Often, the first victims to fall to a Lupine were the friends and family, people closest to the infective. This was a common presentation of the affliction: friends and family first.

Typically, if strangers were being targeted instead, it was a Lupine that was in control of their affliction, and was consciously hunting away from loved ones. These were particularly dangerous targets.

Princess was another matter entirely. She seemed very aware of surveillance, seemed to actually crave the attention, was almost gleefully oblivious of the impact of murdering someone beneath one of the many cameras throughout the city. If anything, she made a point of it, feasting on somebody beneath the camera's eye. She'd done that several times already, looking up at the camera as she fed, bloody-muzzled, a smug gleam in those black eyes.

But if she played it big that way, she had not been positively identified as of yet. She was just the white wolf, she was Princess. So far, she was the only one with white fur that they had seen.

It would be hard to focus on this one target; the way the team worked, if they saw an infective, they would bring them in for processing. Anya had been very clear that Princess was his priority. Zach was a team player, didn't like leaving his buddies in the lurch while he went after Princess.

All the same, he didn't want anybody else bringing her in, either. She was his prey.

Tesco tasked with hunting Big Black, looking like the proverbial cat who'd eaten the canary. The grinning bastard rapped Zach on the shoulder, as they'd rolled out a restrained, tranquilized, red-haired man on a stretcher.

"Tough break, Zach," Tesco said, while Dr. Milkowski strolled up, carrying a clipboard.

"You two better be careful," Mina said.

Not quite 30, yet, her mane of black, curly hair down to her shoulders, black-rimmed, rectangular glasses, sharp nose and pointed chin, white-coated and grey-eyed, Mina was in charge of these prisoners, but never saw herself as their warden; she was a scientist from front to back.

"I should get to hunt Big Black," Zach said. "He killed my partner."

Mina shook her head. "That man was dead. He was pronounced dead at the scene. He was shot dead by the Poles. He came back. That makes him special. Worth studying, Zachary."

Zach watched them roll the man into the elevator, while Tesco looked on.

"Like I said, tough break," Tesco said. "You snooze, you lose, Bro."

Mina was clearly humoring the both of them by lingering even this long outside of her precious lab with her pet lycanthropes.

"How much ketamine will you use to bring him down?" Mina asked.

"250 mg," Tesco said.

Mina nodded, jotted it down on her clipboard.

"He should be dead," Zach said.

Mina tapped her teeth with her pen, shook her head. "He's likely to metabolize it quickly. The regenerative capacity of Lupines is fascinating. Now, if you'll excuse me. Happy hunting, Gentlemen."

Milkowski turned on her heel and walked to the elevators, bound for Research.

"Dr. Milkowski's Werewolf Sanctuary will not be closed down by the likes of you, West," Tesco said, snorting.

"Yeah, well we'll see," Zach said, watching the doors close on the good doctor.

Polly had taken care of it.

After kicking Ansel out, she had cried awhile, mourning her plight, but then she'd gotten herself under control. The thing was: she was not an idiot. She'd been paying attention to the news. The broadcasters were nervously talking about outbreaks of "civic unrest" that were taking place, and mentions of "mass hysteria" as more people in the city reported being attacked by unknown animal assailants. CNN was breathlessly broadcasting it—Panic in the Streets.

Reports of wolves and/or coyotes or even "coywolves" (an altogether poetic name, to Polly's ears) were increasing. People were getting bitten and attacked all over the place. She was not alone. She'd laughed bitterly to herself about the irony of it—Sam had finally managed to be on the front end of something. She must have been so pleased with that.

But she was dead, they all were dead. Polly was sure of that, now. She was the last surviving member of the Horrorshow, and, in her eyes, that gave her some kind of obligation to her fallen comrades.

Not that she was going to write some epic poem about them, but it had offered her some clarity and perspective on her situation, and got her to dry her tears. Something was happening to the city. People were changing. She was changing.

As an artist, she wanted to bear witness to this, to communicate what she had seen, to find or make meaning of it, to make monstrosity her muse.

Of course, her first instinct was to blog it, on Polytician.

I'm the only one left. I think all of my friends are dead, and A is dead to me. Not completely, who am I kidding? I could see how much it pained him, my condition. He was hurting for me. He remains long-term relationship material, but after such be-

trayal, I can't take him into my heart again, at least not yet. He's messy.

At least now I know what he and S had in common. It used to gnaw at me, but since he told me, now I know. And I have it in common with him, too. And with S gone, I don't have to be jealous, anymore.

I have more important things to worry about.

She paused over her words, looked at her painted nails. She'd taken care to paint them red, this beautiful, glossy scarlet. The nails caught her eye as she typed on her keyboard. It had become a bit of an obsession with her of late, in the wake of her condition. Polly always wanted to be presentable and put together, and that Thing inside her kept messing things up, pulling her apart. She'd had Tristan's blood on her hands and underneath her nails. And so, her putting on the nail enamel was a bit of a cosmetic reaction to that, attempting to take control once more.

The problem was that Thing whispered in her ears. She wouldn't shut up. When Polly had come to her senses, standing over what was left of Tristan's body, bloody up to her elbows, blood across her face, her mouth, stomach full, she had understood almost at once, could remember how it happened, like it was a nightmare she remembered.

They had been arguing about Ansel, and that Thing had come bursting right out of her, had lunged for Tristan before he could even react with more than a horrified squawk.

Yes, yes,
I ruined your dress.
And that Thing always spoke in rhyme. It was mocking her.
You and me,
eternally.
That Thing had lodged itself inside her head, and would not leave. It jabbered while she faced the Tristan Problem, which was no small thing.

You've been very naughty.
What's left of his body?
That was the crux of the thing: Polly had been watching the news, was seeing what was going on, could understand in a way that the bewildered broadcasters clearly didn't, or weren't permitted to.

She could have called the police and reported Tristan murdered, and the police would have turned up and conducted a forensic investigation. They would have found the blood beneath Polly's nails, would have unearthed something that implicated Polly in his murder.

And Polly wasn't altogether convinced that if she'd gone that route that she wouldn't end up on some kind of government watch list. It was a paranoid thought, the kind of thing that Lee or Sheldon would have come up with, she was sure. Just the same, she couldn't shake it.

Shake it, take it,
make it or break it.

"You're rhyming 'it' with itself," Polly said aloud, to the Thing.

It could be shit,
if you think about it.

"You're not funny," she said. She'd taken to talking to herself, to the Thing she would not name.

My name is the same.
This fall, I'm Pol, that's all.

"Just stop," she said.

She would not let it distract her. It wanted her to finish what she'd started, to eat the rest of Tristan, but it had been unbearable for her. Knowing that she'd done as much as she had was more than she could stand. She couldn't go further down that dreadful path. Not knowingly.

It's a shame you're so tame.
There's a word for it: LAME.

"Quite the wit, you miserable shit," Polly said. The Thing that writhed inside her looked like Polly. She could see it in her mind's eye, this Vargas girl version of herself, with lacquered black bangs, wearing a black peignoir. An absurd caricature of herself, curlicues of black hair traced to flapperesque points down the side of her face. Dolled up and fanged, but not elegant vampire fangs; rather, brutal, drool-inducing werewolf fangs.

Enough of your kvetching;
I'm really quite fetching.
A dog should be fetching
don't you know, don't you know?
Though it might make you twitch
Understand: I'm your bitch
And think of the places we'll go.

So, with the authorities out of the question, and the Thing's suggestion completely beyond her, Polly went for something rather more mundane, and dug a shallow grave in her backyard, to put Tristan's legs into it. She would bury him in her rose garden, while the Thing blathered Seussian doggerel in her head.

"Leave me alone," Polly said. It was the kind of work Tristan loved to do. Polly loved tending her roses, but let Tristan turn the earth. Physical labor always appealed to him.

Golly, Polly; there's no dearth of earth.

Or mirth, for what that's worth.

"Stop," Polly said. "Get out of my head."

If I left your head,

you'd surely be dead.

As a widow, she would have been privy to Tristan's generous life insurance policy. Death and dismemberment was covered, if she remembered.

Let's take him outside,

we can go for a ride.

She put on some Playtex gloves and put Tristan's wallet in the pocket of his track pants, and then slid his legs into a garbage bag, and, in the dark of the night, she put him in the trunk of his BMW, and then drove him to Harding Park, where the jogging track was, and, careful that nobody was watching, deposited his legs there.

Then she drove off, dumped the bag in a trash can many miles away, and then went home and scrubbed the hell out of the trunk of the car, and the floor where he'd been killed.

Kill rhymes with thrill,

if you only will.

She cleaned every inch of the place, erased every trace of Tristan.

And then she called the police, reported Tristan missing.

She was ever the dutiful wife, a role she had played even when she'd been seeing Ansel.

Tristan was found the following day. A jogger had come to Harding Park early the next morning, a young man, and had found the legs. He'd called it in immediately.

The police had come, and they'd broken the news to her. That something had attacked her husband, and they'd found what was left of him in the park. The police officer had said that it looked like his body had been dropped there; that he hadn't been killed in the park, but there were clear signs that something had eaten him. Maybe a bear, or a wolf. They were still investigating, and would let her know if they learned anything more.

Polly played her part well, cried and spoke about the stuff she'd seen on the news, wondered aloud about what was going on.

Nobody quite knew, not even the police. There had been a wave of animal attacks, and they had seemed to be escalating.

Polly had looked into Tristan's insurance, had begun the sure-to-be-lengthy process of filing a claim. The insurance agent had been polite on the phone, had explained that they would have to confirm that his death had been accidental upon an autopsy, and would investigate the police report of it. She accepted that, knew that the insurance agent would have bitten off more than he could chew with this one. There would be no denial of claims, here—something had eaten her husband.

In fact, she was glad she jumped on that, because she figured if the rash of attacks were on the rise, insurers would surely be inclined to revise their policies on such claims. But she wasn't about to miss out on that.

So, she had handled it. With the death and dismemberment policy as well as the life insurance policy, Polly stood to receive many hundreds of thousands of dollars, more than enough to live comfortably for a long time. Tristan had been meticulous about investments and insurance, so Polly was more than covered, and took some security in that. Despite the mayhem that this Thing had wrought in her life, Polly had some measure of protection.

All the same, she could feel the Thing squirming inside her, wanting to get out. Her fur had not been jet black, as she'd expected; it had been like the very darkest chocolate. The Thing liked to think about itself, liked to push those images into Polly's consciousness, led to them having a bit of a catfight—or was it a dogfight—inside her soul.

But it bothered Polly. Her hair was lustrous black. Why didn't her Lupine incarnation follow suit? Why dark brown?

Brown makes you frown?

"I just don't understand why your fur isn't black."

Our fur: yours and mine.

Together, we shine.

Polly clutched her temples. The Thing was driving her insane with its rhyming.

"I can't live like this," she said. "I can't possibly live with you going on like this in my head."

There's really no need to shout;

please let me out and about.

If you'll just let me feed,
I'll spare you this screed.

Polly wanted to scream. She stalked upstairs in her big, empty house, barefoot on the ivory carpeting on the steps, gripping it with her toes, and she went into the cavernous bathroom that Tristan had insisted that they get, and the big, round bathtub, and she drew herself a bath, poured lavender bath salts into it, and took off her clothes, turned on some classical music on her surround stereo, and slipped into the bath, relishing the feel of the hot water, the immersive nature of it.

But the Thing was in there with her, too, taking a soak, listening to Schubert with her.

"I am Polly Drinkwater," Polly said. "I am no one but who I am."

Ain't that quaint?
You're not without taint.

Polly felt the anger well up in her again, wild and fierce. The Thing was goading her, trying to wind her up. It fed on those base emotions.

The bath was meant to soothe her, but it only made her feel more restive.

Restive, festive, it's all the same game.
Set me free, and I'll leave you be.

"I won't be free," Polly said. "I'll just be taken along for the ride."

You'll hide inside,
but oh, what a ride:
Breaking the laws
raking our claws
Snapping my teeth

Polly was frustrated, was not used to being at war with herself this way.

We're a dream team.
I'll be the trap,
and you'll be the bait.
Let me out,
I swear it'll be great.

"No more rhymes," Polly said. "Please."

Just say my name
I swear I'll be tame.

"Pol," Polly said. "It's what you called yourself."

Pol, Pol, Pol, Pol
once and for all.

It was like a switch inside her, as Polly let out a scream, felt something trigger within her, quite against her will, as she sat naked in the tub, gripping the rim of the tub with both hands, surrounded by fragrant bubbles and steam, feeling her slim body become ribboned with flesh, muscle, fur and meat. Her scream became a howl as she held out her hands, saw them become clawed paws, saw her reflection change, her face turn to a snout, her whitened teeth growing whiter, long and curved, watched her beautiful self become something ghastly and monstrous, her smooth, ivory skin bursting with darkest brown fur.

Wet and wild, Pol leapt from the tub, left a splash on the floor, just like before, and ran right out the door on all fours.

There'd be time for bathing later.

8

From the safety of the shadows, Zooey watched the *Wilkołak* Brothers do their thing at a mechanic shop in Avondale. It was Sam's name for them, and boy did she ever hate them. Only they knew what they actually called themselves, and she'd never left any of them alive long enough to question them. They were Polish, and they were dead serious about hunting down Lupines. She had made a special effort to track these guys down, after all the trouble they'd caused her and Sam. She'd wanted to know where they were, what they were up to. She didn't know if they were somehow responsible for tracking down and killing Sam, but she wanted to find out.

Of course, with all hell breaking loose in the city, the Wilkos had been busy smithing silver bullets and putting together teams of hit men. There was a war brewing in Chicago, and Zooey had tracked this place as a base of operations of the Wilkos, the hub for all of their silver spokes.

She'd studied them covertly, wanted to get a sense of their routines. There were about 20 men, by her count, and they ran in five cars or vans.

Where she watched them was from an abandoned neighborhood pharmacy that was across the street from their hideout. She hadn't wanted to be seen just yet, since the Wilkos were serious, packing silver bullets and daggers and all of that werewolf-busting stuff.

She'd broken in through the back of the place and had just kept an eye on them. Because she'd been seen with Sam years ago, and those guys had been hunting her, Zooey assumed they would shoot her on sight, which was why she was bucking her usual approach to things by observing them before confronting them.

All the same, she was itching for a fight. It was just that she had to be perfect on this one, because those guys just had to take a lucky shot at her and she'd be dead. Part of her thrilled to that now-unfamiliar fear; since the transformation, Zooey had felt like nothing could come close to harming her, but she'd known that silver was deadly to the virus that had remade her.

It was clear that the norms were upping the game. She'd sent Looper, a new minion, downtown to gather a pack and start working the lakeshore, but he'd gotten killed by Wilko snipers or something. The other Lupines had said that silver bullets were raining down on them from everywhere, from all directions. Zooey assumed that they must have had guys up on the skyscrapers, and cursed Looper for being an idiot for assembling a pack out in the open. But he was cocky that way, and paid for it, clearly.

Zooey had already put word out to the other packmates not to gather in the open like that, and not in big packs. As satisfying as it was to see that many lycanthropes in one place, it was just too risky at the moment. For now, she put her sisters to work infecting people. She'd gotten even smarter about it—a lycanthrope could spread the infection with a bite, so she was having them bite everybody they could. Like even when they were normal, she was having them bite people they knew, like during sex and stuff. Just so long as blood was drawn, the infection could be passed. It might take longer if somebody wasn't badly bitten, but it kept victims out of the hospital, which was key, because the doctors were paying attention, now.

These stealth infections were proceeding beautifully. She insisted that everybody infect others. In a way, she felt like a saleswoman, and her packmates had nightly quotas to meet. She'd told them that each of them had to infect 15 people each night. She wanted 15 new infectives each night, did the math in her head, figured they'd be able to control the city in a month that way. Anybody who didn't deliver the quota, Zooey killed. She only wanted motivated members in her pack, and after killing the first three or four squeamish souls, the message was loud and clear, and nobody questioned her. They were meeting their quotas, one way or another.

She hadn't tracked how quickly the infection spread in a person, but it seemed to do so pretty damned fast—depending on the severity of the infection, it seemed like they manifested within a week from a typical werewolf attack. And about a month in the case of a love nip.

She'd been calling newly infected "Nippers," since she'd been careful to have her packmates just give them a nip or two, instead of eating them outright. It paid to show a little restraint during recruitment drives.

She'd been very clear:

1. Eat the fat ones
2. Nip the fit ones

It was her own bit of triage, a prelude to her own grand plan. She wanted her packmates to live off the fat of the land, and to be lean and mean killing machines. Fit for Fat.

Three of the Wilkowagons were gone, which meant that this cell had 12 men in the field, and probably four at the hideout right now, with the remainder resting somewhere. These men had day jobs, had lives of their own, above and beyond this secret society. They were family men, good men, trying to fight the good fight.

Zooey smiled to herself. She understood that, even though it didn't make a bit of difference to her. Let them be good norms, and she'd be a good werewolf, and let the chips fall where they would.

She wanted to confirm that this was where the Wilkos seemed to be operating. As much as she wanted to, she couldn't strike at it directly, not simply because of the risk, but because if she took down the hub, then the spokes would realize that their hideout had been compromised.

So, she had to cut off the spokes, nip them off one by one, until the hub was the only thing remaining, and then she would finish that off.

That seemed safer to her, more sensible. If the Wilkos were all in there at one time, that would be one thing, but they never seemed to be; these guys were always coming and going, and maybe that was because things were keeping them busy that they had to have guys in the field, or maybe it was part of their strategy.

Either way, it didn't matter. These guys were major buzzkills, and they had to be dealt with as such. She'd seen their creepy-ass logo—it was like a cross with arrows, a circle and a crescent moon on it. The guys had it tattooed on their shoulders or over their hearts, in a simple black tat. After stumbling on it while searching the body of one of the Wilkos she'd killed, she'd made a point to check every time, and every one of those Poles had it on his body. She'd seen the symbol as graffiti on walls, and realized that it was all part of it. These creeps had safe houses throughout the city, apparently, but there were a lot in Avondale.

Zooey had ordered her packmates to bring her a Wilko alive, but none of them had pulled it off. The Wilkos didn't allow themselves to be taken captive; they died fighting, and her packmates would get carried away and end up killing the targets, anyway. You just couldn't get good help these days.

She took off her clothes and put them in a plastic bag, set that bundle on a dusty shelf at the pharmacy, and she crouched, letting herself transform, grinding tendons and muscle and sinew into her larger, snowy-white form. She hardly felt the pain, anymore, almost relished the fleeting agony of shapeshifting. The hybrid shape: part woman, part wolf. Unlike the others, she had a unique challenge in this form, for she was very visible, a snow-white monstrosity.

Sniffing the air, she could smell the stinging scent of silver in one of the cars, knew that the four Wilkos in there were planning a field trip. In fact, the men were closing up their headquarters, carrying bags, everybody dressed in black. That creepy logo, painted on a sign over the shop. Graffiti to the norms, but a call sign to the Wilkos, for sure.

They were men on a mission, moving with precise purpose.

Watching from the safety of the shadows, Zooey laughed to herself. These men were so serious, so earnest. They made the BEE agents look like tourists. Taking out the BEE Wardens had been easy by comparison. Those feds had been operating right out in the open—overtly covert, and their agency had been easy to infiltrate, easy to track. Reports came back throughout the country, as packmates told her what they'd found. Zooey had made it easy for them, told them to hunt down the BEE agents without hesitation, and to shut them down. She'd also told them to be on the lookout for that weird glyph, to see if they saw it in their areas.

According to what she'd heard, and what they'd seen, the glyph had been seen in New York, Philadelphia, Milwaukee, LA, Toledo, Phoenix, Pittsburgh, San Diego, Cleveland, Houston, Detroit, Baltimore, San Francisco, Boston, Seattle, Las Vegas—basically, anywhere there were a lot of Poles, the glyph had been spotted, and the Wilkos had been active.

She'd tried to see if she could find the glyph on the Internet, but it was hard to do a search for a glyph, so she recently had her packmates blog about it, to take pictures of it and ask. She knew she was onto something when three things happened:

1. Nobody had a clue to what it represented

2. Nobody said a word about what it was (besides a few conspiracy theorists who claimed it was some Satanic cult or Illuminati thing)

3. Her packmates who had posted the pictures all ended up dead

Zooey had been startled by that, but had seen her packmates falling silent, one by one, usually a week or two after they'd made their posts about the glyph. Clearly, the Wilkos didn't want word getting out about them, and had no compunction about killing her packmates—and worse, they were good at it.

Black Sheep was researching it at the University of Chicago, said they had old books there that nobody read, but if it was anywhere, it would be there, and he'd find it. Black Sheep was a good boy.

The Wilkos got into an old pea green Lincoln, and went off on their way, heading east, as they always did, toward the lake shore. They were working hard to try to keep the werewolves from moving westward. They were failing. Zooey had made sure of that—it was like trying to hold sand in a fist; her pack only kept growing.

Climbing up a fire escape, Zooey crouched in the rooftop shadows, followed the men as they drove. It would do no good to attack them so close to their hub; the others would know that they had been made.

As much as she didn't want to do this, she had to be patient. It was not in her nature to be this way, but she jumped from rooftop to rooftop, building to building, shadow to shadow, always keeping that Lincoln in sight.

When they had crossed the river, she would attack them. There would be no margin for error. At the bridge, they would be bottlenecked, and she'd be able to do away with them more effectively.

Thankfully, she had arranged for one of her packmates to be the bait. It was a young man Zooey had bitten on the El. He had found her, sniffed her out, and Zooey had explained to him what was what, showed him who was boss. It's all these people really wanted: someone to make it all clear to them, to do their thinking for them.

What she had in mind for this one was a simple ambush. The Noob would draw their attention and fire, and Zooey could get behind them and kill them.

The Wilkowagon was one stoplight away from the bridge, and Zooey was alongside them, on a rooftop, behind a billboard, watching. She took the scent of the air, hoping to spot the Noob, but her nose didn't register him.

The bridge was near a water reclamation area, where some kind of chemicals were sprayed into the river water, decontaminating it, turning it into some fizzy, toxic chemical concoction. The tingly stink of the chemicals made her nose twitch.

From this point, there were four lanes of busy road to cross before she got to the bridge, which was a two-laner. To the south, the city sprawled out in the darkness in the distance, an architectural anaconda hugging the horizon, glowing gorgeously in the night.

The traffic lights turned, and the Wilkos crossed the intersection, and Zooey leapt from the building she was at, landing at the far side, near an old, unused gatehouse, where she supposed at one time, some tender may have worked to raise this bridge, back when this bridge needed raising. It didn't look like that had been raised for 50 years.

There was no sign of the Noob, so Zooey simply acted, charging from the pedestrian walkway of the bridge, cutting across traffic, and ripping off the passenger rear door of the Wilkowagon, behind the driver.

She was gratified to hear the spray of Polish from the startled men instead of a hail of silver bullets. They had not expected an attack so soon, and she wasted no time, snapping the neck of the nearest man with a single bloody bite, then clawing at the other man in the back, stuffing herself into the Wilkowagon, even as cars honked behind them, people reacted to the sight of a monstrous white wolf-thing seeming to come out of nowhere, attacking a car.

The Wilkos were screaming, the driver floored the accelerator, and they raced over the bridge, the car zig-zagging, crashing into and clipping parked cars, while Zooey finished off the man in the back seat, and sank her teeth into the meaty shoulder of the man riding shotgun, who had been trying to draw a dagger to stab her with when she bit him.

"*Potwór znalazłeś nas,*" one of them shouted.

Zooey liked to talk when she hunted, but where the Wilkos were concerned, she had to be all business, because these guys were all business, themselves.

She reached around the passenger seat and clawed the man's face, finding his throat a moment later, rending it as she was savaging his shoulder with her teeth.

"*Jest Biały Wilk!*" the driver said.

The driver turned the car a hard right, past a row of parked cars, and as the car turned, he threw open the driver's side door and tumbled out, sending Zooey and the Wilkowagon racing down the street.

She shoved her way out the opposite side of the car, throwing open the door and leaping out, tumbling, herself, as the Wilkowagon sped down the way, crashing into a phone pole near some kind of scrapyard.

Zooey had her feet immediately upon exiting, had the driver's scent as clear as day. He was running toward a parking deck, shooting at Zooey with a pistol as he fled. The bullets sparked on the sidewalk, but did not find their mark. He was panic-firing, was calling someone on his phone.

Springing after him, Zooey closed the distance in seconds, and had her teeth clamped down on the man's gun arm before he could get off another shot. One flex of her jaws, and the man's forearm snapped in her teeth like it was a twig.

The man howled, and Zooey, inspired, let him go, despite wanting to take off his head with her monstrous jaws. By wounding the man, one of three things would happen:

1. He'd go to the hospital and the doctors would mark him as an infective, and he would likely disappear, like the others who became infected and went to the hospital

2. He'd be euthanized by the other Wilkos

3. He'd try to keep it hidden and would eventually become a lycanthrope, and would become part of her pack

In any of those scenarios, it amounted to a win for her, one way or another.

Without wasting another moment, Zooey ran across the street, into the comforting shadow of an alley that ran parallel to the river, while horrified drivers and pedestrians gaped at the carnage they had just witnessed.

The whole attack had only taken about a minute.

She ran into the Noob, who was coming up the alley. She knocked him on his ass. He was in his human form.

"You're late, Noob," she said, breathing down on him, bloody-muzzled.

"My bus got stuck in traffic," he said.

"I took care of it," she said. "But you owe me."

She raced away from the bewildered man, wasn't in the mood to talk further with him. It was something she'd learned already—if you wanted anything done right, you had to do it yourself.

One Wilko spoke snapped.

Best of all, they would wonder how she managed to ambush them. They wouldn't know that she had hunted out their hideout, could do them all in at her convenience.

Police cars and fire trucks howled somewhere, no doubt called in by terrified onlookers. Zooey joined the howling vehicles with her own howl, raising her head skyward, giving a full-throated rendition of it.

Howling invariably felt good. It was like the primal screams her mom and dad had been big on doing, back in the day. Thinking on her parents gave her momentary pause. They'd not approve of Zooey's lifestyle choices of late. They would really not approve of this, although she hardly cared.

After all, this was awesome.

Zach had been so pissed about Tesco being tasked with taking Big Black that he had gone out hunting for Princess, just to get her out of the way. As a BEE Warden, it was a privilege he was afforded. Only the Wardens were authorized to hunt the Lupines, had the training to even have a prayer of surviving an encounter with them.

He'd been driving around in his car, listening to the police reports as well as the BEE dispatcher. These days, there was so much Lupine activity being reported, one only had to wait. When the reports of Princess operating up in Avondale had come through, Zach sped toward it. Tesco may have a chance to bag Big Black, but if Zach could bring in—or bring down—Princess, that was something he could live with.

"Houndstooth to Dogcatcher, I'm inbound to Avondale," Zach said into his radio.

He could see the police sirens and ambulances at the bridge, and went to a nearby park to observe. He took out his Remington rifle and slipped on his body armor, checked his sidearm to be sure it was there—a Colt Python. He had his BEE Warden badge on him as well, just in case Chicago PD crossed paths with him. The BEE had authorization to do what they did, very much a wink-and-nod deal with the local police, who thought they were all full of shit before, but nowadays, with the outbreak spreading, maybe they'd changed their tune. Enough of them had seen Lupines to know that something was out there.

Zach slipped his night vision goggles into place. Everything swam into view, that swampy shade of green that was the hallmark of night vision.

Back and forth he scanned, looking for Princess. For a white wolf, she was notoriously evasive and hard to spot. In the shadows of the park, with only the strobelight of the police cars and ambulances and firetrucks there to illuminate the shadows, Zach scanned, undaunted.

If Princess had been here, she was long gone.

Then he heard something that made him grow cold all over.

It was a growl, behind him.

Zach cursed himself for his fixating on searching for Princess, as it had let something get behind him. He knew from experience that in the time it took him to pivot and bring his rifle to bear on the Lupine, it would already be on him.

So, he turned his head and could see it, a lean, dark lycanthrope in the shadow of his car, eyes brightly illuminated, stalking him. From the size, he judged it to be a female, possibly an adolescent. It was easily within jumping distance.

"Now, now," Zach said, his mouth dry.

"Who are you?" the thing asked, her voice a syrupy hiss.

Zach took some solace in that. The Lupines that didn't talk were particularly savage; the talkers had enough presence of mind to retain at least a sliver of sentience. It gave Zach the chance to treat this as a hostage scenario, with himself as the hostage. If he could talk to the thing enough to get himself turned around, he might have a chance of shooting it.

"I'm Zach," he said. "Who are you?"

"I'm Pol," she said. "That's all."

The two of them moved at the same time, but as fast as Zach was, Pol was faster, and he spun around, only to have Pol break his rifle in half as she'd charged. He'd brought up his rifle in a defensive gesture and she'd cracked the thing in half with her jaws, spittle flinging from her maw as she cast aside the broken weapon and clawed at Zach, who had fallen to the ground and was trying to draw his pistol.

In the light of the night vision goggles, her green-white muzzle loomed horribly. Her face shifted to a lurid, monstrous smile. Despite being lean, she was fiendishly strong, and managed to pin Zach's arm, the pistol drawn but pressed into the grass by an outstretched paw. Her other paw tore away his night vision goggles, her bloody breath in his face.

"Are you a hunter?" Pol asked.

"Yes," Zach said, grunting, trying to free his weapon.

"I'm not hungry, Hunter," Pol said. "I've been hunting, have eaten my fill. I couldn't eat another bite, couldn't make another kill. But, still…"

Then she bit him, right on his gun arm. Zach cursed and flailed, crying out, trying to free himself. Her teeth burned where they touched him, the cellular outrage of those big teeth sinking into his flesh and muscle, her head shaking, making the wound worse. He struggled to free himself, but was at her monstrous mercy, which offered him no hope at all.

She tossed him into the grass.

"Now we both have a problem," she said, grinning at him, before bounding off into the darkness, leaving Zach writhing on the ground, cursing, switching his pistol from his mangled arm to his other hand, and took aim at the fleeing Lupine, but she was already lost in the shadows

There was no vaccination for lycanthropy. BEE had been trying to find one, but nobody had come up with it, yet.

Zach swore, tugging at his clothes, looking at the grievous wound Pol had given him, cursing his misfortune.

She was lost. He was lost.

Infected.

Even the word gnawed at him, made him nauseous.

He got himself to his feet, dizzy, now. Even a small bite from these things could be dangerous, and she'd made a point to make it a big wound, right up his arm, to maximize the infection.

Zach went to his car, to the glovebox, dug out a first aid kit. He tore open an iodine swab and rubbed it on the wound, yelling at the sting of it. It was futile prophylaxis, he knew, but he couldn't just take her attack without doing anything about it.

His radio crackled.

"Dogcatcher to Houndstooth, come in."

"This is Houndstooth," Zach said, straining to sound composed.

"What is your status? Do you need backup?"

"Negative," Zach said, trying to stop the blood flow. He'd need to do a field dressing out here. There was no way in hell he was going back to the Kennel like this. He was not going to end up in one of Milkowski's observation cells, or get euthanized.

Zach understood that it was a breach of protocol. But he figured since Anya had wanted him to be in the field, anyway, tracking and capturing Princess, he wouldn't break protocol if he didn't actually head back to the Kennel.

It was why he was a Warden to begin with. He liked being out and about, couldn't imagine sequestering himself behind a desk.

Having stabilized his injury, Zach made his way to the driver's seat, watched the first responders leave one by one, oblivious to his presence in the park near the bridge. To be blindsided by a Lupine was serious rookie Warden shit. Tesco would never let him live that down. None of them would.

Zach broke out into a sweat as he tried to move his arm. The pain was almost more than he could bear. He closed the door, wincing at the agony in his arm, and went to start the car.

He got as far as reaching for the ignition key before passing out.

10

Ansel was on his deck, drinking a Pimm's Cup, listening to the chorus of howls. Each night he went onto his deck—it was part of his routine. Not the drinking, so much as the listening. He had to take stock, to see how it was developing. The numbers kept growing. It was astounding and hard to comprehend just how fast things had gotten out of control.

He had been naïve to think that he could stop the plague on his own. Things had escalated too quickly. Someone was shepherding this process through at an alarming rate. Somebody had been going out of their way to make a mess of things, to infect as many sheeple as possible.

Every night there were more howls. So far, they had been smart enough to stay the hell away from him, to understand that there was danger in this place, but sooner or later, someone would enter into his territory. It would come down to that. It always did.

That was the prickly problem that he faced. He could not stop what was happening; not by himself. He wasn't goddamned Batman. It wasn't his responsibility; okay, maybe it was a little bit, or even a lot, because of what he'd done to Sam, what had gotten this ball rolling to begin with, but the fix was him going out and killing werewolf after werewolf, until his own fur was matted with blood, until he either killed every one of the infectives or was, himself, killed by one he couldn't beat.

He didn't want to go there. Ansel was an artist, not an assassin, not a warrior. Art was where his heart was. If the city wanted to turn itself inside out and become some kind of lycanthropic playground, who was he to stop it? He would simply paint what he saw, would show the downward spiral of the city in his art, would communicate the monstrosity of the moment that way. Mapping the descent into madness with paint and brush was, to him, the only sane thing he could do.

He had nothing to fear from the breakout, unless the feds went crazy and nuked Chicago. Of anybody in the city at that time, the one with the least to worry about was Ansel. He had plenty of money. He had been a Lupine his entire life. It was as natural to him as breathing. Yes, he'd had a low time that had led him to try to medicate himself, to keep the Beast under wraps, but look what that had gotten him? That had led to Sam.

There was nothing to be done. He would not rise to some higher moral challenge, wouldn't save humanity. Ansel had never been a human being, had only appeared to be one. What was humanity to him, besides a threat and an obstacle to navigate around? People got in the way, got in his way, and Ansel didn't like that.

He cared something for Polly, and Polly had kicked him to the curb. Beyond her, his moral obligation ceased. A cruel calculus, but Ansel was beyond caring at that point. He'd been attracted to Sam, and he enjoyed his time with Polly. And now one was dead, and the other despised him.

He'd crept back to Sam's place, had found his painting of Polly, where Polly had secreted it away, for some reason. He'd taken that painting back, had put it up on his wall, in the empty space where it had belonged, where Polly had stolen it.

Women. The things they did.

Ansel listened to the howls. Hundreds. There were hundreds of them, now. Each night there were more. It was surreal. The norms, the sheeple, had to be shivering in the dark, hearing that racket. Or getting angry. Maybe both.

He understood the call of the wild, that thirst for blood and slaughter that boiled inside him. The Beast wanted to be fed. It insisted on it. He felt that as much as those whelps out there felt it.

There was a ravenous logic to it: eat everything. Infect everyone. Breed and multiply. Kill, kill, kill. Those were the directives of the curse, the imperatives of the affliction. Even trueborn, he was as captive to it as anybody else out there.

He heard someone scaling his fire escape, and he tensed, setting down his cocktail.

A shadow hopped onto his deck, a feral, furry thing, back arched, arms out ahead of it, claws flexing. A werewolf, ears pricked, nose working as it took stock of its surroundings. Upwind of him.

"Hey," Ansel said, and the thing turned and gazed at him, this blue-eyed, brown-furred beast. A bitch.

She caught his scent, emerged into the half-light, the sodium glare of the streetlights below.

"Ansel," the thing hissed, through wicked-sharp teeth. Long, curved claws, the hint of nail polish on them, like bits of blood.

"Polly," Ansel said, catching her scent.

"Pol," it said back to him. "I'm the Apostle Pol."

And she ran up to him, snuffling at him, licking him with her great tongue. She took him in her arms, her claws nicking his skin, drawing blood where she touched.

"Why don't you change your skin for me, Lover?" she asked, her voice a husky hiss. "Slip into something more comfortable?"

Ansel looked into her blue eyes, wild and wanton, her slender form rippling with taut, predatory muscle, and marveled at the transformation.

She nosed at him, nuzzled him.

"Why do you hide?" she asked, her voice a macabre parody of Polly's own practiced, studiously silky voice.

"I'm not hiding," Ansel said. "I'm just not in the mood."

Polly let him go, half-laughing, a ghastly cackle that shook her lean frame. She grinned, all teeth, those wide-set eyes upon him.

"This is what you wanted," she said. "This is what you had in mind all along, Lover."

"Not like this," Ansel. "I wanted to spare you this."

She raised a finger, long and made longer by the lengthy turn of her claw. "I've fed, Darling. I've feasted on the meat of man. I've been busy while you've been cloistered in this place. This was where I should have been born. Sam took my place that night. I'm here, now. I understand."

Polly circled him, her claws carving splinters from the wood of the deck as she passed. She couldn't help herself, kept creating curlicues with her claws as she went.

"What would you have me do?" Ansel asked.

"Ride me," Polly said. "Gods, yes."

The Beast had delighted at the sight of Polly.

Yes. Please do. She's ready for you.

Polly bumped into him, took his scent with snuffs of air. She toyed with him, presented herself to him. The Beast would not take this provocation without responding in kind.

"You want this?" Ansel asked.

"I want it," Polly said.

And, all at once, Ansel willed himself to change, felt the bruising break of flesh and bone, as he was recast into his true self, the Beast, the great big thing that he was, the monster of monsters, growing, sprouting black fur and matching claws, only his teeth white, long and as fiercely overgrown as the rest of him.

Polly watched him change with animal delight, eyes wide, pupils dilated, mouth agape, tongue out, panting, panting, turning herself toward him, turning and yearning. Polly, always coyly sweet and cutely flirtatious with him, now turned into something else, feral and fecund, wild and wanton.

Ansel took her on his deck, sinking his teeth into her shoulder as he mounted her, claimed her, clawed at the back of her neck with his hands, and she yelped and howled as he penetrated her, gazing over her shoulder at him with the wildest of eyes, going wilder with each thrust.

Sex and violence. Violent sex. Lycanthropic lust.

She gave herself to him utterly, and he took her completely, the both of them howling together in the dark.

Dr. Milkowski walked in front of the thick, enclosed containment cells, gazing at the werewolves snarling and howling silently at her behind thick panes of ballistic glass that even they couldn't break.

This part of the BEE was, really, the beating heart of it. This was where the research was conducted, where the infectives were monitored and studied. At the moment, all of them had been induced to transform by adverse stimulus, in this case, electrified panels in the floor. The shock of pain would bring the Lupines right out of their human wrappers.

She had an even split between male and female infectives, the males along the north wall, the females in the south. They were right across each other, with a causeway down the middle where the researchers could walk.

Mina's role put her in two places—biology and psychology. She'd gotten advanced degrees in both from Stanford, had been tapped by the CDC for this role, had jumped at the opportunity. Once you got a peek behind the mask, learned of the existence of the paranormal, it was worth the nondisclosure agreement, frankly.

The Bureau had been a dream job for her, a place where she could study something mysterious and extraordinary. She loved her job.

Typically, the Kennel held, at most, maybe three infectives at one time, since they had been very good about keeping the numbers down, of identifying and dealing with infections as they appeared.

But to have 20 Lupines at one time? It was unheard of, and Mina was making the most of it.

She had a team of assistants, a group of fellow lab rats who were hard at work sequencing the retrovirus that caused this disease. Since the advancements in gene sequencing, aided by ever-growing computer processing power, there had been great strides made in finally cracking the code of the pathogen that had spawned the lycanthrope.

Knowing what it was didn't win the war by any means, but it afforded a vital glimpse into the way the thing worked.

As she understood it to date, the retrovirus managed to carefully insert itself into the host's genome in a way that was particularly distinct. This allowed for a usurpation of the host's genetic code without completely disrupting it. It was like a magic bullet, a marvelous biological dance that turned the target into an ideal transmitter of the virus to other uninfected hosts. That was the entire purpose of it.

Mina paused before Number 7, a brown male, who hurled himself against the glass, tried to claw at it, but could find no purchase.

"What is Seven's problem this evening?" Mina asked.

"He's hungry," Desiree said. Desiree, a young black woman with a close-shaved head and almond eyes, coordinated the containment of the Lupines.

"I see," Mina said. "Hadn't he gotten his rations?"

"He did," Desiree said. "But I think he wants more."

"He wants meat," Mike said. Mike was young and blond, a scar on his chin, legacy of a Lupine, but not enough of an injury to infect him, apparently. Or maybe the bite was the only way to transmit the infection.

All of the infectives in the holding tanks were killers. That was the point of their captivity. Mina's charge was to interview them, take samples from them, study, them, and, ultimately, to dispose of them.

Number 7 had been picked up at the state line, bound for Indiana. He'd killed and eaten three bikers. His name was Desmond La Silva. Native of Pilsen, 23 years old. He had picked up the infection in the mass attack that had occurred in the nightclub, Avalon, when Patient Zero and Princess had entered the place and Princess had transformed, infecting over 200 people in a mass attack that could only be labeled "bioterrorism" in Mina's view.

Patient Zero had filmed the attack, and they had posted it on the Internet, where it, along with Zero's "Transformation" video, had become a viral sensation, one of the first of these types of videos. There were many more, although none shot by the individuals, themselves; rather, just shaky, blurry shots people uploaded.

Mr. La Silva had, by his own admission, encountered the bikers in Pilsen, at an area bar. Whether La Silva or the bikers had initiated the confrontation was not revealed by Mina in her interviews, but he had transformed and had murdered the three men, and had eaten them.

He had been running for the state line when one of Anya's recovery teams had found him and tranquilized him, brought him in.

All of the infectives had their stories. Each one, going about their lives before a fateful brush with the pathogen, and their lives had come to a screeching halt. There was a mix of bewilderment, confusion, anger, fear, regret, and guilt in each of them, in their way.

Mina felt a measure of compassion for all of them, but she also had her job to do. At this point, there wasn't need to do adverse condition assessments on them—those had been done to death (pun intended) since the 1950s.

Werewolves could not drown, could not be gassed, could not be conventionally poisoned (an oral or intravenous solution of *Aconitum* species or a silver-based injection would prove fatal to infectives, however). They appeared to be vulnerable to electrocution, which seemed capable of causing enough cellular disruption to overwhelm the body's amazing ability to regenerate.

However, once the current had stopped being applied, regeneration would begin again. Fire could kill them, again, if administered to a degree and widely enough as to overtax the lycanthrope's astounding regenerative properties, but anything short of outright incineration could leave enough cellular material intact to allow for healing to occur.

Radiation of a sufficient dose could kill a werewolf, but if not administered to the entire body for a specified amount of time, could lead to them to regenerate, as well. Explosives could kill a lycanthrope—basically, anything that disrupted the physical cohesion of the host's body enough, on the order of about 75% of the body destroyed, appeared capable of killing one.

Silver was the most single most effective prophylaxis, although it had to be administered effectively. It both killed the retrovirus as well as prevented its cellular regeneration—but silver alone was not fatal per se; it had to be delivered to a vital region. A prick with a silver needle would harm and anger a werewolf, but would not be fatal. A cut to an extremity with a silver knife would produce an immediate wound and a visible scar that appeared slow to heal, and would cause the Lupine great pain. But to be fatal, it had to be delivered to the brain, the heart, or some other vital organ systems in sufficient volume to cause death.

The recent autopsy of Patient Zero's friend and victim, Reagan Whitehouse, had revealed that she'd committed suicide by swallowing a silver dollar, which had been a novel route of administration. The silver had acted like a poison in that instance, killing her from the inside out, in what must have been a profoundly painful passing.

What people didn't understand with these lycanthropes was that while they had the outward appearance of a conventional organism, they were ultimately viral simulacrums of their original host form, which was what made them so hard to kill. You were fighting a colonized host that was completely viral in nature—so, if you stabbed them in the heart without using silver, yes, you were impeding the host organism's heart from beating, but you were in no way impeding the pathogen's ability to effect rapid cellular repair. The werewolves operated on an entrancingly complex level—a kind of retroviral gestalt organism that had been honed through evolution to be the perfect transmitter of the pathogen.

It pained Mina that she'd not be able to publicly release research papers on it. The amount of classified information she had access to, the secrets she had gathered, was dizzying. Enough data to publish for a lifetime, but she couldn't talk to anybody outside of the program.

Mina watched Number 7 smash against the glass, saw him claw and rend it, the reinforced, specially-formulated ballistic glass able to resist the attacks. The Lupines had attained a purity of evolutionary design millennia ago, and had not adapted themselves to innovations like ballistic glass. Their claws could find no purchase on the smooth surface, and their great strength could not crack it any more than their endless rage could break it.

She walked right up to it, her face only inches away from death, the werewolf glaring at her in the face.

Mina picked up a clipboard. According to the reports, there were another dozen infectives inbound.

"Where are we supposed to put them?" Mina asked. Desiree sighed.

"I don't know," she said. "There's talk of reactivating the Blue Island Research Enclave to take up the overflow."

The BIRE was an outdated relic, shut down when it had been eclipsed by the much-newer facilities at the Kennel, but retained because it had been considered an environmental hazard. The BEE subdivided each part of the country, with a designated command and control facility in each region. As the federal headquarters for Region V, which covered Illinois, Wisconsin, Minnesota, Michigan, Indiana, and Ohio, the Kennel received lycanthropes from all six states. So far, the majority of the infectives were coming from Chicago, itself, which made things somewhat easier to manage. However, the outbreak was spreading rapidly, and they didn't yet know why.

Mina had seen reports from some of the other administrative regions that there were some upticks in activity in other states.

"Except for Cell 13, let's sterilize these cells and make room for the new admissions," Mina said, signing the death warrant for the 20 lycanthropes with a stroke of her pen, handing it to Desiree.

It was part of the job.

Zooey had the burning dream again.

She grinned as she watched BacchUS burn, while her packmates circled around, howling. What's done was done.

"Dudes," she said. "Off to the blood banks with you. I want all of you totally donating. Like any time you can."

She'd been very clear: eat the fat ones, nip the skinnies and the strong ones. It was her own bit of triage, a prelude to her own grand plan.

Having taking care of that last bit of business, Zooey went on her way. While she was Queen Bitch to her ever-growing pack, she didn't want to harsh their respective buzzes—she wanted them able and willing to do what they did independent of her; she was a leader, not an administrator.

She'd already eaten a fatty earlier in the evening, some portly banker who had made the fatal mistake of not keeping banker's hours. Zooey was still picking strips of pinstriped suit from her teeth.

Pilsen was not where it was at; she was glad to see the shitty little gallery go ablaze. Zooey liked the downtown action, craved the scene in the city, with all those people around, all those norms, all of that fresh meat.

She'd taken a fancy to Black Sheep, as she'd named one of her Nippers from the massacre, had taken his phone number from his cell, so she could find him again, put it back into his pocket, called 911, told them about the fire, about the wounded and dead on the street, told them her name was Samantha Hain, and that they had to send somebody quickly.

She did this in the light of the night and the crackling roar of the burning gallery, the fires rising high. In those flames she fancied see-ing devils dancing, fingers of flames and splinters and shards as things ignited, that marvelous molecular dance that heat brought, moving things faster and faster until they had no choice but to ignite. She felt kinship with it, understood what it was about.

"Everybody scatter," Zooey said to her packmates. "Let the paramedics take these people in. They're injured. They need medical aid. And get out there and give blood, you fuckers."

They scattered into the darkness and were gone before the ambulances arrived.

For her part, Zooey hopped a bus and took it back into the city. She'd put her pack to work across town, in cabs, in buses, on the El trains, in restaurants, galleries, bars and clubs. Taking victims, growing ranks. Everything hinged on kicking it up another notch, in infecting as many people as possible, as quickly as she could.

As she made her way into downtown, she was thinking about what to do next. She chewed on a finger as she looked at the commuters who were alternately boarding and leaving. They looked like they were just going through their daily motions, as if they hadn't had their world changed right under their feet.

Sam boarded the bus, her throat slit, blood pouring from her wound as she paid her fare. She looked at Zooey with a sad kind of smile, went to say something, but only blood came out of her mouth, and the ragged wound at her throat, what she'd tried to conceal behind a sloppily knitted scarf, something she'd clearly made by hand.

Sam looked her in the eye, wiped the blood from her mouth with the back of her hand, like she was embarrassed, not like she hadn't already soaked her scarf.

"A goddamned ghost, now? Really, Sam?" Zooey said. "Is that the hip thing to be?"

Zooey awoke with a start, in dusty daylight, now, on the floor of the pharmacy, naked, of course. Bloody from the night's slaughter, but blood long since dried. She was human again, what passed for it, her tall, lanky body filthy on the floor.

She went for the plastic bag, took out her clothes, put them back on. The lycanthropy epidemic she was nurturing would be a boon for the clothing industry, she was certain. Zooey was meticulous enough to strip before she transformed, but she knew that most of the others would not be so careful, would simply transform in whatever they happened to have on. The telltale signs in alleys and curbside, the tattered rags, shoes split like overripe fruit, left behind.

Her head had cleared, and she'd remembered what had happened the night before, her attack on the Wilkos. She had been reckless, she supposed, putting on her bra and her panties, slipping on her skinny jeans and acid-green sneakers.

With her tattoos gone and her piercings a moot point, Zooey paid close attention to her wardrobe; it was one of the only things of her old life she had left to her. Not that she missed what she was one bit, but she had liked her hair, had liked her piercings and her tattoos. It had been the things she'd lost in the wake of her transformation.

Feeling a bit cottonmouthed, Zooey finished dressing, putting on her layers of clothing, not caring that she had blood on her body, only taking a moment to swab off her face, since it would do no good for her to walk down the street with blood on her lips, on her cheeks, in her hair.

She checked herself in a compact mirror, then glanced through the window at the Wilko base. By day, it looked completely innocuous. Nobody would think twice about it.

Staring at the cement walls of that mechanic's garage, Zooey intended to lead an army in there, just in case. She felt that she could have a dozen werewolves attack that place and kill every last one of the Wilkos. Sam would be avenged.

It would be one less thing to worry about. BEE was another matter. She had bitten a number of their field agents, wondered how that was playing out. Maybe those others she had infected had kept it a secret.

Zooey walked out the back of the pharmacy, into the near-wintery light of the day, squinting. She fished out a pair of Persol shades and slipped them over her eyes, feeling better, though she was hungry and tired. The attack the night before had left her feeling muzzy-headed. She had been fortunate to have gotten away with it without a scratch. Had she been any slower, they would have shot her. Or the BEE guys might have taken her, and she'd have ended up in their facility, probably wired to electrodes, strapped to a table. She wondered what they did in that place.

It would be another thing she had to deal with. The Wilkos were her primary target; BEE was secondary.

There were so many things to keep track of, Zooey felt like she needed an administrative assistant.

But first, she needed breakfast. She went up the alley and onto the street, walking along the sidewalk, attempting to look nondescriptly fabulous, in her artful, neo-bohemian, lapsed fashion model couldn't-give-a-fuck kind of way. She wanted to look perfectly human, and perfectly hip.

She walked into Vostok Coffee, treated herself to a tall cup of black tea and an apricot pirozhki, sat at the counter by the window, on a stool, and ate in silence, letting her tea steep, while the staff and patrons went about their business.

Zooey watched the norms do their daily rituals, their drinking and feedings, muttering to themselves about their days, whining, complaining, grumbling, grousing. She made note of the fatties, for future reference. She could smell everybody's fear. The more her tribe worked, the more fearful the sheeple got. Zooey liked that. Fear made people stupid.

It was so mundane, and it made Zooey shiver to think that, even in her own cool way, she'd been like them, once. She remembered a time when the amount of foam in her cappuccino was her biggest concern, or the number of chips in her chocolate chip cookie. Those things had mattered to her once, when she'd been one of them.

Feeling the ache of an all-nighter on the floor of a filthy pharmacy, Zooey needed to crash properly, had to figure out where that would be tonight. Since the goons had tried to ambush her at Sam's apartment, Zooey rarely stayed at the same place twice, and was perhaps glad for that, since everybody was after her, after all.

Sam had paid the rent on her place for November, so Zooey supposed she could go in there if she really had to, although she felt like it would be stupid to do that, since odds were good that Wilkos or the others may have that under surveillance.

Then she remembered Polly, Sam's friend/frenemy/whatever. She lived somewhere on the north shore. That could be kind of perfect. It was a little out of her way, and she didn't quite know where Polly lived, but thought it would be easy enough to find out. Polly the Poet. Polly Drinkwater was an easy enough name to search for.

If nothing else, it was maybe a safe place to stay.

She got to her current crash pad, which was a posh place owned by a Nipper she'd claimed at Avalon, a club kid named Ari Pandolfini, who worked as a corporate spokesmodel for Lavish Industrial Smoothing, which abraded and resurfaced stone facades in corporate settings.

He was pretty enough for her, but when she'd turned up at his door, he was less than happy to see her. He had brown hair and hazel eyes, and was prone to pushups and Swiss ball crunches, and being infected wasn't turning out to be something he particularly liked.

Ari was doing curls on the floor when she showed up, looking him up and down.

"What the fuck?" he said. "This is bogus. You just show up when you want?"

His face looked like chiseled sandstone, owing to much time in the tanning salons, keeping that rosy glow. He looked like a golem to her, a living statue.

"Yes," Zooey said. "That's the deal."

"I ate a goddamned dog last night, Zo," he said.

Zooey looked for her pink Samsonite, which was, thankfully, where she left it.

"What breed?"

"What breed? What the fuck does that matter? It was a fucking dog," he said.

Zooey fished out the suitcase, walked it out into Ari's living room. He'd gotten to his feet, had a towel around his neck, and hair on his chest. He was *not* happy about that, having worked hard to shave himself girlishly smooth. Since becoming a Lupine, he'd had to intensify that hair removal regimen, and he was always complaining about it.

"What do you want me to do about it? Noobs pick on dogs, what can I say?" Zooey said.

"I was out all night," he said. "I've got a gig this afternoon. I'm fucking exhausted."

Zooey shrugged. Ari was a double Libra, which meant that he was particularly unbalanced and doubly shallow, but twice as easy on the eyes. To say Librans were airheads was an understatement; they were more like windchimes, clanging in the breeze—charming in small doses, but irritatingly ornamental and, at heart, hollow, completely at the mercy of the winds of fate and life, itself.

"What do you want me to do about it?"

"I want you to make it go away," Ari said. "I didn't ask for this. I've got my career."

"You don't have to worry, Silly," Zooey said. "It'll all be over, soon."

Ari's face looked somewhat relieved. "Why, how?"

"You'll adjust," she said. "Or you won't, and you'll, like, take a swan dive off a building. Have you been giving blood, like I said? That helps take the edge off."

"Yeah," Ari said. "I don't see how that helps."

Zooey reached out and caressed his man-boy face. It was funny—Zooey was only 19, Ari was, like, 25, but Zooey felt like the only grownup in the room.

"Trust me," Zooey said. "It's like hematochromatosis."

"Huh?"

"A blood disease," Zooey said. "You need to drain off blood or you'll explode. Do you understand me? *You will explode.* Totally."

Ari was still processing that as Zooey went for the door, turning on her sneakered heel. "Actually, you know what? I need to take a shower, first. Then I'm out of here, alright? I'll be out of your pretty hair for good, Silly."

She carried her case into his nice bathroom, leaving Ari looking after her with that stunned and vacant look he had in his eyes. She could almost hear the violins coming, the guiltmongering commencing.

"You did this to me," he said. "You made me a monster. I ate dog. Uncool, Zo. Un. Cool."

"Just let me take a shower and get cleaned up," Zooey said. She was filthy, felt filthier.

"And there's voices in my head," Ari said. "I hear this voice talking to me. He keeps egging me on, giving me shit."

"That's your appetite talking," Zooey said, from the other side of the door. She took off her clothes, got the shower going, let it steam up in there. "You have to just talk your appetite down, show it who's boss. Or listen to it. Whatever."

Ari made good money doing whatever it was he did as a spokesmodel. His condo was beautifully laid out in stone, chrome, and leather. The bathroom alone was palatial, had a lovely glass-enclosed shower and mirrors, and was mostly black, caramel, and ochre tones.

It kind of bugged Zooey; everybody who was a werewolf was always whining about the voices in their heads, these nether selves, telling them what to do. Zooey had never experienced it, didn't know what the hell people were talking about.

For her, the transformation had been liberating, had made her feel whole for the first time. It had brought a kind of clarity she had never known in her life, which now seemed so far away to her.

She stepped in the shower, while Ari was still talking and whining. Librans were always whining about things, always finding that the real world didn't match up with their near-constant delusions and expectations.

Zooey just concentrated on using Ari's nice loofas and pungent, tea tree-infused man-soaps to scrub every lick of blood off her body, until she was pink and fresh again. She still missed her tats, each and every time she got naked. But they were a small price to pay for this.

She got out and toweled herself off, wrapped up her hair, opened the door to let out the steam, so that the mirrors would clear.

Ari had still been talking.

"—and that's why I think it blows," he said.

Zooey patted his pretty face again, a soft, patronizing slap on the cheek. "It's not going away, Silly. You're stuck with it, unless you, you know, like, die."

"I don't want to die," Ari said.

"So, like, live, then," Zooey said.

Then she went down on him, and made him forget for a bit about how much it sucked being a werewolf.

After he'd woken up, the morning after Pol had bitten him, Zach had gone to a drugstore and picked up a pile of medical supplies, had gotten himself properly cleaned up, staying in a hotel room downtown.

He hadn't told a goddamned soul about what had happened, which he understood could get him in deep shit with Anya, but he also knew that if he went in there and told her that he'd been compromised, she wouldn't waste a minute before locking him up, and then it was blood samples and tubes stuck in him until he ended up as medical waste, with Mina on the kill switch.

And that just wasn't going to happen. Zach would find Princess, would bring her in, and he would keep a rein on the infection that was even now multiplying inside him. He'd seen enough of the stuff to understand how it happened, at least on the face of things, since he was neither a biochemist nor a geneticist.

On some level, the lycanthropic retrovirus would affix itself to the normal human DNA in a particular location, and would rewrite the genome. It took some time to reset it, with a strengthening of the adrenal and pituitary glands. Cell production would grow, and the immune response would become more robust. Werewolves never caught colds, didn't get the flu, could literally sweat bullets and eat nails.

This was one of the things that BEE had determined from their study of the specimens they'd acquired over the decades. The retrovirus appeared to make the victim phenomenally healthy, and that ramped-up metabolism seemed to create the need for more protein, which accounted for the endless carnal appetites of the infectives. There were no vegans among their ranks.

The retrovirus exacted a toll on them, which appeared to be a nearly-insatiable appetite, which served as a handy way to spread itself, as there was considerable viral shedding in the saliva. The entire mechanism was diabolically elegant, actually turning the victims into the perfect vectors for the virus.

Lycanthropy was the Rolls-Royce of rabies.

And now it was working on him.

Zach went walking downtown, in Millennium Park, trying to think of what he should do. The honest, professional thing to do was to report in to Anya and tell her what had happened, and take his lumps like a man.

But he didn't want to take himself out of play that way. He'd bring Princess in, one way or another.

Nobody else had come close, yet. At least nobody had done so and lived to tell about it. No, he would find Princess, bring her in, and then, having taken care of that, he'd try to sniff out any wolves in the fold at the Kennel. That seemed like a good course of action.

He walked past the Cloud Gate, also known as the Bean, saw his distorted reflection in it, saw the tourists taking pictures and talking about it. The Bean turned everything into something else, bending light along its seemingly seamless, shiny exterior.

Zach watched people go in and out of it, around it, cooing and oohing, without any real understanding of what was happening beneath their noses in the city.

Moving past the Bean, Zach walked amid tall hedges, a kind of maze demarcated by paths that were either crushed gravel or carefully placed brick between garden plots.

He saw some crows hopping around, picking at something in one of the autumn-withered gardens, and walked over, only to step back in shock, seeing a severed hand barely visible amid the undergrowth. The crows had been nipping at it.

Nobody was any wiser, he saw, watching the tourists mill about. People saw what they were prepared to see. These people didn't want to know about infections and antiseptic lockdowns; they just wanted to take pictures and feel like they were experiencing something wonderful in a world-class American city.

Zach reached down and took the hand, which had been severed cleanly by monstrous teeth, and which the crows had been pecking at, sampling the flesh.

He'd been in Afghanistan, he'd been in Iraq. Zach was used to stuff like this. A war was a war, no matter what they called it, or where it was.

He walked over to a trash can and tossed the hand in. The man he used to be would have called the police, but Zach knew what had taken that man's hand, and there wasn't anything the police could do about it.

His phone rang, and he looked at it. Anya.

"Yeah?" he said.

"Any sign of Princess, Houndstooth?"

"Not yet, Den Mother," he said.

"Where are you?"

"Millennium Park," he said. "She got away."

"Too bad," Anya said.

"There's more," Zach said. "I, uh, got compromised."

Silence on the line.

"Bitten?"

"Yes," he said. There. He said it. He'd done the right thing.

"Bitten by whom?"

"I don't know," Zach said. "I was caught by surprise. It was a talker. Said her name was Pol."

Another silence.

"There are worse things that could happen," Anya said. "You could be dead. Which brings me to a question: don't take this badly, but why aren't you dead?"

"I don't know," Zach said. "She just bit me, that was all. She wasn't part of the Princess pack, was likely just some random infective, aside from being a talker."

"What'd she talk about?"

"Just asked me who I was, told me her name," Zach said.

"I appreciate that, Houndstooth," Anya said. "I appreciate your candor, and your honesty."

"I thought I'd stay in the field," Zach said. "See if I can't bring our Princess in. At least I won't have to worry about getting infected, now."

"I understand," she said.

"I'd recommend doing tests on everybody on-site," Zach said. "Just to be safe."

"I'll take that under advisement, Houndstooth," Anya said. "Keep me posted, and if you start to lose your way, let me know that, too."

"I won't lose my way, Den Mother," Zach said. "I promise."

"I know you won't Houndstooth. Do you require medical assistance?"

"I took care of it."

"Stay in contact," Anya said. "Stay in contact, no matter what."

"Alright, Den Mother," Zach said.

Zach hung up the phone, felt relieved that he'd told Anya. At least he'd gotten that off his chest, had come clean about his infection.

He watched the tourists come and go, oblivious as ever. Then he went back to the hotel and got his case, checked out, picked up his car.

Once inside his car, he opened his cases, which contained the assault rifle, an AK-47. Then he took out some banana clips, turned them over in his hands. He had three clips of ammunition for the assault rifle. The bullets were silver, naturally. He removed one of the rounds, slipped it free of its magazine, held it in his hand.

The 7.62 mm jacketed round rolled in his palm, and Zach touched the silver to his skin. He could feel it burning, a faint sensation, like holding a hot cup of coffee. He took the bullet and put it in his pocket. Then he slapped the clip into the AK-47 and drew the bolt, then put it in the trunk of his car. He drew another box from his trunk, put it in the front seat with him.

Then he went hunting again.

The Director came to Mina's part of the Kennel, a grave look on her face, to the extent that Mina didn't know what to think, until she spoke.

"Zachary's been infected," Anya said.

"Oh, no," Mina said. "Is he hurt?"

"Not badly," Anya said. There were a dozen infectives in the cells, only three of them transformed. "I'm sorry we keep sending them down here."

Mina looked at Anya's face to try to get a read on her. The Director was not an easy woman to read, operated at a high administrative level that was beyond what Mina could fathom, focused as she was on her labs.

"We need more space," Mina said. "Even clearing the cells, we're over capacity."

"I know," Anya said. "I'm trying. This is unprecedented. Right now, I'm just having the identified infectives tranquilized and shipped off to Wolf Island. It's the only thing we can do. There's just no space for them here."

"A rendition operation of that magnitude seems daunting, Anya," Mina said.

Her talent for understatement was undiminished. The logistics of the rendition of infectives was a headache that kept coming, and was only getting worse. Once infectives had been tagged, there was the matter of having a team to snatch them up. Forget due process—the victims simply disappeared. The absence of a cure and the inevitability of outbreak necessitated it.

Anya had access to three transport planes in Region V for this purpose, and that required pulling what strings she had available to her to make this happen.

"At some point, somebody important is going to be infected," Mina said. "And then what do you do?"

"I'll worry about that when it happens," Anya said.

"We should be prepared," Mina said.

Some of the imprisoned infectives were shouting, others sulked, and others tried to reason with their captors. Anya understood their plight, felt their pain. At least here, they were contained.

"I've been working at the Bureau for 20 years, and this is the worst breakout I've ever seen," Anya said. "Nobody's prepared for it. It's why we need to capture Princess."

"I think it's going to be bigger than Princess at this point, Anya," Mina said. "The caseload keeps growing."

"She's still the one behind it," Anya said. "The instigator."

Desiree came up with another clipboard. "Three more infectives, Mina."

"Put them in Cells 7 through 10," Mina said, giving Anya a look that communicated the urgency of the situation.

"I'm trying, Mina," Anya said. "These aren't simple inmates we're talking about, here."

"I'm going to have to simply start euthanizing them immediately upon capture," Mina said. "Forget study at this point."

Anya didn't like having the Kennel turn into a death camp, and knew Mina well enough to know that she would follow through on that statement.

"I'm going to just reroute everybody to Wolf Island," Anya said. "What does it matter? You've got enough data collected for a lifetime's worth of research."

That had taken Mina aback a bit. The prospect of running out of test subjects would put her own position in some jeopardy, knew Mina would not want that.

Anya looked at the younger woman evenly, smirking at her. "Yes, that's what I'm going to do. That way, your overcrowding problem is solved. Just keep a cell open for Princess, should Zachary be able to bring her in. And Big Black, should Tesco succeed."

"Tesco," Mina said, scoffing. "Big Black's going to tear him apart if he sees him."

"If he sees him," Anya said. "That's the thing."

Polly woke in Ansel's bed, aching, exhausted, thirsty, naked and spent.

Ansel wasn't in bed next to her; he was in his studio, painting. She could hear him humming to himself.

She hunted around for clothes, didn't find any, so she wrapped herself in a sheet, walked out into Ansel's living room.

"Ansel?" she asked.

"Yeah?"

"How did I end up here? What day is it?"

"Wednesday," he said. "Why?"

Her head throbbed, and she put a slender hand to her temple. She couldn't remember anything from the last couple of days. The last day she remembered was Monday.

She walked over to the studio portion of his place, where he was working. She saw her portrait on his wall, back in the place where she had stolen it.

"You were at Sam's place," Polly said.

Ansel paused from his painting, holding his brush like it was a scalpel. He smiled at her.

"Had to reclaim my stolen property," he said.

"What am I doing here?"

"You came to see me," Ansel said.

"Fuck," Polly said.

"I would venture to guess that some of you still wants to see me," Ansel said.

"I want you to drive me home," Polly said. "Like right now."

Ansel put down his brush, took a rag with solvent on it and cleaned off his hands, walked over to Polly, stood across from her, about an arm's length away. The physicality of his presence was heady, made Polly feel reed-thin and tiny by comparison.

"Don't you want breakfast?" Ansel asked. "We can get something to eat. My treat, if you're hungry."

"Of course I'm hungry," Polly said. "I'm always hungry these days."

His casual tone irked her. And that her body had betrayed her and brought her to Ansel's. That bothered her, too, the breadth of that betrayal.

"Look, I'm not judging you," Ansel said. "You're going through a tough time. I get it. Let me get my keys, and I'll get you back home."

She gazed at the big bars of his cage, across the far end of his loft. "That cage is for you, isn't it?"

Ansel looked at it, smiled to himself, like it was the most natural thing in the world to have in one's lodging. A cage, sure, why not? Polly felt like an idiot for not seeing it for what it was when she and Sam had first come to his place with him.

"Yeah, that was a rough patch for me. Some nights, I felt a little unhinged. I put myself in there to keep me from doing things I might regret later," Ansel said. "But, honestly, I haven't been in there since Sam. I don't know what it is, but the bullshit with her sort of freed me up a bit. I mean, look at the mess that's happening."

He turned on the television, a big plasma screen set that was on one of his walls, like it was another of his paintings that he had around the place, covering the walls.

The news reported more unrest throughout the city—fires, murders, bodies found in Grant Park, and reports of wild animals loose in the city.

"Compared with all of that, I've got no worries," Ansel said.

Polly saw another mention about the building that hosted BacchUS had been ablaze, that the Chicago Fire Department had finally gotten that fire out. She sucked in a breath.

"BacchUS," she said. "Did you see that?"

Ansel looked at the television screen without evident interest. "That's the gallery in Pilsen, right? The one for your hipster friends?"

"Clay," Polly said. "Oh, why would somebody burn that?"

She felt pain in her heart, thought about Reagan and Sheldon's artworks in there, burning up. The sense of loss was profound.

The news report said that there had been a number of bodies at the scene, and many injured, and there had been no suspects, although someone had called and identified themselves as "Samantha Hain," who had been found dead, herself, in a condominium in the Gold Coast, the scene of an apparent murder-suicide. Authorities were looking for the woman who had made the call, and there was another investigation into the murders of Lee Smathers, found beheaded in his home, and Willa Powers, who had been found burned to death in her apartment. Since they had all been friends of the late Samantha Hain, there was suspicion that the rash of murders may have been related.

"It's a nightmare," Polly said. "All of it is."

"So, do you want me to drive you to Pilsen? Or do you want me to take you home?"

Polly couldn't bear to see BacchUS burning. Clay would have been devastated to see his gallery ablaze. It had been their clubhouse. And seeing Lee and Willa in the news that way gave Polly chills. They would have hated to have been the subject of media sensationalism like that. They would have sneered at it, rolled their eyes. Polly missed them all. She even missed her husband.

"Home," Polly said. "Take me home."

"Alright," Ansel said. "We're not taking my bullet-riddled May-bach, by the way. We're taking my Porsche. But we should get you some kind of clothes to wear, yes?"

He found her a sweatshirt from Brown, which she put on.

"I didn't know you went to Brown," she said.

"I didn't," Ansel said. "It's from an old girlfriend of mine. You'd have liked her, she had a Masters in Rhetoric. Boy, did she ever have a mouth on her."

"Where is she now?"

"I don't know," Ansel said. He fished out some yoga pants, black with a thick red stripe up each side. He tossed those to Polly.

Polly wouldn't be caught dead in yoga pants, hated even holding these.

"Did you kill her?" she asked.

"Don't remember," Ansel said. "Does it matter?"

"Of course it matters," she said, putting on the yoga pants, which fit her well enough, although the woman had been taller than Polly, as it required Polly to pull up the cuffs to keep from dragging them as she walked.

"Good enough," he said. "When we get to your house, you should give me a couple of changes of clothes I can keep at my place."

"I'm not coming back," Polly said.

Ansel smiled to himself, then at her. When he smiled, the wolf that he was came out. The smugness of that smirk bothered her.

"You won't, but she will," he said.

"I won't let her," Polly said.

"Right," he said.

Polly looked at herself in a mirror. Her self-consciously styled hair was all tousled, and she made an effort to fix it, irritated to even be in this situation.

"I look like hell," Polly said.

Ansel sighed. "You look less put together than usual, yeah."

"Take me home," she said.

"I could just call you a cab," he said.

"I don't want a cab," Polly said. "You owe me a ride home."

"Fair enough," Ansel said, taking them to the elevator that led to the garage in his building. He woke a nearby Porsche with his key fob.

He opened the door for her on his grey 911, then went around to his side, got in, started it up. Polly watched him go through these simple motions, underlit by the dashboard.

Aside from wearing some other woman's clothes and waking up in the bed of a man-monster she had no intention of ever seeing again, it was the most normal thing in the world, the two of them, tooling from darkness into daylight in his Porsche, cutting a mean streak in Wicker Park, navigating traffic.

"I'm never doing this again," Polly said. "Do you understand me, Ansel? Never again."

He laughed to himself.

"Sure," Ansel said. "Do you know how many times I've said something like that, myself, Pol? It's not as easy as you think."

There was blood on the street, at the intersection near Milwaukee Avenue. Polly bit her lip, looked away, as Ansel sped through the intersection.

"Looks like somebody had an accident," Polly said.

"Oh, I don't think it was an accident," he said.

"How can you be so calm about this?"

Ansel shrugged, passing a bagel truck, veering back into the proper lane again. "I'm one person who doesn't have to worry about what's happening to this place. You, too, in truth, if you'll just chill out a little."

Polly hid her face in her hands. "This is not the 'new normal,' Ansel."

"Yes, it is," Ansel said. "For you, yes."

"I won't come back here," she said. "You'll see."

"Do you want to bet? Half of you wants to be here," he said. "And I'm going to tell you right now: I'm driving you this time, but you turn up at my door again, you find your own way home."

Polly hated herself for even being in this situation. She'd lost two days, could only vaguely remember what had happened, like images and sensations. She and Ansel fucking, or a ghastly, monstrous parody of coupling between two bestial forms beneath the waxing light of the moon, beneath the open night's sky. Chasing down somebody, biting them, tearing into them, the flesh filling her belly. Running, nosing the wind, homing in on this place.

Ansel put on some music. "She is the New Thing," it said on the player, a song full of macabre, neo-garage braggadocio.

"This sounds like the Sonics on tranquilizers," Polly said.

"Or Monster Machine on ecstasy," Ansel said.

She turned the music off with a pointed push of her finger. Ansel looked at her with amusement.

"They found Lee in his place, his head in his lap, record player on."

Polly gasped. She hadn't seen the details of it. "Did you do it?"

"No," Ansel said. "Sam probably did. I'd say there's more than good money on that."

"Poor Lee," Polly said. "He would have been so insulted to have been killed by Sam."

"That's a weird thing to say," Ansel said.

"Lee was weird," Polly said. "Willa loved him, although she never would have admitted to that."

Ansel yawned, thought all of those friends of hers were douches. Douches in life, douches in death, a whole fleet of douche canoes. Polly's mourning of them was douchy, too. But she was in a fragile place at the moment, so he didn't tell her that.

"They were all assholes, Polly," Ansel said. "You're better off without them."

Ansel had managed to get them to the lake shore, where he could make some decent progress getting Polly up to her house. Northbound traffic was light on a midmorning weekday.

"Weird, huh? Being the survivor?"

"I didn't even know I was endangered," Polly said.

"I think Sam cared about you," Ansel said. "She considered you a friend, or what passed for friendship among your little band of dilettantes."

"Dilettantes," Polly said, wanting to spit at him.

"Hey, I didn't kill any of them," Ansel said. "It was Sam, all the way."

"Why would she even do that?" Polly said. "We were her life."

"It's a werewolf thing," Ansel said. "You always hurt the ones you love. They become targets of opportunity. If you want me to venture a guess, I'd say that her nether self—like your nether self—drove her to do it because it understood that your little gang was the only thing she really cared about, maybe the only thing left that kept her halfway human, or what passed for it in your group. It wanted to free her from that so it could have her complete attention."

It creeped Polly out, having that Thing inside her, making her do things.

Polly crossed her arms, looked out the window, couldn't even look at Ansel. They had fucked all night long. She knew that, could remember bits and pieces of it, which were intruding in her mind. Then she understood why—the Thing, which had been snoozing, was waking back up inside her.

"Get me home," she said. "Get me home, and go away, Ansel."

"What's the problem? You are better than you were before, whether you admit to it or not," he said.

"How can I stop it?" she asked.

"You don't want to go there," Ansel said. "You'd end up messing yourself up, trust me. You can tranquilize the thing down, but it sneaks out eventually. And if you've kept it battened down inside you, it'll really make a splash when it gets loose."

Polly looked at Ansel, glowered at him. She did not like being out of control, did not appreciate being at the mercy of this Thing. This was not how her life was supposed to be going. She looked at herself in the side mirror, at the disheveled wretch looking back at her.

"This is not me," Polly said. "I stopped being me."

"This is a whole new you," Ansel said.

"There's my house," Polly said. "Let me out."

Ansel pulled into her driveway, and Polly hopped out. "Don't get out, Ansel. Goodbye. Again."

Ansel watched her shut the car door, watched her walk up her driveway, for once without her signature wiggle.

"You're welcome, Pol," Ansel said, before backing out and heading back the way he came.

Polly fished out the secret key she had near the door, listened for Ansel's Porsche to growl its way down the street, then she keyed back into her house.

She went in and locked the door behind her, slapped the key down on the table near the door, and let out a scream, a frustrated, desolate thing that had been coiled up inside her the entire ride.

Then she heard somebody in the living room, like somebody getting up off the sofa. It was that gorgeous Valkyrie girl that Sam had at her place.

Zooey.

Zooey had been dreaming when Polly started screaming, which actually scared Zooey, had her jumping to her feet to see what the hell was going on, forgetting for a moment that she was in Polly's place, that she was the intruder, the home invader.

When Polly saw Zooey standing there, her face had gone from pained confusion to white-hot indignation in an instant.

"What the hell are you doing in my house?" Polly asked.

"Sam's dead," Zooey said. "Reagan, too."

"Yes, I know," Polly said. "Now, answer me: what are you doing in my house?"

"I was sleeping," Zooey said. "Why were you screaming?"

"Because I'm very upset," Polly said. "Now would you please leave? Or am I going to have to call the police?"

Zooey looked at her with a grin, her eyes pits of darkness. The casual manner of her was too much for Polly to take right now, her breezy bestiality.

"I don't care. Call them."

"What do you want, anyway? Why are you here?"

"I just, like, needed a place to crash," Zooey said. "What's the problem?"

"You're trespassing," Polly said. "That's the problem. You're not welcome here."

"I know what you are," Zooey said. "Did you know that?"

Polly hated confronting this girl like this, looking like a vagabond. She would have preferred confronting her in a dress and heels, looking sharp as a tack, not like a yoga pants-wearing ragamuffin from Brown.

"Are you infected, too?"

"Yes," Zooey said. "Totally."

"Sam?"

Zooey nodded. "It's like we're sisters, you and me: we have the same mom."

Polly hated the look in this girl's black eyes, this insolent sense of entitlement. Polly went to the front door, opened it, gestured.

"Hit the road, 'Sis,'" Polly said. "Or I will call the police."

"I don't have anywhere I can go," Zooey said. "We have to stick together. We're practically family, now, like I said."

"We are not family," Polly said.

"I'll bet you're a Virgo," Zooey said. "Yes?"

"I'm not going to talk to you," Polly said. "Get out."

"Shaky ground," Zooey said, tracing a pattern on the sofa with a finger. "Mutable Earth. See, you guys are the quakers and the shakers of the Earth Signs. Capricorns are Cardinal Earth, so they're the Earthiest of Earth signs, the good earth, the solid ground. And Taureans are Fixed Earth, so they're the stone-cold Earth signs—they're like bedrock: inflexible, immovable. But Virgos, you guys are Mutable Earth, what I call 'shaky ground'—nobody builds on Virgo because you guys are so unstable, prone to earthquakes. It's like building on sand, living atop a fault line. That's what you Virgos are always about: fault lines. Everything's somebody's fault with you guys."

"Thanks for that astrology lesson," Polly said. "Now please leave, or I will call the police, I promise you that."

"A Virgo likes to complain most of all; that is like their true talent—they find fault in everything, could find unhappiness in Heaven, itself. Virgos complain, and are happy to complain. Virgos get off on misery and woe. Everybody kisses their asses, tries to keep them happy, because they don't want to hear them bitching about everything all the time. I bet you've done nothing but complain since you became infected. You're probably all confused about who you are, now, are busy trying to figure out whose fault this all is, who you can complain to, who you can blame for this."

"Just stop," Polly said.

"You could totally make it work for you," Zooey said. "Virgos have a secret weapon—they're cute. You're all cute, so people put up with your bullshit, and, you know that you guys are all whores. Isn't that ironic? The Virgins are all whores. Everybody knows this about you guys, but are afraid to say it, because it'll send you off on some neurotic freakout. You have an opportunity, here, and you're too chickenshit to take it, to run with it. This life you bought for yourself with your guy, it's gone. This house is a crypt, now."

Zooey picked up her pink suitcase, went to the door, looked at Polly with a mix of scorn and contempt.

"I wanted to give you the chance to do something extraordinary," Zooey said. "To be part of something incredible, to join my pack. But you are weak, aren't you? You're going to end up killed or caught. Or maybe you'll, like, do yourself in like Reagan did. It's not hard. Oh, I took a bath, by the way. I needed to. Hope you don't mind."

"Out!" Polly screamed.

Zooey sauntered back in front of Polly, stared her down.

"Nobody talks to me like that," Zooey said, and grabbed Polly by her sweatshirt, shoved her into the wall, against the mirror, slamming the door shut. "I, like, run this town."

Polly was not a physical person, was caught off-guard by this attack, which sent her into the big mirror she and Tristan had hung in the entry way, to let more light in the foyer. The mirror shattered, raining pieces down on her, crashing on the floor.

Zooey's face was close to hers, teeth set, black eyes flashing, her white hair hanging in her face. She looked demonic.

"Like, Sam told me all about you, Polly," Zooey said. "Totally."

Then Zooey hurled her down the hall, Polly tumbling down the way, bumping into the sofa.

"How dare you?" Polly said, her own eyes animated with outrage.

"I'm calling you out, Sissy," Zooey said. "Come on. Let her out of her cage. Let's see the bitch we both know that you are."

Zooey savored this. She wasn't about to go back on the street. She liked this house, and while she could have taken anybody's home if she'd wanted to, there was something right about it being Polly's pad she'd settled on.

Polly got her feet, glaring at Zooey, who held her arms out, daring her to transform.

"Sam always had a thing for you," Zooey said. "Why is anybody's guess. But Sam was a Sagittarius, and so maybe that flickering flame she had in her, that Mutable Fire, maybe it found something in common with that shaky ground you represent, Earth Motherfucker."

"Why are you doing this?" Polly asked, only to be belted by Zooey, a flat-out backhand that sent Polly tumbling over the sofa, crashing onto her glass coffee table. Polly's face stung from the force of the blow, which had cut her lip.

"I want to see what you have in you," Zooey said.

The Thing inside her was wide awake, now, and was watching this intently, but Polly would not give ground, would not let it loose, would not speak its name.

Polly rolled out of the glass of the table, ran to the phone, only to find that Zooey caught the phone cord, ripping it out of the wall, even as she dialed.

"Nobody's going to ruin this for me," Zooey said.

"What do you want?" Polly said, raising her voice, challenging and shrill.

Zooey smacked her across the face, sending Polly tumbling again. Zooey was taller than Polly, and it was simply a physical mismatch.

Let me out, I'll tear her apart, Pol said inside her.

"This is your life," Zooey said, snarling. "Are you going to let me just take it from you? Sam told me what a fucking bitch you could be. Show me."

Polly ran into the kitchen, went around the butcher's block, drew a butcher knife from the magnet block that held it and others like it.

Zooey, seeing the knife, laughed. "You're going to stab me? For real? With what you have inside you, you're, like, going to use that? On me? I don't know whether to feel sorry for you, or to be pissed, honestly, Bitch."

Zooey charged at her, and Polly swung the knife, catching Zooey across the palms. Zooey paused in her charge, holding up her hands, which had already healed. Her black eyes were wide, alit with a nocturnal, sepulchral flame. Polly could see how much Zooey was enjoying this.

"Can't you even feel this?" Zooey asked. "I'm going to kill you unless you change."

"I won't do it," Polly said.

Polly stabbed at Zooey, who caught her knife hand, wrenched it aside, then brought her nose up close to her, took her scent in deep sniffs of her long, straight nose.

"Ohhhh," Zooey said. "Ansel. Still Ansel's bitch, are we?"

"How?"

"The nose knows," Zooey said, tapping hers.

Zooey forced Polly to drop the knife, then hurled her into the door of her fridge. Polly had never been in a fight, didn't know what she was supposed to do, was terrified of this lanky, gorgeous-horrible girl, who kept dogging her steps. She only wanted to be left alone, not terrorized in her own home.

She grabbed at Zooey's hair, yanked hard at it, which momentarily threw off Zooey's attack, as she grabbed at Polly's hands.

"That's the spirit," Zooey said.

Let me out! Pol howled.

"You can tell by the smell," Zooey said. "If you had half a clue you'd know this, you'd be tapping that. But Smells Like Ansel was tapping you, instead. You have his scent all over you. I know even though I never met the man, because Sam was always chasing after him, would come back reeking of him."

"He'll kill you," Polly said. "If you hurt me, he'll kill you. He cares about me."

"Yeah," Zooey said. "He'll avenge you. Is that, like, what you're saying?"

She threw Polly across the kitchen, knocking her onto the dining room table.

"Man, you have it under wraps, now don't you?" Zooey said, throttling Polly. "I haven't killed anybody like this; you're going to be my first, looks like."

Zooey's hands on her throat, choking her, brought Pol tearing back out of Polly, in the form of claws forming from her hands, her nails curving and fingers lengthening.

Polly gripped Zooey's hand with one of her clawed fingers, and then slashed Zooey across the face with her other hand, raking four cuts over her cheeks and nose, forcing Zooey to release Polly.

Polly scampered back, her hands tearing gouges in the carpeting, while Zooey looked at her bloodily, her face a reddening leer. The blood just poured out of her.

"That is the spirit," Zooey said, spitting blood, grinning. "I knew you, like, had it in you."

Polly still refused to let that Thing out of her, looked at her bloody clawed hand in horror, held it out in front of her. "This is you, not me."

Zooey grinned at her, tasting her own blood, then began taking off her clothes, kicking off her acid-green sneakers, pulling off her jacket, throwing them over her shoulder, as she stalked toward Polly, whose own face was changing, as her teeth were growing.

"No," Polly said slurring. "Not like this. Not so soon."

Zooey's own body began to rip and rend, growing, stretching, and Polly looked on it in horror and revulsion, found her own body responding, fueled by adrenaline and terror, as Pol was not going to let Zooey gain the upper hand in this moment.

For a second, there was a predatory peace as the two of them transformed while glaring at each other, as the human folded up and became the Lupine again. In seconds, there was a white wolf-thing in the dining room, facing a smaller, lithe, almost-black werewolf, teeth bared, circling one another.

Zooey knew this game, even if Polly did not. It was a dominance game fought right here, in Polly's home.

Polly sprang at Zooey, slashing at her again with those marvelous claws of hers, like glamour-length meathooks, catching Zooey on her outstretched limbs.

"Bitch," Zooey said, ducking back, lifting up the heavy dining room table and charging at Polly, smashing her up against a wall and a china cabinet, knocking over plates, which clanged like ceramic bells inside the cabinet.

Polly jumped up and over the table, biting Zooey across her muzzle, an amazingly savage strike that actually pinned Zooey's own formidable jaws shut a moment, but Zooey grappled at the smaller Lupine and hurled her back into the living room, with enough force to send her crashing into a painting on the far wall, near the fireplace.

Then Zooey bounded after her, howling and snarling, blood running down her muzzle.

"This is my home," Polly said, diving through the glass doors in the back, which led to the back patio, where her rose gardens were, where the swimming pool was.

Zooey was hot on her heels.

"Not anymore," Zooey said. "Sissy."

Polly took a swat at Zooey, catching her across the throat with another sweep of her claws. That drove Zooey back a moment, halted her charge. Sensing momentary advantage, Polly jumped at her again, but Zooey struck her, knocking her into her rose garden.

Zooey clutched at her throat, which was badly wounded by Polly's claws.

"Alright," Zooey said. "That's the stuff. This place sucked, anyway, Sissy."

She ran off into the darkness, trailing blood, leaving Polly panting in the dark. From deep within her, unbidden, came a great howl. Polly turned her head skyward and howled in triumph.

Zach had already dropped three infectives in his search for Princess. They were getting more numerous, for sure, as the epidemic was spreading. He continued hunting for her, but figured the overall strategic mission would be met if he bagged targets of opportunity as they came.

And, in his case, it meant tranking a trio of Lupines who had been barreling through Lincoln Park: one grey, one golden brown, the other a middling brown hue. How this trio had ended up a pack was anybody's guess, but they had been charging through the park, terrifying norms and snapping at them, and since he was in the area, anyway, he took the shot he had, having doubled the tranquilizer dose he'd used on Princess.

When the first one went down, the brown one, the other two looked around, startled. The size of the Lupines was impressive, horrifying. They looked like ghastly versions of wolves, a grotesque, gangrel parody of the loping elegance of a wolf.

Wasting no time, Zach shot the second one, the golden brown, right in the back of the head, at the base of the neck, dropping her in seconds.

That left the grey, who turned and had managed to determine where Zach was. It saw him with its big yellow eyes, howled and snarled, charging for him, eating distance in seconds with great, loping strides, a javelin of fur and flesh, tipped with teeth. Zach kept his cool, raised his rifle to his eye again, and he fired again, catching this one in the chest.

It got four more paces before the dart worked its chemical magic, and the great beast did a faceplant, sliding through the faded grass toward Zach, shrinking in size as it slid, until what was inches from his boot was a young man with brown hair.

"Houndstooth to Dogcatcher," he said into his radio. "We've got three infectives here, just off Stockton and LaSalle, near the Ben Franklin statue."

"Copy that, Houndstooth," Dogcatcher said. "Three at once, eh?"

"They pay me by the pound," Zach said, walking over to the other two, looking at them in turn. "Tell Den Mother that these three were running together in a pack. Make sure to tag them appropriately, see if they're related or anything."

He was pleased his wounded arm hadn't screwed him up too badly. Or else, the infection was already augmenting his reflexes and healing him. He didn't want to peel off his bandages to find out.

BEE had been trying to gather as much evidence as they could in the wake of the outbreak, both in terms of individual infections and how the Lupines behaved. Historically, there was often animosity between Lupines, who (perhaps rightly) saw each other as competitors for territory and food in a given area.

Since the lycanthrope was not a normal animal, but was an obscene mockery of nature, a perverse blending of man and wolf, there were inconsistencies in its behavior that made it a challenging subject for observation, which was why study in controlled settings always took a priority. As a thinking beast, it could evade traps and escape scrutiny, could hunt its hunters. It was nearly impervious to physical harm, and its capacity to metabolize even strong tranquilizers, drugs, and poisons was unparalleled.

Dogcatcher had sent a van right away, its red lights flashing. A half-dozen BEE agents emerged from the van, wearing their white jumpsuits, and Zach waved them over. The recovery teams always wore rubber gloves and jumpsuits, had yellow helmets with flip-down plastic visors, just to protect them from bodily fluids, since everybody knew that werewolves were messy and contagious.

The teams knew their business, though. One of them, a young woman with a chestnut ponytail and a freckly face, knelt by the young man and injected him with a GPS tag. They usually did it right between the shoulder blades, in an area where the Lupines couldn't reach. The tagging was essential in the process; once an infective was tagged, the little lozenge inside them would deliver biometric information and would reveal their location on their tracking system. Not that any infective caught by the Kennel would ever go free, but it was useful just the same.

The Lupines would eject the GPS tag upon their next transformation, but until that happened, BEE would be able to gather useful data.

After tagging them, they'd put an identifying bracelet on them, and two of the other members of the recovery team would pick the infectives up and put them in the van. Of course, there were a few bystanders gaping, like joggers and bicyclers.

Mina was on this recovery team, which surprised Zach, since she almost never did fieldwork.

"Needed some fresh air, Mina?"

"You're getting entirely too good at this, Zach," Mina said, while tagging the other two infectives.

"It's what I do," Zach said. "Oh, by the way, we've got about six people bit down the way. Looks like the paramedics are on the scene."

Mina followed Zach's gaze, then whipped out her radio. "Slim, we have a half-dozen infectives about 300 meters south of us. Have an Intercept team pick them up. Be quick about it, too, because there are paramedics there."

That was sometimes the hardest part of the job; dropping the Lupines themselves was pretty straightforward, but dealing with the injured in the wake of an attack, that was particularly challenging. Given that there was no cure for the disease, it meant that BEE had to put them in the DQ—Detainment & Quarantine, where they would be observed before processing.

The scientific arm of the BEE was immense, and Arya had succeeded in communicating the gravity of the situation to Washington, although for now, the storage issue was still a big problem.

Infectives were considered biohazards, so transport and containment of them required rigorous CDC protocols to be in place. Since the Kennel was connected to the CDC, there were procedures they could follow, but the size of this current outbreak had far exceeded anything the BEE had dealt with before, and they were having difficulty processing them.

Of course, calling itself "Animal Control" was euphemistic, intended to keep the public at large from panicking. If people truly understood that there were lycanthropes in their midst, all hell would break loose. That was why the Kennel had been so busy. The longer this disease went on, the farther it spread, the bigger the problem for the organization and for the government at large.

Anya was under incredible pressure to get this thing contained, because nobody was going to be able to quarantine the entire city, and as incidents kept happening, people were beginning to ask questions. One or two stories was one thing, but as the stories multiplied and magnified, people were beginning to wake up and ask questions, and asking questions of the government these days was practically un-American.

"We're losing, you know," Mina said, flipping up her visor. "We can only follow on their tails, barring some kind of large-scale blood test, and we just don't have the resources for it."

Zach wondered if Mina knew about his condition, if Anya had told her. He doubted it.

"I'm doing my best," Zach said.

"Oh, I know it, Z," she said. "Believe me, you field agent guys are something else. There are, what 25 of you out here? We need an army, but the more bodies out in the field, the likelier that people are going to become infected. Anya's having blood drawn from everybody at the Kennel. I don't blame her."

"That's because it's my fault," Zach said. "You know how I'm going after Princess, right?"

"We're not even close to finding a cure for this."

Mina was sharp. She needed to be, since the scientific component of the BEE was as central as the operations aspect that Zach performed.

Zach felt the bullet in his pocket, fished it out, gripped it tight in his fist, feeling the pinpoint burn of the silver against his skin.

She raised her voice when talking to her peers. "Let's go, people. Get them into the van. We've got to get these folks contained. I've got to get back, Z. You want a ride back to the Kennel?"

"No," Zach said. "Anya doesn't want me back there until I've brought Princess in."

Mina patted Zach on the arm. "Okay, well you be careful out here, alright? You call if you need anything."

"Thanks, Mina," Zach said, watching her walk back to the van with the others. They drove off, leaving Zach where he'd been all along, standing in the shadow of Ben Franklin's statue.

He wondered how Mina would react, knowing that he'd been infected. She was too much of a scientist to be frightened of it; she'd probably just want to study him behind the glass.

Zach turned his hand over, opened his palm. The silver bullet had left a burn on his skin. Not a terrible one, but there was a burn there, like he'd put a cigarette butt out in his palm.

He stuffed the bullet back into his pocket, shouldered his rifle, went back to hunting.

Anya watched the status on the big board, the reports that kept coming in. There were over 1000 cases, now. Anecdotal in some instances, but most of them were legitimate. She had managed to get some additional storage facilities, but they were not fully suited to the task. What was needed was a proper containment area. She'd been trying to get an abandoned prison downstate claimed for the BEE, but there was pushback on that, since it was likely not up to the necessary containment standards to keep the Lupines imprisoned.

The caseload was simply growing too quickly. The Wardens were already spread too thin, she didn't have the manpower to get this handled, and Washington was intent on not getting too involved in it, just like they'd done at first with Hurricane Katrina.

Anya had set up a simple test for the personnel at the Kennel: they got to hold a silver dollar. If the person's skin reacted to it, they were infected. This testing had revealed that a dozen personnel in the Kennel were, in fact, infected. She'd had them quarantined and interrogated, since this kind of breach on their part called into mind all sorts of things to Anya, whose mind was prone to racing, anyway.

How had this happened? Why hadn't they told anyone?

That mattered to her. Their answers ranged from fear and ignorance to confusion about it, to denial. None of the infected personnel admitted to being compromised by Princess, to being planted there.

That they even had a screening test, even a simple one like that, was, in her view, a huge stride they had made in the containment of this outbreak.

But, of course, it wasn't being contained at all; it was an open wound and they were simply a bandage.

She could not keep staring at the board. It was too much information, and the situation was too dire. Princess had managed to greatly expand the range of her affliction, and it wasn't clear yet how she was doing this. It was a bloody mess.

Then something occurred to her.

The Kennel was charged with monitoring and tracking lycanthropic outbreaks, and she'd made the mistake of treating this situation along those lines, as if it were simply a super-outbreak, along the usual protocols of dealing with a disease breakout like this. But this was not simply a plague; there was volition in this, a method to the madness. And that made all the difference.

"What would you say is happening, Matt?"

"We can't exactly say what's happening, Ma'am," Matt said. One of her lieutenants, he was a young man, balding, with glasses. He was skinny, prone to wearing blue-grey suits and red bowties.

"Of course we can't," Anya said. "This isn't a disease outbreak; it's a Category A Bioterrorism event. That will bring Homeland Security running. We'll tell them what we're doing, what we have, and they can set up a buffer zone in the city, prevent it from getting completely out of control. And we can tell civilians that there's a hemorrhagic fever loose in the city. We can say whatever we like, so long as it keeps people under wraps. The point is that we'll have the manpower to deal with this. We move this from public health emergency to national security crisis, and we will get action."

Anya went down the hall, to her office, poured herself a drink, composed herself, made the call.

Mina saw the girl when they'd parked the van at the Kennel. She was leaning against the wall outside the gate, clutching her throat. She was bleeding, had scratchmarks across her face, angry, open wounds.

"Get these people into the DQ," Mina said.

She walked up to the girl, who was taller than she was, had blood all over her, had slashes across her face.

"Miss?" Mina asked.

"Help me," the girl said. "Wolf attacked me."

Her voice was a rasp.

"Jesus," Mina said. "Okay. We can help you. Come with me, and try to stay focused. Tell me what happened."

They went inside the gate, and Mina helped the girl into the building, calling out orders to the other personnel.

"We have an infective," she said. "She needs to be stabilized, by the look of things. Have Dr. Stiles paged."

They reached one of the stainless steel elevators, the kind with doors that opened on either side.

"Why didn't you go to a hospital?" Mina asked.

"Just got attacked," the girl said.

"What's your name, Honey?"

"Zooey," she said, looking at Mina with the blackest eyes she'd ever seen on a person. "Call me Zooey."

"Alright, Zooey," Mina said. "We're going to have a doctor look at you. Can you tell me what your attacker looked like?"

"She was a wolf," Zooey said. "A wolf-woman named Polly Drinkwater, in Winnetka. I saw her change. She clawed at me."

"Did she bite you? Were you bitten?"

Zooey looked over her wounds, turned her arms this way and that.

"No," she said. "No, I don't think so."

There was an interesting opportunity, here, Mina could see. She would want to get a blood sample from the girl, to see if the pathogen could be transmitted through cuts alone.

"What's *your* name?" Zooey asked.

"Mina," she replied.

"That's a nice name," Zooey said. "And you have amazing eyes. They're so grey. It's like you can see right through walls with them. I bet you're a Taurus. Are you a Taurus?"

"Scorpio," Mina said.

"Ah," Zooey said. "Bet your Moon is in Taurus, though."

They reached the medical section of the Kennel, the elevator door opening into a busy scene of scurrying bodies as medical staff went about collecting samples and monitoring the condition of the test subjects.

Zooey reached for Mina's hand, gave her hand a squeeze.

"Don't worry, there's nothing to be afraid of in here," Mina said.

"Oh, I'm totally not scared," Zooey said, pulling Mina's hand to her mouth and biting down hard. Mina yelped, gazed in shock at the young woman who was glaring blackly at her, having bitten right through Mina's rubber gloves, finding flesh and blood.

And then, all at once, the girl's flesh rippled and flared, and the girl's lanky body gave way to an altogether monstrous form, billowing like a cloud as muscle piled onto her frame, seemingly out of nowhere, white fur burst from her body, her limbs lengthened, hands became paws, fingernails became claws, and all the while, as her face became a muzzle, the girl kept her grip on Mina's hand, while Mina fought to free herself, screaming.

Zooey released her with a shake of her head, sending her careening across the lab. Then Zooey charged through the place, slashing at and biting everybody within reach. Dr. Stiles, who had been answering his page, looked on in horror as Zooey leaped at him, biting him savagely on the leg, throwing him into some nurses.

Then she smashed open the observation and containment rooms, all 20 of them, ripping off the doors and throwing them about, releasing the infectives imprisoned there. And after that, she went through the medical wing, biting absolutely everyone who worked there, everybody who was wearing white got a bite.

Somebody had triggered the alarm klaxon, and Zooey herself pulled the fire alarm, yanked the thing off the wall, which caused the place to erupt in pouring water from the ceiling.

Then she ran for the stairs, her monstrous, white-furred form knocking down a steel door like it was made out of cardboard. She bounded up the steps, went to the floor above, which was where Security was stationed. She tore that door down and charged the black-clad Security men who were looking at her in naked shock.

She slashed one across the face, bit the other one, then turned on the first one and bit him, too.

With the fire sprinklers on and the alarm klaxon sounding, it was bedlam, and she was making the most of it, jumping from the shadows to attack every person who was within reach.

Several of the Security people fired at her with assault weapons, but Zooey moved far too quickly for them. She was like a bullet, herself, and in close quarters like this, she had the advantage, could spring on the personnel and bite them before anybody could even respond. The norms were so slow, relative to her.

A guard drew a pistol, and Zooey clamped down on his hand, making the man scream as she tore his hand right off before he'd been able to fire a shot.

Then she bounded through the steel doors here and went up another flight of stairs, this time to the Administrative level.

The old line was about how the best defense was a good offense. Zooey remembered her dad saying that, when he was trying to teach her how to play chess. Zooey knew how to be offensive. This was about as offensive as she could be.

Life was good, and getting better all the time.

Anya heard the emergency alert klaxon go off after she'd finished her call to Homeland Security, had explained their situation, what she suspected was going on, and why they needed to get response teams here immediately.

There was shooting going on in the halls somewhere, and she heard that, tried to contact Security on the intercom, but nothing was coming through. Then the fire sprinklers went off, and she knew that, somewhere, they had a breach.

She pulled a pistol from her drawer, a Beretta loaded with silver bullets, and she braced herself behind her desk.

While her administrative instincts had her wanting to go out and take charge of this situation, she felt that in the chaos of the moment, she was better off hunkering down and preparing for the worst.

She heard someone screaming down the hallway, and scotched that idea; she couldn't let any of her people die.

Anya threw open the door to find Matt down the hall, on the floor, shivering in the chill water raining down on them. He had been bitten across his midsection, and gazed up at her, pale as a sheet.

"B-b-behind you," he said.

Anya spun around, shooting, the Beretta coughing bullets, flashing orange. The white werewolf had sidestepped her shots, grabbed her gun arm, and effortlessly twisted it with a flick of its arm, breaking three of her fingers as she did so.

"Princess," Anya gasped, dropping her pistol as the pain shot through her.

"What?" the thing said.

"You're Princess," Anya said. "You're her."

The werewolf's muzzle was bloody, and the water had given her a wet coat, but the ivory fur was thick and beautiful. Even the wolf's monstrous face was somehow beautiful, in a sinister and menacing way—it had pure, clean, predatory lines, though its black eyes seemed strangely at odds with it, giving it a bottomless gaze that bore into the Director, and it had scratches across its face.

"You're the Director?" the werewolf asked. "You're in charge? You're the one who sent the snipers after me?"

Anya winced at the pain in her arm, which had not yet been released by the creature. She was not going to give the thing the satisfaction of crying out.

"I am," she said.

"That, like, bites," the werewolf said, yanking Anya's arm up to her mouth and taking a bite.

"No no no no no no NO!" Anya said, feeling the burning sting of the bite.

Princess almost seemed to grin at her, as the bit down on her wounded arm. It was the last thing she saw, as darkness overtook her and she fainted.

Anya had fainted before. One time, when she had not eaten breakfast, had been running late. She just blacked out, and remembered the sound coming back to her before she'd been able to see. It was like that for her at the Kennel, as she heard the sound of paramedics and personnel, heard groaning and moaning, before she could see.

She saw Mina hovering over her, her own hand bandaged, shining a penlight in Anya's eyes.

"We have a problem, Director," she said. "The entire Kennel has been compromised."

Anya felt her head buzzing, looked around, saw that Matt was gone, although there was blood on the carpet where he had been. Somebody had, thankfully, turned off the fire sprinklers.

"The entire place? Everyone?"

"Reports are still coming in," Mina said. "I'm guessing that about 95% of the personnel in here have been bitten. No fatalities, at least."

"She didn't want us dead," Anya said. "Princess wanted us alive."

"It's my fault," Mina said. "She tricked me."

"What do you mean?"

"She was at the carport entrance," Mina said. "Injured, by the look of it. I had thought she was an infective."

"She was," Anya said. Someone had bandaged her arm. Anya sat up. "I should have been more careful. I counted on our anonymity protecting us, on her not being able to find this place."

"It really was Princess, wasn't it?" Mina asked. Anya nodded, accepting Mina's help as she got to her feet.

"I want to tour the facility," Anya said. "Homeland Security is going to shut us down, cart us off to some control unit prisons. Or maybe we'll get taken to a biological weapons lab, or to Wolf Island."

Anya dug out her cell phone to make a call, but the thing had gotten wet, and wouldn't work. So, she went to her office, went to her desk, and she pushed a button. This opened the Kennel's PA system.

"This is the Director," she said. "One of the infectives, the one we codenamed 'Princess,' has attacked the facility. Many of you, perhaps all of you, are injured. This was her intent. She wanted to infect all of us as a way of scuttling our good work, here. But our work must continue. All of you understand its importance. And I want to be very clear: none of you are permitted to leave the premises. Anyone who attempts to do so will be detained by Security. We are going to remain in lockdown until Homeland Security or someone else from the CDC arrives to take charge of this facility."

She paused, releasing the button a moment, resting her head in her good hand, before she pressed the button again.

"I know many of you are hurt and hurting," she said. "But our mission remains unchanged; all of you understood the risks associated with our service. We must look at this as a kind of opportunity, as unfortunate as that may seem. I want all of you to log your experiences as the infection progresses—and let's not be naïve—it will progress, as it has with every infective. I want everything you feel and experience to be logged. This information that we can provide may prove of value to the CDC and other bodies that investigate, and we must do our duty. I know it will be difficult, but in this way, we can have a kind of legacy for the good work we have done here. I am very proud of all of you, and the work we do here in the wake of this monstrous attack will help us get that much closer to finding a cure for the disease."

Anya sat back, spent, and Mina sat down across from her.

"It's all my fault," she said. "I didn't even think; I just saw somebody injured, reacted to it instinctively."

Anya admitted that she hadn't planned for an infective actively seeking out the Kennel, and could have kicked herself for that simple oversight. She had hoped that secrecy would have been enough protection, and the internal defenses of the Kennel would be sufficient. The place had been built to contain lycanthropes, but had not truly been intended to repel them. Their budgeting had not permitted it, they hadn't faced something of this order of magnitude.

The idea of an infective with an agenda, deliberately carrying out attacks with cunning and precision? That was something else.

"Her name's Zooey," Mina said. "She told it to me."

"Zooey," Anya said. "You saw her in her human form."

"Yes," Mina said. "She's a pretty girl. Tall. Maybe in her early 20s at the latest. She was a bloody mess when I saw her, had scratches on her face and a cut throat. Black eyes, blonde hair, I think. There may be security camera footage from the elevator."

"Of course there is," Anya said. She pushed a button on her console. "Reed? Are you still breathing down there?"

"Yes, Director," came the voice of the Security Director. "We're all chewed up, but everybody's here."

"Get me the footage from the security camera on the carport elevator," Anya said. "The last hour or so. I want it."

"Will do," Reed said.

"I'm not letting that bitch have the last laugh on this, you know," Anya said. "I intend to go down fighting. Mina, I need you to get out of here immediately. Before the DC folks arrive. Phil Sanderson's going to lock this place down."

Mina looked at her a moment, her face uncertain. "Why?"

"You're our best researcher," Anya said. "Grab the data and just get offsite immediately. Once Sanderson's here, you're just another prisoner."

Reed glanced at Anya and Mina, but Anya shook her head.

"Not a word, Reed," Anya said. "On your life, not a word. Go grab a laptop and get those files, Mina, and get out of here as soon as you can."

"Okay, Anya," Mina said, running off.

11

Zooey took a luxurious bath, laughing and laughing as she cleaned herself off. It was even worth the sting of the wounds across her face, which were going to be slow to heal, since they were inflicted by that little bitch, Polly.

But it was so worth it. Zooey had taken her dad's advice to heart, about taking a bad situation and turning it into an opportunity. She'd been so pissed off at Polly actually managing to drive her away, injuring her, that she'd wanted to take it out on somebody. She'd been close to having a moment of self-pity at her situation, when she realized that she could pose as an injured norm and waltz right into that BEE place and fuck them up.

It had been an inspired move, even for her. They hadn't known what had hit them, hadn't even seen it coming. And the way Zooey had the run of the place, with its labs and its serious government contractors busy working away, it had been awesome. She'd infected, like, over 250 people in one pass.

That was totally wicked. She took a sponge and mopped off the blood, watching it turn the bath water pink. It had to be a lycanthropic record.

She'd commandeered a townhome she had come across in Old Town, just broke the fuck in and wasted the gay couple who were living there, these two old guys. She'd thought about just infecting them, but wanted to have the place to herself, and she was hungry after hitting BEE and her fight with Polly, so she just killed them and ate them. It was far simpler that way.

And after the rush that had been the raid on BEE, it was practically a letdown. Her taste for bigger and better had really taken hold. She had visions of taking out Navy Pier, fragging all those fat suburbanites and clueless tourists who flocked there, sending them back to

wherever it was they came from, whether Naperville or the Nether-
lands.

She would get her pack organized, would start staging lycanthropic outrages like that. It would be gorgeous.

Zooey got out of the bathtub and wrapped herself in a towel, went
to the big mirrors that were on the wall there, mopped them off with a
pass of the towel, patted her face dry. Polly's claws had done a number
of her face, which would pose problems for Zooey at the moment, as
she turned her face this way and that.

Angry gashes, right across her pretty face.

The bitch had some serious nails going. And the slash at her throat
could have been fatal, if Polly hadn't been such a pussy about it, if
she'd had the guts to bite down hard.

Still, it would take time to heal, and Zooey thought it might be
useful to hunker down for a few days, let herself get better, so she
could pass on the street without incident. The norms were beginning
to get scared—they were beginning to understand that something terrible was happening, that more and more people in the city were being
injured, that something was hunting them.

They were finding bodies in the parks, body parts and blood on
the streets. They were witnessing carnage, and for a country unused to
carnage, a country that had insulated itself from both life and death,
it would be a rude awakening.

The last thing Zooey wanted at this moment was attention, which
was contrary to everything about her; she loved attention, but would
have to be sure that it came to her in her Lupine form, not her norm
disguise. People would be getting pissed about what was happening,
and lord knows that those BEE twats would be after her, and the
Wilkos.

No, she would lay low for a few days, just chill out, have some
quality Zooey Time. The gay couple's townhome was nice, had a ful-
ly-provisioned fridge and comfortable furnishings. Zooey could camp
out here until the norm food ran out, could watch the news, see what
the norms were busy talking about, thinking about. She could see
how things would settle in the wake of what she'd done, and determine her next move.

She took off her towel and hung the thing up, decided she'd just
walk around the place nude. Why the fuck not? Clothes were for
norms. She cranked up the heat in the townhome and walked about
naked as a jaybird.

She went to the fridge, looked for something to drink. They didn't have any beer, but there were some San Pellegrino sodas in there. She took out a Pompelmo and sat down on their sofa, found the remote, turned on the television, and bathed once again, this time in the HD electron glow of a plasma screen television.

People were definitely going apeshit, and she could see the media people, the broadcasters who were used to reporting much on almost nothing at all, day after day, coming up short, unable to explain, contextualize, or account for everything that was happening to the city.

Police reports, hospital reports, government reports. The Mayor, blustering and fuming, and somebody actually asking if there was a problem with coyotes in the city, them biting people.

Nobody would say it.

Nobody could bring themselves to say it.

Not a single news channel would speak the word on everybody's lips.

It at first amused Zooey, more than anything else. Here it was, happening right under their noses, right in their faces, and nobody could even bring themselves to say it.

"Werewolves," Zooey said to the television. "Say it, fuckers. Fucking say it."

No.

It was "Animal attacks."

It was "Coyote outbreaks."

It was "Rabid dogs."

Some even pushed the envelope and spoke of "Wolf incursions."

There was a naturalist talking about how climate change had brought Canadian wolves across the border and into the Great Lakes region. Something about wolves and coyotes mating, producing "coywolves" that were bigger than coyotes, and apparently more savage, unafraid of Man.

Motherfucking coywolves? Really?

It made Zooey want to attack the broadcasters, next. Give those people something to put the real fear in them.

Actually, as she surfed through the channels, saw the same pile of nothing repeated across the networks, she thought that might not be a bad idea. Give the norms something they couldn't ignore, shove their noses in it.

Coywolves. What the fuck?

She understood that most Americans lived with their heads shoved squarely up their own asses, or up each others' asses. But to deny what was happening to them in the here and now? Out of what? Fear of people thinking they were crazy? Fear of the unknown?

If this had been goddamned Romania, people would have fucking known what was going on, would have known what to do with werewolves. Hell, the Wilkos knew what they were up against. They were like the only ones. There was something offensive about it to Zooey, this idea of going after such clueless prey, these folks who couldn't even give a good fight because they were afraid to look their enemy squarely in the eye.

She'd been running all over town, trying to stir things up, and still people weren't getting it, were refusing to see what was going on. She bet that even if she went on the news and attacked the newscasters on the set, people would still not believe what they were seeing.

Zooey touched the wounds on her face, drank her soda, fumed about it.

It pissed her off.

What the hell was wrong with people, anyway?

Polly had cleaned up the last of the Zooey-mess that had been made at her place, while she tried to compose herself. The Thing had released her after a day, leaving Polly to wake up outside, in a playground, actually laying on a merry-go-round, waking up before dawn, covered in somebody's blood, the merry-go-round gently spinning, squeak-creaking as it moved.

She hadn't known where she was at first, had to suffer the indignity of running naked through town before the sun rose, praying nobody would see her. She realized she was only a few blocks down the street from her house, so she ran there, hiding from early-morning dog walkers. Of course, the dogs could smell her, were barking in her direction, which forced her to hide and try to wait them out, while their owners were looking around, talking to their dogs, trying to find out what their pets were barking at.

Polly recognized one of the walkers as Lane Jeffries, the tax lawyer. He'd played golf with Tristan a few times. Nice enough man, but terribly boring, despite being tall and tan and fit, with gunmetal-grey hair. His dog, a Labradoodle named Diane, was barking furiously at the tree Polly was hiding behind.

"Oh, hush, Diane," Lane said. "You'll wake up the entire neighborhood."

Polly had always hated that he'd named his dog "Diane." It was such a rotten dog name. His wife was Missy Jeffries, who was as avid a golfer as her husband, sold real estate to fill her otherwise painfully empty days.

The pre-dawn light was growing, while Polly shivered in the shadows, and Diane the dog barked, and Lane Jeffries kept cross-examining the dog, instead of just taking her out of there.

Polly looked at her own body, naked and pale and covered in blood. Whose blood was anybody's guess, and it scared her to think about it, since her tummy was full. That Thing had eaten somebody, she was sure, or at least taken some hefty bites out of them.

She wished that her friends were around, so she could talk to them about this, could show them. So she could chew out Sam about infecting her.

Jeffries finally dragged his dog away from the tree, and Polly wasted no time, sprinted away, keeping the tree between her and the lawyer as she went to the next yard, and the one after that, finally reaching her place, sneaking in back, through the broken glass doors she'd gone through after fighting Zooey.

Then she went upstairs and took a long, hot bath, got herself cleaned up, put herself back together, went to work cleaning up the mess.

Having done that, pouring herself a strong cup of coffee, Polly wondered what she should do. She had Zooey's pink Samsonite suitcase, which was locked. Angry at the brazen nature of the attack, she wanted to leave that case at the curb, but thought that Zooey might come looking for it again, and that maybe it could be a bargaining chip or something.

She'd never seen such raw malevolence in a person before; it had been jarring. Zooey was beautiful, but she was pure evil. It was abundantly clear to Polly, who had never seen such a thing before.

Part of her, whatever undamaged fragment of herself remained, wanted to create a poem about it. She'd not written any verse since she'd become infected. Something in her had been broken when she'd become that Thing, and in so doing, had lost her way.

There was no poetry to lycanthropy. Or was there?

She took out her laptop and turned it on, sat down in her living room, faced the blank phosphorescence of the thing as the sun peeked over the horizon and shot amber-colored light into her house.

Polly wrote the word: LYCANTHROPY.

From the Greek word, *Lykànthropos,* literally meaning "wolf-human," and, perhaps the word was drawn from the story of King Lycaon, king of Arcadia, who had been cursed to turn into a wolf because he had dared to serve the flesh of his own murdered son to Zeus as a sacrifice, in an attempt to determine if Zeus was truly divine.

It was an ugly thing, but was kind of a beautiful word.

LYCANTHROPE
LYCANTHOPY
LYCANTHROPIC

She stared at the words a moment, felt her poet's brain playing.

I AM A LYCANTHROPE

I am a lycanthrope
Stalking winsome shadows
Bastard bringer of death
Hungering for ruin
Depravity's daughter

I am a lycanthrope
Running hard on all fours
Feral faith commanding
My nose knows what you are
I'll kiss you with my teeth

I am a lycanthrope
Not zombie, ghost nor ghoul
Trading my flesh for fur
Fangs make my fear recede
O pray for me, my prey.

She paused, saved it. It was her first poem in the wake of her infection, the first stray bark of her muse. Polly drank down the rest of coffee, laughing grimly to herself. She would be the poet laureate of lycanthropy.

POL

Monstrosity's muse
You are no beast of burden
Laying claim to what you will
Must I enjoy the ride?

LAMIA

I saw you tonight, you white-haired harpy:
fell creature laughing:
harridan harlot.

Bringing me only bane in your reckless
lycanthropic livery:
carpetbagging chaos.

Your storm and fury signified nothing,
t'was an empty threat:
vagabond vanguard.

Breathing bloodshed and feasting on slaughter
I defeated you:
lamentable lamia.

Polly stopped, snapped shut her laptop, poured herself another cup of coffee. Maybe there was something to be mined from this nightmare, after all.

She did not want to call Ansel, but after what Zooey had done, she wanted to sic him on her, pure and simple. Ansel cared about her, and, perhaps she could admit that she cared about him, too. Not yet, but eventually.

Polly rang him up, and, to her surprise, he answered on the second ring.

"Yeah?" he said. "What is it, Polly?"

"Sam's plaything attacked me," Polly said.

"Which plaything?"

"Zooey," Polly said. "Did she not tell you about her?"

Ansel shrugged on the other side of the phone, while Polly told Ansel about what she suspected, about how she'd met Zooey, who had shacked up with Sam.

"How'd she find you?"

"I don't know," Polly said. "But she did. It's not like I'm that hard to find. She came here wanting to, I don't know, hang out, and I kicked her to the curb."

"You kicked her out?" Ansel said.

"Yes," Polly said. "I became, you know, that Thing."

"Are you okay? Are you hurt?"

"Believe it or not, I'm okay. I got banged up, but I think Zooey got the worst of it. I drove her off. Who knew I had it in me?"

"So, why are you telling me about this?"

"I want you to kill her, Ansel. For me," she said.

"I see," Ansel said. "For you?"

"Yes," Polly said. "Do that, and I'm yours. How about that?"

She could hear Ansel chewing that over in his head, which was what passed for thinking for him. Ansel was smart, but it was a deliberate intelligence, the plodding, painterly way he had with everything, the world as his canvas, and him with his brushes in hand, taking his time with it, taking everything in, deciding which pigments to use.

"So, you're wanting me to commit murder as a precondition for us to, you know, have a relationship?"

"Pithily put, but, yes," Polly said.

"My kind of girl," Ansel said.

"Look, she home invaded me, threw me around, made a mess of this place, and wanted to kill me," Polly said. "She thinks of me as kind of a little sister, since, I think, Sam infected us both."

"Sibling rivalry," Ansel said. "Oh, I know all about that. You've never met my sister."

"Are you going to do it for me or not?"

"And on a cell phone, no less," Ansel said. "You could have just asked me to come over, we could have talked about this face-to-face."

"No," Polly said. "I don't want to see you until it's done."

"Hardcore, Polly," Ansel said. "Since this 'Zooey' appears to be part of Sam's mess, since she's the price of admission—"

"She is," Polly said. "That is, if you want all of me, not just half."

"Fine," Ansel said. "I'll see what I can do. Happy?"

"Getting there," Polly said. She hung up on him, spent some time thinking how she should tweet this turn of events.

13

Zach had been stalking around Avondale, fruitlessly trying to track down Princess Zooey, when he'd gotten the call from the Kennel, from Anya, herself.

"We found Princess," Anya said. "The dear child found us, I should say. She attacked the Kennel, Houndstooth."

"What?"

"She got in, bit every last one of us," Anya said. "Can you believe that? So much for our protocols, yes? I'd say you might as well come in, now, but there are extenuating circumstances."

"What extenuating circumstances?"

"Homeland Security will be here at some point to take over the Kennel," Anya said. "I'd rather you stay far afield, lest you get caught up in the reorganization directly."

Zach felt a mix of concern and admiration at the sheer brass balls of Princess Zooey. That had been an audacious throw of the dice, to be sure.

"Is Princess dead?"

"No," Anya said. "Nobody hit her. I want you to stay in the field. Don't come back in. Phil Sanderson is going to be moving in, taking over. They're going to be locking us away somewhere, I'm sure of it. I know that's what I'd do. They are going to lock this place down, take all of our accumulated data, and send us all away. I can't just disappear; they'd find me. And, honestly, I want to be found, so at least I'll be of some use for the research arm. But you are most useful in the field. You come back, and your talents are wasted."

Zach was upset at hearing Anya talk like this, the finality of it. He liked his job, didn't want to lose it, as absurd as that might seem to somebody looking in on the outside.

"Why can't I just reach out to him on this?" he said.

"You could, but if he found out that you're infected, you'll be shipped off like the rest of us," Anya said.

"They might not," Zach said.

"They will," Anya said. "We have over 300 personnel here, nearly all of them infected. The only sensible precaution is to quarantine this site, evacuate the personnel to Wolf Island, and shut this place down. The alternative is letting us all run wild, watching the infection take hold of us, and watching us lose control and compromise the Bureau."

Zach took out the silver bullet, pressed it into his palm, winced at the pain, almost dropped the bullet. He had a welt on his skin where the bullet had been. He put it back in his pocket.

"Keep after her," Anya said. "Bring her to Sanderson and maybe they'll let you in. I can't guarantee it, but you are one of the few Kennel personnel who were not on-site when Princess attacked—that's reflected in the duty roster. So, you're one of the only ones who could plausibly claim to not be infected. Do you see my logic?"

"But I am infected," Zach said.

"And only we know this," Anya said. "That's my point."

"I don't like it," Zach said. "I don't like the idea of Sanderson coming in on this. Those DC clowns don't know shit. They can't possibly cope."

"I made the call," Anya said. "It was the only thing I could do under the circumstances. Once we'd been compromised, that's all I could do. The other directors of BEE have their hands full—our Princess has been scattering infectives like dandelion seeds. We're getting preliminary reports of outbreaks in Detroit, Cleveland, Pittsburgh, Philadelphia, St. Louis, New York, Seattle, Los Angeles, Atlanta, New Orleans, Boulder, Las Vegas. It's all over the place."

Zach could only imagine. How could it have spread so fast?

"I know what you're thinking," Anya said. "You're wondering how. Mina's working on theories on that."

"Fuck," Zach said.

"Yes," Anya said. "I'm sure she'll figure out how she's doing it, or if she even is. There's talk about some kind of conspiracy among infectives, a kind of infective insurgency. That's why Homeland Security needs to be in on this, why it's blown bigger than the Bureau, Zachary."

"Fuck," Zach said.

"It's not something you need to worry about," Anya said. "Just bring her in. She's a bioterrorist, now, Houndstooth. She remains your top priority."

"And after that?"

"You go to the new admin—Sanderson—and give her to him. He'll take care of it, and you'll probably get a new assignment."

"I should turn myself in," Zach said. "I'll be fully infective by then."

"Do what your conscience tells you to do," Anya said. "We are in the midst of an epidemic and a war. I trust you, Houndstooth. Good luck, and goodbye."

She hung up on him, leaving Zach shaken.

He was completely alone.

Phil Sanderson thought there was no epidemic that couldn't be cured with stacks of barricades, gallons of bleach and loads of bullets.

When word had come through that the Kennel had been compromised by a coordinated attack by one of these metamorphic bioweapons quaintly referred to as "werewolves" or "lycanthropes," Sanderson made sure that they had a counterinsurgency plan in place.

It had been Anya's ball, and she'd fumbled.

He sent his Hazmat teams in fully garbed and masked, and they went about spraying down the Kennel, while he had personnel load the Kennel employees into buses for immediate evacuation. They were to be shipped downstate, where they could be more effectively quarantined before being flown to Wolf Island. That was the official plan.

Sanderson had never seen such a sorry group of people; they looked like they'd been in a war—every one of them was bandaged, all of them had pales faces and hangdog looks. They were scared, and were rightfully so; even Sanderson couldn't guess their fate, since the protocol for dealing with this epidemic had not yet been fully written.

He assumed the Vice President and Attorney General were in a bunker somewhere drafting it, and was surprised that they didn't crank up the threat level color to red at this point, putting the whole country into a politically-motivated panic.

Frankly, the lack of response from Washington wasn't surprising; they had been so busy chasing phantoms and milking people's adrenal glands that when something real finally happened, they didn't know what to do—the Boy Who'd Cried Wolf had gotten his comeuppance, it seemed.

That wasn't something Sanderson shared with anybody; in the current administration, he understood his role all too well:

1. Follow orders
2. Protect the higher-ups

3. Fuck the consequences

Since the epicenter of this biohazard blowout was in true blue Chicago, Sanderson sensed that his bosses could give two shits about it, and were already figuring ways of turning this to their political advantage.

The bands of partisan troglodytes had to be loving this, while the Secretary of Defense was barking orders about how they had to get these lycanthropes contained, controlled, and deployed in the Middle East, assuming that something like this would be the perfect way to break the backs of the insurgency, destabilizing enemy regimes with an influx of infectious, almost invulnerable agents. They hadn't ruled out that terrorists had somehow brought this disease here.

The problem with that theory was that everybody in the know knew that the lycanthropes had come from an old Nazi "Super Soldier" experiment gone wrong, their *Werwolf* program circa 1944.

That was exactly Defense's point—they had been intended as a nasty little leave-behind for the Allies, working behind the scenes to cause chaos and wreak havoc. While most of the commandos had been miserable failures, and the concept as a whole served more as a propaganda tool than a practical weapon. But some part of that otherwise benighted program had been dazzlingly, dizzily successful, as was clear from looking around the Kennel.

The lycanthrope was a nearly perfect living weapon—almost immune to conventional weapons and attack, equipped with enhanced senses, claws and fangs, and able to blend seamlessly into a civilian population. They were like homicide bombers—you could take them and drop them into someplace you wanted to destabilize and watch them go off like the killing machines that they were.

Anya, for her part, had at least been thoughtful enough to give him all the data they had gathered to date. She'd presented it to Sanderson, herself, her arm in a sling, since she'd apparently been bitten by this rogue Lupine, herself.

"You did the best you could with the hand you were dealt, Anya," Sanderson said. He was shorter than she was, had brown hair he kept close-cropped and wore round, rimless glasses. Sanderson took advantage of his endomorphic physique to work out a great deal, maintained a muscular build that nonetheless made him seem kind of lumpish in a suit, but he took pride in his strength: it gave him confidence, was to him a badge for his discipline and determination to succeed.

This lycanthrope business was no different. When Anya had raised the white flag on it, Sanderson had jumped at the chance, bringing himself up to speed and eager to go to work, to hit the ground running.

The first order of business was that they were no longer going to capture and study the lycanthropes, nor ship them off to Wolf Island; he'd put word out to his teams that they were going to simply kill any lycanthropes they encountered. That came by way of an Executive Order.

He felt that the Kennel had enough samples gathered already, had enough prisoners—and with the Kennel personnel themselves infected, he had all the test subjects he needed for now. Logistically, it was just so much simpler.

What mattered now was reestablishing order. Civilians were getting scared by what was going on, even if they couldn't quite explain what was happening. And with an election year looming, they didn't want anything that could risk the election coming out to literally bite them on the ass.

The scent of bleach was making it hard to breathe, so Sanderson walked Anya outside, let his teams do their thing.

"This isn't just some band of hooligans, Phil," Anya said.

"Oh, I understand," Sanderson said. "I'm treating this very seriously, Anya. They're up in arms about this, they want this shut down without raising a stink. Everybody has Katrina on the brain. They're worried about becoming more of a laughingstock if word of this slips out."

"Nobody's laughing, Phil," Anya said. "A single infective decimated my facility."

"And whose fault was that?"

"It wasn't anybody's fault," Anya said. "It just happened."

She looked pained when she said it, and Sanderson felt professional sympathy for her: of course it was her fault. She was in charge, so it was her fault. In the school of moral management, that was how it was played out. Anya always played the high ground that way.

In Sanderson's experience, it was the other way around—when somebody down the food chain fucked up, they had to pay for it; those up top had to be protected at all costs, and Anya's biggest failure was not finding someone to fall on their sword for her. What was the point of being powerful if you didn't have immunity from responsibility and consequences? That's what made you powerful.

"Right," Sanderson said. "I'm changing the focus of the operation, effective immediately. We're going to be deploying kill teams out there; they've got standing shoot-to-kill orders for any lycanthropes spotted."

"That will get messy, Phil," Anya said. "The biggest problem we face with a kill of an infective is that they return to their human form when slain. So, if you send death squads out there, people are just going to see everyday-seeming people murdered on the streets. That's why we put a high priority on recovery and incarceration before shipment to Wolf Island."

"Yes, I get it," Sanderson said. "I do, Anya, I really do. But you tried it your way, and look what you have to show for it. It's not like we're going to do this loudly; we're going to have our guys deployed covertly—people will just disappear. Speaking of that, do you still have any Wardens out there?"

"I do," Anya said. She handed over a file that contained the dossiers of the surviving Wardens. There had been about 15 of them remaining, including Zachary.

"Great," Sanderson said. "Are they still in radio contact with you?"

"Of course," Anya said.

"Call them in," Sanderson said. "I want them to meet their new boss."

Anya took out her radio, cleared her throat, while Sanderson looked on, amused at his colleague's unease. She didn't like the way he was going about this. Anya's problem was that she was seeing the lycanthropes as victims in need of curing; like this was a medical problem.

Sanderson understood them as enemies in need of killing. Nobody yet had a cure for the condition, and he couldn't bank on it coming anytime soon, so it was a no-brainer in his view. If you had gangrene, you had to excise the diseased tissue in order to save the rest of the body. Sanderson was going to save the body politic, one way or another.

"All field units, this is the Director," Anya said. "I need you to report back to the Kennel immediately. Cease all fieldwork and report here. Phil Sanderson is taking over operations going forward."

She held out her radio, but Sanderson wouldn't take it.

"Worried about catching cooties?" Anya said.

"Yes, frankly," he said, holding out a small biohazard baggie, into which she dropped the radio. He sealed the baggie, put it in his pocket. "How many Wardens are we talking about here?"

"About 15," she said.

"About?"

"At last count," Anya said. "Sometimes they don't make it back. You'll learn about that soon enough, Phil."

"Don't worry about my guys," he said. "I'm going to get this wrapped up before year's end. We're putting a firewall around this, although I tell you, I think if it bleeds into next year, they're going to use it as an excuse to declare martial law and put off the elections."

Anya laughed bitterly at this. "You're a cynical man, Phil."

"Count on it," he said. "My orders are to get this contained as soon as possible. And if that doesn't pan out, they'll go public with it and declare a state of emergency until it gets sorted out, and that means, you know, extreme measures. They'll call it bioterrorism officially and that will be that. The procedures for this are all in place."

"You're loving this," Anya said.

"It's my job," Sanderson said. "I love my job. How long until your Wardens come in?"

"Should be about an hour," she said. "Two at the most."

"Let's get some coffee," Sanderson said. "You can bring me up to speed on what you've seen so far."

———

It took an hour and a half for all of the Wardens to turn up. They were a mix of men and women—12 men, 3 women, all of them with military backgrounds. Sanderson could use that.

"Homeland Security is officially taking over," Sanderson said. "I don't know how much your Director shared with you, but the Kennel was attacked and compromised by the infective your Director code-named 'Princess,' who I believe is actually named 'Zooey.' By the way, how was this determined?"

"She spoke to one of my personnel before she began her attack on the Kennel," Anya said quickly.

"Which of your personnel?" Sanderson asked.

"Dr. Mina Milkowski," Anya said. The name didn't register with Sanderson, although he glanced around them.

"Where is Dr. Milkowski?" Sanderson asked.

"I don't know," Anya said, nodding to Reed. "Get on the intercom and see if you can locate her, Reed."

Reed nodded and went about that.

"I see," Sanderson said. "So, you 15 are the fortunate ones; if you had been at the Kennel at the time of the attack, you'd have been infected, or maybe killed. At any rate, you'd have been taken out of the equation. But you were lucky, so now you're going to work for me, since, as you surely know, we can't have you following orders from a Director who has been compromised by the very infection we are trying to contain."

He looked at Anya a moment when he said this, and she returned his gaze evenly, without evident emotion. Sanderson liked Anya, felt bad that it was going to end for her this way. She surely thought she was going to end up in a lab somewhere, as a specimen. She deserved better than that.

"With a change in leadership comes a change in direction and emphasis," Sanderson said. "Two things: first, we're going to pursue a straightforward shoot-to-kill policy with these lycanthropes. You find them, you kill them. No more tranquilizer nonsense. You see one, you kill one. We'll worry about the retrieval of the bodies. You just shoot them, and call those in, and we'll have somebody scoop them up. Second, I want you to brief my own shooters about what you've encountered out there. You guys are the veterans of this insurgency, and I want every bit of intelligence you've gathered about what we're facing to be passed on to my own kill teams, so we can get this going as smoothly as possible. If we're viewing the city as a game preserve, you guys are the wardens. I've got 75 men at my disposal—all Special Forces, every branch. Seems like everybody wanted in on this opportunity, so we're bringing them all in. Any of you folks former Special Forces?"

Eight of the Wardens raised their hands.

"Fabulous," Sanderson said. "I'll have you brief your respective peers, then, if they're here. Have everybody speaking the same language, get this going quickly. We have Green Berets, SEALs, Rangers, Delta Force, Marines SOR, Air Force CCTs. We've even got the brand-spanking new Coast Guard DOGs in on this, since we've got Lake Michigan and the Chicago River to contend with, and lord knows those Lupines know how to doggy-paddle."

Sanderson smiled, let the team laugh at his little joke, before continuing.

"You should all be proud of the work you've done for the Bureau. Believe me, I understand how hard this has been for all of you, and you, more than anybody, know how much is riding on this. But my hope is that by hitting these things fast and hard, we'll be able to cauterize the infection before it spreads."

"It's already spreading," Anya said. "We had reports coming in from across the country."

"Homeland Security is handling this nationwide, trust me," Sanderson said. "We are going at this systematically. That's why the ground role on this is so vital, why leveraging the situation here is critical. Your agency has been active for the past 50 years in keeping this lycanthrope thing under wraps and out of the headlines, and we all respect the history and the dedication behind that critical mission, what has been happening here right now is something nobody's been prepared to deal with. Not at this level, at this intensity. That's why we're employing such measures. The quicker we stop this, the quicker things can get back to normal—or back to paranormal, anyway."

That got another laugh out of the Wardens, which Sanderson used to segue to his closing statement.

"I'd like to welcome you each to my team, and I'm confident that we'll be able to work together effectively in carrying out this mission," he said.

Sanderson then worked his way from agent to agent, shaking their hands and meeting them one by one. All of them looked tired and stressed, but each of them had clearly performed well in their role. Sanderson had hoped that by simplifying their mission parameter for them, some of the stress would be alleviated—it was far easier to simply kill a target than to wound one. Bullets offered surer ballistic prophylaxis when contrasted with tranquilizer darts.

He reached Zachary West, aka, Houndstooth, and shook the man's hand. Zach looked a little ragged, was very tightly wound.

"Anya tells me you're her best Warden," Sanderson said.

"She's exaggerating, Sir," Zach said.

"You're the Green Beret," Sanderson said.

"Formerly, Sir," Zach said.

"But it never really leaves you, does it? The training?"

"I suppose not, Sir."

"Call me Phil."

"I suppose not, Phil," Zach said.

"She tells me you're tasked with hunting this 'Princess,'" Sanderson said.

"I am," Zach said. "I was tasked with tranquilizing her and bringing her in. The Director felt she was central to the epidemic. Princess and Big Black."

"Yes," Sanderson said. "You shoot them dead if you see them."

"Sir?"

"The Director said you lost your partner weeks ago, when you were attempting to apprehend 'Big Black,'" Sanderson said. "And that you failed to locate Princess after the Avondale Assault."

"That's true," Zach said. "He's unbelievably fast, Sir. I'm not making excuses; but you have to get it out of your head that we're hunting wolves, here. These aren't wolves; they're werewolves. They move differently, they think differently. And they're fast and very strong. Some of them are even smart."

"So, you hunted Princess, but she got away," Sanderson said.

"Yes," Zach said.

"How'd you lose her? I want to know how her best Warden managed to lose his target."

Zach looked at Sanderson, who was looking back at him with an eager, unreadable expression. Zach didn't know what to say, could see Sanderson sizing him up.

"We were near Horner Park, just east of Avondale," Zach said.

"Why Avondale?"

"Why anywhere, Sir?" Zach said. "She goes where she wants."

"Don't you Bureau people have folks up in Avondale?" Sanderson asked.

"We had some operatives, yeah, but Princess killed them," Zach said.

"So, go on with your story."

"I got up there as soon as I could, and while first responders were there to deal with the wounded and dead, there was no sign of Princess," Zach said. "Princess is always very hit-and-run. That's her style of attack."

"Don't beat yourself up about it, Zach," Sanderson said. "If you'd been authorized to use lethal force, any shot you had taken would've put an end to it."

"If you say so, Sir," Zach said. "It would take a lucky shot, even if I'd seen her. She's damned quick."

"I can vouch for that," Anya said. "Like a blur. I fired at her at nearly point-blank range, and caught nothing but air."

Sanderson looked over his shoulder at Anya, laughed. "But you're not a soldier, Anya. Nobody would expect *you* to hit anything."

"Neither are you," Anya said, meeting his gaze. Sanderson smiled at her, turned his attention back to Zach.

"Don't beat yourself up about it," he said again, patting Zach on the shoulder. "Better luck next time. We have 10 Green Berets here. I want you to brief them in a couple of hours. Take a break, get something to eat—oh, but don't go into the Kennel; we're shutting that down, sealing it up. I have hazmat teams in there taking everything they can use and hosing down the rest with bleach. We're going to have that place sealed up tight. Also, we're setting up shop at the Water Filtration Plant, once we shut this place down."

Zach nodded. "Nice to meet you, Sir."

"Likewise," Sanderson said, watching Zach walk over to talk to some of the other Wardens.

"They're good kids," he said to Anya.

"Yes," she said. "I'm going to miss them. I'm going to miss everything. You know, you can leave me in place until—"

"Now, Anya, you know that wouldn't be prudent or possible," Sanderson said. "I'm having you and all of the other infectives taken downstate. We're putting you in a special quarantine facility. Forget all of this fancy business; we're sending you infectives underground. We'll put a few biologists in there to play zookeeper, give them some ledgers and a stopwatch, let them see how long it takes for you to manifest the infection."

Reed came back, glanced at Anya.

"No sign of Dr. Milkowski, Anya," Reed said. Sanderson looked at Anya for explanation.

"Did you call her cell?"

"Yes," Reed said. "Went to voicemail."

Sanderson crossed his arms, flexed them a bit as he did so.

"So, I'm confused," Sanderson said. "You said Dr. Milkowski talked with Princess right before the attack, and now she's missing."

"Apparently," Anya said.

Sanderson pulled out a radio. "Dylan, I want Dr. Mina Milkowski found and detained. Check their personnel files."

"Mina wouldn't have been cooperating with Princess," Anya said.

Sanderson shook his head. "You don't know that. You can't know that."

"Mina's one of our best researchers," Anya said.

"Was she bitten by Princess?" Sanderson asked.

Anya looked Sanderson in the eye, could see him trying to read her face, to see what her play would be.

"I don't know," Anya said. "But no way was Mina working with Princess."

"We'll find out soon enough," Sanderson said. "The more important thing right now is dealing with your own team."

"What, we don't at least rate a supermax? We can help your team. We have the expertise."

"Honestly, my bosses don't want to risk contaminating a supermax with a bunch of infectives. We are quarantining you as quickly and quietly as we can. If Congress gets wind of this, can you imagine? I mean, they're in the President's pocket these days, but you never can tell how they'll react in a crisis."

"But where are we going?"

"Downstate," Sanderson said. Anya wondered where. Joliet?

Sanderson smiled. "Sorry, Anya. If you'd been more careful, you wouldn't be in this situation, now would you? Think about it when you're down there. Goodbye, Anya."

He gestured, and some soldiers carted Anya away, put her in line with the other infected BEE personnel. There were buses waiting for them, motors running.

Ansel didn't know who he was looking for. It was part of the problem. Sam had been very careful to conceal Zooey's existence from him, knowing that he would have not approved of her making herself a little protégé, especially so soon after she'd been infected.

The problem was, he didn't know what to look for, beyond the description Polly had given him. Tall girl, pretty, whitish blond hair, black eyes, and the most sinister grin Polly had ever seen, and slashes across her pretty face, thanks to Polly. Prone to wearing Chuck Taylors and offbeat colors and clashes of patterns, dressing (as Polly put it) like a "hipster who fell into a Cuisinart."

It wasn't much to go on, but he hoped it would be enough.

He didn't hunt Zooey in his natural form; he stayed as a man, hoped he'd just run into her. There was more mayhem than ever on the streets. He could see that people were getting shot, kept seeing their bodies, seeing unmarked trucks picking them up.

There were men in the trees, men in the bushes, men on rooftops. He could sense them, could see them. Even in his disguise, his senses tended to be sharper than normal, and he could see these shadowy men with rifles.

Ahead of him, he saw a young woman, naked, lying face-down on the sidewalk, dead. She had been shot through the heart.

"Oh my god," Ansel said, more for the benefit of anybody who was nearby than for himself. He was familiar enough with slaughter.

He could also pick up the stink of silver on her, where her wound was.

Playing the part, he took out his cell phone, dialed 911.

"I wanted to report a murder. I'm at Lincoln and Armitage. There's a woman who looks like she's been shot through the heart."

The dispatcher asked for his information, and he gave it, and sat down on a nearby bench, shaking his head, going through the motions of mourning, waiting for the authorities to arrive.

He called Polly, felt like he had to warn her.

"Just so you know, it looks like people are getting shot down here. I'm seeing bodies," he said.

An unmarked truck came up, parked on the street across from the body, and some men in biohazard suits and gas masks got out, and, without a word, picked up the body of the girl. Ansel got up, walked over.

"Hey," Ansel said. "I called 911. You can't just take that woman. Somebody shot her."

"If you know what's good for you, Sir, you'll move along," one of the men said, gazing at him with his gas mask, his voice muffled.

"What?" Ansel asked, pretending he couldn't hear him—a norm would have had trouble hearing the man.

The man pulled the mask up a moment. It was a young man under there, sweaty-faced. "I said you should move along, Sir. We have this handled."

"Who are you?"

"Homeland Security," he said. "Now, move along. It's not safe to be out right now."

Ansel could peek into the truck from where he stood, and could see that they had a number of bodies in there.

"Move along, Sir," the man said, gesturing.

Ansel complied, walking away, shaking his head, maintaining his shocked charade. The police didn't come, so he assumed Homeland Security had briefed the cops on it. This wasn't the Poles, now; these were government agents.

He was relieved he hadn't come barreling through the place in his Lupine form, and was more grateful than ever that, as a natural lycanthrope, he had full control over his transformations, versus the ones who'd been bitten, who had varying degrees of control based on circumstance and force of will.

From his own experience, the more willpower a person had, the less vulnerable they were to the transformation—that wasn't quite accurate; the less fully bound by the transformation they would be. They could still change under particular circumstances, but they weren't completely tethered to the glandular time bomb that lycanthropy represented.

The less willpower a person had, the more they would give themselves over to it. That was, perhaps, the X on the lycanthropic axis. The Y on the axis would be their intelligence, which manifested in the character of their werewolf form—if you were an idiot, you would become a mostly mindless monster, this ravenous beast completely at the mercy of its appetite.

The dumb werewolves operated purely on an instinctual level—full-on charge, usually in the four-legged form, only rarely in the hybrid, two-legged form. The irony being that the dumb ones were often the most likely to infect fresh victims, when they weren't busy devouring them. This was because they were operating out of pure, predatory animal cunning. The Z on the axis was the stimulus—usually hunger, lust, pain, rage, or terror—these were the likeliest triggers. These would challenge even the most disciplined and intelligent of souls, could compel a transformation.

Ansel rarely thought so much about his condition; for him, it was mostly a non-issue. But he thought about this because what it meant was that the government guys would be shooting the dumbest lycanthropes first, the ones least able to control their transformations, the ones likeliest to make a big mess, the ones likeliest to be caught.

As a selection factor introduced into the mix, these men didn't realize it, but they were making their jobs harder, not easier. It was why they had yet to successfully wipe out werewolves—the more determined they were to hunt them out, the more readily they drove them underground. Only the dumbest, sloppiest lycanthropes would fall to the hunters, leaving behind the canniest, savviest, deadliest ones to endure.

It was like that story he remembered about the old man in the South who hated rattlesnakes, and had taken to tracking them down on his property and killing them. He had been so thorough that he'd managed to kill most of them.

But the problem was because he was old, his hearing wasn't so good, and he'd only managed to kill the rattlesnakes on his property who had the loudest rattles. He'd found that he had to start using a listening device to track down the remaining ones. And, eventually, even that didn't work, as he had become a selection factor on his property, creating, over time, a rattlesnake that didn't have its telltale rattle. That would be his gift to the world, the reward for his obsessive, misguided bid to wipe out the snakes on his property: silent rattlesnakes.

These government guys were like that; they were only ridding the world of the least cunning lycanthropes. The smart werewolves, the most disciplined, would continue to survive. They would evade this dragnet.

Not that these qualities were actually transmissible from werewolf to werewolf—but what it meant was that the surviving ones would be the most dangerous of werewolves, and the likeliest to carefully select their own victims.

From what he'd gathered, Zooey was intelligent and seemed fairly disciplined; she didn't seem at all conflicted or captive to her infection the way that, say, Sam was. There was a "supernaturalness" to her, an ease with her affliction that was rare with infected lycanthropes. Or else maybe there was another element to the bar graph in his brain: The W axis—how evil a person was.

It seemed sort of old-fashioned to think in those terms at all. But there was an inverse relationship to morality and lycanthropy, which norms didn't understand, something that Ansel had seen in his life.

Paradoxically, the more moral and upright a person was, the greater their vulnerability to the transformation. Which was to say that the greater the moral conflict between who they were and what they did as a werewolf, the more stress and trauma that would induce in them, which would make them more susceptible to bouts of the affliction.

An evil person felt no conflict—they would face turning into a werewolf as a welcome addition to their lifestyle: they didn't care what effect they had on others, had no sense of a categorical imperative, and they would appreciate both the power that it would bring and the secretive, exclusive nature of it. They would see themselves as a part of a powerful elite, with the ability to kill with near-impunity, if they were smart about it. They could see themselves as superhuman, and they would be right about that.

The moral individuals were likeliest to recoil from their affliction, to try to hide from it, to do whatever they could to avoid it, to live in terror in the shadow of what they had become, and, perhaps, the likeliest to kill themselves rather than succumb to the darkness of the disease, and also the likeliest to both have loved ones nearby who were at risk, and to be most vulnerable to the Z axis, the stimulus triggers.

But immoral and amoral individuals would find lycanthropy to be a thrill ride, something that validated their own sense of special-ness and self-worth, a marvelous ace they could literally hide up their sleeves until they needed to put it into play, whenever and however they wanted to.

That was one of the tragedies of it, which was why Ansel was always so reticent about infecting someone, why he was so careful in selecting anybody: just like you wanted a happy drunk for your drinking buddy, instead of one prone to crying in the hallway or starting fistfights with strangers, so you had to choose your partners wisely, where lycanthropy was concerned. You wanted someone who could handle their high.

Of her friends, Sam had clearly infected Polly, Reagan, and Zooey, and, at least anecdotally, the four of them vindicated Ansel's analysis of the situation. Amoral Sam had been thrilled to become a lycanthrope, but she'd lacked the willpower to control herself, and was fairly quickly overcome by her affliction, until what had been "Sam" had been replaced utterly.

Polly was both more intelligent and willful than Sam, and had been seemingly more successful than Sam at controlling herself, but she was also more conventionally amoral than Sam—she was horrified by what she had become, not really for what it was, but as a violation of herself and her aesthetics. This amoral outrage made for a more traumatic schism between her old self and what she'd become, greater than it otherwise might be. Instead of an integrated whole, there were now two Pollies in play, time-sharing in her body.

By way of contrast, Reagan, judging from her alleged actions, had strength of will, intelligence, and a strong morality. But the stimulus of her murder of her girlfriend (which Ansel suspected; often loved ones are the first to fall with an infective lycanthrope), coupled with her strong moral view, had created a moral precipice for her, and she'd jumped off it by taking her own life, rather than succumbing utterly to the infection.

Conversely, Zooey was fairly intelligent, had reasonably strong willpower, was a rampant thrill-seeker (which likely meant that she was seeking stimulus, for which lycanthropy would readily provide), and was completely immoral, could have been a psychopath—for her, lycanthropy was as easy as putting on a pair of sneakers. No trauma, no painful loss of identity, no moral qualms to nag at her. Full-on assimilation.

Hence the "supernaturalness" Ansel saw with her. Zooey was the most natural infective he'd likely ever face, someone completely comfortable with their affliction.

That would make her the most dangerous prey he could hope to hunt, the likeliest to be a genuine threat to him: there would be no hesitation between them, no second-guessing, no misjudging. Like two gunfighters facing one another.

There could be only war between them.

Anya was fretting the whole time they were on the bus. She'd sat with Reed as they went downstate.

"I'm so sorry this all happened," she said. "This is all my fault, you know."

"It wasn't your fault," Reed said.

Anya gave her hands a squeeze.

"It's my fault," she said. "None of this would have even happened if I'd been better at my job."

Anya patted Reed's shoulder. Seeing Phil take over her operation had left Anya's pride stinging. The man knew his job, would get things done. It ate away at Anya that she had allowed herself to lose her job by losing focus on what she was doing, by underestimating her enemy.

That was always something she had to come to terms with. With lycanthropes, you could never afford to underestimate your opponent. She looked at her bandaged hand. This was the reward for forgetting that.

The buses turned off the highway, headed toward a seemingly endless darkness that was broken only by the periodic streetlight.

"Where are we?"

"Downstate," Reed said.

"I wonder how far downstate he's taking us," Anya said.

The buses pulled off the road, toward a staging area that had been surrounded by four bright, generator-powered lights.

"Everybody off the bus, head for the reception area," the soldier said. "Everybody out. Director Sanderson has something to say."

Anya was surprised Phil had bothered to come out with them at all.

The BEE personnel were lined up, while Sanderson paced with a bullhorn, talking. Shadows loomed beyond him, wind-powered fans in the distance, great big things, whirring, lit by lone red lights to mark their position.

Anya looked at the ground. They were in some kind of field, with freshly-turned earth. Where was the facility?

"Where's the prison?" she asked.

"I want to thank all of you for coming out here with us," Sanderson said. "I know you've been through a lot, and all of you did the best you could with what was already a desperate and dangerous situation. If you hadn't been so diligent in your duties, I can only imagine that the outbreak would have been far worse. In that respect, you are all heroes, and are owed a debt of gratitude from me and my team, and from the country at large. You tried your best; it just wasn't good enough. It's why I can only extend my condolences to you and to your families, at how undeserved your fate is, given how hard you worked to try to do the right thing."

In the shadows, beyond the reach of the lights, was a whirring sound. It came from all sides, this mechanical whir, like the turning of a turbine. All at once, fire emerged from all four sides, the chattering, horrible bark of machine gun fire, bullets moving at unbelievable speed.

All around her, Anya heard people screaming, panicking, saw blood as people were chewed up by the machine guns. Reed cried out, was almost cut in half by gunfire. Anya grabbed for him, they fell together, as people around them were mowed down.

"I'm hit—" Reed gasped, blood on his teeth and lips, and his eyes went blank.

Anya could not believe Phil had done this. It took maybe a minute's worth of gunfire, and all of them were dead. All of them, that is, except Anya, who had Reed's blood on her, was forcing down her gasping sobs, was playing dead. All around her, a sea of BEE uniforms, covered in red.

The machine guns stopped firing, went back to the whirring, and then silence. It had been a massacre. Rage boiled in her heart, but Anya would not move, could hear Sanderson talking.

"I think the miniguns were definitely the right call," he said to an unseen confederate. "That took, what, a minute and a half? Astounding firepower."

"They fire almost 70 rounds a second, Sir," one of the soldiers said.

"Damn," Sanderson said. "That's a lot of silver we just threw away."

The soldier acknowledged that with a grunt.

He clicked on his bullhorn. "I know this seems shocking to you, but I want you to understand something: this was euthanasia. We don't have a cure for this disease, and we couldn't ship these folks off to some far-flung facility, and Wolf Island's no longer a possibility, by executive order. Our job here is to clean up this mess, as quickly as possible. With the infectives, the longer they are around, the worse, the more difficult they get, and the likelier they are to infect others, including you. It makes our job harder. We have shoot-to-kill orders with regard to the infectives. That is exactly what we're going to do. All we did here was kill these infectives before they had a chance to infect anyone else, before their disease could manifest. Nobody said this job was going to be easy. Now, get the bulldozers going. Dump them into the pit."

Anya heard the bulldozers, felt the rumble on the ground as they approached, let herself be pushed along with the rest of the dead, toward a pit that had already been dug. Phil had arranged this from the start. All that talk of a downstate facility was so much nonsense. She felt bitterness and rage bloom in her heart, at all of her colleagues tumbled down into the freshly-dug pit with her.

She knew what she had to do—she had to let them bury her alive, for she was confident that Phil had men around the perimeter, watchfully waiting for anybody to flee. Several wounded people did try it, a couple who had been playing possum like her. She heard them get dropped by snipers and sharpshooters from the shadows.

Then the bulldozers rolled everybody onto each other, and lime was tossed on the bodies. Still Anya would not move. She had to wait this out. It was the only thing she could do. She just let herself be rolled over with the other bodies, part of this wave of carnage, tried to have herself be at the top as the dirt came pouring in.

It was hard to hold still, as she knew there were soldiers stationed at the lip of the pit, could see them through slitted eyes, watching. They were keeping watch, no doubt as Phil had ordered them to.

She just held her breath, tried to shield herself as the dirt came piling down on her, tried to keep from choking, horrified to be sprawled atop this pile of bodies.

Your deathbed, some ghastly part of herself said, deep in her head. It took about a half an hour for her to be entombed, and it took every bit of control Anya had to not let out a scream, to not claw her way out right then. She could not risk detection, though she could not stay there for long, as the air would go soon. The horrid silence of it, all of her peers and colleagues dead around her, beneath her, bleeding into the earth. The alkaline sting of lime in her nostrils spurred her upward, ever upward.

Excelsior, that voice said.

In this silent, unholy place, she hid, working her way up like a worm, tucking her face into her shirt, forcing herself to breathe calmly, while, overhead, the bulldozers rumbled. She managed to snake her way to the top, breaking the surface with two fingers, taking a fresh breath of air, trying to stay quiet.

The bulldozer rumbles faded, and she just waited in the dark, breathing, bracing herself, afraid to move another inch, waiting.

Eventually, she heard the bulldozers shut off, saw the big lights turn off, heard the portable generators shut down, heard men talking, heard doors slamming, heard cars and trucks driving off, until there was only darkness.

In that darkness Anya breathed, acutely aware of the deafening silence beneath her, this abominable tomb of the newly dead. She waited in the darkness, listening, until the only sound she heard was her own breathing.

Then she used what was left of her strength to push herself out of the earth, her knees creaking, her arms aching. She pried herself out of the widening hole she'd made, and birthed herself from the ground, a chthonic quickening.

Free from Sanderson's tomb, she rolled onto her back and breathed, exhausted, waiting to see if anyone shot her. She waited for minutes, and nobody came.

Then she rolled onto her belly and listened.

Sure enough, she could hear a couple of soldiers talking quietly to each other, on the other side of the pit.

Anya crawled in the opposite direction of the soldiers, taking her time, not wanting to make too much noise. Overhead, the stars shined beautifully, and nearby, those wind fans were quietly, cleanly generating power.

She kept going until she was off the freshly-turned dirt of the mass grave, and onto fallow farmland. Anya could not believe that Sanderson had done it, and what was worse, the man didn't breathe without orders, so someone higher in the food chain had given him the latitude to take such extreme measures.

Although she was angry at Phil for murdering her team, she knew that someone higher up was really deserving of her wrath. But she also knew that the actual decision-maker would have been protected by many layers of organizational chaff that would inoculate them from any dangerous side effects that could have resulted from their decision. And if that failed, they could always claim that it was a matter of national security. Or that Sanderson had "gone rogue" and exceeded his mandate. Or they could kill Sanderson. And so on.

Anya belly-crawled across the fallow field until she felt that she was far enough away from the scene of the massacre to risk standing up and walking. And so she did, completely filthy—dirt, powdered lime, and blood drying on her clothes. But she was alive, and that mattered.

Anya gonna get Philled up? Came the voice inside her head, this intruder, gleeful, macabre, madcap. It was not her. She chalked it up to her brain letting off steam, reacting to the trauma she had just experienced.

Anya sure?

It was something she couldn't shut off, like an itch she couldn't scratch. Somewhere deep in the shadows of her mind, the dusty corners, way in the back, in the older parts of her brain. The human brain was a marvelous thing, the way evolution and natural selection built out new real estate within the skull, with the brain stem and the cerebellum representing mankind's inheritance from more primitive lifeforms, and the cerebrum being where the thinking got done, compared with the synaptic stenographers in the lower parts of the brain. And most of the higher reasoning happened in a thin layer of cells in the prefrontal lobe, the executive suite of the brain.

This thing talking to her couldn't talk if it was banished to the brain stem, but she could feel it wending its way through those autonomic brain functions, lounging in the pituitary gland. It was in her.

The virus. Of course.

It was already working her over, transforming her into just another vector.

What's our vector, Victor? Roger, Roger.

She looked at her wounded arm.

That bites, doesn't it?

She could almost see it in her mind's eye, this shadow Anya, in silhouette. Unseen, but lurking, wanting to be seen and heard, eager to come out.

I can help you take down Sanderson, if you let me. If you're patient.

As she stood in the dark, in the shadow of the great big wind towers that were quietly catching the breeze, Anya could see that there was a problem she faced.

As an infective, by her own definition, she had a moral and professional obligation to put herself down, or at the very least, to quarantine herself so that she would not be a risk to others. That was precisely her priority. But Phil had taken charge of the local operation, and there was no way Anya would go to him; that would be a death sentence. She could jet to Atlanta and go directly to the CDC. That would be morally responsible. It would mean the end of life as she knew it, but then, that seemed a moot point. She could get herself to Wolf Island.

Or she could create a splinter cell with Zachary and Mina, try to coordinate their efforts.

You know they don't need you, you know?

It sang it like it was a song.

You should avenge your team. You should take down Sanderson. Kick some Sanderson in his face.

Revenge felt so petty to her; Anya was not vengeful, was not spiteful like that. This thing inside her was. It was thirsting for revenge, even now, newly infected.

I won't let you go.

It knew where she was headed before she even thought it through. It knew what she wanted to do, where she wanted to go. It was her, this alien thing. Or it was becoming her, learning her language.

She saw herself going to the CDC and turning herself in. Of testifying at a hearing about the massacre Sanderson had perpetrated. She saw Sanderson being brought to justice. And her detainment in a lab somehow allowing a vaccine for this disease to be discovered, the epidemic stopped in its tracks. Maybe a Congressional Medal of Honor.

Golf applause. You really think that's how it's going to go?

The intruder spurred her to imagine going to the CDC, them taking her to a Level 4 containment lab, where her blood was drawn, where they hooked her up to electrodes and gathered data on her transformation. Where they took X-rays and CT scans of her in her Lupine form, studied, poked, and prodded her. And, finally, administered a shot that put her to sleep, so they could autopsy her.

It wouldn't go that way, Anya told herself.

It all depends on Sanderson, the intruder said. *You have to find out if he was acting on orders or not. If not, then we'll do it your way. If so, then, that's another matter.*

He must be brought to justice, she thought.

What if there is no justice? What if he was acting on orders? You have to see him. You have to know for sure.

Then there would be a reckoning. One way or another, there would be. Her first order of business was to determine where in the hell she was, and, having done that, getting back to Chicago.

And after that, finding Sanderson.

And after that, finding out.

Knowledge is power. Ignorance is strength.

It mocked her from the shadows, made her mouth water.

Salivation is salvation.

4

Something was up. Zooey got that. She could tell, because she'd see dead people on the streets that weren't mauled and half-eaten. The news was reporting it. People were being shot. There was talk about people not going out after dark, about the city imposing a curfew, and how everybody had to stay put after hours, for their own safety. They wouldn't say precisely why, only that there were terrorists rumored to be loose in the city.

There was no mention of werewolves. Not a single goddamned word about it. It was really pissing her off. She went through every channel, and there was nothing.

Homeland Security had apparently been called in to follow rumors of a bioterrorist incident that had supposedly occurred in the city, perpetrated by some unidentified terrorist cells.

Zooey paced back and forth in front of the large plasma screen television. She'd been laying low for days, letting her skin heal—by now, the scars across her face were only thin lines. She wondered if they would ever completely go away. She wasn't sure. She was busy emptying the fridge of norm-food, resting up, and watching the news.

Any time the shooting victims were found naked, she knew that one of her own had been taken down. Somebody out there had gotten wise, had decided to play for keeps. It was bullshit. Sure, she expected the norms to fight back, but it was still bullshit.

The newspeople wouldn't talk about it. Nobody breathed a word. They just talked to the cameras the way that they did, bland as buttered toast, and pretended that nothing unusual was happening. Did they give them scripts for this?

Zooey understood at once that she hadn't gone big enough. She'd made a splash, yes, but her insurrection required a more robust approach.

She had to attack one of the news stations when they were going live. That was clear. She had to do something that they couldn't possibly ignore.

She was pissed that she'd left her suitcase at goddamned Polly's. Her wallet and everything had been in there. Her laptop.

Zooey would have to steal some new clothes, or just content herself with wearing some of the gay guys' clothes. She was tall enough that she could get away with it. She fit one of the guys' outfits well enough, looked herself over in the mirror.

She looked good in anything she wore; that was one of her many gifts. The men's clothes paired with her beauty gave her a kind of androgynous, fey look. She liked it, although, without makeup, she felt a little boyish. Whatever. Fuck it.

Zooey went through the guys' place, took about $50 from their wallets, pocketed that, and carefully closed the front door she'd kicked in. That door wasn't going to close properly again, so she just pulled it shut, wedged it that way.

Then she sniffed the air, walked across their tiny yard, went to the gate, opened it, and got to the street.

It was late afternoon, and this street was already dipped in shadow, despite the sun still gracing the sky. Zooey looked downtown, thought about where she should go. NBC was the obvious choice. They were right down there. Or NPR—they were at Navy Pier. No, fuck radio: although she thought it would be funny to tear somebody apart on the radio, could only imagine the Baby Boomers being upset to hear their smooth jazz interrupted by somebody noisily chewing up the host.

It had to be television. The sheeple had to see.

But she had no idea how to get in there, where she could go. Then she remembered—one of the other channels she'd watched, was it ABC? They had their broadcast area down on State Street, streetside, a big window behind them.

Yeah, that would be fucking perfect.

She hailed a cab, and told the guy to take her downtown, to the ABC News building. The cabbie, a patchouli-scented young man of what looked to be Middle Eastern, gamely took her down there, while the cab, which itself had a little television screen in it, played either bottled news or a live feed.

"Crazy shit going on, yeah?" Zooey said.

"Yes," the driver said. "Very crazy. Very bad."

"I saw somebody get eaten the other day," she said.

"Really? By what?"

"You'd think I was crazy," Zooey said.

The driver looked at her through the rearview mirror a moment, and in that moment, Zooey was sure that he'd seen something like that, too.

"It was a werewolf," Zooey said. "A big, white-furred werewolf."

"I've seen that, too," the driver said. "Big fangs, huge thing. They're huge. I had one chase my car three nights ago. Chased me for two and a half blocks. All the cabbies have seen them."

"They're not coyotes," Zooey said. "I don't care what they say on the news."

The driver nodded. "No, not coyotes at all. Werewolves. *Kurt adam.*"

She looked at his ID badge, thinking he'd given her his name, but it wasn't Kurt Adam.

"Zooey," Zooey said. "My name's Zooey, Kurt."

"No," the driver said, laughing. "*Kurt adam* is 'werewolf' in Turkish. I'm Turkish."

Kurt Adam. That was curious to her. Was everything strange in Turkish?

"For real? Wow," Zooey said. "So, uh, like, how do you say 'vampire,' then?"

"*Vampir,*" the driver said.

"Of course," Zooey said. "Typical. Fucking vampires. What about 'Ghost?'"

"*Hayalet,*" the driver said.

"Zombie?"

"*Zombi,*" the driver said.

Each time he said them, Zooey would mouth them to herself. "So, you have *Vampirs* and *Zombis* and *Hayalets* and *Kurt Adams* in Turkey."

"*Kurtadamlar,*" the driver said. "One werewolf, *Kurt adam.* Many, *Kurtadamlar.* One ghost, *hayalet.* Many ghosts, *hayaletler.*"

It was fun hearing the man talk, his accent.

"*Hayaletler,* like, sounds kind of like 'Heil, Hitler,'" Zooey said. "How do you say 'monster?'"

"*Canavar,*" the driver said. It sounded like "Janavar" to Zooey.

They reached her destination, and Zooey paid the man $50, way more than the cab ride was worth. The man was thrilled.

"You want change?" he asked.

"Keep it," Zooey said. "Thanks for the language lesson."

She watched the man drive off, then went across the street. Sure enough, there was the brightly-lit news station, right at the street, with pylons in place to prevent anybody from driving through their studio.

Zooey watched them talk, their backs to the street, the newspeople there, brightly lit, the cameras on them. Above the place was a Jumbotron, broadcasting the broadcast.

It would be perfect. Let them, like, ignore THIS.

She looked either way. The Chicago Theater was down the street, and the El was up the street. There were people walking up and down both sides of the street. Cars coming and going, a crowd of onlookers gathered by the window, doing their usual gapemouthed "Look, Ma, I'm on TV" thing, the pantomimes.

Zooey grinned. This was going to be fantastic. She positioned herself across the street from the studio, and took a deep breath, began running for the station. As she ran, she transformed, ripping the clothing from her body, flesh becoming fur, muscle rippling, limbs stretching and cracking.

She was gratified to hear the honking of horns, the squealing of brakes as the drivers swerved to avoid her and ran into each other. She was pleased to hear the shrieks and see the norms pointing at her as she sped toward the station.

Her speed multiplied as she crossed the street, her strides eating up distance. She cleared the street in seconds, and tore through the onlookers with her teeth, and dove right for the great window that separated her from the newspeople.

The window exploded inward from the force of her charge. It was built to stop bullets, and had no chance against Zooey, who went flying through it in a sparkling rain of glass nuggets.

She wasted no time, biting Isaiah Hall, the local anchor, right on his arm, as he'd been turning. And she bit down hard on Martinique Andrews, his co-anchor, catching the leggy brunette right on her thigh, throwing her aside with a toss of her head.

But Zooey wasn't finished; she jumped onto their desk and gazed into the cameras, where the stunned cameramen were still filming, and it looked to be going out live. She glared into the bright lights, blood on her muzzle as the anchors screamed and crawled through the broken glass, as the wounded bystanders reacted from the street.

Zooey remembered something about digital delay, like how anything broadcast had at least a seven-second delay from broadcasting, maybe more, so the production people could prevent something unwanted from being broadcast. Zooey had to ride out that limit, started talking.

"Don't you dare switch channels," Zooey said. "The worst is yet to come. Producer, if you switch this off, I'll kill everyone in this room, starting with you."

She could see the broadcasters looking around, unsure what to do, could smell their fear and confusion. But it looked like the cameras were still going.

"You sheeple think you can just ignore us," Zooey said. "That we're not out there. We are. We're here. We're haunting your steps. We're watching you while you sleep. We're hunting you. You're meat for us."

The norms just watched, frozen, frightened, paralyzed at this thing that glowered at them from atop the desk of the anchors, blood dripping from her muzzle as she slurred her words, teeth bared. The newscasters moaned and wailed, unseen, on the floor.

"You'd better start paying attention before we finish you," Zooey said.

Then she howled and charged deeper into the studio, snapping at the cameramen, catching one on the foot as he was running away from her.

Zooey then leaped back to the desk where the anchors had been, and jumped through the open window, out into the street, terrifying bystanders and onlookers, who had crowded around the broken window, had been looking in. Zooey took to biting them as she ran north, then bounded up the steps to the nearby El platform.

There were startled commuters standing on the platform, gazing in horror and disbelief at the great, white wolf running toward them.

There was an El train on the platform that had just started rolling out of the station. Zooey ran after it, leaping as the train had cleared the platform. She hung onto the back of the thing, then climbed onto the grooved roof of the El train, riding it to its next stop.

This train appeared to be heading north, which suited Zooey just fine.

She let her tongue loll out of her mouth as the train raced forward, tasted the city, the cascade of flavors and sensations dizzyingly diverse.

Zooey crouched on the moving train; it was almost too easy for her to do this, reveling in her superhumanity, in her paranormal prowess.

She gripped the side of the train and swung herself down, propelling herself through another window in a shower of safety glass, landing in the fat lap of a commuter.

The people in the train were stunned and shocked at the sight of her, and Zooey dropped to the floor, feeling their fear, savoring it.

"Little piggies," she said. "My juicy little porkchops."

Commuters screamed and shoved at each other to get away from her. Zooey loved when they ran, or did what passed for running among the norms.

She charged through them, claws slashing, mouth stealing bites of their flesh as she made her way through the car, from one end to the other. There was bedlam on the train as people tried to get away from her, but in the close confines of the car, there was no place to go.

Someone pulled the emergency door release and the train halted, and commuters jumped from the car, some of them landing on the third rail, electrocuting themselves in a shower of sparks and a whiff of ozone and burning flesh. Zooey watched a moment, gazed out the open door at the twitching corpses, and then jumped from the train car, onto the tracks.

Another jump and she had reached the ground. She ran hard beneath the El train, straight north, vaulting from shadow to shadow.

Anyone she saw, she bit, snarling, calling them "bitches" as she went.

Just let them try to ignore that.

Ansel had gotten wind of Zooey from all the sirens, all the chaos happening downtown. He hadn't been sure where he was going, but when he saw the El train stop, saw the sparks on the tracks and the fleeting glimpse of the great white wolf jumping from the open door of the train, running down the street, he knew it had to be her.

Without hesitation, Ansel went after her. She was racing northbound, leaving wounded people in her wake. She was biting to wound, deliberately. He could tell this much.

He just needed to see where she went. Ansel wasn't about to transform in the streets like this; it struck him as somehow graceless, even gauche, to do that like this, out in the open. Perhaps his caution from experience informed his decision, but Ansel could not bring himself to do it.

The irony of it chewed at him a little—the only natural lycanthrope in the city, and he was the one who was unwilling to transform.

Zooey was a blur ahead of him, having reached a stretch of soccer field that was near the El tracks.

"Zooey!" Ansel yelled, fairly confident that she'd hear him.

And he was not wrong. She paused in her headlong running, turning, glancing back the way she'd just come, past the columns of wounded commuters, to see Ansel running for her.

He reached the fence that cordoned off the soccer field a minute or so after Zooey. She'd occupied herself by lurking in the shadows, watching him, sniffing the air.

"Zooey," he said. "That's enough."

"Ansel," Zooey said, the great white thing that she was looking at him, grinning toothily. "You're, like, the guy."

Ansel went around the fence, catching his breath.

"You've got cast-iron balls to come at me without your skin on," Zooey said.

"I don't need to suit up to put you down," Ansel said.

Zooey's black eyes shone brightly in the dark, against the ivory white of her fur, and her bloody-wet muzzle. She circled him, like a shark, in the hybrid form, but on all fours, slavering.

"Did you come to spank me, Dad?" Zooey said.

"This is my place," Ansel said. "My city."

"Not anymore," Zooey said. "I took it from you."

"I want it back," Ansel said.

"Come take it, then," Zooey said. "Like, show me what you've got."

Ansel drew a pistol, cocked it, pointed it at her.

"Silver," he said. "Silver bullets. Can you smell them?"

Zooey's confidence didn't waver. She just looked at him, still circling.

"I'd kill you before you got off a shot," Zooey said. "I'm faster."

Ansel fired at Zooey, who was, indeed, faster. The bullet went over her shoulder, and Zooey struck Ansel with a backhand that sent him into the chain link fence. He fired shot after shot at her, but Zooey evaded each with deft turns and supernatural dexterity. She was astoundingly fast, faster than any lycanthrope Ansel had known. He emptied the pistol trying to shoot her.

"Coward," Zooey said, as he clicked on the empty gun. "That was, like, cowardly. Come take back your city."

He threw the pistol aside, and his body flexed, and as his skin began to change, Zooey attacked him, not sitting idly by while he transformed. She sank her teeth into his leg as his slacks split and he grew, her claws at his chest, which had grown furry. Zooey clawed at his throat, gripped at it, throttling him, only to find her grip slipping as his neck broadened.

In moments, Ansel was towering over her: this big, horrible, black-furred abomination, a wolf gazing at her with blue eyes, and long teeth.

"Now we dance," Ansel said, overpowering her with a thrown shoulder that knocked her on her back.

Zooey twisted around, protecting her belly, her teeth bared. The two of them circled each other.

Then they sprang at each other, mouths agape. Ansel was larger and stronger, but Zooey was faster. She bit him in the leg, a savage tear of flesh, letting go before he could bring his claws down on her.

He shifted his stance, protecting his wounded leg, while Zooey danced out of reach.

"Old man," Zooey said, drooling. "I don't know what Sam saw in you."

"It doesn't matter," Ansel said, leaping at her. She jumped out of his reach, and he'd caught only handfuls of turf, where she had been.

"You leave this city," Zooey said. "Tuck your tail between your legs, and, like, maybe I'll let you live."

Ansel charged Zooey, cut her across her back as she'd dodged. He whirled around and tried to follow up, only catching empty air where she had been.

"Slow," Zooey said. "So, like, slow. Like Earth Sign slow."

She showed Ansel what fast was, darting in at him, biting him on the forearm, tearing a chunk of him loose, and releasing him when he tried to counter.

As much as he hated to admit it, she was good at this. He had not faced a proper rival in Chicago in years. Part of him welcomed the challenge, while another part wondered if it was even worth it—she'd made such a mess of the city, it would be a prize not worth having.

Zooey lunged at him again, dodging a swipe of his claws, only to slash him across his belly. He managed to get a blow in on her, a rake of his own claws that cut her across her shoulder and made her yelp.

But she'd slipped out of reach again. She had obviously fought some other lycanthropes already, was using hit-and-run tactics on him, trying to wear him down.

"You're ruining everything," Ansel said. "There are hunters throughout the city. They'll kill you. Your little insurrection is stillborn."

"Not yet," Zooey said. "I haven't even gotten started."

And then she howled, and there were answering howls around them.

Ansel ran at her while she'd howled, but she scampered out of reach yet again. Every time he charged her, she'd dodge, and every time his charge would break, she'd turn back on him and attack again. It was like working a ratchet: there was no give to her.

She had given a lot of thought to this night, this moment.

Ansel became aware of other lycanthropes appearing at the edge of the fencing. There were three, then five, then a dozen. Then more. Many, many more.

They watched from the shadows, this massive pack of werewolves, of grey and brown and tan and honey brown.

"I have a pack," Zooey said. "You're a lone wolf, like, totally."

Ansel kept his face to hers, while they circled again, the other lycanthropes watching. She'd been so very busy.

He feinted to one side to draw her away from that and into a strike of his jaws, only to have her grab his jaws with her hands, pivoting hard and flipping Ansel to one side, sending him to the ground.

Ansel went to reach up for her, but she pried open his jaws again, straining them. She had leverage, could break his jaw if she'd wanted to.

"Submit," Zooey said. "Bitch."

Ansel was not ready to die. He thought of Polly, of his promise to her. He had not considered the possibility of failure. He was trueborn. Zooey was a fresh-faced pup, newly infected. It was not possible for him to be beaten by her. And a she-wolf, no less.

"Submit," Zooey said, straining harder on his jaw.

Never in his life had Ansel met his match, never had he faced such an opponent. It was not that she was more formidable than he was. Rather, he had never seen such an absence of conflict in her nature. Even he, a natural lycanthrope, faced some duality in his manifestation, faced some uncertainty. There was no uncertainty with Zooey, and no hesitation. It was the key to her speed.

He would not surrender. It was not in him to do such a thing. Ansel kicked out Zooey's legs from beneath her and clawed at her arms, forced her to relinquish her grip.

Zooey grunted at the force of his attack, as they fell into the grass. Ansel spun around and sprang at her, tore at her with his claws, creating bloody furrows in her ivory coat and making her cry out.

The rage was building in him, the savage instinct, and Ansel pressed his attack, while Zooey leaped out of reach in a splash of her own blood, yelping.

The other lycanthropes were howling, as Zooey rallied, struck out at Ansel with her claws, caught him in the ribs. It sounded like a pistol shot, this violation of bone and sinew.

Seeing his injury, satisfied, Zooey howled in triumph, and the others joined in.

Zooey looked around at her packmates.

The agony of it was beyond belief, and still Ansel did not fall, and he jumped at her again, snapping at her with his great jaws, while his claws slashed the ground in his bid to run her down.

He tackled her and brought her down, and the two of them hacked at each other with their great claws, bit at each other with their great fangs, blood spattering on the grass.

Zooey let out a howl, and a dozen of her packmates began to run across the field, while she forced herself out from under Ansel, who pressed his attack, only to have other Lupines crashing into him, attacking him.

"Kill him," Zooey said to her pack, and not one of them hesitated at her command, and, in moments, the field became a churning mass of fur, dirt, blood, and grass as Zooey's Lupines attacked Ansel, while Zooey sought to put distance between herself and him.

Ansel tore the head off a caramel-colored Lupine male, tossed it aside with a flip of his jaws, hacked at a grey male with his claws, and fought to reach Zooey. But more of her packmates were attacking Ansel, who, mighty as he was, could not hope to prevail against so many Lupines at once.

He feinted away from Zooey, hoping to draw her packmates after him, only to reverse direction and run hard for her, while Zooey herself circled to his right, toward her remaining packmates. There were as many as 50 Lupines on the field, now, a chorus of snarls and growls and yips and howls.

Ansel had nearly broken through Zooey's packmates when machine gun fire rang out from the shadows, striking some of the lycanthropes nearest him. Ansel dove for Zooey, who ran into the underbrush and headed toward the river, while machine gun fire rained on the Lupines in the field, including from a helicopter which had knifed into the clearing overhead, shining a spotlight down on the scene of carnage.

Ansel kept after Zooey, while the helicopter pursued them, the blinding spotlight on them both.

Zooey glanced over her shoulder, seeing that Ansel was still pursuing her, and then ran beneath a bridge to shield herself from the incoming fire from the helicopter. Ansel redoubled his effort to pursue her, while zigzagging to avoid the helicopter.

Zooey vaulted up and over the bridge from the far side, while their attention was fixed on Ansel, who was on her tail beneath the bridge.

In moments, Zooey crossed the bridge and leaped up the steel supports and threw herself at the helicopter, crashing through the cockpit and tearing the pilot and copilot out of their seats with swipes of her claws, which caused the helicopter to lurch hard to the left, causing the gunner to tumble out the side and fall to the ground below with a crunch, landing near Ansel.

The helicopter came down on the other side of the river, and Zooey threw herself from it as the thing chopped into the ground and detonated in a plume of fire, to the terror of pedestrians and automobile drivers on the bridge.

Backlit by the fire, Zooey stared at Ansel, who faced her, panting.

Then Zooey let out another howl, and her remaining packmates howled in turn, and chased after Ansel, who, seeing them coming, turned and ran, leaving bloody pawprints in the dirt.

Polly had been watching the evening news when she'd seen Zooey come smashing through the window. The sight of it frightened her. The channel didn't cut away, and Zooey had threatened to kill everybody if they did, so they kept the cameras on for a few seconds, until Zooey chased one of the cameramen and the screen went to static for a moment, and then ran a TECHNICAL DIFFICULTIES message.

"Fuck," Polly said. She tracked it on her Twitter feed for the next few hours, and saw people reacting to it. Already people were posting the attack on the news channel on YouTube and some of the other social media.

Nobody was believing it, people were thinking it was some bizarre kind of stunt, or that somebody had hacked the news channel and put some produced piece on instead. People were blaming hacker groups and some were saying it was some marketing thing for a new movie. The part where the thing talked was chalked up to somebody off-camera, or some overdubbing.

Polly saw from other news channels that a mad dog had attacked a bunch of commuters on a northbound El train, and that several people had died when they'd attempted to leave the train, had been electrocuted on the tracks.

Police were searching for the animal, which had last been seen heading northbound, and had bitten everybody in its wake, and was considered extremely dangerous, and not to be approached.

Polly heard a knock at her door, and when she answered, saw Ansel fall in toward her, naked, bloody.

He smacked the ground, and Polly could see that he was terribly wounded. There were bites and cuts all across his body, deep gashes and slashes.

Polly helped him to his feet, took him to Tristan's car, put him in the passenger seat, ran back into her place and got a blanket, threw it

176 | D.T. NEAL

on him. Polly was no doctor, but it looked like maybe he could be in shock.

Then she drove to the nearest hospital emergency room, which was heavily populated with people who had been bitten and clawed and otherwise attacked. The triage nurse, a bony, hatchet-faced woman with her brown hair cut close, looked at Ansel and sighed.

"My god," she said. "I'm amazed he's still alive."

"Do something for him," Polly said. "He was attacked by wolves."

"Everybody here has been," the nurse said.

"But he's been hit worse," Polly said. "Look at him."

"I can give him some morphine," the nurse said. "We are neck-deep in trauma cases right now."

"I want somebody to see him," Polly said. "Look at him."

The nurse did, and shook her head.

"He's lost a lot of blood," Polly said. "Look, he needs your help. Where are the doctors?"

The nurse called in one of the emergency room physicians, who, upon seeing Ansel's wounds, immediately asked her how it happened.

"He got attacked by wolves," Polly said, not bothering to offer up some kind of cover story—he looked like he'd been attacked by wolves, so she went with it.

"We'll take care of him," the doctor said.

They gave Ansel a sedative and whisked him away, leaving Polly to handle the paperwork, since Ansel was in no condition to do it, himself.

Polly felt terrible; it had been her idea to send Ansel after Zooey to begin with, and now he was a mess. She couldn't believe she'd done that to him.

She should never have sent him on that fool's errand. She turned in the paperwork, what she knew about Ansel, and sat back down, waiting. Everybody in the place looked like hell. Only Polly looked good by comparison, although she was feeling anything but good.

In the waiting room there was a television, and they were talking about the event that had taken place downtown, where people believed they had been attacked by a rabid coyote or coywolf, which was the hybrid offspring of coyotes and wolves, and had been lately seen throughout the Chicagoland area.

Apparently, there'd been machine gun fire, which was attributed to gangland activity, and a helicopter had crashed near the river. Firefighters were on the scene, and it looked like dozens of people had been shot in a nearby football field.

Polly sat in the waiting room for five hours, when the surgeon emerged, told her that they'd taken care of his injuries, given him blood, and that he'd been stabilized, was resting in his room.

They didn't let her see him, told her she could come by in the morning, so Polly left, glad that at least Ansel wasn't going to die.

Meantime, she went home, surfed the Web while having the television on, watched the reports about these coywolves, which were said to be highly aggressive but with no aversion to man-made areas.

Gun-toting groups in the suburbs and collar counties were busy hunting down the supposed culprits.

Polly went on her blog, since she had time to kill (so to speak) and had a lot on her mind.

> *The world is going crazy. A got himself hurt badly going after Z. I don't know what to say to that.*
>
> *He looked terrible, and I can't imagine him recovering from it.*
>
> *I do care about him, as angry as I am, about what he did to me. But I didn't want him to get hurt, don't want him to die.*
>
> *People are losing their minds about what's happening in the city. There are people being shot in the streets, people hanging from trees, like Christmas ornaments. I've seen it. Lynchings and public executions.*
>
> *The norms are watching. They are paying attention, looking at who looks different, who seems out of place.*
>
> *There has been a run on silver. People are buying it up wherever they can, people are carrying it. There's a simple test: clutch some silver in your hand—if it burns, you're infected, and they'll string you up or shoot you down.*
>
> *I'm trying to be calm about all of this, but I'm seeing ugliness abound in our world, something monstrous shamble around in the shadows, claiming what was left of American innocence.*
>
> *Maybe we never had that. After all, our nation's heritage is steeped in blood and slaughter, in genocide and slavery. Maybe the wolves are a kind of revenge inflicted on us by the Native Americans, reparations for our conquest. Or some side effect of slavery. We were never innocent.*
>
> *I'm as guilty as anyone else.*

Polly missed Sam, who would lurk her blogs. No doubt Sam never knew that Polly knew, but she had set up analytics on her site to monitor her traffic, and could always tell when Sam was around, would look for when something she'd written about had impacted or irked Sam, for Sam to talk about it, while never mentioning that she'd found it on Polly's blog. The remembrance of that game made her smile for a moment.

Now she was simply a friendless widow.

A were-widow.

The news channel reported that their broadcast had been hacked, and that what people had seen was a CGI rendering that some hackers had perpetrated. Their news anchors, having been targets of this outrage, were in protective government custody as they were being asked what might have made them the target of this cyberattack.

Polly sucked her teeth at this, rolled her eyes. The mendacity of it was breathtaking. There had been eyewitnesses downtown, people who had actually been there to see it. But when some reporters from other channels had come down to find those people, they had disappeared. There was no sign of anything unusual. The window down on State Street had been replaced overnight, and a dozen armed guards were stationed by it, now.

> *It's quite striking how far people will go to maintain a pretense of normality. I think I understand what Z was doing. She's a monster, but I know what she was doing, because it's something we artists try to do—we try to raise the bar, try to raise people's awareness.*
>
> *But it's like trying to throw off a tar-soaked curtain that blankets the world. The apathy, the inertness—these things keep people stupefied, blind to the beauty and the horror of the world.*
>
> *Nobody will admit that werewolves exist. Not publicly. I am convinced that the government knows, that there are agents in the field who are shooting them, but nobody else will speak about it. I feel squeamish even using the word.*
>
> *Where are the werewolves? They're everywhere and nowhere. Nobody says it, because to admit it is to admit that there's something higher on the food chain than we are. It's like admitting to the existence of the Bogeyman. No adult will willingly go there.*

Polly brewed herself a pot of coffee and stood in her kitchen, arms folded, leaning against the counter. She'd worked hard to keep herself contained, to not lose her cool. She would not let that Thing out of her.

Pussy. You can't be a norm.

I'm not a norm.

You're a total norm.

I thought you said you couldn't be a norm.

You're a wannabe norm. Like you're a wannabe poet.

I am a poet.

Right.

I've never been a norm.

Prove it.

I don't have anything to prove to you.

Meh.

What does that mean?

I don't believe you.

Polly caught herself. The Thing would try to draw her out that way, would try to anger and offend her, get under her skin—to be sure, it was already under her skin—but it would seek to get a rise out of her.

You make that sound like it's a bad thing. Zooey was right about you.

What?

You're a neurotic Virgo twat. No Virgo has the stones to go to the mat for something like this. And here I am, stuck with you. A lump of coal in stockings.

Fuck you.

Fuck YOU, you FUCK.

Such language.

You love language. I hate you.

You hate me?

It's what you want. In addition to complaining about everything and everyone, self-reproach is the Virgo's favorite pastime. Self-loathing is better than sex.

Stop with that nonsense.

Yes, a werewolf shouldn't believe in astrology; it's unseemly. Don't you dare think that you have me under wraps, though, Sweetie. I can come out any time I want to. We could have killed that bitch if you'd let me go with Ansel. The two of us could have done it.

She poured herself a cup of coffee, took a long drink of it. The venom of that Thing inside her, the malice of it, it alarmed her. It was pure malevolence. To be known so intimately by some alien part of her, it made Polly terribly uneasy.

She needed to get out, to circulate. To see and be seen. That was one of the things that was bothering her the most about the chaos in the city—it was forcing her to shut herself in, to hide. She did not like to hide. It made her feel like less than herself.

Even Ansel's injury and hospitalization had made her feel like that. It made her feel hampered and contained. She did not like to be stuck at home, sitting around, wondering whether Ansel would pull through or not.

No, she needed to get out. She needed some Polly time, needed to think of herself, for once.

Zach was not feeling like himself. He had gone to his place, taken a shower, scrubbed the blood from his hands. Not literal blood, but the metaphorical stuff. Since Sanderson had taken over, their kill teams had bagged 150 lycanthropes altogether. His operation was savage and smooth, procedurally efficient, rigorously ruthless.

Sanderson had put up a kill board in his operations center, with tally marks for each strike team. He'd made it a kind of contest: bottles of scotch for the winners.

Right now, Zach's team was in first, having taken down 45 lycanthropes. He didn't relish this straight-up death squad stuff. Zach understood the logic behind it—the infectives had to be stopped, or they would continue to infect more people. And the quickest, surest way to stop a lycanthrope was with a silver bullet.

But he still didn't feel like the Lone Ranger when he did it. These people deserved better than what came to them. They needed to cart them off to Wolf Island.

Sanderson didn't do that, though, because it would take time and cause uncertainty. He wanted quick results and definitive outcomes, and that meant bullets.

He'd already set up a remote distribution center in Gary, Indiana, where the bodies of the infectives were being cremated. Again, Sanderson's logic was that the CDC was already getting piles of caseloads and specimens, and the Kennel's own labs, having been emptied, had been shipped to Atlanta. There was no compelling scientific mission left to undertake in Chicago. His mission was clear: eradicate the lycanthropes.

The downtown meltdown by Princess had only intensified Sanderson's intention to sterilize the city. He was so pissed off about that, especially since he'd caught some heat from on high about it, that he'd sent some armored cars downtown to patrol, each with a squad of triggermen in it, so that if anything like that happened again, he'd be ready for it. He deployed plainclothes operatives on the El trains and on some of the buses.

He was sending kill teams into the suburbs, as well, doing whatever he could to stop the infection before it got completely out of control. The loss of a helicopter had been particularly galling for him.

The problem was that there was a threshold issue for him—it was one thing to shoot an active lycanthrope that was hunting people on the street. But as the recent rampage by Princess had demonstrated, where she'd actually infected about 200 people as she'd made her escape north for parts unknown, what happened to those 200 people she'd bitten?

Zach felt like even Sanderson would be reluctant to take those 200 victims and simply kill them out of hand.

In his own case, while his infection was definitely spreading, and was manifesting itself more and more each day, Zach felt that he was not the same as the beast rampaging in the park. He'd not infected anyone; why should he get the same treatment as someone who had actually hunted and killed and infected others? The BEE protocols were clear on this, but Sanderson was not following them. Zach thought about checking himself into Wolf Island, if he could get there on his own.

"I am not a lycanthrope," Zach said aloud, running his face in the water of the shower, but the troubles wouldn't wash away.

You are a killing machine. We have so much in common.

He'd taken to calling the voice in his head Lupus. He rather liked that, putting a name to his infection.

I should fit you like a glove, Zach Attack.

He rinsed his hair, turned off the shower.

His hand was scarred where he'd held onto the bullet, until he'd decided he didn't need it anymore to tell him how bad his infection was. The worse it got, the louder Lupus got in his head, the more he talked. And Lupus loved to talk.

What are you going to do, anyway? Your mates wouldn't think twice before shooting you.

"I'll think of something," Zach said.

What about Sanderson's loyalty test? Are you ready for that?

Sanderson wanted everybody on the team to take hold of an ingot of silver he'd brought. He called it "Passing the Bar." It was a simple test: you held the bar. If it burned you, you were a lycanthrope, and you were dead. Shot on sight. If you refused to take the bar, then you were taken off your existing team and held for questioning and placed under observation.

He'd come up with it when it had been determined that one of the receptionists in his operations center had turned out to be an infective, had transformed and threatened operations personnel. She'd been put down, but this had made Sanderson paranoid, and without the means of identifying the infectives through blood testing, the silver ingot was the easiest way.

Zach had been sweating this the moment Sanderson had brought it up, since there was no way in hell he'd be able to hide his infection.

If you don't pass the bar, we're dead.

"There's no way I can," Zach said. "You've seen to that."

I can't help but be what I already am.

It bothered him. Zach had been a good soldier, had done right by the team. Even when he'd done things that he could not condone. He had followed orders, wherever they took him. Wasn't that what heroes did these days? The bad guys were the ones who overturned the apple carts; the good guys were the ones who cleaned up the messes, without question or hesitation.

He got out of the shower, wrapped himself in a towel, stepped out of his bathroom, into his living room.

"Zachary," said a voice in the dark. Anya's voice.

"Anya?" he said, turning on a light.

She sat on one of his chairs, dressed in a filthy-dirty grey skirt suit covered with dried blood, her hair tied back in a haggard ponytail, stray wisps hanging loose on her forehead. She looked at him with a grave expression.

"Sanderson killed everyone," Anya said.

"Huh?"

"He had us executed," she said. "I can show you where, if you don't believe me."

Zach knew Anya well enough to know that she was telling the truth.

"Are you a ghost?"

"Don't be ridiculous," Anya said. "Reed took bullets meant for me. Sanderson had men with machine guns murder the entire team. They buried us. I crawled out of the pit."

Zach sat down on the sofa near Anya, looked her in the eye. Her grey eyes gazed levelly into his own.

"He wouldn't," Zach said.

"He did," she said.

"You're infected," Zach said.

"So are you," Anya said.

"Why are you here, then?" Zach asked.

"I have to find out if Sanderson was acting under orders," she said. "Obviously, I can't do it, myself."

The breadth of her ask was clear to him, but Zach was, himself, walking a tightrope. He had to make inquiries without Sanderson getting wise to it. But Sanderson was looking hard at everything and everybody, had gotten more paranoid than ever, in the face of the escalating crisis.

"You realize that I'm taking a hell of a risk, here, Anya," Zach said.

"I do," Anya said. "I wouldn't ask it of anybody else on my team, Zachary. Only I don't have a team, anymore; I only have you. I tried to reach Mina, but she's not answering her phone."

He held out his hand, his scarred hand, and shook hers. He liked Anya, wanted to help her, didn't like to think of all of the Kennel people shot down someplace, left for dead.

"Did anybody else get out?"

"I don't think so," Anya said. "Sanderson had people stationed to shoot the survivors. It was just blind luck that I managed to crawl out of there. Or maybe it was my determination to endure. Maybe both. You know how stubborn I can be."

"I'll do what I can."

"Can I stay here?" Anya asked. "I snuck into my place when I got back into town, but I don't want to risk going back there. I need to get cleaned up."

"Fine," Zach said. "But if you're caught, it means both of our heads."

"Our heads are already on the chopping block," Anya said. "Sanderson's going to sterilize the city one way or another. His career is riding on this, and he's always been a career man."

Zach went to the Water Treatment Plant, the base of operations Sanderson had set up in the wake of shutting down the Kennel. The scent of bleach was in the air, smelled like Sanderson had done some cleaning in his office.

An ingot of silver sat on a stand at the edge of his desk, front and center.

Sanderson looked up at him.

"Hey, Zach," he said. "What can I do for you? I saw your latest kill counts. Your team is doing great work out there. Even though we lost three guys in the chopper, they managed to shoot nearly 24 Lupines. I can live with an 8:1 kill ratio."

"I tried calling Joliet," Zach said. "They said there was nothing there."

Sanderson stopped working. "Of course not. Nobody's authorized to go down there. You're worried about Anya?"

"Yes," Zach said. "I want to see her."

"She's finished, Zach," Sanderson said.

"I'd just like to know that she's alright," Zach said.

Sanderson shrugged, leaned back in his seat. "There's all sorts of things we'd like to do, but we can't, Zach. Anya's not your problem; she was my problem."

"Was?"

"In a manner of speaking," Sanderson said.

"That's my point," Zach said. "Regarding my team's kill count. What about the wounded victims?"

"We're taking care of them," Sanderson said. "It's not something you need to worry about."

He had expected that kind of runaround from Sanderson, of course. He reached out with a couple of fingers and touched the ingot of silver with them, tracing a pattern along the surface of it.

"Suppose I am worried, though," he said, watching Sanderson watch him touch the silver ingot. "I need to know whether I need to worry about the victims. You know what I mean."

"Ah," Sanderson said. "Just report on your kills, and give us estimates on the damage. And then we'll send recovery teams. It'll be like what you did before, almost."

"Almost," Zach said.

"So, what about Anya?"

Sanderson sighed. "You're muscle, Zach. Not the brains. You just do your musclework."

"She was my friend," Zach said.

"Was," Sanderson said. "You have new friends, now, Zach—powerful friends. Look, don't worry; I've got you covered on this stuff. You keep bagging Lupines, and we'll tag the infectives and clear the scenes. You're completely covered on this stuff. Local law enforcement has been brought up to speed on this. They're not going to get in our way."

"Alright," Zach said. He gave the ingot a last pat, held up his unmarred skin. "Does this mean I passed the Bar?"

Sanderson laughed. "Sure looks like it."

"Did you, you know, have the Kennel folks put down?" Zach said. Sanderson put down his pen and steepled his fingers, looked Zach in the eye.

"I did not," he said. "We send them to a rendition facility."

"Which one?" Zach asked. "You already said you weren't sending them to Wolf Island."

"It's classified," Sanderson said. "She's in good hands, I promise."

Zach looked the man over, imagined taking his pistol and shooting him with it, just on general principles. Sanderson was a good liar, a smooth one.

Sanderson gestured to a report. "Do you believe this? Somebody's buying up silver in droves. It's not the norms, either; I think it's her. Your Princess. Her people. She's directing them to do it."

"You think?" Zach asked.

"I do," Sanderson said. "She's hitting us on so many fronts at once. It's uncanny. This silver thing, I don't know—it's just disappearing from the market. People are purchasing it, the prices are climbing, and it's vanishing. She's preparing for all-out war. We lose our silver bullets, we're in a fucking jam, Zach. The Outbreak is spreading out of control. I went over some of the missing Dr. Milkowski's notes, and she thinks your Princess is tainting the blood supply with the retrovirus. Why she didn't report that is not clear to me, but from what I read, it looks like she was trying to come up with a blood test for the retrovirus."

Zach thought about it, imagined if she had enough of a rein on her pack to drive them to do something like that.

"Guess that would explain why it has spread so widely," Zach said.

Sanderson shrugged. "I don't even know how I'm going to communicate that upstream. Can you imagine how they'll take that, once I tell them that our little bioterrorist is poisoning the blood supply, making more of her?"

Zach didn't know what to say to that, but had to hand it to the audacity of Zooey to do something like that, imagined how often donated blood got used, how that would work. She'd found a way of replicating herself on a level that no Lupine had done before.

"There's more," Sanderson said. "Dr. Milkowski discovered that a female who is infected by lycanthropy can pass it along to any progeny. They become what she referred to as 'natural lycanthropes,' versus 'infective lycanthropes.'"

"Wow," Zach said. "Mina was on it."

"Why this didn't show up in reports to the BEE higher-ups is rather peculiar," Sanderson said.

"Mina's a researcher," Zach said. "She probably wanted to be completely sure before passing that on."

Sanderson smiled to himself, glanced up at Zach. "Maybe so, maybe so. I sent a team to her place, and she wasn't there. Do you have any idea where she might be? I sure would like to talk to her."

"No idea," Zach said. "Mina kept mostly to herself."

"Once I figure out how to write this stuff up, I'm sharing it with Washington," Sanderson said. "They have to know what's going on. You Bureau people screwed it up. Not you Wardens; I just mean the rest of the BEE. Milkowski was concerned that the Kennel was compromised. What do you think about that?"

"Could be," Zach said, picking up the silver ingot. "A lot of people have been infected over the years. Have you Passed the Bar, Sir?"

Sanderson looked at the ingot, which Zach held out to him. He laughed at Zach.

"I'm not touching that fucking thing," Sanderson said. "I know what I am."

"Yeah, I do, too," Zach said, striking Sanderson over the head with the ingot. He bludgeoned him to death with it in a half-dozen blows, before dropping the silver ingot on his chest.

Zooey nursed her wounds, watched Sam's "Transformation" on You-Tube, which was the first of the viral lycanthropy videos, but was now one of hundreds that were surfacing. Seeing that video had been an epiphany for Zooey. It had literally changed her life.

Seeing Sam on the screen, transforming into her werewolf self, was enough to move her. She had been there, at the supernatural vanguard.

Now there were clips galore, people transforming, filming attacks. Nobody did it the way Sam did. Sam was the first, and would have loved knowing that.

Every lick of everything that the mainstream media was ignoring, the Internet and the blogiverse were covering. Twitter was on fire with tweets about werewolves.

Zooey kicked herself for being naïve that she could stir the pot by way of the broadcast media. She even saw clips of her attack on the news station online, watched it and relished it, the comments from people. Reading the comments, she didn't know whether to laugh or to cry. There were actual debates about it, whether it was real or not.

It hardly mattered; the clips were multiplying, were turning up across the country. Sam's video had gotten several million views, now. She'd have been so proud to have been at the front end of something.

Seeing her on the computer screen, alive again, a ghost, now; it was surreal.

Meanwhile, it was up to Zooey to try to shake the sheeple up, to move the norms out of their collective stupor.

She had gone to the third floor deck of the townhome she'd taken, sipping a San Pellegrino, a stolen laptop in hand, and listening to the howling in the darkness. It didn't matter that there were snipers around; the werewolves were multiplying.

Zooey's "infect everybody" policy had been bearing fruit.

After her bout with Ansel, Zooey got particularly aggressive about that. She was surprised she'd done as well as she had against him. Sure, she had to sic her pack on him in the end, but it was great seeing the big bad wolf running for his life.

He'd managed to evade her packmates, who had lost him somewhere north of the city, when he'd used the river to mask his scent. It didn't really matter; Ansel was finished, as far as she was concerned. Chicago was Zooey's playground, now.

Black Sheep came out to join her. He was the hipster boy who had been at the BacchUS Gallery slaughter, the one she'd made a point to take. The way they all did, he turned up at her door, drawn by the salivary siren song of the infection.

She didn't know how, but there was a bond between her and her victims, and they came to her, wanting explanation and direction. They weren't under her control, of course—nothing could control a werewolf—but as their creator, there was this link that they had, and she exploited it.

Zooey had felt it when Sam was alive, and had felt it when Sam had died, that sense of being untethered and free to be on her own.

"We should take over Cabrini Green," Black Sheep said. He had a name, but Zooey wouldn't call him whatever it was; that was the old way. He was Black Sheep to her, now, and for the rest of his days.

"Go for it," Zooey said. "They're, like, in the process of tearing it down, Dude."

"Yes," Black Sheep said. "But that's perfect. It's the perfect staging area. We fill that up with packmates, and we can keep knifing the Loop right in the back, over and over again."

There had been some culling Zooey had done with her pack. There were those who weren't comfortable with their transformation, those who wrestled with their affliction, thought it was a curse. Those folks weren't welcome in Zooey's pack. She let them live, but didn't consider them part of her pack; and had to take their chances with the snipers out there.

The ones Zooey welcomed in her pack were those who were bloodthirsty, had a taste for outrage and mayhem, who welcomed the change. She wanted only the wolfiest of werewolves in her pack. Forget the navelgazers or the "why did this happen to me" whiners; she wanted the ones who immediately understood the gift that had been bestowed upon them, the ones who knew that they had become ultimate killing machines, and just exactly what that meant.

Black Sheep was one of them. Sly and cunning, he had thrilled to his discovery, that he could become a fucking monster. And he'd been one, had been taking people day and night—his day raids were particularly ballsy, since most of the lycanthropes, including Zooey, had preferred to hunt at night.

But not Black Sheep; he went after people in broad daylight, all but daring the various hunters to gun him down. To date, none of them had, because he'd been very careful in his target selection, would scout things out before acting. He was brazen, but he was no fool.

He'd nearly finished off the Wilkos, at least that cell that had operated in Avondale. Black Sheep had just waltzed in there and butchered every Wilko he'd seen, had eaten his fill, and pissed on their walls for good measure.

Zooey was sure there were still Wilkos out there, but that Avondale crew were either finished or driven underground. She'd been pleased by Black Sheep's initiative. It had saved her one more thing she'd had to worry about.

Zooey had taken down two of the sniper teams, too. These clowns would tree themselves or occupy rooftops, and Zooey would have some of her packmates stalk them, get a feel for where they went, who they were, so that when the time was right, she and her crew could finish these guys off with a minimum of fuss.

In a way, it worked to her advantage to have some of the crybabies out on their own, because they'd draw the fire of the snipers, and Zooey and her pack could then take them down, using the whiners as bait. She didn't have interest in wounding the snipers; yes, it might be useful to have some soldiers in her ranks, men used to following orders and trained to kill, but she didn't want anybody who'd been shooting Lupines to be in her pack. She wanted to be sure that everyone in her pack knew where their interest and allegiance resided.

Black Sheep sat down next to her, stroked her leg. Since the fight with Ansel, Zooey had been laying low, healing. Although she thought he'd taken the worst of it, she had her share of injuries, and didn't want to be out there if she wasn't at her best. She told herself she'd beaten him, but dreaded facing him again. If her pack hadn't been present, he would have killed her. Although she was faster than he was, he was bigger and stronger than she was. That tipped the scales in his favor, unfortunately, and she had been grateful for her pack's assistance, even if she chafed at the symbolic risk that assistance brought to her rule.

One of the perils of her selection process was a degree of ruthlessness and opportunism among her packmates. To show weakness before them was to present an opportunity for challenge. She'd already fended off three challenges from wannabes in the wake of her fight with Ansel.

That was something she hadn't fully reckoned with. Zooey had been so assured of her supremacy in the chain of command that she hadn't expected there to be challengers to her authority. When it was just her and Sam doing their thing, it hadn't come up. They'd been friends and lovers, and Sam had been her sire. It had been a non-issue.

But among strangers, there had been an issue. And Zooey had realized that she'd made a mistake in the indiscriminate nature of her approach to filling out the ranks—having males in the pack meant that there would be an alpha male, sooner or later. Ansel was the resident alpha, the strongest of the strong, and Zooey couldn't beat him toe-to-toe.

There was no doubt that Zooey was the alpha female of her pack, but there was a slot open for an enterprising alpha male.

What it meant, in terms of the brute force of lycanthropic politics, was that Zooey would have to face down more and more challenges from striver alpha males. And sooner or later, it meant that she'd come up against a lycanthrope fellow who was bigger, meaner, faster, and tougher than she was. Ansel had been a taste of that.

Zooey had relied on her own natural talent, youth, and speed to prevail against a monster like Ansel, and it hadn't been enough. But as the numbers of lycanthropes swelled, thanks to her efforts, a proper challenger would come along, and she'd be in the position of becoming his bitch, or dying.

It galled her to think of it that way, but she'd be forced to share power with a male, because he'd simply overpower her. Or she'd die trying to maintain her authority. Zooey didn't want to die, yet; she was having far too much fun.

She should have only infected females, formed a proper sisterhood. Sam had been starting that, perhaps unintentionally, but it had been going that way. Zooey had needed to build herself a proper pack of sisters to protect her, to insulate her from challenges from rogue males.

But she'd been so thrilled to be in the game at all, so eager to spread the infection as widely as she could, that Zooey had overlooked that. Two of the three challenges to her authority had been from males. As the pack grew, there'd be more. They were watching her, waiting for their own opportunity to lead.

Obviously, werewolves were not the same as wolves; she understood this. However, there was a particular transformational tyranny in place in her evolving world: the strong would survive. She had kicked over civilization's candle and returned things to a shadowy world of might makes right, but in so doing, had jeopardized her own supremacy in the were-world.

It was something that weighed heavily on her.

"You're brooding," Black Sheep said, rubbing her feet.

"I'm, like, thinking," Zooey said. "I see why Ansel went solo. I mean, like, I get it."

Black Sheep had wonderful hands, and it felt great, his hands on her feet. "What's to get?"

"Pack politics are complicated," Zooey said. "Like, everybody wants their slice. I just wanted to, you know, stir the fucking pot. I didn't plan on being, like, a short order cook, ringing up fucking tickets all day."

Black Sheep smiled to himself. "Oh, is that what you're doing?"

"Feels like it," Zooey said.

"You're not an administrator, Zooey," Black Sheep said. "That's all."

"I'm not supposed to be," she said. "It's not, like, what I'm about."

She thought Black Sheep was probably right about that. She had told her pack to go out and do awesome things, but they kept coming back, wanting to know what they should do, next. Or they came back and tried to give her the boot.

"What are you about?"

"Freedom," Zooey said. "Liberty. Anarchy. Fuckin' shit up."

"Ah," Black Sheep said. He kept working her feet, then her calves. Everything was sore after Ansel. It would take weeks to fully heal the damage he'd done to her.

"You think the norms sweat this? Part of, like, being sheeple is that they get in line. No questions asked. Whoever their new commander is, they're giving orders and people are following them. There aren't any challenges to their authority. Not like that."

Black Sheep laughed to himself. "Part of the cost of playing your game of Anything Goes. Anarchy is a transitory state; order inevitably imposes itself, one way or another. It may not be an order you're familiar with, but it's order, all the same."

"What are you, Dude? Socrates?"

"Philosophy major," Black Sheep said. "University of Chicago."

"Ha," Zooey said. "Bet you're regretting going to that gallery."

"Maybe just a little," he said. "I thought it was going to be some soft-core performance art porn. Didn't expect, you know, what came after."

"Yeah, well," Zooey said. "Sorry."

"I'm not," Black Sheep said. "But I admit that it's weird how this all works out. Post-post-structuralism or something."

"Whatever," Zooey said. "It's a pain in the ass is what it is. I'm not a politician or an administrator; I'm a revolutionary."

"Right," Black Sheep said. "I get it."

"That's just your Moon in Pisces talking," Zooey said. "Blowing smoke right up my ass."

Black Sheep winced. "Lovely image, that. I'm just saying, your heart's not in the political game, and werewolves are pack animals, aren't we? Packs mean politics. You must become a politician to succeed at this."

Zooey hadn't reckoned with that aspect of it. She just felt the world would take care of itself down the line, once the infection had sufficiently spread. For her, it was the trip, not the destination. That's where it mattered.

The howls kept growing in number, punctuated by gunfire.

"The gangs aren't happy about the turn of events," Black Sheep said. "They're not liking this invasion of their turf."

"Fuck them," Zooey said. "Fuck everybody who's not us."

Black Sheep smiled at that, was working on her calves. "That's their attitude in a nutshell."

"Are my people still buying silver?" Zooey said.

"They are," Black Sheep said. "Buying it and hiding it, just like you said."

"Throw it in the lake or something."

She knew that the norms were stocking up on silver, despite the mainstream media's refusal to air the story properly. People were hoarding silver, and her pack was acquiring it whenever they could, and burying it or throwing it into deep water.

"Dude, I fucking talked on the television," Zooey said. "I was there, in full regalia, and I fucking talked. And they still wouldn't cop to it. The cameras were, like, totally rolling."

"People see what they want to see," Black Sheep said. "And were-wolves are people, too."

"No, we're not," Zooey said, sniffing the air. "It's chilly. Smells like it wants to snow."

She kicked his hands off her feet, snapped shut her laptop, and got up, went inside. Black Sheep tagged along, closed the sliding glass door behind them.

Zooey plopped the laptop onto one of the chairs in the living room, made her way to the sofa. She ached. Ansel may have gotten the worst of it in their exchange, but Zooey still felt like shit. He had hurt her badly.

Like everything, this would pass. The vitality that they possessed was a true marvel. Even grievous wounds would heal rapidly, given enough time. She had not been critically wounded by Ansel, but it had been enough to ensure she was in pain for awhile. She would pay him back for that.

Black Sheep started working her shoulders.

"You're stressed," he said. "Very stressed."

Zooey let him work her shoulders. She didn't feel a thing for him, but she let him tend to her, anyway.

"I'm just, like, frustrated," Zooey said. "People are lame."

"And tame," Black Sheep said. "It's the legacy of thousands of years of agricultural civilization. The hunter-gatherer cultures are the pack animals of human civilization; agricultural man becomes livestock."

Zooey batted his hands away, glowered at him. "We're not, like, livestock."

Black Sheep shrugged. "We're in this comfortable townhome—sure, you killed and ate the owners, but we're still lounging on their furniture, enjoying their creature comforts. It's not very badass."

"You're saying we should, like, travel to the Third World or something? Rough it? This place needs us," Zooey said.

"I'm saying that we're werewolves in a barnyard," Black Sheep said. "We're not in the forest or even in the urban jungle. We're running wild on a farm. The suburbs are a golf course, and the city's a farm."

"Farms are, like, rural, not urban," Zooey said.

"That's the old way of looking at things," Black Sheep said. "I'm saying that, to us, there is no difference between cities or farms—a farm may be rural, relative to the city, but it's still civilized. A farm is not the wilderness. We're the barbarians at the gates, now; whether we're at the gates of a farm in the country or at the metaphorical gates of the city, it doesn't matter. Everybody's livestock nowadays, and we're the wilderness."

Zooey just let him talk. Black Sheep was a talker.

"The wildest city dweller today is probably tame compared with yesterday's farmers," he said. "Everybody's tame today. It's the price of admission into civilization. You play nice, you don't run with scissors. You live and let live. That's how civilization functions. Cooperation, collaboration and reciprocity: it's how civilization evolves. Now, we come along and we upend that whole thing. You're trying to swap out Live and Let Live for Kill or Be Killed, and then you're wondering why people aren't rushing to embrace that, why the livestock aren't taking up that banner?"

"I'm trying to force, like, a change," Zooey said.

"It can't be forced," Black Sheep said. "You're just trying to roll the clock backward, not pushing things forward. People always want to move forward, whether they admit to it or not. That's why it's called progress. People have to feel like they're going someplace worth heading. You're all about the trip, without paying attention to the destination."

"You, like, read my mind," Zooey said. "Are you a mind reader?"

"You have to take people someplace where they want to go," Black Sheep said. "This isn't it."

"Dude, you seem to be handling it alright," Zooey said.

"I never had a choice," Black Sheep said. "You took it from me at that shitty fucking art gallery. This isn't a place where I'd ever have wanted to go. Now that I'm here, I'm making the best of it, but this isn't what people want. Most people don't want to become killing machines. Most people don't want to become fucking cannibals, man. They don't want to be reminded of their animal natures. Civilization banks on mankind believing, thinking, and feeling that it has left those animal trappings behind. All you're doing is reminding people of what they used to be. Nobody wants that."

"Philosophy major," Zooey said. "Are you still going to class?"

"Hell, yes," Black Sheep said. "Philosophically, it's fascinating. I'm getting to watch humanity with a degree of objectivity I didn't have before."

"Werewolf professor," Zooey said. "That's what you're going to be?"

"I definitely have a deep understanding of duality," Black Sheep said. "I mean, look at you. You're 19, Zooey. You dropped out of college to do what? Become a monster? A rabid revolutionary?"

Black Sheep's laugh was scornful, contemptuous. Zooey turned her head to look at him, her black eyes raking up and down his body.

"I threw off society's shackles, Dude," Zooey said.

"And, you've, what, infected hundreds, maybe thousands of people? Murdered hundreds? Eaten dozens?"

"Fuck, you're talking like a norm," Zooey said.

"That Ansel guy," Black Sheep said. "He's a painter. He's an artist."

"I'm an artist," Zooey said.

"You're a murderer," Black Sheep said. "And a cannibal. And a terrorist."

Zooey was getting pissed off at Black Sheep. If she hadn't been as achy as she was, she'd have gone right at him.

"I'm a revolutionary," Zooey said. "I'm overturning the established order."

"Right," Black Sheep said, like he wasn't even believing her.

"Alright, you can just leave now, Dude," Zooey said. "You have officially, like, pissed me off. I gave you a gift, you fucker. Now you're, like, throwing it back at me."

"You infected me," Black Sheep said. "That's not a gift. You're thinking like an addict. It's like a rapist telling his victim that at least she got laid."

"You fucker," Zooey said, getting to her feet. "Get the fuck out of here."

"Or what?" Black Sheep said. "You'll kill me?"

As he spoke, Black Sheep split his skin, transformed in front of Zooey, becoming a splendorous black-furred werewolf with green eyes that matched his eyes in his human form. Not as bulky as Ansel, Black Sheep was long and sinewy, with a shaggier mane and a longer snout. His legs were long and rippled with muscle. He was an impressive lycanthrope, she admitted, although not her type.

He grabbed Zooey by the wrist before she could react.

"Is this what you want?" he snarled. "The Hobbesian war of all against all?"

Zooey willed herself to change, if only to have a chance against Black Sheep, looming over her, holding her arm like she was a rag doll. Although it pained her to change again so soon after her brawl with Ansel, she would not let herself be cowed by this upstart.

"That's the spirit," Black Sheep said, grabbing Zooey's other arm, pinning her as she'd transformed. He shoved her into the sofa, face-down, while she snarled and snapped at him, straining to free herself.

He had leverage on her, and he bit down on her shoulder, forced her head over with a shove of his own head.

"I'll kill you," Zooey said, muffled by the cushions of the sofa.

"Maybe," Black Sheep said. "Maybe you will."

He entered her, thrust into her from behind, making Zooey cry out. She fought against him while he fucked her, took his pleasure on her. Zooey did not like men, so this violation was doubly infuriating to her.

Black Sheep rode her and rode her until he came, his body snapping against her as he did, his claws digging into her arms as he held her.

"You are dead, Aristotle," Zooey said.

Black Sheep leaned in and took Zooey's head in his mouth, gently gripped it in his teeth. He could crush her skull from this position. She felt the heat of his breath on her head.

"I'm more Protagoras than Aristotle," Black Sheep said. "Not that you'd even know the difference; it's all Greek to you. This is what you did to me."

And then he showed her.

Polly went to see Ansel, had given him a whiteboard and an erasable marker. He looked so sad with his jaw all wired shut, and bandaged up from all the wounds. He took the whiteboard and wrote something on it, turned it so she could see it.

FUCK

She laughed, despite the sorry spectacle in front of her.

"What happened to you, Ansel?"

He rolled his eyes, like he was weighing whether or not to respond.

FUCK

ZOOEY

"Zooey did that to you?"

He shrugged.

"How?"

PACK OF FRIENDS

"Why?"

He turned the board back to himself, wrote again, underlined the word.

TURF

He erased the board, wrote some more.

I TRIED TO KILL HER

He showed it to her, and Polly nodded, looked over her shoulder, gestured for him to erase that. He did, turned it back to her.

ALMOST DID IT

"I know you did, Ansel," Polly said. "I should never have sent you to do that. That was terrible of me."

He wrote again.

WE HAVE TO LEAVE. NOT SAFE HERE. CHICAGO.

"We can stay at my house," Polly said. "I mean, it's not in Chicago."

He laughed, a silent shaking motion, his shoulders heaving. It made Polly laugh, too.

"I mean it," Polly said. "Stay with me, Ansel. Please? When you get discharged? I'm sorry I went a little crazy before; I'm alright, now."

ALRIGHT.

"Yes," Polly said. "I'm alright."

Ansel shook his head, wrote some more.

ALRIGHT. I'LL STAY WITH YOU.

Polly nodded, smiling. "When are they discharging you?"

SOON.

"Great," Polly said. "I'll wait."

Ansel erased his board, wrote on it again, turned it and showed her.

THAT RHYMED.

GREAT

I'LL WAIT

Polly nodded, grinned a little. "Guess I haven't completely lost my touch as a poet."

It was funny, seeing Ansel there, but him not being able to speak.

"How did Zooey even beat you? I didn't think that was possible."

Ansel shrugged.

SHE DIDN'T BEAT ME.

FASTER THAN ME.

LOTS OF FRIENDS.

LONER LOSES AGAINST A PACK.

He erased it. The shame of that, coupled with the headlong flight through the city, chased by Zooey's packmates, still stung. Ansel could heal from almost any wound, but his pride would always hurt in the face of that.

Polly reached out and touched his wounded face. Her hand was gentle and cool against his skin.

"Does it hurt much?"

Ansel sighed.

I LIKE DRUGS.

"What if you transform? What would happen?"

Ansel shook his head.

MESSY. I WILL HEAL, BUT IT'D BE UGLY. THAT'S WHY I HAVE TO GET THE HELL OUT OF THE CITY. NEED TIME TO CHILL OUT. HEAL.

Polly accepted that, ran her hand along the contours of his jaw. Even wounded and damaged, Ansel was still very handsome.

"I'll take you home," she said. "I should have been with you."

She drove them through the city in her BMW. The discharge had occurred without incident. With all the injuries occurring in the city, the hospital staff were probably more than eager to have a bed open. They'd picked up his painkillers from the pharmacy, and had gotten out of there.

It was mid-afternoon, and things weren't completely out of control, but there were signs of the city getting ragged around the edges: more bodies on the streets, being put into white, unmarked trucks by masked workers, wearing hazmat suits.

Some of them were shooting victims, others were torn apart—it made for an odd juxtaposition, two sets of victims, tied to the same pestilence.

Ansel watched without comment, and Polly just focused on the traffic. They had stopped by his place, where he'd put a bunch of his clothes in a duffel bag. She looked around his loft, at his paintings, saw hers on the wall.

"Can we take that one with us?" she asked.

Ansel nodded, walked over, picked up the painting. Polly looked at it, admired it. He had captured her so perfectly.

"It's me, before my fall from grace," Polly said.

Ansel rolled his eyes, and they locked up his place, went to his garage. He put the painting in the back seat, and his duffel bag in the trunk.

Then they got out of there.

"It's getting ugly outside," Polly said. "Nobody's saying anything official about it. But there's a kind of curfew going on. Not that it matters. I mean, werewolves aren't like vampires; they can go anywhere they like, anytime."

It galled Polly to even be talking about werewolves. There was something terribly gauche about them. Werewolves were uncouth. They weren't cool, like vampires.

"Here's a question for you: do vampires exist, too?"

Ansel laughed to himself, a silent shaking of his shoulders. He took out the marker, wrote on the board, held it so she could see it.

YES.

"You're kidding me. Have you seen one?"

Ansel tapped it again, underlined it.

"Vampires, Werewolves," Polly said. "What is this world going to?"

Ansel erased the word and wrote another, held it out for her.

HELL.

"Quaint idea, that," she said. "You really saw a vampire?"

YES.

"Male or female?"

CHICK.

"Ah," Polly said. "A past girlfriend?"

HAHA.

"Aren't werewolves and vampires enemies?"

COMPETITORS. RIVALS.

The idea that such things walked the earth and she'd never believed in them or run into any, at least with her knowledge, unnerved her.

"What happens if a vampire bites a werewolf?"

HAHA.

"No, really? What happens?"

NO CLUE. VAMPWOLF? WEREPIRE? WEREVAMP? LYCANTHRORATU?

Polly laughed at the names. Such a silly notion. It was fun quizzing Ansel, though, despite herself.

WEREWOLVES KILL VAMPIRES. CAN SNIFF THEM OUT. VAMPIRES DON'T LIKE US BECAUSE WE CAN TEAR THEM UP, SPILL THEIR PRECIOUS BLOOD. VAMPIRES ARE LIKE CADILLACS.

"What do you mean?"

PRETTY, BUT THEY GUZZLE GAS, ARE HIGH-MAINTENANCE.

Polly laughed at that, and Ansel erased his words.

"What are werewolves like, then?"

SAM CALLED US THE EL CAMINO OF MONSTERS. SHE TOLD ME THAT.

Polly felt a wistfulness at the memory of Sam. It was such a Sam thing to say.

"How so?"

MISFITS. PARTS DON'T QUITE FIT. NEVER GET THE RESPECT WE DESERVE.

"I don't like El Caminos," Polly said. "Okay, since we're going that way, I have to ask: what about ghosts?"

YES.

"I knew you were going to say that," Polly said. "You've seen them?"

YES.

"Werewolves, vampires, ghosts. Oh, my," Polly said. "What a weird world we live in."

Ansel erased the word without a sound, while Polly drove them out of the city, heading north.

She didn't like to think of these other things in her world, at the edge of her vision. She especially didn't like that one of those things had irrevocably altered her world.

"The vampires won't like what's happening here, will they?"

NO.

"Will they stop it? I mean, how does that all work itself out?"

Ansel thought about it a bit before he responded.

VAMPS TEND TO RUN GOVERNMENT, VERSUS GO-ING ROGUE. THEY CO-OPT POLITICIANS AND TRY TO KEEP THINGS GOING SMOOTHLY.

He thought a bit more before replying.

BLOOD IS BLOOD TO THEM, BUT IF THIS STUFF MESSES UP THEIR SUPPLY, THEY'LL STAMP IT OUT.

"So, who wins?"

Ansel sighed.

THEY HAVE THE CONNECTIONS, WE HAVE THE NUMBERS AND THE POWER.

"Werewolves are stronger?"

IN FACE-TO-FACE, YES. WE CAN TEAR VAMPIRES APART, TOE-TO-TOE. BUT VAMPIRES WORK BEHIND THE SCENES. THEY'RE LIKE CHESS PLAYERS, WHERE-AS WE'RE MORE LIKE RUGBY OR HOCKEY PLAYERS. THEY SCHEMERS, WE BRAWLERS.

That she'd even be having this conversation gave Polly bitter amusement. Lee would have had a field day with it.

VAMPS CAN PLAY THE WAITING GAME. WE STILL GROW OLD AND DIE. THEY JUST GO ON AND ON.

"It's all so strange," Polly said. "I don't even like to think about it."

Ansel erased his board, looked out the window. They were driving through Evanston, which still looked like itself, although Polly sup-posed anything could be happening behind closed doors. It was like her place—nobody would have guessed what she'd done to Tristan.

"I'll be glad to have someone there with me," Polly said. "That house is too big to live in alone."

WHY NO KIDS?

"I didn't want any," Polly said. "I suppose I don't have much of a maternal instinct."

TOO BAD.

Polly shook her head. "No, I think I made the right decision. I mean, can you imagine where I'd be right now if I had a child?"

IF YOU HAD A CHILD, YOU WOULDN'T HAVE BEEN OUT HANGING WITH THOSE DILETTANTE BUDS OF YOURS. WOULDN'T HAVE GOTTEN INFECTED BY SAM.

"Ha," Polly said. "I would have been home changing diapers or taking my child to piano practice or ballet or something like that. Funny set of circumstances. Dilettante lycanthrope, werewolf poetess, or domestic goddess? I'd have had Tristan hire a nanny."

She knew Ansel didn't approve of the Horrorshow, thought they were all just poseurs. And she understood that. He was a serious painter. Perhaps not enormously talented, but he was a legitimate artist. Sheldon and even Reagan were just strivers in the realm of painting, and the others had themselves coiled up in knots about their relevance in the art world. Sam, most of all, because she was the performance artist, wanted so badly to be taken seriously, even though she was mostly the mascot of the group.

DIFFERENT WORLDS.

They reached Winnetka, got to her house. Polly drove them in the back, and they got out, Ansel tucking the whiteboard under his arm, getting painfully out of the car. Polly went to help him, but Ansel waved her off.

She let them in, and Ansel went into the living room.

WATER?

Polly nodded, went into the kitchen, got him a glass of water. He took out a slender straw and carefully drank some water.

"You certainly are going to lose weight like this," Polly said.

LIQUID DIET.

Polly laughed and when back outside, got her portrait, brought that inside, rested it beneath the mantle in the living room.

"I'm putting it up here," she said. "I'm moving Reagan's painting, I'm afraid. Sorry, Reagan."

She got a stepladder and set it up, carefully removed Reagan's painting. It was a large painting, a figure of gold and green, fairly abstract, but with something lurking there within the canvas, gazing out at the onlooker.

WHAT IS IT CALLED?

"'Thrasymachus Rising,'" Polly said. "Reagan had a whole dissertation about it, was thrilled when Tristan bought it, although I had just told him to buy it so she'd not feel bad."

Ansel thought the painting was alright for Reagan, whose work lacked much finesse, but was at least technically proficient.

Polly put Ansel's portrait of her up, leveled it out, and then stepped back down, looked at it from across the room.

"You captured me perfectly," Polly said. "I just love it."

Ansel watched Polly admire herself, shook his head.

SILLY.

"No, I like it," Polly said. "It's lovely. You made me immortal."

NO, YOU ARE SILLY.

"Me? Why?"

He wouldn't tell her why, just laughed to himself. It bugged Polly that she couldn't even make him talk if she wanted to.

She put away the stepladder, and leaned Reagan's painting on a wall. She'd find a place for that one, later, maybe in the dining room.

"I like having real paintings," she said. "Even ones done by my friends. There's just something captivating about it. Someone made this, took the time to create it. I'd die before I had a print of something on my wall."

She sat down across from Ansel, who just looked at his painting in silence. It was kind of fun for her, the three of them in the room—the artist, the subject, and the artwork. Polly soaked up that vibe for a bit.

"You really did capture me perfectly," Polly said. "I can remember the sitting for that. How you set things up so carefully. You are a marvelous painter, Ansel. I respect that."

GOOD PAINTER, LOUSY WEREWOLF.

"There are worse things to be," Polly said.

I CHOSE ONE; COULDN'T CHOOSE THE OTHER.

"I choose to be exactly who I am," Polly said. "I won't let that Thing usurp my world. We can protect each other that way, you know? Keep each other honest. Keep us from falling off the wagon, and doing something we might regret."

Ansel hadn't thought of that before. He had been so used to being a lone wolf, going at it on his own, nobody knowing his secret, it simply hadn't occurred to him.

NOT A BAD IDEA.

"Yes," Polly said, warming to it. "We can make our own scene, do our own thing. Watch each other's back. I'll write my poems, you'll paint. We can just be there for each other."

A COUPLE?

"A quartet," Polly said. "You and your beast, me and mine. The four of us, living together. Our own pack."

It wasn't the worst idea he'd heard.

11

"It worked, Anya," Zach said, holding out his unmarred fingers. She'd painted his fingers with super glue before he'd gone to see Sanderson, and the glue had been enough of a barrier between his skin and the silver to prevent his skin from reacting to it.

"The important thing is that he didn't suspect you," Anya said. "What did you learn?"

"I think he's operating under orders," Zach said. "That was my impression."

"A cog," Anya said. "He's always been a cog."

Anya took Zach's hand, inspected it.

"That's a relief," she said. "At least we have something for it."

"He's definitely pursuing a policy of extermination, though," Zach said. "Or he was, anyway."

Anya steepled her fingers, was deep in thought. "Was?"

"Was," Zach said.

"What did you do, Zach?"

"It's coming," he said. "I can feel that much. I know it's only a matter of time before I completely lose it."

She nodded. Anya wished she had access to a lab again, but couldn't risk it. She'd still not been able to reach Mina. It bothered her to think that they were willfully flouting protocols by not quarantining themselves, but Sanderson had changed the rules of the game.

"How did you kill him?"

"I beat him to death with his silver ingot," Zach said.

"You're a latter-day Judas, Zachary," Anya said.

Zach sighed. He didn't feel bad about it. Sanderson had murdered his coworkers, and had it coming to him, as far as he was concerned.

"The skin changes," Anya said. "That's another of the tells with the lycanthropes: no tattoos. Any previous tattoos are lost when the transformation occurs. It's no guarantee that you're dealing with a lycanthrope, but it is a way of outing them."

"What does that have to do with anything?" Zach asked.

She turned over his arm, revealed the tattoo of a mermaid he had on his forearm. "When I see that this is gone, I'm going to know that you've lost it. You won't be able to hide that."

"I'm not hiding anything from you," Zach said. "You are all I've got, here."

"How is the extermination program faring?" Anya asked. She was pacing in Zach's living room, while Zach was sitting on his sofa.

"We're still getting hefty kill ratios," Zach said. "Although we've lost two more teams. The infectives are fighting back. I'm sure Princess is targeting the kill teams."

"Who's the new director?"

"Minton," Zach said. Anya nodded. Troy Minton was a rival of Sanderson's, so she could only imagine how that would go. He was a young black executive, a former Marine.

"He wants to escalate, of course," Zach said. "He's been calling to bring more manpower in here. He's been having the coroners reclaim the silver bullets, having them resmelted. He's pushing for a frontal assault on this."

Anya laughed. That was very Minton. Wage war but be mindful of the overhead. Minton would do his job to completion, could only wonder how it must have been perceived in Washington, losing Sanderson so quickly.

"Do they suspect you?" Anya asked.

"No," Zach said. "The Director's office was one of the only places without surveillance over there. I took out Sanderson while his admin was out getting lunch. Nobody saw. Minton is checking everybody out, thinking Princess has an agent in our midst."

"If Minton brings back the Bar, you'll be outed," Anya said.

"I know. What's our next step?" Zach asked.

"We can't simply keep squatting here," Anya said. "If nothing else, his building management will get suspicious, and so forth. The Kennel was our main base of operations, but we could go to the Blue Island Research Enclave. It was the original BEE headquarters before we'd migrated to the Kennel. It's older and smaller, but could meet our needs."

"Assuming that Sanderson hadn't already commandeered it," Zach said.

"Why would he? It's outdated," Anya said. "It's from the late 1940s, when the Government first got wind of the real nature of *Werwolf*, during Operation Paperclip—that's when the United States brought over Nazi scientists for our space and engineering program. Once the Nazis had their backgrounds bleached, they were recruited. That's when *Werwolf* got exposed. It was intended as a kind of super-soldier project, another of those crazy Vengeance weapons. Create a super soldier, an early biological weapon, who could then effectively deploy behind enemy lines and sow discord and chaos."

"Ah," Zach said. "Let's check out this BIRE, then."

They packed up some supplies and Zach drove them to Blue Island, with Anya navigating from the back seat. She was nervous about being out in the open. Both of them were virtual shut-ins from all the hours they'd booked at the Kennel. It struck him as kind of ironic— they were working hard to help free people of this infection, but were themselves trapped in the organizational amber of the BEE. They were as captive as the subjects that they studied.

As he drove, Anya talked about the *Werwolf* program. He admitted that he'd not read up on the history of it. As an operations guy, the context of a situation didn't really matter to him; he just had to know who the target was, didn't need their life story.

"As a program, *Werwolf* was a failure," Anya said. "The commando operations intended to work behind Allied lines never took off. Apparently the Nazi propaganda arm was unwilling to even concede that the Allies could take Axis land, which made them very reluctant to speak of their guerrilla operation at all."

"Did the Lupines originate with that program?" Zach asked.

"No," Anya said. "I don't think so. I think some of their scientists had managed to find a few lycanthropes and subjected them to tests. They couldn't sequence genomes back then, of course, but they could test infectivity and so on. From the records that survived, they had volunteers who willingly were exposed to the pathogen, after a first round of tests on prisoners. At least a dozen men, maybe more. But, as the infection took hold, they were impossible to contain or control. Several of them escaped."

"We're going to find ourselves in that same situation," Zach said. "As the infection takes hold, we're going to be out of control. The virus, as much as it can want anything, wants to be spread. It doesn't kill its host, but the changes it causes in the biology of its host makes infection likelier—heightened emotional response, physical transformation into a form that increases the chance of infecting others, which, itself, takes a toll on metabolism, requiring massive intake of protein, which, again, completes the circle."

"Schizophrenia," Anya said. They all had the voices in their heads, she was sure. Whether anybody spoke of it, they all felt it. "That psychological dysfunction as a side effect of the disease is interesting. I'm not sure whether it is the brain's reaction to the virus or else some odd manifestation of the virus, itself. Not that it's talking to you per se, but that it represents the infected part of you talking to the rest of you."

"I don't hear voices," Anya said. When Zach looked at her, she got diffident. "I don't."

"Right," Zach said. "I don't believe you. Mine won't shut up."

"I'm trying to find a way of addressing that," Anya said. "Tranquilizers have some effect, at least temporarily."

"I'm not doing that," Zach said.

"We're here," Anya said, pointing.

It was an old, fenced-in property with a faded metal sign on the front that said Blue Island Research Enclave (BIRE). The fencing was topped with barbed wire. The building beyond was old yellow brick, three stories, with graffiti on most of the lower walls, and a smokestack in the back.

"We can't just drive up here," Zach said, driving around the place. "You sure Minton doesn't know about this place?"

Anya sighed. "I don't know what he knows. I just don't think he cares. But what he needs is state of the art, not an old facility like this. This place shut down in 1984."

"But they didn't tear it down," Zach said.

"It was considered to be a biohazard," Anya said. "One of those Superfund sites. So long as it was shut down, they figured they could let it languish and save money on demolition."

Zach took them behind the place, parked the car, gazed at it. "It's creepy-looking."

Anya laughed. "No need to be scared, Zachary; we're the only monsters, here."

Four hours. Black Sheep raped Zooey over a span of four hours, before he bounded off into the darkness, cackling and howling. All the time he was assaulting her, he was talking, giving her a dissertation about the duality of man, bestiality, lycanthropy as a metaphor for man's discomfort with his animal nature, and other things. He wouldn't shut up the whole time.

And when he wasn't yammering about that stuff, he was telling her that she deserved this, because she'd infected him to begin with. How he'd been happy and she'd come along and ruined his life by making him this diseased monstrosity, and how he'd done things he had never even thought possible, and how he'd killed and eaten people, and how he knew she'd done that, too, because he'd watched her.

As far as potential protégés went, Black Sheep was a letdown, Zooey conceded, recovering in her wolf form, covered in bites and scratches, aching. She was not going to give Black Sheep the satisfaction of having broken her.

Yes, he had dared to assault her in a fashion that was particularly hurtful and bestial, but if his goal was to put her in her place, Zooey wanted him to know that he'd failed.

Black Sheep had only killed himself by doing this.

He was a dead man.

Zooey crawled across the living room, joints aching, and willed herself to her feet. Her body had healed the worst of Black Sheep's assault, thankfully; the pain was more spiritual than physical, and she could cope with that. One of the blessings of lycanthropy was a capacity to deal with pain, and to heal more rapidly from things that would have killed norms.

As she thought about Black Sheep's effrontery, she got more angry.

She had taken him under her wing—under her paw, at any rate—and this was how he'd repaid her? She would find him, and she would kill him. Or, perhaps better, she would maim him. She imagined taking his legs and arms, leaving him a lycanthropic torso. There was something marvelous about that, this image of Black Sheep transforming, without arms or legs, just this dreadful wolf-thing—limbless, helpless, hopeless.

Zooey willed herself back to her original form, went to the fridge and took out another of those sodas, drank it down, crunched the can. No more men. She would get the word out, that only females should be infected. She kicked herself for not acting on it earlier, for being so high on her own monstrosity that she'd not thought it through. It should be a sisterhood, a supernatural sorority, with herself as the alpha female, the pinnacle of the pyramid.

It may have gone too far for that; with her blood drives, she couldn't determine who the recipients would be, but she didn't worry about that; rather, in the day to day, she would have her packmates only infect women. It might be a difficult order to enforce, ultimately, since a lycanthrope could not necessarily control who fell victim to them. But for the ones who were able, the ones with volition and will, perhaps it would be enough.

Zooey took an hour-long shower, filling the apartment with steam as she scrubbed her body clean, angry at its latest betrayal of her. For the first time since her transformation, she had felt at odds with her body in a way that was reminiscent of her life before her infection, which, to her, had felt like a communion of sorts, a biological epiphany that had helped her understand her role in the universe.

Black Sheep was a Cancer Sun with a Pisces Moon and Leo Rising. She'd been a fool to think that there was anything she could do with that worthless, watery fuck. He was weak, not strong, and given over to impulses he could not hope to control. She should have known that any clown who turned up at the BacchUS Gallery was worth next to nothing, a scenester-hipster-wannabe, a cowardly coattail rider, a lickspittle, a sycophant.

No doubt he raped her as a way of trying to reclaim some measure of himself that he'd lost from cowering in her shadow. She finished bathing, wrapped herself in a towel, looked herself over in the mirror after mopping off the steam. The scars across her face were healing well, looked like just thin lines, now. The marks from her battle with Ansel would heal in a few weeks. The injuries Black Sheep had done her might take longer to heal, but she'd deal.

In a few more days, she would be all better. She didn't think Black Sheep would have the balls to stay in Chicago. But she hoped he did.

She turned on the laptop she had, went to Twitter, immediately tweeted:

Black Sheep = Dead Meat. #promise

She didn't want to be more obvious than that, since she was sure that agents would be monitoring the social media. She didn't even know if he bothered with Twitter; it just felt good to write it out, to think it. Zooey had to rally her pack to her, to tell them how it was, what it was going to be, what they were going to do.

Zooey transformed again, throwing aside the towel, and felt the rejuvenating pain of the passage from woman to wolf, and could feel the restoration of herself in the change. It was curative, restorative and holy.

Then she went to the balcony and slipped out there, quietly, and scaled the roof. Once there, she bounded from rooftop to rooftop, until she found an old Victorian building with a pointy, copper-clad tower, and she scaled that and turned her head to the heavens and she howled. She gave a full-throated summons to her pack, the ones she'd infected, herself, the ones who felt that tug on their leashes toward her, the ones who belonged to her, just a little.

She waited, heard answering howls, smiled to herself. This was the right thing to do. Whatever Black Sheep had intended with his assault, she would not let herself be cowed by it. She howled again, a beckoning cry, and waited for them to come.

Her people.

HER people.

They gathered around the yard of the house, while Zooey stayed on the roof, so she could look down on them.

And come they did. Hundreds of them, despite the snipers, the gunmen in the night, the urban assassins. Like they did with Ansel, these packmates, pawns in her grand game, a mix of men and women, of course, her earlier thinking.

"Siblings," she said, "I understood something today. Something clear and pure and true. All of you must infect only women. Don't infect the men."

She could see them looking up at her in confusion, animal eyes upon her. Zooey knew she had to be quick and clear in her messaging, for she knew that the government hit squads would be scrambling to catch them in one place like this.

"Infect the women, because the gift of life is in woman," Zooey said. "Yes, we spread our gift through our bite and through our blood, but there is another way. We must infect women because that will bring us trueborn as well as infectives. Do you understand me? Infect the women, and the world will follow, because every child they have will carry us in them as well."

It was so simple, so obvious. It was another avenue of attack, another way of spreading the disease so that even if they caught the bloodborne passage of infection, even if someone evaded being bitten, themselves, the lycanthropes could still pass themselves on through progeny. It wasn't simply enough to create packs; she had to build families. Families of lycanthropes would be stronger than infective packs. It would make the revolution inevitable.

"Go," Zooey said. "Go and do this thing. For the future. Our future."

She howled, and was pleased at the cacophony of howls that rose in unison. That sense of unity and belonging healed her heart, let her cast off the wounds inflicted upon her by Black Sheep. There was power in solidarity. No one would ever know what had happened to her, no one would believe it. Black Sheep would be rendered impotent before her.

"Go," Zooey said. "Hide from the hunstmen; scatter."

She went into the shadows, herself, crept back to the townhome, willed herself to appear human again, slipped back inside, closed the door. The undisputed mistress of the city, she was terribly pleased with herself. Her pack knew her will; they would carry it out.

Black Sheep could not have imagined what he had released in her. He would have been dismayed and shocked, but then, it was why she was who she was. It was why she had actively hunted out Sam in the first place, in her understanding of what Samantha had represented, and why Black Sheep had turned up at a no-name gallery seeking some pointless, puerile stimulation. Zooey was the artist, after all. She was creating a masterpiece of mayhem, on a scale that Sam herself would never have been able to imagine, or have had the courage to undertake.

Zooey was reshaping the world, itself, recasting it red in tooth and claw.

Triumph flowed from taking adversity and spinning it into opportunity. It was how she wrestled her own violation to the ground and tamed it, put it to work for her. Yes, she had been hurt by her would-be protégé, but she was tempered by it, not broken. Everything they threw at her only made her stronger, more resolute. The future was hers to have.

Hungry, she went to the freezer and dug out a frozen rack of ribs, found a recipe for it online, and went about making herself a celebratory feast, and it didn't matter one bit to her that she was the only one there to enjoy it.

Polly had put Gang of Four on the stereo, which Tristan had gotten wired so that it could be heard throughout the house. The spectral guitars and throbbing bass perfectly suited her mood. There was a rightness to her idea.

She had created a new blog, too, to commemorate it: Pollyvore.

Turning it toward Ansel for approval, he looked at it and shrugged, wrote on his board.

SILLY.

"It's not silly," Polly said. "Blogs are authentic expressions of the zeitgeist. Absolutely everybody has them."

WHAT ARE YOU GOING TO TALK ABOUT?

"Being a lycanthrope," Polly said. "Being me. I'm a thinking person's lycanthrope."

Ansel rolled his eyes.

LAME.

"It's not lame," Polly said. "Don't make me kick you back onto the street, Ansel. Pipe down over there."

She went about writing a little bit, warming herself up.

> I decided to move to this new blog because I've become a
> werewolf. There, I said it. Don't judge me, don't fear and hate
> me. It's simply what I am.

Polly didn't like that, deleted the line, tried again. Maybe she could just write poems about lycanthropy, as she'd started to on her other blog.

DOUBLETIME

Seeing double

In two places at once
Doubletalk
Two-timer, Janus-faced
What have I forgotten?

Double Trouble.
There's you and me
You're me and I'm you
Just the two of us
Closer than sisters.

You won't let me rhyme this time
You speak in guttural growls
You think forbidden thoughts
You talk in doggerel.

I keep the peace
I hold myself together
I pull ourselves apart
I wax lyrical about our miracle.

You drowse in the dark,
I lie awake at night.

Polly stopped, could feel the Thing within stirring. Her poetry woke it up, but she did not know quite why. Perhaps it was because it was part of her attempt at normalcy, trying to find herself again. Whatever it was, it woke the Thing up.

Would you just stop trying to be you? We're us, now; not you.

She glanced over at Ansel, who had laid back on the sofa, eyes closed, while Gang of Four sang about capitalism.

I am in charge, here, Polly thought. *I make the rules.*

I change rules as readily as I change skin.

You can't tame me. Not with your verses. No lycanthropic lullaby for me.

Polly felt herself hit the delete button, deleting her poem, aghast at this silent usurpation.

It works both ways. You repress me, I can repress you, too.

Polly felt her fingers move on their own, typing:

DEAD MEAT

I don't like dead meat
Live kills are far better
For I am a hunter
And not a scavenger

I take what I want
and I won't ever ask
You'd know that, my Lamb
When I took off my mask.

The Thing released her fingers.

I can do that all night. Is that what you want? I can wear you down until you're exhausted, asleep at the wheel, and I'll take it and you won't come to for days. Is that what you want?

Polly deleted the Thing's poem, tried again.

HUNGRY FOR MORE

I'm hungry for more
I'll admit only that.
The price of admission:
My lies of omission.

She stopped. It wasn't working. The Thing didn't want to be composing verse; it wanted to be running outside, chasing down prey, quaffing blood and eating meat.

"Ansel?" Polly said, snapping shut the laptop. "Can you tell me something?"

He wrote his message on his board.

WHAT?

"How do you deal with the, you know, cravings?"

DRUGS.

"I won't put myself in a stupor," Polly said. "I simply won't."

Gang of Four sang about anthrax, while Polly dreamed of hunting people.

IT'S NOT LIKE QUITTING CIGARETTES.

"I never smoked," Polly said. "I mean, not for real."

ONLY SO MUCH YOU CAN TAKE.

"The more I fight the Thing, the more it fights me," Polly said. "But if I give up, it wins. If I fight it, it wins."

IT'S A BITCH.

Polly put her hand on her hip, cocked her head at Ansel. "Is that right?"

He cocked an eyebrow and nodded.

WANT TO SEE MAGIC?

"I don't believe in magic," Polly said.

Ansel put down the whiteboard and the marker, held up a finger, and then began to transform, breathing heavily as he did so.

"No, Ansel," Polly said. "Your wounds!"

He looked at her as his skin began to buckle and boil, his tendons throbbing, bones creaking and stretching. The wires in his jaw snapped and sprung, flinging across the room, and screws that had been placed in his jaw as well flew free of his body, hitting the ground with clattering sounds.

Ansel became his bestial self, glossy-furred and monstrous, big blue eyes and gaping jaw, massive teeth.

"Better," he said with a baritone hiss. "Much, much better."

"Oh, my god," Polly said, feeling herself compelled by Ansel's transformation in a manner that concerned her. "You healed your injury?"

He had to crouch to keep from hitting the chandelier, he was that big. How Zooey had managed to fight him at all was a marvel, as he was huge. His claws alone were at least two inches long.

Ansel caressed his jawline, which was restored.

"Amazing," Polly said, reaching up to stroke his face. "Marvelous. Why did you wait?"

"I wasn't ready," Ansel said. "It wasn't ready."

He accepted her hand on his muzzle, let her pet him, her hand in his fur, impossibly pale in that sea of black. Something stirred within her, unbidden. It was the Thing, watching Ansel from behind her eyes.

Gang of Four blared as she gazed up at her beastly boyfriend, sinister, stuttering guitar flaring feedback and swaggering, strutting bass.

The Thing was a bitch forever in heat, could not fail to respond to Ansel this way. He was more than compelling in this form, she admitted to herself, something she had not reckoned with before, had not properly seen.

This was the real Ansel; she could see that, now. What had drawn her to him was precisely this, only glimpsed in his everyday disguise. She had always seen this, the lure of the beast.

He panted before her, arms at his sides, built to rend and tear in a way that was only a ghastly approximation of his apparent Lupine form, but Polly was not afraid. There was comfort and familiarity, here.

Proto-Polly would have felt terror at this thing standing there in her home, hulking and horrible. But she was not now who she had once been. She was Post-Polly.

Her hands traveled across his muscular frame, impossibly large, no trace of the man she had only thought she knew, and as his arms enfolded her, Polly knew him anew, kissed his chest, ran her tongue across it, could see him harden, felt his hands grip her arms almost gingerly, turning her and bending her over her own sofa, his breath on her ear.

The bitch in her blood wanted to fly out of Polly, but she would not let it, refused to release the limbic leash that kept her collared. Instead, she shoved her ass at Ansel as he mounted her, cried out as he entered her.

She was in control, here. Polly, not the Thing. She gave herself to him as herself, though he could tear her apart with a shrug of his shoulders. To be at the mercy of the merciless intoxicated her, this supple surrender to the supernatural, on her own terms, giving herself to her lust, while the Thing within her seethed and raged, demanded to be free, to face him on her own terms.

There would be no such thing. The Thing had stolen kisses from Ansel before, and that usurpation was unforgiveable to Polly. She was in charge, here, not the Thing, and not Ansel. It was Polly.

Pollynomial.

Pollychromatic.

Pollymorphic.

Pollyamorous.

Pollyannaish.

And she showed him as she accepted him inside her, turning her hips and crying out not as an animal, but as a woman. She gave herself to him, and took him entirely for herself.

She loved a man in uniform.

14

There was no power at the BIRE, and from the look of things, it had been decades since there had been. They worked in the dark, cordoned off a working space after Zach had gotten them some lanterns they could set up.

Walking through the old halls, rendered in retro institutional greens and beiges long given over to decay, past the individual cells that were like little vaults, with thick steel doors, past rows of barred cells, the walls scratched, the bars bent.

"I would love to have access to the BIRE files. We had them at the Kennel," Anya said. "I had Mina take what she could. The research back then was more physical—electroshock and what-not, stimulus assessment, that kind of thing. Triggers and so forth."

Most of the equipment was long gone, but the windows with chickenwire within them had still held, kept the place in good condition, despite the decades of disuse.

The architecture of the place spoke to its mission. The proximity of cells to labs, the gurneys with thick leather straps, themselves cracked. And down the hall, the ovens.

"They burned the subjects who died, of course," Anya said. "Couldn't leave any traces."

"Why are we here?" Zach asked.

"We needed a safe place to make our base of operations," Anya said. "This will do. Minton likely has far too much on his mind to worry about the BIRE."

"We can lock ourselves up in here," Zach said, gazing in one of the cells. "When we lose it, I mean."

"Yes," Anya said. "We certainly could."

Zach knew he was going to lose control. He could feel it coming.

"It won't be long," Zach said.

"Why don't you?" Anya asked. "We can observe it."

224 | D.T. NEAL

"No way," Zach said.

Anya sighed, ran a hand through her hair. "I'm talking about a controlled transformation, of course. Most of the time we saw induced ones, or accidental ones. Zooey presented with a willed transformation, a deliberate one. That was the first one of those I saw."

Zach nodded.

"I'd like to see if an infective can maintain sentience in that situation," Anya said. "I know Zooey said, but she was near Patient Zero. How about it, Zachary? Want to try? It's not like we have to worry about you infecting us. Me, I mean."

"Not a chance," Zach said.

"We can't do much good here, anyway," Anya said. "This is a hideout, not a lab."

They had gathered in what would have been the administrative offices of the BIRE, set their lanterns around them. The conspirators, underlit, surrounded by shadow, with only a skylight overhead, and the moon above.

"Action items," Anya said. "Zachary, bring Zooey to heel. I'll try to contact Mina. She's got the data, has done the research. If anybody can find a cure for it, she can. She has the laptop and a ton of data. She's the scientist, and while this is hardly a lab, maybe there's a chance that there's something worth finding in it that we might be able to use."

"You think?" Zach asked.

"I'll work on it, anyway," she said. "There must be something worthwhile in there. But first, I have to find her."

"Right," Zach said. "You should lay low."

Anya could feel the anger boiling up inside her, the infection spreading, fueling her feelings, shaping her thoughts. There was a sliding scale of Anya/Not-Anya, a graph inside her brain that reflected her reality. She knew where she was on the graph, at which point she'd slip into the domain of not-Anya.

And yet, having dug herself from a mass grave, Anya wanted only to have revenge for this. Thanks to her spreading infection, she could not know whether this was the human or inhuman part of her that was driving this thirst for revenge.

She could not let Zachary know that she had these feelings in her. For Zachary, her blood-soaked warrior, it was so commonplace as to be unremarkable. Protocol demanded that Anya throw herself on a pyre and put a halt to the infection, or her portion of it.

So long as she lived, she had her imperatives, her moral requirements. But these clashed with the brute reality of what Sanderson had done to her and her team.

Was it simply wounded pride, or administrative anger at having been sound roundly outmaneuvered? She'd made the call, had acted in good faith, expecting honest outcomes, not arbitrary assassination.

"I want revenge," Anya said.

"I took care of that for you," Zach said.

Zach sighed. He hadn't been able to track Zooey down again since their earlier encounter, and he was afraid that the only way he'd be able to do it would be to give himself over to the infection and become a fucking Lupine, which would then put him at risk of getting popped by one of the sniper teams, or maybe even by his own team. That didn't sit well with him.

Hit squads or not, he intended to carry out his mission, but was having grave doubts about the efficacy of it in the face of the evolving situation. Despite everything they'd been doing, more infectives were appearing, and it was beginning to look like the situation was getting completely out of control, whether or not Minton or anybody else copped to it.

Part of him wanted to simply pack it in and resign, but he figured there'd be some kind of rider on his commission with the Bureau that would require him to remain in service until his administrative leads determined that he could step down.

Or, at the very least, there'd be a confidentiality and nondisclosure agreement he had to sign, where he didn't speak about anything he'd seen while in service.

There was always that route, but, to Zach, that felt like a surrender, and he simply wasn't the type to surrender, regardless of the circumstances. He didn't like the idea of giving up, and so he tabled that and steeled himself to finding Zooey, one way or another, dead or alive. What he would do once he'd bagged her, of course, was almost meaningless in his eyes—would he present her to Minton (who didn't care) or Anya (who couldn't do anything about it).

It was fucked up, and he knew that. It frustrated him, and, magnified as his emotional states were, thanks to the growing infection bursting in his blood, he was feeling it more strongly than ever. There was a way out, he knew. He could throw duty and honor to the ground and give himself over to his infection, become one of them, run wild and spread the disease, which was to give in completely to the evolutionary imperatives of the virus. Or he could stand fast against that particular pathogenic priority and heed the organizational insanity of Homeland Security, keen to cauterize the epidemic before it could spread completely out of control—in case it hadn't, already.

That was the thing: to Zach, despite their efforts, they were sweeping back the sea. The infection was spreading past their firewalls. Princess had found a way to bypass the standard routes of transmission, and until they figured that out, they would always be playing defense, would always be playing catch-up ball with Zooey.

He was the triggerman, he was the professional; she was the amateur. But, somehow, she had found some way to elude the authorities and to propagate her cause—that's how he saw it, clearly—and advance it.

Maybe that had been his mistake. He had been trying to resist the infection, trying to resist becoming one of them. Maybe what he needed to do was to become one of them, so he could become the perfect assassin, could slip into the pack and get close to Princess and deliver the deathblow.

There was an incendiary logic to it, an incandescent inspiration that might make it not the most half-assed of ideas he'd ever considered.

Anya watched Zach wallow in his own mire of concern and duty and responsibility. To her, it was simply a matter of medicine—this epidemic was like any other, and what mattered was getting ahead of the organism, finding its borders, the places where it could not or would not go, and surrounding it with those barriers, and then using them to shut the thing down.

The others had their own agendas, their own priorities, but for Anya, it was a simple matter of containment. And the only real containment for this epidemic was finding a vaccine for it. Yes, she lacked the resources for it, but she understood that you could treat the symptoms of a disease indefinitely, but what mattered was finding a cure for it.

Zach could not deliver a cure for it; Mina could, at least in theory. Anya had to find Mina, no matter what.

As it happened, Mina called Anya. Her cell rang and Anya answered.

"Where have you been?" Anya asked.

"Where have *you* been?" Mina replied.

"Sanderson killed me," Anya said. "Or thought he did, anyway. He killed everyone at the Kennel. There's a mass grave downstate. Where are you, Mina?"

"I'm safe," Mina said. "That's all that matters."

"Zachary and I are at Blue Island," Anya said, not quite caring if anybody was eavesdropping.

"Why?" Mina asked.

"We had to go somewhere," Anya said. "I didn't trust going home. Troy Minton's in charge at the BEE, now. They're operating at the Water Treatment Plant, because Sanderson had shut down the Kennel after the attack."

Anya heard Mina working it out in her head.

"Are you showing symptoms?" Mina asked.

Anya chewed on that thought a bit before swallowing. "Are you?"

"Not yet," Mina said. "I don't think so."

"Minton will be looking for you as surely as Sanderson was."

"Was?"

"Sanderson's dead," Anya said, glancing at Zach, who shrugged sheepishly.

"I can cure it," Mina said. "I know I can."

"Right," Anya said. "You already said that it impacts several areas on the genome."

"Yes, yes," Mina said. "I'm going to stop this."

Anya and Zach just looked at each other like Mina was insane, this blend of contempt and bemusement that Mina would find infuriating, had she been there.

"You don't believe me," Mina said, and, bizarrely, Anya felt her nether self chafing at the prospect of curing the affliction. Of all people, the infection that wanted lay claim to her soul was the very thing that was spurring her to put the lie to her peers, to show them that, yes, she could create the cure for their affliction.

Anya understood that her own judgment was impaired. As an infective, she could not trust her own appraisal of her situation, but she was resolute in her determination to beat this thing that was besetting them all. She hoped Mina felt the same way.

"It's not a matter of belief," Anya said. "We just don't have the resources here."

"A theoretical model is still a workable tool," Mina said.

Mina would not give the last laugh to Zooey, who had tricked her. That the girl had so effortlessly betrayed her, caught her off-guard in that manner; she should have been better than that. That the girl had managed to sideswipe her the way she did had cost Mina considerably, in terms of her own view of herself, to say nothing of what it cost the Kennel.

She wanted to make amends for that lapse, and that meant finding a fix for this epidemic. A vaccine would render everything that Zooey had done moot. A vaccine would put an end to the lycanthropic revolution before it had even begun.

"Naturally," Anya said. "Supernaturally, I should say."

"Fuck semantics," Zach said. "I'm sick to death of them."

"I will cure us," Mina said. "I will make this right. I need to get to Wolf Island. Or at least Atlanta."

She could see their caring for her, in their different ways. Anya, like a sister-mother, and Zach like a brother, in a way. He got it, got her. They got each other.

"Maybe if something bubbles up in that brain of yours, we can make use of it," Anya said.

Mina didn't like how Anya thought about it, but, at heart, she was right. The larger, worthier goal was to put an end to this infection. It meant isolating the nature of the virus, inhibiting its ability to override the host's genes and triggering an infective transformation whose sole purpose was propagation of the infection.

That's where the infectives were getting confused. They saw everything in terms of their own lives, their own experience. The virus was simply using them as a means of spreading itself. Everything else was subordinate to the overriding goal of propagation. The virus wanted (as much as it wanted anything) to be spread far afield.

It didn't care how; it only knew that it wanted to be spread, and modified its hosts to be able to infect as effectively as possible. For all of the attendant horrors associated with the claws and fangs of the Lupine form, it was merely the most expedient means the virus had for increasing its likelihood of infecting potential hosts.

Ears to hear, a nose to smell prey, teeth to bite and infect; claws to rend and infect, and a means to heal to ensure that the vector would be able to infect more hosts again.

It was a marvelous adaptation. Whatever the Nazis had done to magnify the virulence of the pathogen, however narrow their focus, the core of it was marvelously adapted to spreading the disease. For an unthinking thing, a mindless pinpoint of protein, the virus was sublimely suited for virulence. Everything they had experienced to date was reflective of this.

That she was trying to find a cure for it, even as it was rewriting her body to suit its own ends, was itself significant to Mina. Anya and Zach approached it as a problem to be solved, but to Mina, the retrovirus was operating at another level. That was the place where she sought to fight it. At some point, she would be unable to conduct her research, but until that line had been crossed, Mina intended to find a fix for it.

"We won't have long," Mina said. "Sooner or later, one of us will succumb. And when that happens, all bets are off. Maybe we'll attack each other, or maybe we'll go off into the darkness and attack anybody we see. Maybe we'll join Princess."

"We'll stay out of your way," Anya said. "How about that? Zachary and I both have our respective tasks; we'll leave you to your work, Mina, and will only check in when we have something worthwhile to report."

"Fine," Mina said. "I only want to cure us. All of us. We should stay remote from each other, I think. Just to be safe."

"We know," Anya said. Zach only looked on, wordless, like a Sphinx.

PART FOUR

Troy Minton looked over his kill counts. Something was going wrong, and he was unable to account for it. He had lost 75% of his kill teams over the past few weeks, and he understood that the Lupines were actively targeting them, and not simply infecting them, but actively killing them.

Nobody knew who had killed Phil Sanderson, and none of the surveillance tech they had in place had shown a thing out of place. Somebody on the inside had gotten to Sanderson and had murdered him. Minton had instituted a mandatory check on all of the remaining staff, just in case Princess had some agent operating in their ranks.

It had been a source of frustration, because clearly the things were getting smarter. His kill teams had dispatched over 750 infectives in Chicago alone. That was a higher kill rate than anybody else had garnered in the other cities. But it had not been enough. The epidemic was continuing to spread, and he was both at a loss as to how to account for this and also how to deal with it, and was the last person in the world who would communicate this confusion up the pipeline. He didn't want to see some other striver getting his post; Minton understood exactly how good a deal he had, and was loathe to give it up.

He sat in his office in the situation center, where the data was showing that the infectives had managed to bypass his firewall, and, if anything, were growing their numbers. It was one thing to be able to consign a top-secret government facility to an unmarked grave. Sanderson had understood this. But he could not take all of these new infectives and scoop them up and drop them into yet another unmarked grave. People would ask questions, would want to know what had happened to their loved ones. Sanderson had overstepped himself, and somebody had gotten him because of it.

And he was not confident in his superiors' ability to insulate him from the consequences of his own actions. He feared reprisals, whether from enraged infectives, outraged relatives of the disappeared, or the umbrage of his superiors. One way or another, it was going to come his way. He was operating in a kind of shadow world, outside of the realm of proper law and order, on the path Sanderson had paved.

In the face of this, Minton kept his composure, kept adhering to the mandate he had been issued, kept his kill counts high, raised his kill quotas, kept the disposal teams busy, had a constant pipeline in place, to ensure that, destination unknown, the bodies kept going through the system, so that he could offer rosy reports to his deniable superiors, who cloaked themselves in procedural camouflage that enabled them to take the credit for successes while leaving him to shoulder the blame.

Minton felt the weight of his predecessors' plights in this, the need to show progress even when progress was proving to be elusive. Princess was infecting people on a scale that nobody could yet account for, least of all his shooters. Nobody saw, and nobody knew. He'd had his scrubbers look through the Kennel data, trying to find something he could use, but nobody yet knew, nobody had connected the dots. The missing Dr. Milkowski had been the closest to it, and she was nowhere to be found. Minton had dispatched two Wardens to keep 24/7 surveillance on her home, and she hadn't turned up.

With this nipping at his heels, Minton was feeling the heat. It had become standard for him to heft that ingot of silver with him, to press it into the palms of his subordinates, halfway-hoping for one of them to wince at the sizzle of silver in his palm.

If he could net himself a scapegoat, he could pin the blame on that hapless soul's shoulders, and buy himself some time. He was convinced that if he only had enough time and enough firepower, he could put an end to this epidemic, and let the Administration rest easy. More money, more manpower, and he'd be able to quash this infective insurgency.

That's how he saw it, and rightly so. He understood where the money was coming from, and what the expectations were. For him to fail at this was unthinkable, and he wasn't even factoring in the costs in terms of public health; he was only thinking of himself.

Minton sat in his office, processing the numbers, the kill counts, the losses to his own men, and forecasting what he needed to make things right.

That most of his kill teams had, themselves, been killed, caused him no end of uneasiness. These weren't new recruits; they had been seasoned professionals, impeccably trained. For them to have fallen to the infectives made him worry more than a little. If his best weren't good enough, where did that leave him, exactly, in terms of staffing?

His intercom sounded. It was Elissa, his receptionist. "Houndstooth is here to see you, Sir."

"Very well," Minton said. "Send him in."

He was glad at least Zach's team had survived. They were one of the last teams still out there in force. Zach had a good instinct for this work. Minton thought he should bring him in from fieldwork and have him train new shooters. That made all kinds of sense.

Zach came in, looking like his usual careworn self, took a seat in one of the chairs across from his desk, looked up at him, without a word.

"What is it, Zach?" Minton asked. "Something happen?"

"Anya's escaped," Zach said.

"What? I thought Sanderson had liquidated her."

Minton felt his blood chill at the very idea of it. He didn't agree with what Sanderson had done, but orders were orders. She was a witness, now.

"You've seen her?"

Zach nodded.

"Where?"

"At her place," Zach said. "I was set up on a rooftop in Bucktown, and that's where her place was. I didn't think it was her, but I looked with my scope. It was."

Troy's mind was reeling.

"She must have gotten out of the Joliet facility somehow," Zach said.

"Yeah, I guess so," Minton said. "Why didn't you call it in?"

Zach sat back in the chair, looking Minton in the eye, trying to gauge the man's reaction. Minton gave exactly nothing away, steepled his fingers before his face, elbows on his desk.

"I wasn't sure that was the kind of thing you wanted broadcast on the radio," Zach said.

"You're right," Minton said. "Thanks for showing some discretion."

Zach watched Minton processing this information, saw the wheels turning. He decided to tweak the man a bit.

"Maybe I should go down to the Joliet facility? See how this happened?"

"No," Minton said. "I need you up here; you're my best man out there. What was she doing at her condo?"

Zach made as if to try to recall, squinted a bit.

"Just seemed to be packing up some stuff," Zach said. "She was hunkered down in there, but definitely had a suitcase. And a laptop."

"And this was?"

"Last night," Zach said. "Last shift."

"You're a good man, West," Minton said. "I'll look into this. Good work. Go get some rest."

Zach got up. "I can help you, if you need it."

"No, I've got it," Minton said. "Thanks, West."

Minton watched him go, tried to compose himself in private. He'd read Sanderson's report, had seen how thorough the man had been. How Anya managed to get out of the pit was anybody's guess. The woman was nothing if not stubborn, but the prospect of her actually having gotten out of there and trekking back to Chicago, of all places? It showed serious determination on her part. What was she up to?

It didn't matter. She was infected, and on top of surviving a massacre that wasn't supposed to have had any witnesses, she was a danger.

He wasn't about to let her skip town. Not with what she carried in her head, to say nothing of what she carried in her blood, now. It wasn't like she could run somewhere and implicate anybody; he was protected higher than his pay grade by big players who had more than a little skin in the game. But it could be embarrassing if she went public with it, and she knew where the bodies were buried. All the same, she was a biohazard, now, too. Minton could call down the thunder upon her.

He flipped his intercom switch, told Elissa that he'd be out the rest of the afternoon. Then he took a chromed Walther PPK out of his desk, loaded it with a clip of silver bullets, slipped it into his coat pocket, and looked up Anya's address on the computer.

Bucktown.

Zooey chased down the Segway tourists on a whim. In the light of everything that had been going down in the city, seeing a dozen people wearing day-glo vests and helmets, puttering along on their Segways was too much to bear.

She saw them near the Art Institute in mid-afternoon, practicing their moves in Grant Park, driving in circles, and in columns and lines.

Seeing this, in the mood she was in, Zooey could not stomach it. She had taken to wearing clothes she couldn't give a shit about as a way of being able to transform without feeling like she was leaving something nice behind. That meant that she'd been going thrift-store shopping lately, picking out stacks of dresses and slacks and tops for cheap.

It made her happy, knowing that she could turn at any given moment, and not sweat the details. She never carried a wallet or a purse; the only thing she left behind was her pink suitcase that was still up in Winnetka with pretty Polly. She would eventually go back for it, once she got her nerve up, and pay Polly back.

But seeing those Segway tourists just brought it out in her, had Zooey transform under cover of some bushes and emerge, snarling, chasing down the Segway tourists.

Somebody had seen Zooey charging for them, as they yelled and pointed, and one of the Segway tourists looked over his shoulder, gaped at seeing this big, white wolf-thing racing for them, cranked up the throttle and puttered along.

Zooey could see the warning travel up the line, as each rider looked over their shoulder and reacted to the sight by accelerating, the Segways purring as she panted after them, charging, clawed feet devouring distance.

She wanted to laugh, watching these human lollipops scoot up the street; she barely had to work to even overtake them. Of the 12 riders, seven were women. Zooey simply ran up to them and bit each one of them on the leg, marveling how they would tilt one way as she attacked, only to pop back up, thanks to the gyroscopes, and then they would stumble and fall, thanks to Zooey's attack.

Zooey simply shouldered into the guys piloting their Segways, knocking them aside, forcing them to dodge. She scattered the Segway tourists effortlessly, then ran into the park, while people on their lunch breaks pointed and looked and snapped photos with their phone cameras.

Zooey had wanted to kill the tour leader, but didn't want to risk lingering, since it was broad daylight and it was crowded downtown, and there were already police sirens sounding somewhere, probably for her, and sure to be snipers around.

She raced into the park, which, downtown, was hardly thick and woodsy enough to offer a great white werewolf much in the way of camouflage, but she ran past Millennium Park, where there were some clusters of trees and massive hedges that could screen her from most observers.

When the bullet tore through the ground, missing her by inches, Zooey understood at once that the same qualities that made this a good place to evade scrutiny also made it a prime sniper's nest.

She abruptly started zig-zagging, scenting the air to try to track where the shooter was, training her ears for anything that was out of the ordinary.

Zooey heard a chuffing sound that she understood well enough, now—the sound of a silenced rifle—the bullet struck near one of her paws, missing by millimeters. Zooey tried to zero in on where that shot had come from, and triangulated it to an oak tree near some unused tennis courts.

Glancing upward, she saw that a man in camouflage had set up a roost for himself up there, a full 20 feet off the ground, upwind, in a tree blind. Smart man, reminded Zooey of her brothers and her father, back in Wisconsin.

She dove for the base of the tree, putting the tree between herself and him, and turned herself into the hybrid form, the she-beast, and clawed her way up the tree, hoping that this man didn't have teammates on other nearby trees, since she could not dodge or maneuver well while scaling a tree.

She could hear the man talking into his radio.

"Tagteam, this is Nimrod Six," he said. "I've got Princess inbound in under a mike. Repeat, Princess inbound. Need backup."

Zooey leaped into the forked tree branches, where Nimrod Six had placed his little sniper post, and batted away the man's rifle as he'd turned to shoot her. She moved so quickly, it was like he was a statue.

The man, to his credit, didn't beg or cry out. He drew a silver dagger from his belt and tried to stab Zooey, a short, quick, underhanded jab, but Zooey caught his hand in hers and turned it, causing the man anguish as she broke the hand with a savage twist that cracked bone and snapped ligaments and tendons, rending muscle.

She caught the man with her jaws, under his chin, and snapped hard, watching his head come right off, landing in the tennis courts below with one bloody bounce. Then she took a few big bites out of him, spitting out his camouflage clothes as she chewed. A nonsmoker, he tasted fit and delicious: good, fresh meat.

While she ate, she listened on the radio, could hear the other sniper teams responding.

"Come in, Nimrod Six, Over," the radio said. "We have three men inbound in 5 mikes."

Zooey left a crescent-shaped hole in the man before shoving him out of his perch. His body caught on the tall chain-link fencing that surrounded the tennis courts, and it hung upside down at the waist, like she'd draped him over the fencing, while blood rained down on the weathered clay courts.

She knew what to smell for, the telltale tang of silver. She jumped out of the tree, landing in some bushes nearby, while Nimrod Six's body bled out on the tennis court, with only his severed head to bear silent witness, eyes open, mouth agape. His death had come so quickly, was he seeing it, even now?

As a white wolf in daylight, Zooey understood her disadvantage, slipped into the foliage nearby. Without any snow falling, it was particularly dicey.

She caught wind of the strike team. They were approaching from the north, had set themselves up in a triangular pattern, widely dispersed, a fairly standard approach. That tended to be how the shooters went, as it gave them a chance to cover one another. She watched them from the screening cover of the yew bushes she'd hidden within.

Even as fast as she was, she doubted she could take all three of them before one of them got a shot off at her, and she felt that these men were good enough shots that one of them would be able to carry it off.

But the thrill of that uncertainty meant that she had to try. She understood that at some point, her luck might run out, and she would finally get tagged. Breaks of the game, as she saw it. To the victor went the spoils. After Black Sheep's betrayal, though, Zooey found that she didn't give that much of a shit. There were things to fret about, and things to deal with.

The men were carefully approaching their fallen peer's nest, moving very carefully, ears attuned to everything around them.

Zooey watched them, thinking that she could have slunk off and evaded these men, and they'd be none the wiser. But the man had called her "Princess" on his radio. They had known her, had named her. She couldn't disappoint them.

Hit-and-run was the most logical attack method, here. Catch them while they were still reacting to their peer's condition.

"Fuck," one of them said. "Six is a mess, Lodge."

Zooey sprang at the nearest one, whose back was turned to her. She bit him in half, wasted no time hurling herself at the second man, who was on one side of the black chain-link fencing. Him, she slammed into the fence, knocking him off his feet, even as she charged the third man, the one who'd been on the radio.

He had seen her coming, pivoted to try to crease her with an assault rifle, the silenced gun firing silver bullets, a spray of them tearing up the ground beside Zooey. She was on him a half-second later, and actually took his head into her mouth and snapped it off him in one bite, reversing direction in a mid-air pivot where she used the man's falling body as a kind of springboard, throwing herself back in the direction of the man at the fence, who was only now finding his feet again.

Zooey spat out his teammate's head at the gunman, the thing catching him in the chest with a thump that took the wind out of him. He had dropped his assault rifle when she'd slammed him into the fence, and Zooey could see him looking at it, and at her, trying to decide if he had the time to reach for it.

The man was older than Zooey, but still young, wearing woodsy camouflage. He had a helmet strapped to his head, like his peers, and what looked to be some kind of flip-down nightvision goggles.

"You know how many of my pack your men have shot?" Zooey said, relishing the man's terror at being spoken to in this manner, by such a creature. The man gaped at her, adrenaline shakes going up against his training and experience.

"We're just doing our jobs," the man said, drawing a silver knife from his belt, a long blade.

"I used to just maim and infect you guys," Zooey said. "No more. Now, I'm playing for keeps. You see your pals?"

The man glanced at the bodies of his buddies, and at his rifle, and at Zooey. "That's going to be you."

They didn't need to say more, and, to his credit, the man didn't beg or plead; instead, he dropped hard to the ground, in the direction of his assault rifle, using the knife for defense, just as Zooey jumped for him. Fast as the man was, Zooey was simply faster. She was blessed with this gift of speed, and she took the man by the throat and shook him hard, hearing his neck snap, and she took a bite out of his throat, just to be extra-thorough.

He died instantly, blood gushing from him. She tossed him aside with a turn of her head, and stalked around the kill site, bloody-muzzled, pleased at her work. One less kill team to worry about, as far as she was concerned.

Not that Zooey was worried; she was long past worrying. She wanted to enjoy herself, to really cut loose.

She ran across the park, toward Lake Shore Drive, toward Lake Michigan, bounded across traffic, gratified by the squealing tires and honking horns as people strove to dodge her or to gape at her as she passed. Zooey loved to remind the norms that monstrosity stalked the streets of their city.

In three easy leaps she cleared Lake Shore Drive and was in the park, while cars were crashing into one another in reaction to the sight of her.

Then she ran north, along the strip of green that was the park here, headed toward Navy Pier, where the Ferris Wheel was. She ran along the bike path, where joggers and bikers gasped and screamed at the sight of her, charging along, or where they just looked at her in mute awe.

Not wanting to get bogged down here, but still with her grand plan in mind, Zooey took swipes at the women she saw, taking a bite here, a bite there. Little infections, just appetizers, but they would grow and spread.

The scent of fear intoxicated her, the taste of terror. She saw that there was a chokepoint up ahead, a bottleneck where the bike path crossed a bridge, went over the river. She charged through there, pleased to see the bikers and joggers blanch and give way as she went through, her white fur covered red with blood.

Clearing the bridge, she cut to the right, went back into the strip of green that counted as a park, screened by trees and a wall, Navy Pier looming, brightly lit. She loped in that direction, mindful that she had water on one side of her, and highway and city to the other, and, were she more cautious, she might have worried that she'd trapped herself.

But Zooey didn't feel trapped; she understood that if anybody actually tried to stand in her way, she'd tear them apart.

She bounded out of the park, past the public art (she took a moment to relieve herself on one of the pieces, a giant fire hydrant, counting on her contribution to turn it into a piece of performance art, hoping that some terrified tourists had captured that with a camera), and then she ran into Navy Pier, actually taking a moment to push the handicapped entrance door opener.

Let's see a coywolf do that, Bitches, she thought.

Then she ran in as the doors opened, could smell the food from chain restaurants and the assorted scents of commerce throughout, saw chubby suburbanites in sweatshirts and baseball caps gaping at her, arms laden with bags.

It was Christmas time, after all, shopping season. Hunting season.

Zooey ran through the lower concourse, biting the women as she went, slashing and savaging them, killing none, infecting all. The workers in their rolling sales carts, peddling baubles and trinkets, like Gypsies in the Old World, perhaps, she bit the women there, too.

The whole place was a long strip of stores, confining, without leaving anybody much place to run. Even the stores weren't overlarge. It was a one big, fat buffet.

And Zooey sank her teeth into every thick, suburban slab of woman-thigh, every pudgy hand or forearm, set those double chins wagging as the women shrieked and fished out their pepper spray or tried to defend themselves from her teeth.

One woman even pulled a pistol from her purse, a pink pistol, an automatic, and fired shots at Zooey, which really put people into an all-out panic, the din of the firearm deafening in the close confines of Navy Pier.

Not wanting to trust to chance, that maybe this women hadn't picked up silver bullets somewhere, Zooey sidestepped her shots until she clamped down on the woman's shooting arm and sniffed the gunpowder stink, found the dull scent of lead, not the painful aroma of silver.

She shook hard on the woman's arm as the woman shrieked, punching at Zooey's muzzle. The woman did have on silver rings, and so Zooey felt a couple of those blows, let go with a bark, let the woman nurse her ravaged arm in peace.

Then Zooey ran into a burger joint, which was packed with panicking people, and made herself a happy meal of every woman she could reach in the store, although the norms were in full flight, now, were trampling each other trying to get away from her, running through the outside doors, hysterical.

Zooey stalked through the food court, finding spiritual nourishment in the terror she was creating. It was so easy to frighten people, so satisfying to see their faces creased by chaos, broken by bedlam. She was a true terrorist, now.

Navy Pier's security had been called, and there were uniformed men running in Zooey's wake, calling on radios, riding her way on souped-up Segways, with laughably thick tires.

Zooey did not want to linger, but, instead, took off running deeper into the place, following it to its end, wanting to go to the very end of the pier, itself, despite the risk.

She ran through, everything blurring around her, until she came to the end of it, where a ballroom sat empty, where there was no more pier, and only a great anchor, a host of flags, and the churning, chopping waves.

Zooey smashed her way through the glass doors and went outside to see, to taste the fresh air. Out here, the wintery wind was abominably strong, tearing at her, and the waves surged. This was wilderness, right there in the faces of the norms.

Waves crashed, and Zooey, warmed by her fur coat and her own dire condition, welcomed it. Wave after wave, a mindless crashing din, elemental explosions, wearing down the pier. She wondered if she could drown, or if the lycanthropy protected her from such a mundane fate. It was a strange and morbid musing, unbecoming to her carnival spirit, but facing the roaring waves and howling wind, Zooey wondered just the same.

She raised her head and howled, fully voiced her feelings, made the windows shake. At the edge, here, there were no norms; they

244 | D.T. NEAL

stayed safe within the bowels of the pier, enclosed, clutching close the things they most certainly didn't need.

Zooey stalked around the edge of the pier, into the wind shadow of the building, knowing that the huffing, puffing security men would be coming soon, since she'd left them in the dust, and none of them really wanted to face her down, anyway.

She could hear sirens, could see the red and the blue, the fire trucks, the police cruisers, the ambulances, the security Segways, flashing lights and clarion calls.

She had given them something to talk about, gave them a memorable taste of Chicago.

Out here, the air was sweet, the wind danced across her face and she felt at home. For all of her urban renewal efforts, there was something in this call of the wild, this siren's song of storm and wave that spoke deeply to the thing she had become.

Zooey did not want to charge back down the way she'd come, back into the noise and the screaming and the inevitable gunfire. It could be that she had sated herself for the moment, wanted to settle down and slumber, for she had never known herself to avoid a confrontation.

Instead, answering her wolfish whims, she ran across the pier and dove into the wild waters of the lake, landing with a monstrous splash, and swam across it to a spit of wildness, a bit of undeveloped beach that was near the water reclamation plant, where, unbeknownst to her, Sanderson had set up his Homeland Security operation.

She swam through the chilly waters, washed the blood from her body, and bounded up on the beach, shook herself dry, savored the cold and the wind and the wet. There was oneness she felt in this that defied anything she had yet experienced.

Zooey had been so caught up in her war on humanity that she'd forgotten to take in the scenery. Across the lake was Michigan, and that made her think of Detroit. Detroit was a place that could fully belong to the lycanthropes. She wondered if Black Sheep had gone there. He was a Michigander, and like all Michiganders, talked ceaselessly about Michigan.

She could easily imagine him claiming Detroit for himself, going through there and making that place his own.

The scent of silver distracted her from her daydreams, and made her turn around, looking, nosing her way around, ears pricked.

The norms hadn't seen her jump into the water; nobody knew where she'd gone, which was for the best, in her view. Let them wonder and fear the specter of her, let the SWAT teams and whatever else they had go skulking through the mall, looking for her to pop out of the shadows.

That degree of distraction was all she needed, as she slipped down this neighboring jut of land, devoid of people, following the stink of silver, finding a gunman on a radio, eyes skinned in the direction of Navy Pier, confidently informing his superiors that he'd be able to bag the bitch when she got out of the pier, that he and Nexus had the place covered.

They did not know that Zooey had outflanked them. They crouched by some chain-link fencing and bushes, most definitely did have Navy Pier under surveillance, past the flash of lights and the panicked mass of shoppers, these two hunters waited, tuned to their radios, not knowing that death was creeping up behind them.

Zooey had always been fortunate in her rampages; it was almost as if because there was no hesitation in her, she was able to fully enjoy and benefit from her lycanthropy in ways that more conflicted souls could not.

There was no gloating, no taunting or posturing. Not with these men, this pair of hunters, rifles at the ready. They were killers as surely as she was.

Zooey jumped them both, grabbing them by the head with her claws, snapping both their necks with her strong hands. Then she nipped off their heads and, in a bit of wicked whimsy, swapped their heads, put one on the other's body.

She backed away, surveyed her handiwork, saw two dead men already prone, crouching by their rifles, their heads awkwardly propped on their lifeless, twitching shoulders. Zooey could hardly wait for their teammates to see it.

Then Zooey ran along the fencing, away from the noise of Navy Pier, watching as the tree-lined area widened into some kind of chunk of trees, thick enough that one could not see through it. Perhaps it was a bird sanctuary or something, a peaceful, natural place.

Zooey jumped the fence and slipped into this patch of trees, scented her way through it, and, for a moment, could pretend she was not even in a big city, but could pretend she was in wilderness once more.

She found a place in the heart of these trees, were no man traveled, where she could be fully screened from prying eyes, and she did something she had not yet done as a werewolf: she fell asleep, sated, spent, and satisfied, having fully indulged the dark spirit that had infected her.

Polly ran her hands on Ansel's jawline, which had completely healed. They were in bed, Ansel eyeing her with sidelong amusement as he flipped through channels.

"I can't believe how quickly you heal," she said.

"We all do," he said. "The transformation heals, somehow. I'm not complaining."

Ansel was back to his beautiful, masculine self again, like a block of Italian marble, there in her bed.

She had been barely able to stand after Ansel had taken her in the living room, but now she was alright.

"What would happen if I shot myself?" Polly said.

"Provided it wasn't silver, you'd be okay," Ansel said.

Polly liked silver, didn't appreciate a life without it.

"Gold and platinum are still okay, right?"

Ansel nodded, laughing to himself, like it had been some sort of idiot question. "Only silver is trouble."

"I wonder what it does?" Polly ask. "Why it's lethal?"

"Who cares?" Ansel said. He'd stopped on the local news, which spoke of a coywolf attack along the lake shore and Navy Pier, particularly savage. Dozens of people had been injured. Eyewitnesses cried on-camera, talked of a white coywolf running through the place, biting everybody who had gotten in reach.

"When are they going to do something about this?" a fat man in a baseball cap wanted to know. "We need somebody to do something."

"Zooey," Ansel said. "Up to her bullshit again."

Polly rested her had on Ansel's chest, looked on. "Should we do something about it?"

"Yeah," Ansel said.

Zooey had stirred up the hornet's nest so much that Ansel doubted he'd ever be able to get the place back to normal. Even if he and Polly went after Zooey, Ansel didn't think it would make much of a difference; she'd done too much damage, had worked too hard to fuck things up in the city for it ever to fully recover. He could only imagine how much the Mayor was sweating the loss of tourist dollars as the footage of the bloodbath in Navy Pier got shown.

"Coywolves," Polly said. "That's what they're saying?"

Ansel shrugged. "Better than wolfyotes, I guess."

"That sounds like a snack," Polly said.

The newspeople said that over 200 people had been bitten by the animal, which had not been caught nor located, although authorities were continuing to investigate.

Polly got out her laptop and checked her Twitter feed, and, sure enough, people were losing their shit about it.

WEREWOLF. MOTHERFUCKING WEREWOLF.

I SAW IT. IT LOOKED RIGHT AT ME.

THING OPENED A DOOR, MAN.

IT ONLY BIT THE WOMEN. I DIDN'T SEE ANY MAN GET BIT.

FUCKING WEREWOLVES. THEY ARE EVERYWHERE.

I'M ONE.

DID YOU SEE THE NEWS? WOLF ATTACK. AGAIN.

ONLY WOMEN GOT BITTEN.

DOWN THE BIKE PATH, TOO.

SEGWAY TOURISTS WERE ATTACKED.

WOMEN.

ILLUMINATI!!!!!!!!!!!!

ALIENS. THEY ARE ALIENS.

BUSH MAKING THIS UP. ELECTION YEAR.

WEREWOLVES.

Polly looked up. "They're tweeting it, alright. I think Zooey's only going after women, now. By the sound of it, I mean."

Ansel understood what she was up to, he got it. "She's reducing the risk of competition. If she targets only women, she ensures that she's the alpha female when everybody manifests. She brings too many males into it, and one of them is either going to unseat her or else force her to split the city."

"Werewolf male chauvinists?" Polly said.

"Hierarchies do come into it with lycanthropy." Ansel said. "Even more so, because you have the human tendency toward hierarchy and you have the Lupine hierarchical impulse, as well. And the males are bigger, what can I say?"

Polly could only imagine how that all shook out between lycan-thropes. Bloodily, she presumed.

"That's why she took you out," Polly said.

"Tried to," Ansel said.

Ansel hated to think of himself as a kind of exile from Chicago, would not stay safe up in Winnetka when he had his place in Wicker Park, his life there. He wasn't going to let Zooey think that she could actually run him out of town. Yes, she'd gotten the drop on him before, but it had been more his fault than her triumph, in that he'd underestimated her, hadn't thought she'd bring her pack into it.

He felt confident that, were they to cross paths again, the outcome would be different. Ansel didn't think it was simply his wounded pride telling him this. She was a noob; it was absurd to think that a lifetime member could be displaced by the new kid on the block.

"You aren't thinking about getting back at her, are you?" Polly asked.

"Yeah," Ansel said. "All my stuff is down there. Who is she to kick me out of my own town?"

Polly immediately worried. She liked knowing that they were, at least for now, safe up at her place. With the insurance money coming in from Tristan's death, she could live comfortably for the end of her days.

"You can move up here," Polly said. "You can move your studio here."

"My gallery's in Wicker Park," Ansel said. "My life is down there."

"Your life can be here," Polly said. "With me."

Ansel didn't like to think of himself as a suburbanite, although he thought the prospect of setting up a gallery in Winnetka, with all the well-heeled would-be art patrons there, perhaps could pay off. It wasn't even that he needed that; Ansel did art because he was able to, not because he actually needed the money.

He had picked Polly, that was true. When he'd crossed paths with her and Sam, she'd been the one, even though Sam had been the one he'd slept with that night, and, ultimately, infected, Polly had been the one he wanted.

In a way, it was for the best that Sam had infected Polly. Had it been Ansel who'd done it, it would have created a breach of trust between them that might have been hard for him to mend. As it was, he had become something of a bridge between the life she had and the life she was going to have, and that put him in a better place.

And she would be the only girlfriend he'd had who actually, for real, knew just what he was from the start. She would go into it with eyes wide open.

Some of his girlfriends had found out what he was, and that had been bad. Most of the time they just thought he was skipping out on them, didn't even guess what he really was. Those were the lucky ones. The less fortunate ones actually discovered what he was. One of them was institutionalized, another had committed suicide. One had tried to call the police, had barricaded herself in his bathroom, dialed 911. Ansel had turned himself human again, had met the cops, had told them that she'd had some kind of psychotic breakdown. It had been awkward, the cops managing to talk her out of there, walking her out, while she gazed at him with pinwheel eyes and quivering lips, and Ansel gaslighting the hell out of her, acting like nothing untoward had even happened. He'd not wanted to do that, but he had no choice—what was he going to do, blow his cover?

That's what made Zooey's rampage so irritating; that bitch had blown the lid off of everything. She was trying her damnedest to get the norms to pay attention to her, to accept the reality of their condition; but nobody wanted to think of themselves as prey, least of all the norms. It didn't sit well with them, and they'd fight back hard to try to reassert themselves, to try to put themselves at the top of the food chain again.

"We still have Zooey's suitcase, don't we?" Ansel said.

"Yes," Polly said.

"She'll come for it, eventually," Ansel said.

"For that thing? What's even in it that should matter that much to her?"

Ansel smiled. "You mean you haven't looked? It doesn't matter; it's the spirit of it. You drove her out of here. It means she'll be back. She won't let that kind of thing sit."

"We should throw it out," Polly said. "That would really piss her off."

Ansel got out of bed, stretched. "Where is it? I want to see what's in there."

The two of them got dressed and Polly fished out the pink Samsonite while Ansel went into the basement and brought up a pry bar from Tristan's workshop.

"This should do it," Ansel said, after Polly checked to be sure that, yes, it was locked. It took some doing, but Ansel eventually cracked the thing open, and they went through Zooey's stuff.

There was an eclectic blend of clothes, mostly t-shirts and jeans and skirts of odd and mismatched quality, a welter of patterned and distressed couture, piles of tube socks, brightly striped at the top. Bras and panties, every one of them animal patterns—tiger, giraffe, zebra, leopard, cheetah, snake, crocodile.

"She sure likes her animal patterns," Ansel said.

There was a laptop, and there was a diary. The diary was thick, leatherbound, red.

"Ooh," Polly said. "Treasure."

Ansel turned on the laptop, which was not password-protected, he was surprised to see. "She's not the most cautious of souls, for sure."

Polly paged through her diary, fascinated despite herself. She never would have broken into the case, even after Zooey had attacked her in her own home. There was a violation of protocol in doing that which struck her as beyond the pale, but Ansel had no such problem with that kind of impropriety, and after he'd done that, Polly's curiosity compelled her to nose through it.

5 November 2007

Samantha's totally a werewolf. Her wicked video, people don't believe it, but I totally do. It's her. It's for real. It's the most real thing I've ever seen, and I'm totally going to see her. I've already bought the ticket. Can't fucking wait. I'm going to get her to infect me. One way or another, it's happening. It's like the ultimate body piercing, right? Fuck everything else. I'm going to Chicago to GET MADE.

6 November 2007

Mom's whining about the college thing again, wanting me to go back to Madison, square it all up. Fuck that noise. Come on, like for real? College, Ma? We're talking lycanthropy, here. Hello? I'm gonna major in Damage, Ma, with a concentration in Mayhem.

WEREWOLF
EREWOLFW
REWOLFWE
EWOLFWER
WOLFWERE
OLFWEREW
LFWEREWO
FWEREWOL

Totally gonna watch every werewolf movie before I got. Like every last one. So excited, I can hardly fucking stand it. Can barely focus on my job.

7 November 2007

Went to Flying Saucer Video and scored every werewolf movie they had. I must learn the lay of the land. Here's the list:

Werewolf of London (1935)
The Wolf Man (1941)
She-Wolf of London (1946)
The Werewolf (1956)
I was a Teenage Werewolf (1957)
Werewolf in a Girls' Dormitory (1962)
Werewolves on Wheels (1971)
The Werewolf of Woodstock (1975)
American Werewolf in London (1981)
The Howling (1981)
Wolfen (1981)
The Company of Wolves (1984)
Teen Wolf (1985)
Silver Bullet (1985)
Wolf (1994)
Bad Moon (1996)
Ginger Snaps (2000)
Dog Soldiers (2002)
Underworld (2003)
Big Bad Wolf (2006)
Blood and Chocolate (2007)

Rex the Clerk already sniffed that "Wolfen" wasn't really about werewolves, but that I should see it anyway, since it explores predation in an urban setting.

Clearly, I have my work cut out for me, since I have to see all of these before I catch my bus on Friday. So, I decided to quit my job and just go on a movie bender. Totally!

Polly shook her head.

"She's like the ultimate lycanthrope fangirl," she said. "She watched a bunch of werewolf movies before heading to Chicago to get infected by Sam. She apparently knew—or at least hoped—that Sam was for real."

"She's a sick puppy," Ansel said. "What can I say? Some are drawn to it."

He looked through her computer. Her laptop had a picture of herself on it as wallpaper, lavender-haired, pierced and inked, looking coyly at herself, posed half-nude, inked sleeves showing mermaids and octopi, robot women and gryphons and fish men with harpoons on one arm, and some kind of metallic man, a portal to a distant world, a beautiful woman in a box and a starship on the other arm. She had little tattooed stars across her clavicle.

Ansel turned the monitor so Polly could see it.

"Zooey before," Ansel said.

"Wow, she would have lost all of those tattoos and piercings," Polly said. "Right?"

Ansel nodded. "Sam lost her shit about that, too."

He looked through her computer. Most of it was just photos of herself in Wisconsin, mugging with her friends, dicking around in college. She had tons of schoolwork in there as well.

She was so young. That stuck out at him.

Ansel saw a file she'd labeled "Operation Wolfsbane."

Opening it up, he looked it over.

OPERATION WOLFSBANE

Phase I: Become One
Phase II: Learn the Ropes
Phase III: Run Wild
Phase IV: Expand the Franchise

"I think she's got some kind of manifesto, here," Ansel said. Each Phase had a lengthy dissertation, where Zooey talked about what she'd do. "This is like her *Mein Kampf* or something."

He opened Phase IV.

PHASE IV: EXPAND THE FRANCHISE

Physical Man, you have met your match in the face of the lycanthropic revolution. Your days are numbered on the back of your hand, and there is nothing you can do about it except, of course, fight back. That is a fight we welcome, because, simply, we are better at it than you are. You have turned yourself into livestock, and are expecting the rest of us to assume that role, to assume your place on the animal farm. But there is no room on the animal farm for the Wolf.

As it should be.

It ends with us.

We are the remedy.

The treatment modality is, as ever, through numbers.

The problem that werewolves face is that they don't think things through. Born in emotion and pain and saddled with a diabolical duality, the Werewolf faces obstacles right from birth. Maybe they are at war with who they are.

The point is that so many Werewolves face their struggles alone, they wallow in isolation and confusion and fear—fear of what they have become, fear of what they have done, fear of what they might do, fear of being caught.

These Four Fears are the shackles the Werewolf puts on himself, to try to keep the beast at bay, and these are exactly what keeps most Werewolves from effectively organizing.

First step for expansion of the franchise, then, is abandonment of the Four Fears. Lose those, and instead of a cage, one finds oneself in a bigger, better, brighter, bolder place.

We can afford to be fearless; almost nothing can kill us. We are superhuman—more than human, quite literally. We must embrace paranormal politics if we are to survive.

I'm not talking about Werewolf politicians per se; because, if we get our way, there won't be politicians anymore. But rather, there will be an upending of the existing social order.

A New Order.

This can only be attained if everyone becomes a Werewolf. Or at least there are enough to create a kind of carnal quorum. When this tipping point is reached, this furry fulcrum tips the balance in our favor, then we shall see the change.

If everyone's a monster, then monstrosity itself is overcome. Then "What Have I Become?"—the first and most hobbling of the Four Fears simply withers away.

When that horror is overcome, then a world of possibility opens up, and everything is up for grabs.

"Yeah, it's a kind of manifesto, alright," Ansel said. "She was probably planning to post that on the Web at some point, if she hasn't already."

"She'd probably die if she knew we were going through this," Polly said.

Ansel wasn't so sure. Zooey seemed to crave attention, would probably love knowing that the two of them had seen where her head was at, even if it was in a messed-up place.

"She's an attention whore," Ansel said. "She'd love this, I bet."

"We should use this as bait," Polly said. "Draw her out with it."

"Or leak it to the media," Ansel said. "Put somebody else's name on it. Put Sam's name on it. That would drive Zooey crazy."

Polly playfully batted Ansel on the shoulder.

"You are wicked," she said. "That would bother her, wouldn't it?"

Ansel was sure that it would.

"Check to see if she's posted this online, already," he said. "If not, then we can have some fun with her."

Polly took her own laptop and did some searching on it, and apparently Zooey hadn't.

"You do know that that plagiarizing is altogether abhorrent to me," Polly said.

Ansel laughed. "You're a lycanthrope, now, Polly; stop thinking like such a norm. Don't be held captive to the First Fear. Besides, we're going to credit it to Sam, not take the credit, ourselves."

"Ah, I see," Polly said. "For a big dog, you can sure be catty."

Ansel went into the file and took Zooey's name off it, put SAMANTHA HAIN on there, instead, then saved it.

"Meow," Ansel said. "This will piss Zooey off so badly that she will come running at us. Did you know her full name's Zooey Louise Hummel?"

Polly admitted that she didn't. She'd only met the girl that one time, at Sam's place.

"We should print these out and send them to the television stations and the newspapers," Polly said. "I'll write a press release for it, hope maybe they do something with it."

They got dressed and went about their little scheme, printing up six copies of Operation Wolfsbane and then packaging it up and putting a press release to it, something Polly cooked up about the Werewolf Organized Liberation Front (WOLF) and announced that Operation Wolfsbane was their declaration of war on the world, and how this would be the start of something big.

"You know," Ansel said, "Putting Sam's name on this will not only be a declaration of war, but will likely have the media hounding you, because if they actually track down who Sam is—and we should give them contact information, yes? You can always come forward as Sam's friend."

"Oh, I intend to," Polly said, reapplying her red lipstick, giving him the most devilish of grins.

4

Minton brought a team down on Anya's place: a half-dozen of his best shooters.

"Target's in there," Minton said. "Use extreme caution."

The fire team set up a perimeter, with two Wardens covering the back, and three approaching from the front.

They went up the steps, guns at the ready.

"Just smash down the door and charge in there," Minton said.

The men did as ordered, and stormed into her building. She lived on the third floor, so they ran up the stairs, with Minton at the rear.

The team reached the door to her place and kicked it down, and inside was Anya, wearing shades, her head wrapped in a red patterned scarf. She held up her hands, which were gloved.

"I surrender," Anya said.

Minton entered the room, saw her for himself.

"Walker," Minton said.

"Troy Minton," Anya said. "I wouldn't get too comfortable in the Director's chair if I were you."

"You're going to need to come with us," Minton said, nodding toward his men.

"And what? Get taken somewhere and shot? Again?"

Minton raised his pistol, pointed it at her.

"I'm sorry about what happened," Minton said. "That was not my call, but Phil was just following orders."

"Is that what you call it?"

"It's what it is," Minton said.

Anya cleared her throat.

"I just wanted to be deported to Wolf Island," Anya said. "Not murdered. I wanted to help, but Phil had other intentions."

"He had orders," Minton said. "And so do I."

"Let me help you," Anya said. "We know I'm infected. So, let me help bring down Princess with you. She's the key to the whole thing, I'm sure of it."

"I've got a team," Minton said.

"Nobody on the inside," Anya said. "This was what I was trying to tell Phil. Yes, I'm infected, but I'm not yet one of them. So, I have no fear of what they might do to me, and I fall into area of being a resource Princess might use. Let me at least try."

Minton considered it. Although Sanderson's orders had been clear, the actions he'd undertaken had been his own. Minton wasn't obligated to cover up for what Sanderson did, and Walker would hardly be seen as a reliable witness, in the sense that she was infected.

"Let me assist in this enterprise on the condition that when it's over, I'll be safely deported to Wolf Island," Anya said.

"You're not a field agent," Minton said. "You're an administrator. I don't see how you can help us."

"You're a warrior," Anya said. "I understand that. And this is a war. I understand that, too. But let me be a weapon in your war, and maybe we can win this thing. Think of it, Troy: you'd be the hero. The senior leadership of this administration would look at you as the man who got the job done, where others had failed. They don't even need to know about me."

"You and your BEE teams weren't able to find Princess before," Minton said. "With the resources at your disposal, you failed. How am I supposed to believe that you, on your own, can somehow succeed when before, you couldn't?"

Anya smiled. "Granted, that's a legitimate concern. But I have better insight, now. Let me be a hunting dog for your operation. You haven't had that before. I certainly didn't have it before. I'll bet there's been attrition among your Wardens, yes?"

She knew it had been the case, as Zachary had told her.

"We experienced the same thing," Anya said. "And there's something else for you to consider: Princess has people on the inside. Somebody killed Sanderson. Don't you want to know who?"

Minton considered this as well. The woman was a good negotiator, he had to give her that.

"Do you know who?" Minton asked.

"Let me be your gundog, Troy. I'm newly infected—I don't think I'm at risk of transforming for a few days, yet. Let me put those few days to good use for the sake of our country."

"Okay," Minton said. "Alright, here's the deal: First, you try to find Princess for me; second, you find me who killed Sanderson. Do those things, and I'll charter the flight to Wolf Island for you myself."

"So, we have a deal?" Anya asked. "No funny business, no bullets in the back of the head?"

She extended her gloved hand, which Minton shook.

"There, was that so hard?" Anya asked. "No, as to the second matter, I can make it very easy for you: Zachary West killed Phil."

"What?"

"He did it," Anya said.

"What the hell for?" Minton asked. "He's working for Princess?"

"He's working for me," Anya said.

Minton gestured to his men, who grabbed Anya.

Anya struggled, but there were several soldiers, and they were stronger than she was, and were able to restrain her.

"You ordered Zach to kill Sanderson?" Minton asked.

"No," Anya said. "I wanted to do that, myself. Zachary is very loyal, and when I turned back up, I think he was seeking some kind of revenge on my behalf."

"Fuck," Minton said.

"He's going to help me find Princess," Anya said. "We're working as a team, he and I."

"Does he know you're infected?" Minton asked.

"Of course he does," Anya said. "I've been nothing but honest, both to you and to him."

"Take her to the Facility," Minton said. "Lock her up."

"Wait wait wait," Anya said. "Our deal?"

"Is off," Minton said.

Zooey woke up shivering in the grove, naked in the night. She'd never dozed off in her Lupine form, found that strange, but after the excitement of her rampage downtown and through Navy Pier, it had left her sleepy.

As a lycanthrope, she rode her adrenal glands hard, thrived on death and danger; slumber wasn't something that was part of that equation. She wondered why that had happened.

Crouching, she transformed into her Lupine self, grateful for the fur to warm her skin, and for the wash of sensation as she turned her eyes, nose, and ears to the city. She was ravenous, and knew that she must eat soon. She slipped from the copse of trees and cleared the fencing and was back in the park proper, taking advantage of the strange capacity of sodium lights to actually magnify the shadows, to illuminate without enlightening.

There was some aftertaste of an epiphany that she had, like something she had dreamed, this idea that lycanthropes must always live in two worlds, maybe more. She was no more wolf than she was human; she was both and neither at the same time. She was deprived of the elegant simplicity of being a beast—yes, she could get near it, could approximate it better than any person could, but she was not a wolf; she was a werewolf. And she was as remote from human civilization as a person could be—she had long since thrown aside that mantle and embraced monstrosity. She could no longer walk the world as she had as a human being.

It was more than duality; it was something else entirely. She was not plagued with conflict between the sides of her spirit; she was unified in acceptance of what she'd become. Rather, she also felt more than ever that she did not belong anywhere.

She caught the scent of joggers, who, despite everything that had been happening in the city, still braved the night to run. Increasingly, runners had been taking to the gyms, to inside tracks, where they could feel safe.

But others still ran, and she watched them as she crept between the crabapple trees, lurking in the dark, listening to the crash of the waves. She was not in a good place; there remained for her the trek home, which meant cutting through the city somewhere. It meant more chaos and mayhem, which she didn't object to per se, but which would make things inconvenient for her, would have police and government agents pursuing her. Or Wilkos.

First things first. A light snow began to fall, crisp, beautiful flurries dropping from the sky, lending a splendid silence, making Zooey smile inwardly as she felt the flakes melt on her muzzle. Camouflage.

She saw a Baby Boomer man, overtanned, running, wearing a navy blue track suit. Her decision was reached in a half-second, and she sprang for him, knocking him on his back. The man, faced with her fanged face looming over him, let out a gratifying squawk of uncomprehending terror, when she bit down on his throat, crunching his windpipe and snapping his neck, dragging him back into the shadows, just out of sight of the bike path, screened by trees and some bushes.

Zooey unzipped his track suit and tore off his tee, and gazed at his thoroughly tanned and waxed chest and shuddered a moment. Then she ate her fill, amused that the police would find him and wouldn't have been able to do a thing about it. She left what was left of him in his track suit, and had eaten while joggers ran by, oblivious, their iTunes in their ears, while the snow fell.

Snow in the city always made the place magical, made it beautiful, at least when it first fell, before the soot and the grit made the snow ugly. But right now, it was like a fairyland, and was the perfect accompaniment for her meal, made it feel almost cozy to her.

Having finished, she then sniffed the air, wanted to know which way she should go, and what she should do. Lake Point Tower loomed behind her, visible but remote behind a curtain wall that screened its innards from the outside world. She doubted she could readily break into that building, but it was tempting, since it would eliminate the need for her to cut through Streeterville and work her way west and north to Bucktown, where "her" townhome awaited.

She would, instead, take advantage of the snow and just creep her way west. Zooey ran through the traffic corridor, went beneath a bridge, then went up through the city, moving from shadow to shadow, comforted by the thickening snow that fell all around her.

It would be Christmas soon; Zooey thought for the first time in awhile about her parents, up in Wisconsin, surely awash in snow, no doubt wondering and worrying about their daughter, wondering where she had gone.

Thinking of her parents cast a pall on her mood; she had been so busy with, like, being a wicked thing, she had forgotten about that. Her life had irrevocably changed the moment she'd crossed paths with Sam. That old life was dead, but her parents weren't, and the love they bore her, and the love she still had for them, that was something she couldn't completely cast aside, and that inability to do this caused her some unease, even a bit of turmoil.

They would, at the very least, be wondering where she had gone. They might have even called the police. And there was the gaping gulf of what she had been up to, how impossible it would be for them to understand just how important the happening was, how vital it was, and how central a place in it Zooey was. They only knew her as their daughter, and loved her for that.

It made her lycanthropic soul curdle, thinking of that. Simply put, it harshed her bestial buzz. And yet, it made her want to see them. Her family all got together for Christmas.

This was the chain that pulled on her, and in so pulling, earned her ire. She could not be fully free or fully formed while she still had family, those who knew her when she was just a nobody and a norm. How silly she'd been, thinking with her ink and her piercings and her pink or lavender hair that she had been anything unusual or different—she'd been just another norm, playing dress-up.

Having completely transgressed as she had—murder, cannibalism, terrorism—how could she ever think that there would be a place for her at her family's table? But there would be. Mom and Dad would be there for her, the way they always were. And her siblings, and their kids. They'd all be there. They'd wonder where Zooey had gone.

Humbug, a voice said inside her, an unfamiliar thing.

She had never had the voices, felt a measure of alarm at that, ran across Michigan Avenue, past honking horns and Christmas lights, scaring the fuck out of tourists, who pointed and shouted and screamed, but she didn't stop running, didn't even take the time to take a bite out of any of the women; she just ran. Running made everything better; it was the antidote to her angst.

You have to, like, call them, Zo-Zo, the voice said. *You can't leave them in the lurch. You already missed Thanksgiving, you bitch.*

264 | D.T. NEAL

Fuck that sentimental bullshit, Zooey thought back. *What the hell are you?*

I'm, like, what's left of you, Dude. I'm the Ghost of Christmas Past.

Ha ha. Are you, like, my conscience? Is that what you're trying to be?

I just told you; I'm what's left of who you were. The wannabe. The norm.

The sting of that bit down hard on her. She'd heard enough of the noobs whining about it, the nether voices inside them, gnawing away at them. Zooey had never been troubled by that, had reveled in her unity of purpose, in being completely committed to her new life.

But this thing, this nagging scold inside her, this little killjoy? That was all kinds of annoying.

Killjoy to the world, she said. *I like that. I am Killjoy, hear me roar.*

Fuck you. This is my place, now. There's no room for you here.

You sure about that?

Killjoy conjured up memories, thoughts of her family, her older brothers (Zane, Carter, and Joel), giving her shit, as they always did.

Are you going to kill them? Infect them? Have you thought that far ahead?

Zane and Carter both had families, six kids between them, her nieces and nephews. The kids always loved Aunt Zooey, who used to do magic tricks for them, sleight of hand, juggling. Zooey always had a natural dexterity to her.

Stop it. Fucking stop that.

But the memories kept coming. Killjoy kept piling them on, Zooey doing card tricks, Zooey reading to her nieces and nephews, playing games at her parents' place. Sledding.

Killjoy transformed those idyllic visions, showed her family set upon by werewolves, chasing down her nieces, biting them, tearing apart her nephews, her brothers roaring in terror and agony, Zane trying to shoot the wolves, Carter trying to save the kids, Joel throwing himself at the wolves. A huge pack, ravening and savage, and tearing everyone apart.

Quite the family reunion, Killjoy said. *I don't think your nieces will appreciate what you did for them.*

Zooey ran harder, trying to drive the visions from her head. It wasn't fair; she'd come along so far, had made such progress. Bringing them into it wasn't fair.

You hadn't factored them into it, had you? Or imagine this, maybe....

And Killjoy brought another vision, with her family learning about what Zooey had done, and the reproach they would feel at such abominable crimes.

You crossed that path. You chose it. They love you, Zooey. And you love them.

It was intolerable.

Who gets to make them, Zooey? You? Black Sheep? Somebody else? Somebody worse? You know your brothers; they'd fight it. They'd die fighting it.

Zooey reached the townhome, the shelter of the canopied trees, slipped into the back, down a narrow alley that separated this townhome from the one next to it, and turned back to her human disguise, slipped in the back door, which she'd left unlocked, shivering, chilled bare feet on the freshly-fallen snow.

She paused, gazed at the ground, which now had an inch or two of snow on it. Her wolf prints changing to bare human footprints. It was beautiful in the snow, like art.

Then she went inside, closed and locked the door, scuffed her bare feet on the doormat, went upstairs, grabbed a shirt from one of the gay men's closets, a snow-white button-down, and found some navy blue striped track pants, and slipped those on, pulled the drawstring tight.

You're a mess, Zooey.

"Get out of my fucking head," Zooey said. "This isn't fair. I'm clean. I had a clean break with my past. We're through."

You only forgot, that's all. You weren't always a monster. Well, not on the outside, anyway. Mom's worried about you. Dad's upset. Your brothers might even be looking for you. Can you imagine what would happen if Black Sheep found them?

She would not be held captive to this. Zooey went to the fridge and pulled out another of those sparkling sodas she liked. At some point, she'd move on from the townhome, would crash someone else's pad. This is how it would be, this was the future: the strong would take what they wanted, and the weak would just have to take it. It wasn't much different from the world as it was; the only change was the directness of it.

You have to protect them. To warn them, at the very least. Don't you think you have to do that, Zooey? Don't you owe them that?

Maybe this was some outgrowth of the infection. Some kind of psychosis that afflicted the victims, and it just took longer to affect her.

I'm not a psychosis; I'm Killjoy, the angel on your shoulder. You nearly did it; you nearly were the uncarved blockhead Sam wanted so badly to be, but I'm here, now, and I'm not going anywhere.

"Fuck you," Zooey said, turned on the television.

Then Killjoy had her pick up one of the cell phones. Zooey, aghast, tossed it aside, only to have Killjoy pick it back up again.

Call them. They're worried about you. Tell them you'll be home for Christmas.

"I'm not going home for goddamned Christmas."

If you do, I'll shut up for a week.

"I'm not being guilted into going anywhere," Zooey said, amazed that she was even talking to herself. "And I'm not being extorted, either. Fuck you."

The news just spoke of more killings, shootings, bombings. Somebody firebombed one of the buildings in Cabrini Green, which was apparently being frequented by coywolves.

"Goddamned coywolves," Zooey said, swigging her soda. "How long are they going to keep going with this bullshit?"

As long as it takes. Until everything seems normal again.

Zooey found that Killjoy had snuck the phone back in her hand, and, realizing that, tossed the thing away again.

One phone call, so Mom doesn't worry. You know how she worries.

"Fine," Zooey said, snatching up the phone. "Fucker. If it will shut you up."

She dialed home, and her mom answered on the third ring, as she always did.

"Hello?" her mom's voice, something she hadn't heard in over a month.

"Mom, hey, it's Zooey," she said.

"ZOOEY! Jack, it's Zooey! Let me put you on the speaker," her mom said.

"No, don't do that, Mom," Zooey said, but she's already done it.

"Zooey," Jack Hummel said. "Where in the hell have you been? Have you been watching the news? What's happening in Chicago with all those coyotes biting people?"

"Coywolves, Dad," Zooey said, rolling her eyes. Even she was saying it, now.

"Where are you?" Her mom asked. "We can't believe you hadn't called us. We tried your cell phone, but you didn't answer, it kept going to voicemail."

Zooey had left her phone in her Samsonite, which was at Polly's. That was something she had to get back. There was serious payback in store for that skinny bitch.

"Are you coming for Christmas?" her mom asked.

"Susan, don't nag her," Her dad said.

"Your brothers are. Everybody's been so worried about you, Baby. I have most of all. Would it kill you to call us? And what about school?"

"Mom, I dropped out. Fuck college," Zooey said. She put the phone on speaker, set it on the coffee table.

"Don't say that, Zooey," Her mom said. "What are you doing? How are you living?"

"I'm working, you know, just little jobs here and there," Zooey said. Lying to them was the easy part, keeping them on a low-information diet.

"Odd jobs," Her dad said. "That's what they call them, Zo."

"Right, Dad," Zooey said. "See, I, uh, don't think I should go home for Christmas."

"Do you need money? Is that it? We can buy you a bus ticket," Her mom said. "Jack can drive down and get you. You'd do that, wouldn't you, Honey?"

"Absolutely," Her dad said. "I'll get you, Zo."

"No, Dad," Zooey said. "Seriously, like, don't even do that. Okay, I'll come up there, okay?"

"Attagirl," Her dad said. "Just come home. Everybody's going to be there. But stay out of Milwaukee, would you? Things are getting bad there, too."

The thought of going home to Oxblood, Wisconsin, made Zooey cringe. For Christmas, no less.

But if she wanted a clean break with her past, perhaps it was an opportunity. If she killed her family, she'd have no family to worry about, and nobody in this world would have that to hold over her. It was something to consider. Or she could infect them, let them be prepared for the wave of the future, the First Family of lycanthropy.

Or you could warn them about it. Tell them about the happening.

I'm not doing that.

"This is great news, Zooey," Her mom said. "When will you get up here?"

"The 23rd," Zooey said.

"That's wonderful," Her mom said. "Perfectly timed. I can't wait to tell everybody."

"Zooey," Her dad said. "You be careful down there. There's perverts and creeps at the bus station."

"I'm not worried, Dad," Zooey said.

"Yes," Her mom said. "Do you have pepper spray? Do have your rape whistle?"

"Guys, I've got it covered," Zooey said. "Seriously. Don't worry about it. Don't worry about me. I'll see you guys in a couple of days, alright? Bye, now."

She hung up on them before they could say another thing, and tossed the phone away again.

There, was that so hard?

"Fuck you," Zooey said.

6

Minton called Zach in from the field, and when Zach turned up, Minton had some of his men seize him and put cuffs on him.

"You're under arrest for the murder of Phil Sanderson, West," Minton said. "Anya sold you out, man."

Zach sighed, looked Minton in the eye, decided it best to come clean.

"You'd be better off shipping me to Wolf Island," Zach said. "And Anya, too. We're both infected."

"Both?" Minton asked.

"Yeah," Zach said. "I got bitten, so, yeah, it's only a matter of time."

Minton watched the soldiers react to this, a sudden wariness.

"So, you haven't turned, yet?" Minton asked.

"No," Zach said.

Minton gestured, and the soldiers walked Zach to one of the holding tanks they had at the Facility, where they put him inside. Anya was in a cell next to it. They were thick-barred titanium cages.

"Sorry, Zachary," Anya said. "I was trying to negotiate, but Troy wasn't amenable to it."

Zach thought about fighting the soldiers, about trying to get free—in fact, the thing inside him dearly wanted this, but Zach refused to give the thing the satisfaction, let them put him into the holding cell.

Minton pulled up a chair, looked at them in turn.

"I'm not Sanderson," Minton said. "Although the executive order is pretty damned clear, I'm going to take an administrative action, here—I'm going to have the two of you shipped off to Wolf Island. Now, you tell me where Dr. Milkowski is."

"We don't know," Anya said. "She's gone missing."

"That's what I keep hearing," Minton said.

"I haven't seen her since the Kennel was attacked," Zach said.

Minton didn't look like he liked that answer very much.

"You two are infectives," Minton said. "As far as our government is concerned, you're already dead. I could just put silver bullets in you both and we're done."

"We don't know where she is," Zach said.

"She's trying to find a cure for this disease," Anya said.

Minton held up Anya's cell phone, slid it to Anya.

"You call her," Minton said. "Bitch still has a phone, right? You call her, you tell her to come in."

Anya looked Minton in the eye, who stared right back at her. For a few moments, the two stared hard at each other, then Anya picked up the phone, dialed Mina, who answered on the second ring.

"Mina, it's Anya."

"What's up, Anya? You sound stressed out," Mina said.

"It's been a trying day, Mina," Anya said. "Now, I want you to listen very carefully to me."

"I'm listening," Mina said.

"Zachary and I are prisoners of Minton, the new BEE Director, at the Facility headquarters. They're going to ship us to Wolf Island," Anya said. "They're looking for you, Mina. Whatever you do, don't let them find you. I'm afraid they may try to kill you. They think you had something to do with the compromise of the Kennel."

Anya disconnected, then deleted Mina's number from her contact list and her call log, and then stomped her phone beneath her heel, cracking it, while Minton had some guards go for her through the bars, jabbing her with cattle prods, which sparked and shocked her. Once she was stunned, they pulled out the remains of the phone, while Zach cursed them from the neighboring cell.

"You bastards," Zach said, watching them try to salvage the broken phone.

"Fuck you both," Minton said, signing a digital clipboard. "I just signed your rendition papers. You're going to Wolf Island, and that's that. I'm done with you."

"Why not just kill us?" Zach asked.

Minton looked at them both a moment, before replying.

"It would set a bad example for my men," Minton said. "You were our best Warden, West. And I think Anya's sincere in her desire to help out. Maybe having you two shipped to Wolf Island might do some good."

Mina worked by the light of her laptop, crunching data as she noshed on some bagels Patryk Landa had brought earlier, like it was just another day at the office. The *Synowie Srebra* had the safest of safe houses, borne of hard-won experience and a long history. Landa, one of the most successful and dedicated of the werewolf hunters, looked on in his unassuming, utterly normal way. Landa was anything but that, but he knew how to blend in, and for the Sons of Silver, blending in was everything.

Landa was middle-aged, blandly handsome and very fit, with sandy blonde hair and glasses that made him look like a philosopher, especially when paired with the black ribbed turtlenecks he was fond of wearing, and the khaki pants. He always carried a silver dagger at his belt.

The survival of his ancient brotherhood depended on their ability to do so. When you hunted prey like the Lupines, the ability to be inconspicuous was a necessity.

The call from Anya had thrown her off, had made her more nervous than ever. That the Bureau was hunting her while she was hunting for a cure made it all the more harrowing for her, while she sifted through the data.

She'd been noting the presentation of lycanthropy, aggregating the incubation periods to time of onset of symptoms. The data showed that, on average, symptoms began appearing 24 hours to 72 hours from time of infection. That was where the majority of infectives fell. She assumed there may have been some genetic susceptibility to the retrovirus on the part of some infectives, which might account for why some of them manifested earlier, versus ones who manifested later.

It was a fascinating thing, this virus, rewriting the host's code so radically as a way of propagating itself. How odd it was to think that the lycanthropes were, for all of their furry fury, really a virus delivery system. Mina posited that the nature of the transformation could have reflected its origins, much the way that the malaria organism clearly had some kind of ties to plant life in its past.

Perhaps it had been some kind of wolf that had carried this infection, long ago, and had bitten a caveman, transmitting it to him, and thus the retroviral chain was forged. And, back then, there would have been considerable survival value for a prehistoric lycanthrope, a skinchanger who would find himself immune to conventional disease, able to more effectively hunt. And, if he'd infected his whole clan, then they'd be unassailable, particularly in an era when silver was unknown. They would be effectively immune to the conventional weapons of the day, and would have a measure of protection from predators of that time, whether the saber-toothed cat or the short-nosed bear.

Mina found herself imagining those prehistoric infectives. Maybe the original one, the true Patient Zero, would have lost control of himself, would not have understood what was happening to him (or her; it could have been a woman). Maybe they would have killed some of their tribe members and been cast out, surviving on their own. Or maybe there would have been some kind of superstitious awe about their skinchanging, and they would have held places of authority within the tribe, like shamans. The possibilities were dazzling.

However it presented, it did not take over the human genome, in the sense that the clear survival benefits of lycanthropy conferred a competitive advantage over uninfected humans. That was very apparent. In a fight with a normal human, a lycanthrope had a decisive edge. Evolutionarily, then, there would have been a genetic rout of conventional humanity.

So, there was some kind of selection factor in place that prevented this from occurring. Possibly it was the unruly nature of lycanthropy itself—the thirst for blood, the desire to spread the infection as widely as possible; those did not lend themselves to a comfortable tribal existence, but spoke to war and bloodshed and mayhem.

Maybe there was the innate competitiveness between lycanthropes themselves—while the average lycanthrope had a definite physical advantage over an uninfected human, if you had two lycanthropes facing each other down, then odds were good that one of them would not survive. Lycanthropes would prey upon themselves in efforts to establish dominance, reducing their numbers that way.

But even that could not account for how this had not taken over the human genome. Maybe it first sprang up in an isolated place, or maybe the Toba supervolcano eruption had cut off the lycanthropic strain from the rest of humanity. Toba's eruption had nearly made mankind extinct, and while cannibalistic lycanthropes would have, once again, a definite advantage relative to their peers, if the thick snows had fallen in the wake of Toba, if the Ice Age had come and cut them off, then it would have inhibited their ability to spread. They would have dominated in their particular habitats, but would not have been able to get past the natural barriers that separated them from the rest of the survivors.

Mina ate her bagel and thought a lot about this, imagining that snowbound survivor. Maybe if it had been bad enough that lycanthrope had been forced to kill and consume his or her entire tribe, and it was reduced back to one survivor carrying the retrovirus, causing a setback in the infective chain again. It was impossible to know, except in the folkloric chain of it, the references to these things.

Or it was possible that their cannibalism was such that they didn't leave many survivors of their attacks to actually get the infection. It was possible that the prehistoric lycanthropes hunted their peers and simply ate them, didn't actually consciously infect them, and their very advantages in battle made it likelier that they would kill their opponents versus infect them, especially in advance of the development of armor.

There were so many tantalizing roads to go on this, as she walked back through time, imagining this thing walking in mankind's shadow. Civilization itself could have been a reaction to the early lycanthropy, as mankind banded together to seek protection from the savage world around them. She could not see a lycanthropic tribe abandoning its hunter-gatherer organization in favor of an agrarian way of life.

The discovery of silver in antiquity had at last offered normal humanity a defense, a weapon against these seemingly invulnerable marauders. The antimicrobial qualities of silver presented prophylaxis against the retrovirus. Silver had a longstanding association with fighting and warding off the supernatural.

An understanding of silver could give her an understanding of the retrovirus, itself, but while the antibacterial properties of silver had been researched, no one yet quite knew how silver inhibited viruses, only knew that it did. The Greeks and Romans in particular made use of it to prevent infection, which Mina assumed included lycanthropy.

In her own research, it did not take much silver to cause a catastrophic breakdown of the retrovirus. Even at molecular levels, it was devastatingly effective. She wondered if there was the possibility of designing an oral vaccine. The problem was navigating the toxicity of the silver relative to the virus. It could be as likely that a vaccine could prove fatal for anyone infected by the retrovirus.

Someone came into the safe house. It was Patryk, carrying a pizza.

"Perfect thing to wash down the bagel I just had, Patryk," Mina said. "Your timing is excellent."

Patryk smiled, sat down near her. The pizza did smell heavenly.

"Five meat pizza," Patryk said. "Sausage, pepperoni, ham, meatballs, and beef."

"Had a craving?" Mina asked. She opened the box and watched Patryk open a screwtop bottle of red wine. Patryk was looking ragged, a little rough around the edges.

"Yeah," Patryk said. "Heard from Anya, yet?"

"Yes," Mina said. "She and Zach have been captured, and they're hunting for me."

"That's no good," Patryk said.

"I'm going to turn soon, Patryk," Mina said. "Do you have a place where I could go?"

"Of course we do," Patryk said. "We have…a place…where we could put you, until the madness passes. While *Synowie* hunts werewolves, we do have a place to study them. Not a lab, so much as a cell."

"That'll do," Mina said. "I just need a place where I can, you know…."

Landa nodded. "I've already told my brothers. They know about you. It'll be safe."

Mina shook her head, sank her teeth into the pizza. It was exactly what she'd needed. They gorged on the pizza in silence, and when she'd grabbed the wine from him, he did not drink from it again.

"I think there's probably a way of administering an oral vaccine for the disease," Mina said. "But I'm sure as hell not going to be the one who invents it. It'll take a real lab, with full resources, and years of clinical trials. The Phase I of the trials alone should be a bloodbath."

Patryk ate the pizza by way of a response. "There's only one way I'm going to be able to find the White Fang."

"Zooey," Mina said.

"She'll always be 'White Fang' to me," Patryk said. "Anyway, I need to catch her. That's what I need to do."

Mina stopped eating, looked across at him, half-wrapped in shadow. "She'll kill you."

He nodded. "She might."

"Why risk it?" Mina asked.

Patryk hadn't exactly thought about it that way, but he supposed he agreed.

"Sounds kinda crazy, Patryk," Mina said. "Kinda desperate."

She took a deep drink of wine, and he nodded.

"What are we, if not desperate, Mina? We're in a safe house, trying to hold off this epidemic on our own. To what end? What's the point of it?"

Mina nodded, finished her piece of pizza. The infection was changing her, too; she was feeling it as surely as the others were. All she wanted to do was eat lately, which she suspected was a sign of the infection. On a molecular level, the virus was rewriting her, adapting her to its needs. She did not like to be in this position, changing from who she was to this viral simulacrum of herself.

"Silver is the key," Mina said. "Something about it kills the virus. I don't know what it is, but it destroys it, stopping it on a molecular level. I'm beginning to wonder if there's a window of time when one could administer an oral or nasal vaccine. If we delivered the vaccine—the hypothetical vaccine—before the victim was fully changed, maybe there would be a way of saving them."

Patryk took another piece of pizza, curled it up in his hand into a "U" shape, and ate it. "Which means that you're doomed, even if a vaccine did appear."

"Yes," Mina said. "We are either fully or nearly fully assimilated."

"Why haven't you changed?"

"Willpower," Mina said. "Luck. Drugs."

Mina had been taking ample tranquilizers to keep them from reaching the stimulation threshold to trigger the metamorphosis. It wasn't a cure, but it was at least a treatment, up to a point. Sooner or later, she'd cross a threshold and a transformation would occur.

"The period of intervention would have to be from that first point of infection," Mina said. "It's kind of like rabies; the sooner you act after point of infection, the better."

Patryk watched her swig the wine.

"And then there's a point of no return, yes?" Patryk asked. Mina nodded, handed the bottle back to him, but he waved her off.

"It rewrites our genome," Mina said. "Once it's in, it can't be evicted."

"So, no cure? That's what you're saying?" Patryk said.

"Once it's braided itself into our genome, no," Mina said. "I don't think so. Maybe someday, but not now."

Patryk laughed. "So, there it is, then. You're doomed."

"Pretty much," Mina said. "Sooner or later, I'll develop enough tolerance to the tranquilizers and I'll go through it. The only difference between us and anybody else is that we're aware of what's happening to us; we know how it's going to end." Patryk gobbled another piece of pizza.

"Do we?"

"More or less," Mina said.

"So, you aren't you, anymore?" Patryk said. "You're viral imitations?"

"Chimeras, I suppose," Mina said.

"Werewolves," Patryk said.

"No, a chimera is a term geneticist use for an organism that is made up of distinct genetic components," Mina said. "It's hard to explain. There's what we were, Subset A, and there's the virus, Subset B—they're distinct. An infective is then an AB organism. Interesting issue, if infected women are able to give birth to AB babies.

"Were-babies?"

Mina nodded. "Zach, Anya and I are all infectives; we were bitten and became infected. But suppose we had children—both of us would pass on that infection to our offspring, because we stopped being fully human when the infection changed us. We became, in effect, half-human, half-virus."

"That makes sense," Patryk said. The *Synowie* had plenty of accounts of Lupine families and clans.

"The virus has actually given itself two pathways," Mina said. "There's a real problem here, with the breakout of infection from this whole Patient Zero event. None of the infectives should be allowed to breed, because they'll be birthing natural lycanthropes. Shapeshifters from birth."

"Litters?"

"Kinda," Mina said. "God, this is worse than I thought."

Patryk finished his piece of pizza, slid the box to Mina, who took another piece.

"What happens if somebody who's infected kisses somebody else?" Patryk asked.

"Nothing," Mina said. "Unless there was a break in the skin. Such a minute infection like that might take longer than the 24–72 hours I put on traditional transmission."

Mina shook her head as she pondered the complications of it. The virus was marvelously adapted for transmission.

"All infectives should be sterilized," Mina said. "Or any children they have will be lycanthropes. We have to tell somebody," Mina said. "There has to be more stringent protocols around this. It's not just a pathogen; it's worse. It's a genetic disease, fully heritable."

She drafted an email to send to some peers who worked at CDC, thought that would be prudent. Someone had to know.

LANCE, THIS IS MINA. I'M UP TO MY NECK IN EVERYTHING HERE IN CHICAGO, BUT I WANT TO BE SURE THIS DOESN'T GET LOST. I KNOW YOU ARE BUSY WITH THE INFECTIVE SITUATION, BUT I WANT TO BE SURE YOU UNDERSTAND WHAT YOU'RE DEALING WITH: THE RETROVIRUS IS HERITABLE; IT'S NOT SIMPLY AN INFECTIVE ORGANISM. ANY INFECTIVES CAN PASS ON THE DISEASE TO THEIR PROGENY. I'M PUTTING MY RESEARCH IN A DROPBOX FOR YOU.

NOTE: I'M SUPPOSED TO BE DEAD, APPARENTLY. THE KENNEL WAS COMPROMISED, AND I'VE BEEN INFECTED. I'M DOING WHAT I CAN ON THIS WHILE I STILL HAVE MY WITS. USE THE FILES, AND TRY TO FIX. I RECOMMEND SOME KIND OF SILVER-BASED SUSPENSION, ORALLY OR NASALLY ADMINISTERED WITHIN 24 HOURS OF INFECTION, IDEALLY. WHEN YOU GET THE NOBEL PRIZE, DON'T FORGET ABOUT ME.
~MINA

She sent it, watched the files upload, while Patryk watched her. Mina was studiously pretty, with no-nonsense black-framed glasses and a thick mane of tightly curled black hair. Her face was spade-shaped, with a sharp chin and a widow's peak. She caught Patryk eyeing her, gave him a smirk.

Outside, snow was falling heavy and hard.

"It's gonna get cold as hell this winter," Patryk said. "We may all be sporting our fur coats sooner than later, if it gets really bad."

"Promise me you won't let it come to that," Mina said.

"I promise," Landa said.

With everything that was going on, Zooey couldn't even believe she was thinking of taking a bus to Oxblood, the tiny farm town where she grew up. But such was the power of family, to pull you where you couldn't possibly want to go.

It was like when her folks made her get piano lessons, out of some benighted sense of her learning something like that, even though there'd be no reason for her to ever play piano.

The bus station had been packed with people, norms to her eyes, by the look of frustration and boredom they had, none of them radiating any kind of predatory grace to her.

Televisions were everywhere, talking about the news of the day, about how all the snow that had come in was making holiday travel a nightmare.

Even getting down to the station had been difficult for Zooey, who was wanting nothing more than to transform and bound through the growing banks of snow, but was forced by circumstance to remain disguised. She'd put on some knee-high snow boots to manage, which she'd bought with some of the money she'd stolen from the men she'd murdered, made sure they were nice boots.

"This is stupid," Zooey said. "I belong here."

You belong with family, Killjoy said, making Zooey wonder if Killjoy was really just guilting her into visiting her family in hopes of increasing the likelihood that she'd infect them, herself.

I wouldn't do that, Killjoy said.

She was trying to decide which line she should enter when she saw Sam's face on the television, saw talk about a manifesto she'd written—an Operation Wolfsbane—some kind of terrorist manifesto.

"What the FUCK?" Zooey said aloud, shoving past a family of fatties to get a better view of the television, to actually hear what they were saying.

"The station—in fact, all of the broadcasters in the city as well as the newspaper publishers—received an identical manifesto penned by area performance artist, Samantha Hain, who had recently been found murdered in the Gold Coast condominium of Reagan White-house on November 12, along with Gretta Moore, in a scene authorities had described as some kind of grisly murder-suicide. Ms. Hain appeared to be at the head of some kind of performance art troupe that referred to itself as WOLF—the Werewolf Organized Liberation Front—which had delivered the manifestos to the news media with a press release."

Zooey stomped her feet and glared at the television, felt herself nearly lose control right there in the bus station.

Those twats had broken into her suitcase after all, had actually stolen her stuff, had put Sam's name on her manifesto? Why in the fuck had they even done that?

Then she saw Polly's pretty face on the screen, talking to a reporter.

"Polly Drinkwater, of Winnetka, and friend of Samantha's, had this to say:"

"Sam was a performance artist; we had a little group of people—you know, poets, painters, that kind of thing—and I think Operation Wolfsbane was intended to be some kind of big happening for Sam—that's what she called her events: Happenings. It's a term performance artists use. Anyway, we were all very shocked when she died. Shocked and horrified."

"What do you know of WOLF?" the reporter asked. Polly grinned radiantly, her cute face absolutely loving the camera, her eyes flicking into the camera every now and again, seeming to look right at Zooey.

"I can't speak to that, but Sam was always coming up with new things," Polly said. "She staged a YouTube video of herself transforming. We still don't know how she did it."

The television station showed a clip from Sam's "Transformation" YouTube, her becoming a werewolf, noted that the video had been viewed millions of times, now.

"She was really proud of that," Polly said. "I can only guess that Operation Wolfsbane was going to be the next step of her happening. As for how it got out after her death? I have no idea. Maybe she left some instructions with some other friends, to have them distribute it today?"

Zooey fumed, balled her hands into fists. Those claimjumping motherfuckers.

"Is there any tie-in to the spate of animal attacks that had been occurring throughout the city and the nation at large for the past few months?" the news reporter asked.

"I really wouldn't know that," Polly said. Smiling prettily out at everyone, her pale face, red lips, and immaculately coifed black hair working perfectly. She looked like the picture of retrosexual flapper charm.

The news shifted to events in Iraq and whether Iran would have a nuclear reactor by March.

Zooey was losing control, right then and there, surrounded by all of those norms. She let out a scream and split herself wide open, right in front of everybody, trashing those nice, new snowboots she'd purchased that same day, shredding her clothes, causing the norms to scream and panic, shoving against themselves and each other to get away from Zooey, who had become her great, white self, the hybrid form, the monster, slavering jaws and claws like steak knives, hunched forward, arms out.

She looked around at the mob of people, who were gazing at her in horror and terror, the fear flowing off of them in great waves.

"I'm the face of your future, you fucks."

Then she charged toward the exit, knocking norms out of the way, smashing through the entry doors, racing out into the snowstorm, into the thickening banks of it, blood in her eyes, hate in her heart.

She had become death.

Ansel and Polly toasted each other with champagne, watching the news reports, Polly's place beautifully crusted with snow. They had been playing house all day, putting up Christmas decorations, including three trees—one a towering green tree in the living room, one a white tree in the foyer, and a third, vintage metallic tinsel tree in the study.

It had kept them busy most of the afternoon, while they'd waited to see if the media had picked up the whole WOLF thing.

"Sam would be so tickled by this," Polly said. "I mean, not the manner of it, but to finally get the kind of recognition she'd always been fighting for. Her YouTube channel is on fire. She'd absolutely love that."

"I hope Zooey saw it," Ansel said.

There was breaking news about a white coywolf appearing in the crowded bus depot, getting trapped in the bus station, only to smash its way out of the place. Herky-jerky footage showed Zooey stampeding through the bus station, a snarling blur.

"Oh, she saw it," Polly said. "She's probably running right for here, like a bullet."

Ansel smiled at her over the lip of the fluted champagne glass. "We'll be ready for her. How far is it from Chicago to Winnetka, anyway?"

"Maybe 16 miles," Polly said.

"Ah," Ansel said. "So, if she's really booking, she'll be here pretty soon, then."

"If we have to fight her, Ansel, I want it outside. I don't want her ruining Christmas," Polly said, grinning at him.

Ansel nodded, finding a grin, himself. He had completely healed from the injuries he'd suffered at Zooey's hand, and looked manfully dashing in his fitted black sweater and grey slacks.

"You'll be the bait, and I'll be the trap," Ansel said. "She will be expecting you, she won't be expecting me."

"She won't be expecting US," Polly said, putting Mission of Burma on the stereo, turned up. Ansel seemed to approve, the room filling with anthemic guitars and hiccupping tape loops.

"If she's alone, we'll doubleteam her," Ansel said. "If she's with a pack, I want you to stick by me."

"Alright," Polly said. They took off each others' clothes, embraced, looked at one another, kissed.

"The snow is a gift," Ansel said. "If she's running up here on her own, she'll be tired out. It's tiring, running through the snow. Especially this much snow."

Then they went to the front door and opened it, shivering in the chill, stepping out into the snow, together, hands entwined, the flurries enfolding them.

Zooey had howled as she'd stormed northward, had managed to draw dozens of packmates to her, younger Lupines eager to prove themselves worthy to run with her. The blood rage was filling Zooey, fury at Polly for doing what she'd done, for invading her world that way.

Yes, she had invaded Polly's first by actually showing up at her place, but that was a trifle in the face of this violation that Polly had perpetrated on Zooey. To actually doctor her documents and try to steal Zooey's thunder that way, to give it to Sam? It was so bitchy of her, and Zooey was going to kill her for it. It was as simple as that.

The pack ran through the thickening snow, through whipping wind and curtained flurries, the others eager to follow Zooey's lead, eager to follow her example, to become, to belong. She had not even told them where they were going, or why; they understood that she meant death, and that was something they could comprehend.

This was how it was done, Fuckers, Zooey thought.

They were maybe minutes away from Polly's place, having stayed close to the lake shore, rather than contending with the serpentine coils of the city streets. They followed her without question, without her having to explain what she was doing, where she was going—they only wanted to be with her.

That filled Zooey with pride, satisfied that her reputation alone could move mountains. She was the alpha, and this was her city for the rest of her days. Her army would lay claim to it and hold it tightly. Once tonight's challenge was dealt with, she'd rule unopposed.

Zooey nosed her way to Polly's place, remembering the scents and sights, the avenues and trees, the broad yards and pretty promenades.

"Polly's mine," Zooey said. "Mine mine mine."

And she ran harder, panting, heart beating, crashing through the snow, which was falling furiously, now, made running difficult, even for them.

Polly's palace rose into view, that great big house her late husband had bought for them, gorgeous and slate-roofed, stone and brick, comfortably crouching on a great big, verdant yard that looked like a park of its own.

In the center of that front yard, like an ornament, was Polly, lean, dark chocolate, snarling at Zooey, who reached her, breathless, her packmates around her—three greys, four browns, and more packmates on the way.

"You fucking bitch," Zooey said, panting. "Couldn't, like, leave it alone, could you?"

Polly gazed out at Zooey through yellow-green eyes, teeth bared, claws out.

"Came back for more, Bitch?" Polly said.

The other werewolves circled Polly, all of them full of bloodlust, whipped up by the frenzy of the chase, feeling the rage of Zooey, absorbing it.

Then there was a shuddering howl, a great and dreadful thing that shook snow from the trees, like a klaxon that boomed in the darkness. Zooey whipped around, knew the sound, felt a fist of ice clamp around her heart.

Ansel.

Polly took advantage of her distraction to draw first blood, going right for Zooey's throat, with a speed that even Zooey did not think possible, taking a savage bite that would have killed Zooey then and there, had she not pried herself loose before Polly had fully clamped down.

Ansel appeared behind them all, massive, ghastly, a specter in black that visibly intimidated her packmates: unharmed and whole, unbent and unbroken.

Zooey could not speak, her throat gushing blood, the damage done to her vocal cords by Polly's attack.

Polly was on her again as Zooey's focus was split between Polly and Ansel.

"Walking pelt," Polly snarled.

Polly jumped right on Zooey's back, raking her with her long claws, while Ansel tore into Zooey's packmates, sending one of the browns flying with an almost contemptuous toss of his head, and nearly splitting one of the greys in two with a swipe of his claws.

Ansel was in his element, moving with deadly, practiced purpose. Seeing that through the red veil of rage and pain added a curtain of fear to Zooey, even as she tried to pry Polly off her back, who was savaging her, turning her beautiful ivory coat red with her own blood.

"Fur-lined cage," Polly hissed, spitting Zooey's blood.

The fight was a monstrous brawl, with Zooey's packmates piling onto Ansel, who slashed and bit at them with a savagery Zooey had never seen before. He broke a grey and shattered two browns with ease, while some tans and reds surged at him, snapping at him, clawing at him.

Ansel moved like a black blur between the packs of minions, but they were too new, too inexperienced, and, Zooey admitted as she half-monitored the slaughter, they were too small to prevail against mammoth Ansel.

Polly kept after her, but Zooey slammed her against a tree and clawed at her exposed belly, her own claws tearing into her and making Polly yelp.

Zooey backhanded Polly and sprang for Ansel, as she understood that she had to do this to buttress her sisterhood militia against the power of Ansel. It had to be a fight of alpha against alpha, and though she was wounded by Polly, she had no choice but to throw herself at Ansel.

He was in the midst of decapitating a tan when Zooey ran for him, marveling at his great power. She would consume him and take it into herself, make it her own.

Ansel was ready for her this time, though, and countered her speed by charging for her, smashing into her, knocking her backward, into a snow-bedecked spruce that buried Zooey in an avalanche.

He did not wait for her to rise, but forced his way past her minions and ran right at her, and Zooey, not wanting to let her own fear be seen by her pack, charged him with her fanged mouth agape, her white fur covered with her own blood.

Ansel caught her with his claws, while she clamped down on his arm, and the two of them went to the snowy ground, rolling and rending.

Her surviving packmates formed a circle around them, none of them wanting to intrude on this fight to the death between alphas.

If her throat hadn't been savaged by Polly, Zooey would have ordered them to help her against Ansel, but she could only manage a mangled snarl.

Ansel flat-out broke one of her arms with a monstrous twist of his own arm, and Zooey cried out, blood flying from her lips as the lightning pain coursed through her wounded limb.

Then, still holding her broken arm, Ansel brought his jaws in at her neck and finished what Polly had begun, his jaws tearing into her throat.

Zooey clawed at his face with her good arm, jabbed at his eyes with her thumbs, kicked at him with her feet.

But Ansel would not be denied—he threw her with a toss of his head, launching her hard against an unyielding oak tree in the yard.

Zooey, bloody and broken, fought back to her feet, eyes blurring, and saw wounded Polly trying to get to her feet, clutching at her clawed and bleeding belly.

She jumped for Polly, catching her with her wounded limb, while Polly struggled against her, too weak from blood loss to evade her.

Ansel bounded for them both, steam rising from him in the chilly air. He was panting, but far from spent.

Zooey wanted so badly to taunt him, to threaten to kill his little bitch, but it would take days for her throat to heal. Even now, she was amazed her head was still attached to her body, after what Ansel had done to her.

Ansel loomed over them, rising to his haunches, while Zooey's packmates shuffled around them, uncertain, unwilling to intervene.

I'll kill her, Zooey seemed to say, her long claws at Polly's neck, like a fistful of steak knives.

"Do it," Ansel said, a guttural growl. "And die."

Zooey gazed into his great blue eyes, and sank her claws into Polly's throat without hesitating, for if it was her fate to die in this place, she would meet that fate uncaring, unencumbered by fear.

She drew forth her claws, watching the fount of blood flow from Polly, feeling her shudder as she fell into the snow, and met Ansel's charge, which came on in what felt like slow-motion, the tableau of her terrified packmates, her sisters looking on in confusion and dismay, while snow fell thickly from the sky, like they were in a great snowglobe. Bodies and blood were strewn upon the yard, torn and broken, while Polly bled out in the snow, and Ansel, fangs bared, surging toward her, blotting out everything as he neared her, Death Incarnate.

Zooey turned her head up to the sky, felt the snowflakes hit her face even as Ansel crashed into her, finding her exposed and bloody throat, severing her head.

It was an awesome way to die.

Like, totally.

Polly felt the man strain against her as her teeth snapped his wind-pipe, felt the blood gush down her throat as she slammed him against the side of the shower, drove him down to the floor of it as the hot shower water flowed and she fed on him, without him so much as getting to scream.

It was an immaculate, extraordinary kill, and she crouched over him, feasting on his fresh, tough flesh, forged in who knew how many hours of exercise he dedicated himself to. She devoured him from the neck on down, her teeth sublimely suited for the task at hand, while blood pooled in the shower.

Polly had gorged herself on his arms and his chest, until there was only a torso left, then she paused, for the Thing within her had filled her stomach, and, momentarily sated, was content to heed her counsel.

"If he simply disappears," Polly said. "There's next to nothing I can do. The man has to die."

She turned off the shower and stepped out, forced the Thing back inside her, toweled herself off.

Then, wrapped with their thick towels, she walked into Tristan's closet and got out one of his favorite pairs of sweatpants. Then she dried the man's legs off and put them in the sweatpants, like she was dressing a doll. She put on some Playtex gloves, then she ran down-stairs and got out some trash bags, and slipped the man's torso into the bag.

She would take care of it. His body thus removed from the shower, she turned the shower on again, so it would, she hoped, rinse the rest of the blood down the drain.

The thing was, she may have been a murderer and a cannibal crea-ture, but she was not an idiot. She'd been paying attention to the news, with the broadcasters going on and on about outbreaks of "civil unrest" and "mass hysteria" as more people kept reporting about attacks by unknown animal assailants. CNN was breathlessly reporting it as Panic in the Streets.

The reports of wolves or coywolves continued. People getting bitten and attacked almost daily. She laughed to herself as she carted the man's remains down the stairs, at the irony of it all—Sam had finally managed to be on the front of something, and hadn't lived to see it.

Not that she was going to write some epic poem about them, but it had offered her some clarity and perspective on her situation, and got her to compose herself. Something was happening to the city. People were changing the way she had changed.

As an artist, she wanted to bear witness to this, to communicate what she had seen, to find or make meaning of it, to make monstrosity her muse.

Of course, her first instinct was to blog it, on Pollyvore:

ODE TO APPETITE

I'm so hungry, night and day
Yearning for a place at your table
Will you serve me, I can't wait!
To see what you put before me, Love

I'm not finicky, I swear
I'll take the scraps that you leave for me
You will not hear me complain
Knowing just where I stand: on all fours

I'm starving for you, you see
Waiting with vernacular abandon
You should really give me a taste
Don't you ever dare deny me.

She eyed herself in the mirror, could see the scars at her throat, where Zooey had tried to kill her. She'd taken to wearing scarves to cover her wounded throat, at least until it healed.

She'd been as good as dead, but Ansel had saved her, for some reason only he knew.

Her memories of him were blurry, dreamlike—he'd tended to her, had nursed her back to health, but, increasingly, he'd been gone, until he'd gone away.

"I've got to make this right," Ansel said, his voice cutting through the haze.

She couldn't talk then, as her throat was still healing. The wounds she'd received would have killed her as a norm. She squeezed his hand, and he smiled at her.

"It may take awhile," he said. "Just try to keep out of trouble while I'm gone."

She'd tried to find him, but he'd vanished. She did not know where he had gone, could not track him, even when she looked for him.

Polly had gone to his place, and there was no sign of Ansel. She'd sniffed the air, tried to catch his scent, but he hadn't been there for weeks.

In the dark of the night, she took the man's body, put him in the trunk of the BMW, and drove him someplace far away. With so many bodies, it hardly mattered, anymore. And she found if she fed monthly, she attained a measure of control of the Thing within her.

All the same, she could feel the Thing squirming inside her, wanting to get out more and more. Satisfied with the turn of events, Polly fought to bring her life back to normal, or at least to paranormal, to something she could control and understand.

When the cravings came, she indulged them, did not fight them, careful to feed the Thing regularly, so that it did not get out of control, did not become sloppy or careless or greedy. And, in that way, she reached a symbiotic harmony with the monster within her. With all of the chaos afflicting Chicago, and, now, from what she'd seen, cities and towns across the country, she felt a measure of safety in her periodic forays.

She took a bath and watched the news, something about the National Guard being mobilized to maintain order. The sight of it, the blood and slaughter, it stirred the Thing within her.

Pol slipped from the tub, shook herself dry, and bounded out the bathroom door, twice as hungry as before.

Ansel made his way to the meeting place. He passed up the stairs between a pair of bronze statues of wolves that stood where one might have thought lions may have better belonged. Instead, the wolves gazed out at any who passed them with a mute look of predatory appraisal. They were old statues, impeccably crafted long ago.

The place was called *La Galleria delle Anime,* and it was curated by the Rupinos. The endowment they provided for *La Galleria* ensured that it would continue to remain a fixture of Detroit.

While much of Detroit had descended into ruin, *La Galleria* was untouched by graffiti, was otherwise unharmed and unsullied. No one dared to harm *La Galleria.* Even the most relentless of vandals and thieves gave *La Galleria* a wide berth.

It was an old bank building, a stately structure from a bygone era, now repurposed, now an art gallery, where a number of his paintings and the paintings of others were on display, carefully lit and presented between white marble columns. There paintings were all along the walls, and hanging suspended. Every painting was a portrait.

Over the entrance, etched in stone letters, was *"Lupus Ad Ostium"*—the wolf is at your door. Ansel took a deep breath before crossing the threshold. He was the big, bad wolf, after all.

A young woman waited inside, wearing a caramel-colored leather skirt and a matching jacket and gloves over an ivory blouse. She had black hair like Ansel, and ice blue eyes, and a strong nose. Her face was sternly Italian, square-jawed and big-toothed, her strong features compounded by smoky eye shadow and burgundy lipstick, with a rugged, almost feral beauty to her.

"Ansel," she said. *"Fratellino.* What have you been doing in Chicago? Are you here to sell me more of your paintings?"

"There are problems," Ansel said. "I need help, Gia."

Gia Rupino looked her brother up and down, sniffed at him a bit.

"You smell like death, *Fratellino*," Gia said.

"Problems," Ansel said. "Like I told you."

"I've been watching," Gia said. "We all have. It's very bad."

Ansel looked Gia in the eye, feeling ashamed to even be at *La Galleria* like this. She reached out with her gloved hand and stroked his brow, brushing some of his hair from his eyes.

"You need *Us* to assist?" Gia asked, with a special emphasis on that word.

"I do," Ansel said. "There are too many for me alone."

Gia gestured, welcomed Ansel into *La Galleria*, and they walked down the center of the gallery, her heels clacking as she walked, taking his arm in hers.

"Of course there are, *Fratellino*," Gia said. "Now, tell Gia all about it."

Ansel told her everything.

ACKNOWLEDGMENTS

I would like to thank all of my readers, who offered their time, attention, and opinions to the writing and revision of this novella. I would also like to thank Christine Marie Scott of Clever Crow Design Studio in Pittsburgh for her wonderful cover art and her invaluable assistance with the layout of these pages.

ABOUT THE AUTHOR

D. T. Neal is a fiction writer and editor living in Chicago. He won second place in the Aeon Award in 2008 for his short story, "Aegis," and has been published in *Albedo 1*, Ireland's premier magazine of science fiction, horror, and fantasy. He is the author of *Saamaanthaa*, *The Happening*, and *Norm*, known collectively as the *Wolfshadow Trilogy*. He's also written the vampire novel, *Suckage*, as well as the Lovecraftian cosmic horror-thriller, *Chosen*. He has written three creature feature/eco-horror novellas, *Relict*, *Summerville*, and *The Day of the Nightfish*. He continues to work on several science fiction, fantasy, horror, and thriller stories.

NOSETOUCH PRESS

Nosetouch Press is an independent book publisher
tandemly-based in Chicago and Pittsburgh.
We are dedicated to bringing some of today's most
energizing fiction to readers around the world.

Our commitment to classic book design in a digital
environment brings an innovative and authentic
approach to the traditions of literary excellence.

*The Nose Knows™
NOSETOUCHPRESS.COM

Horror | Science Fiction | Fantasy | Mystery
Supernatural | Gothic | Weird

THE WOLFSHADOW TRILOGY | BOOK 3

It's been eight years since Zooey's lycanthropic insurrection--known as the Happening—broke out across the country. Werewolves are everywhere and nowhere at once, ignored and disregarded by the media and officially denied by the government. Norm Stockwell, an elite, paranormal counterinsurgency agent, is desperate to reclaim his former life in the face of the ongoing lycanthropic epidemic. Working with members of the secret society of the Synowie Srebra, Norm hunts down the ever-elusive Ansel Rupino in an effort to put an end to the Happening once and for all. All that stands in his way are highly organized pack-gangs of Lupines who prowl the bloody streets of Chicago by the light of the moon, in their relentless, instinctive search for prey.

LUPINIA

*The Selected Poems
of Polly Drinkwater,
2007–2015*

A WOLFSHADOW BOOK

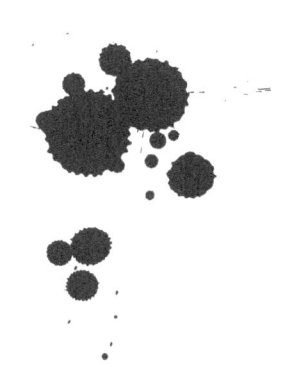